Lady Avely's Guide
to
GUILE
and
Peril

MATRONLY
MISADVENTURES
BOOK 3

ROSALIE OAKS

First edition
Cover design by Lena Yang

eBook ISBN 978-0-6453005-4-3
Print ISBN 978-0-6453005-5-0

Contents

In which peril threatens

When peril threatens, one may discover inner resources, previously unknown.
— from *Lady Avely's Guide to Guile and Peril*

THE KITCHEN at Garvey House was rather full of people, but it was dreadfully empty of one person in particular. Where the Duke of Sargen had stood only moments ago was an empty space, his glass of brandy still half-drunk on the wooden bench.

Judith's heart thudded as she stared at the vacant stone. Dacian's warning gaze was sharp in her memory. He had been trying to tell her to keep away, even as he couldn't speak, held immobile by the very same Gift that he himself possessed.

Her fingers clenched around the topaz ring in her skirts, her nails biting into her palm. The ring was a Travel charm, and it would enable her to follow him into the fort. If, indeed, that was where 'Captain Drumpellier' had taken him. The softly-spoken captain had turned out to be an agent of the Musor Custos, which Judith had not known when she had pleaded for his help: a secret officer who prosecuted crimes of magic. Unsuspecting, she had led him straight to the duke. So it was all her own fault, really, and she had a duty to rectify her mistakes.

Her hands fumbled as she pulled the ring out of her pocket. She slipped it onto her middle finger, where it weighed heavily with its dark blue stone. She would have to muster up some of Dacian's own daring. He was made up of arrogance and strength, audacity and boldness, and she must pretend she had some of those qualities now.

But before she could say the word for Travel, Marigold spoke up. Judith's tiny vampiri companion—curly-haired, usually cheerful, and usually naked—was standing on the kitchen table. She was wrapped in a flannel handkerchief, and her voice was sharp with anxiety. "Judith, wait!"

"Why?" Judith twisted to face her. "They might do something awful. I must hurry."

Traditionally, the punishment for magical felonies was to strip the culprit of their Gift, and even their memory, with a mind-altering dose of Lethe. She couldn't bear to think of it. She *must* go back into the fort, even if it meant landing right in the nest of the Custos.

"I will come too," said Marigold staunchly. "You might need me."

"Fine." Judith was too distraught to weigh the risk carefully. Marigold might, in fact, be useful.

With alacrity, Marigold transformed into a bat and lurched into the air, dragging her flannel handkerchief along with her. She managed to cram both herself and the kerchief into Judith's gown pocket. Her curly head popped out again, looking around with triumph. "Time to rescue a duke," she said. "Let us be off!"

First, Judith drew a breath and faced the remaining occupants of the kitchen. Mrs Selina Southcott stood by the table, her apple-green mobcap twisted in her hands, her face a picture of guilt. She, after all, had failed to stand her ground in the duke's defence. Robert lay on the bench by the door, his injured leg swaddled with bandages and blankets, his cup of chocolate now cooling and forgotten next to him. His complexion was still pale from blood loss. He was Judith's husband's illegitimate child, and although she had been distraught to discover his existence a while ago, she was now very upset to see him wounded.

Miss Georgina Garvey sat beside him. She was the only person who truly had a right to be in the Garvey House kitchen, as the daughter of the house. Her eyes were wide and her mouth open at the scene that had just unfolded before her: a duke accused and then snatched away before their eyes.

"Georgina," said Judith firmly. "You must use your Healing to help Robert as much as you are able, for he intends to follow me to Castle Lanyon. It is a good three days' drive from here, and I don't want him travelling in his current condition."

"Nonsense," said Robert vaguely. "Right as rain. Already feeling better."

Judith suspected it was the brandy speaking; he had consumed copious amounts of it to deal with the pain. His blue eyes looked heavy, and his chestnut hair was tangled.

Georgina cleared her throat. "I will do my best, Lady Avely, and I fancy that my Gift is not unequal to the task."

"Good. Robert, dear boy, travel in easy stages." Judith cast her eye around the room, landing on Mrs Selina Southcott. "Selina, give me one of your rings." Her tone was peremptory, for she was angry with Selina.

"A ring? Whatever for?" Selina put down her mobcap and splayed her fingers. "I only have my wedding ring. I cannot part with that; Mr Southcott would notice."

"I need a trinket to renounce," explained Judith shortly, "should that dastardly captain ask for my Travel charm again. He was eager to confiscate it last time, but I cannot let him have the topaz." *That* ring belonged to Dacian, and Judith might have need of it again. And she was determined not to cede anything to Drumpellier.

Selina curled her hands in repudiation, and Judith turned away in disgust. Upon inspection, Georgina too had nothing to offer, her youthful fingers bare of adornment. Judith contemplated the silver thimble on the table, wondering if it could pass as a Travel charm. It held traces of brandy, as it had been a drinking receptacle for Wooten, Dacian's vampiri. At least Wooten was with Dacian, hidden in his pocket. Though God knew, the vampiri might have been hurt by the restraining Impact, or soon discovered. At least he had his velvet cloak with him, so his dignity would not be too impaired, which was always Wooten's first concern.

Then another small voice floated down from the roof. "I could fetch a suitable ring, if you like."

Judith looked up to see Miss Yvette Belfleur peering from behind a rafter. Her black hair fell in waves around her face, hiding her expression.

Marigold's curly head craned upwards in affront. "You! We don't want *your* help, you fraudulent female! You've done nothing but lie to us!"

Yvette's tone lowered, with guilt perhaps, or maybe boredom; it was hard to tell with her French accent. "It could be a small recompense for the ill I have done you both." She pushed her hair away from her face, the gesture slightly defiant.

Judith examined her: the elegant cheekbones and full lips, now closed and wary. "I would appreciate it, Miss Belfleur. I take it you are going to steal one of your companion's rings?"

Yvette did not blink. "I regard myself as freed from that bond, and I do not balk at the necessity."

"Ha," muttered Marigold. "Of *course* you don't balk at stealing. Duplicitous, double-dealing, deceitful..."

"That's enough, Marigold," said Judith.

Yvette's expression remained inscrutable. "In my defence, I was acting in the best interests of my companion, as you are about to do, Miss Cultor. Surely you can understand?"

"My companion isn't about to murder someone!" huffed Marigold.

"As I say, I did not suspect that that was the case."

"And how do we know you're not *lying* again?"

Judith coughed gently. "*I* know that she's not lying; I'm a Truth Discernor, remember?"

Marigold wrinkled her nose and receded into the pocket in a huff. Her voice came out muffled. "Fine. Fetch us a ring. It's the least you can do."

Without further words, Yvette dove from the rafter. A glimpse of a small, naked, female form showed before she transformed into a bat and swept out of the kitchen.

Judith busied herself, despite the agony of waiting, with marching to the stables and giving orders to Dacian's coachman, so that the poor man could deal with the villains currently tied up in the Garvey House drawing room. When she returned, Yvette was on the kitchen table, a deep blue silk cloak pulled tightly around her. She held a gold ring set with diamonds, heavy in her tiny hands.

Marigold's head popped out again and she eyed the ring with annoyance. "Good to see you didn't restrain yourself," she said, with mingled approval and scorn.

Yvette ignored her. "This used to be a Travel charm," she explained to Judith, "but it has lost its potency. It should show traces of the Musing, however, and lend credence to your story."

"Thank you." Judith took the ring and slipped it on her middle finger, where it fit snugly, the diamonds glinting in the candlelight.

"Hmph," said Marigold.

"One more thing, my lady," said Yvette hesitantly, her head bowing. "Could I accompany you too?"

Marigold drew a breath of outrage. "You may certainly not!"

Judith hushed her and examined Yvette closely. "Why should you wish to do that?"

"They will expect you to have one vampiri, not two, and I could assist if you need to distract the guards." She met Judith's eyes. "And I don't want to stay here. It is too painful."

Marigold grumbled something indistinguishable but otherwise remained silent. Judith put out her hand. "Very well. I am not in a position to refuse any offers of help."

Yvette walked onto the back of Judith's wrist and then clung on as Judith transferred her to another pocket. She did not think it wise to stuff Yvette in a small space with Marigold. Goodness knows what might happen. Fisticuffs at the very least, or something even more scandalous.

Now she had her pockets stuffed full of vampiri. What would her children say if they could see her now?

She turned and gave a last farewell to Robert. "Goodbye, dear boy. You mustn't rush to Castle Lanyon, but you can be assured of a safe harbour there once you reach it."

He nodded. "I'll bring the duke's luggage, and yours."

Judith couldn't even begin to think about luggage. She gave a distracted nod, then tucked her lapis lazuli pendant into her bodice, keeping this sign of her Gift hidden. It was time to Travel into Pendennis Castle.

"*Veho*," she said firmly, and twisted the topaz ring on her finger.

It was time to rescue Dacian.

THE WORLD TREMBLED AND DARKENED, then righted itself again.

Judith opened her eyes to a familiar sight: the round tower room of Pendennis Fort, built of heavy stone, with a large desk opposite her. It was Captain Drumpellier's desk. He, fortunately, was not present like the last time she had appeared here: he must have his hands full escorting Dacian to wherever they intended to incarcerate him. One lantern glowed steadily behind the desk, indicating that its owner might soon return.

She had been here earlier in the day, a lifetime ago. Dacian had slipped the topaz ring on her finger and sent her here, whisking her out of danger. Only she had brought a greater menace back to him: the wrath of the law down upon his head.

Never mind that the Musor Custos would probably have caught up with the duke at some stage; he had, after all, killed three men with his Gift. There had been mitigating circumstances, however, especially for the last one. Judith was determined that the Custos should hear her testimony. Surely, then, they would have no choice but to pardon him.

She looked around, wondering if there was any weapon or tool she could requisition. A rifle hung on the wall, but she was not a practiced shot, so reluctantly she discarded the idea. Also, her first attempt must be to reconcile Drumpellier, not commit treason by aiming a gun at an officer of the Crown.

From her pockets, two heads emerged, one curly brown and one dark. Yvette clambered out, clinging to Judith's skirts and looking up.

"I will reconnoitre," Yvette said briefly, and shifted into her bat form to fly out of one of the windows set deep into the stone. Judith only hoped it wasn't a partial truth, and that Yvette wasn't going to abandon them now that she had escaped from Garvey House.

Outside, the night was black, the full moon now set. It was

very late, or very early. The air was cool, and Judith could hear the sound of waves shushing in the distance. They were in Falmouth, Cornwall, having traversed days of carriage travel in mere moments.

"Hmph," muttered Marigold, still in her pocket. "We should make a plan, before flitting off like that."

"We do need to know where they have put Dacian. If, indeed, he is even here." Worry gnawed at Judith's innards. With him taken from her, all her dithering and self-delusion over the last few weeks seemed terribly foolish. It was apparent to her now that Dacian was dear to her, completely and utterly, and that she would do anything to gain him back.

She gritted her teeth to keep herself from succumbing to maudlin emotion. The years spent apart from him—in stupid misunderstandings and anger—must *not* be compounded now.

Striding to the desk, she rifled through the papers there. They seemed to be in some sort of code: nonsensical sentences strung together. Was this how the Custos communicated? Was there anything about the duke, some hint as to how they intended to deal with him? Impatient, she opened the drawers, finding more papers closely inscribed with gibberish. Useless to her, and no weapon either.

She turned in time to see a black shape flap through one of the windows.

It wasn't Yvette, however. A black silk cloak billowed out as the bat tumbled onto the desk. Judith was pleased to see it resolve into the form of Wooten Willoughby. She shut the drawers.

His long face peered up at Judith. "My lady, you came."

"Of course I did. Where is he?" She ran her eyes over Wooten, ascertaining that he seemed unharmed. "Are you all right? Is *he* all right?"

"Below, six flights down." Wooten didn't answer her other question.

She narrowed her eyes. "Take me there."

"That is...inadvisable."

"Why?"

Wooten winced nervously. "His grace is not quite...himself."

Her heart leapt to her throat. "What have they done?"

"Administered the first dose of Lethe." At her aghast face, Wooten hurried on. "Not enough to be irreversible; just enough to keep him docile. It is probably standard procedure: Impact to contain the threat, Obruo to neutralise it, Lethe to make him forgetful. I have hopes that it will wear off in a day...unless they renew the dose."

Judith closed her eyes momentarily in aguish. "I must talk to him. Warn him."

"I *have* warned him, and I don't think his grace would want you in his presence, my lady."

Marigold scoffed from her pocket. "Don't be ridiculous, you bofflehead. If you don't show us the way at once, I'll rip off that black silk until you're as naked as the day you were born."

Wooten grimaced. "Was it really necessary to bring Miss Cultor?"

"Miss Belfleur is here too," warned Judith. "She said she could help us with a distraction. Are there any guards?"

"One," admitted Wooten.

That news only made Judith feel more apprehensive. Clearly, Drumpellier thought one guard was sufficient, despite Dacian's power. The Defences on the cell must be strong, or he was dreadfully weakened. Her heart quailed. "I will not wait, Wooten. Lead the way. Marigold, here—take the topaz ring and keep it safe, in case I am apprehended." She handed Marigold the heavy masculine ring, adorned with the dark blue stone. "If we are separated, find your way to Castle Lanyon."

"Pfft," said Marigold. "I am not leaving you! Not with only Sir Long-Face and Lady Liar to help you!"

With a lugubrious sigh, Wooten turned and stepped off the desk, transforming into his bat form. He floated over to the door, waiting for Judith to open it, his cape trailing behind him.

The door did not make a sound as she swung it open. Stone steps led downwards, lit by a single sconce. She trod down them quietly, following Wooten's shadow.

In which a duke forgets himself

The accoutrements of age and station can be their own disguise.
— from *Lady Avely's Guide to Guile and Peril*

AS THEY DESCENDED THE TOWER, the icy cold of the stone crept through her thin slippers. Her blue silk gown—from the day—did nothing much to keep out the chill. At least she had her matching blue mobcap on, to give a little warmth and a semblance of respectability, despite the fact that she had just illegally entered a military fort before dawn.

Wooten pulled to a halt after six flights of stairs and gestured with his wing. Judith stilled and carefully peered around the corner of the landing.

A soldier stood to attention before a narrow wooden door, set into thick stone. He wore the red military costume of the infantrymen: one of the garrison stationed at Pendennis. His posture was ramrod straight, though perhaps more from habit than attention, as his eyes were dreamily focused on the upper right corner of the wall. The same wall led down a further corridor to another stairwell, presumably ascending to the ground floor and the way out.

An ominous silence came from the cell. Why was Dacian not ranting and raving, or throwing things about? It was dreadfully out of character.

Judith swallowed and drew back. What now? Should she march out there and tell that pesky guard that his presence had been requested by Captain Drumpellier? That is what Dacian would do, and he'd have the arrogance to carry it off. Could Judith manage the appropriate level of hauteur? It might just work, at a pinch, to send the guard off and give her some precious minutes to discover Dacian's state and talk to him.

She drew a steadying breath, conjuring a ducal attitude. Just as she did so, she felt the brush of air by her cheek, and a small weight landed on her shoulder.

Yvette's voice came in her ear, low and melodious. "I can lead him off."

Marigold's white face popped out of her pocket, looking up. "Don't be stupid," she hissed. "Vampiri aren't supposed to expose themselves!"

Yvette's voice warmed with amusement. "Who said I was going to *expose* myself?"

Judith let out a breath of warning. "Shh!"

"Let me," said Yvette quietly in her ear. "It will be easy enough to distract him, then I can fly off."

"I bet," grumbled Marigold, barely audible.

Judith simply nodded. She was too desperate to see Dacian to cavil at Yvette's suggestion.

The weight of the vampiri lifted, and a black shape floated to the ceiling. Judith waited, pressed against the stone, still and anxious.

A moment later, a gasp issued from the guard. Judith craned her neck to peer around the lintel. He was still standing at his post, but his eyes had moved to stare, wide-eyed, at the far corridor.

A glimpse of pale flesh showed there. Yvette was in her human form. Her midnight cape swung open to reveal her shapely, naked figure, as she strolled towards the stairs.

From Judith's pocket, Marigold huffed crossly. "The hussy! She *is* exposing herself!"

"Marigold!" hushed Judith, under her breath. Marigold was in no position to censure nakedness, but Judith dared not remonstrate further.

By the stairs, the miniature vision of feminine beauty had completely transfixed the soldier. Yvette began scaling the steps, her cloak fluttering behind her. When she had just about vanished from view, the soldier slowly crept after her, his face intent.

Marigold muttered something. Judith felt the tug at her skirts as the vampiri whisked herself out and swept up to Judith's ear.

"I'm going to follow her."

Judith nodded again. "Look after the ring!"

Marigold drifted quietly up to the roof and away. Judith waited a long moment. Then she stepped down from her own hiding place. Her pulse thudded loud in her ears as she crossed to the barred door. It was impenetrable wood and adorned with a lock approximately the size of her own head. She did not think for a moment that she would be able to gain entrance; even Dacian in the fullness of his power would find it difficult. Moreover, there would be Defences on the cell, comprised of the very same Impacting power he ordinarily wielded.

Fortunately, there was also a low, narrow ledge, jutting into the deep stone and interspersed with iron bars, as a way of viewing the prisoner and also passing food to him without risking the door. A plate sat there, ignored, with bread and a slice of some kind of meat pie. There was even a bowl of candied sweets, which seemed out of place. It was a reconciliatory gesture that did nothing to allay Judith's fears.

She knelt on the floor and looked through, her hands grasping the cold iron.

Inside was a strange juxtaposition of elements. A dank, stone cell was strewn about with rugs and cushions, as if to try to hide its real purpose. A hard stone bench was covered in a red carpet, and a table bore a decanter of whisky, two glasses, and some long candles, lit. Someone had been in here with Dacian, perhaps persuading him to drink. Was that how they had managed to give him the Lethe? Judith doubted he would have been so stupid. They must have forced it on him somehow. Or perhaps they had used Diplomacy, that Musing which could transform the tenor of a room—or a person—into benevolence and acceptance. It would have to have been a very strong Diplomacy Gift, however, to soften the duke's ire, and it did not look as if it had lasted long.

Dacian sat on the floor, his back rigid against the wall, staring unseeing before him. His black hair was in wild disarray, and he was still dressed in Robert's plain shirt, donned as part of a disguise from earlier in the day. With dismay, Judith saw that his coat and cravat had been stripped from him, and with it the Illusion charm that Robert had hidden within a button. So they could not rely upon that trick. But Dacian was conscious at least, thank God, and he wore a heavy scowl.

"Dacian," Judith murmured softly.

His head whipped towards her. His eyes widened slightly—possibly at the sight of a well-dressed, middle-aged matron kneeling by his cell—then his expression became inscrutable and aloof.

"Dacian." Her heart sank. "It's me. Judith."

"Oh? I'm afraid that I cannot remember your acquaintance, ma'am." His voice was harsh. "Do I know you?"

She blinked back sudden tears, her hands tightening on the bars.

"Fairly well, I promise you. I have come to help. They have taken you here against your will, as I'm sure you can guess. Do you remember anything at all?"

He stared at her for a long moment, unmoving. "They tell me I killed a man. If that is true, perhaps I ought to remain here to meet my punishment."

She shook her head quickly in repudiation. "You were provoked, and the punishment is too severe. But I cannot explain it all to you now, dearest. I must simply warn you not to drink or eat any of their food, as that is how they may keep you forgetful, with their dreadful drug. I will offer testimony in your defence, and we must hope they will listen."

"Dearest?" He pushed himself off the ground and moved with sudden rapidity towards the grate. "Do you claim a relation with me, ma'am?"

"Er, no," she said after a moment under his intense inspection, for indeed she could claim nothing, even as she knelt before him. "Only a very long friendship. And you are very dear to me," she added, in case she should not be able to tell him again. Her hands gripped the bars with the effort not to start crying like some foolish female.

"Oh, is that so?" He squatted by the ledge, leaning forward with interest. "Odd that I cannot recall your visage at all..." Doubt and scepticism flashed across his face, then his eyes narrowed in calculation. "How do I know you are not some trick they have sent to further confuse me? A beautiful woman to soften my temper; I confess that I am not so averse to this tactic. Perhaps if you remove that mobcap, I may see your face better?"

Judith raised her brows, ignoring the moisture in her eyes. That was more like him. Trust the man to attempt to remove her mobcap within minutes.

"I will not remove my mobcap." She managed a watery smile, and his eyes became hard again with suspicion. "I must remain respectable if I am to speak in your defence."

Wooten chose that moment to clamber up onto the ledge, fumbling with his black silk. He cleared his throat as he swept it around himself. "If I may say, your grace, you are well acquainted with Lady Avely, and you are extremely fond of her."

"Is that so?" Dacian tilted his head back suspiciously and his eyes traced down to her bodice. "I can see you have many qualities to recommend you, my lady. But how do I know you're not trying to seduce or trick me?"

"It is usually *you* trying to seduce *me*!"

That won a smirk. "I can believe that. I like your—" his gaze flickered down, then up again— "eyes."

"Never mind my eyes," she said with asperity, though the heat in his gaze was familiar, and a welcome relief. It was *much* more like him. Though it hurt a little to know that he did indeed flirt with every woman he came across. "Do you know when they will hold your trial? I must know how much time I have to prepare your defence."

Dacian's expression darkened again, and he rose abruptly. "I don't know much, I am afraid. All I know is that there is evidence of my felonies, and I risk death." He paused. "Yet it is hard to trust in these assertions when I have no memory of them."

Wooten spoke up again, diffidently. "The trial is three days from now, I believe. And if they find you guilty, they will ensure that you never recover your memory, or your power."

Dacian's fists clenched involuntarily. "I do feel strangely impotent, as if they have taken some vital energy from me."

Judith bit her lip. "Yes, that is your Impact, by which you can move and crush almost anything. They must have given you a drug called Obruo; it dilutes your Gift."

He stared down at her. "Perhaps you can help me recover this force? I feel enlivened by your presence already, I confess..." He examined her face again, then his lips tightened. "Are you weaving some spell to manipulate my mood? The bat here says that I must be wary of such enchantments."

"No spell; just myself." Judith tried to reach through the bars to offer her hand, but she met with an invisible resistance: a Defence spell, heavy and impenetrable. Under Dacian's suspicious gaze, she withdrew her hand again, gesturing to the meat pie. "Please take heed, and do not eat this."

He folded his arms, his handsome face grim in the shadows. "You recommend similarly to the flittermouse." He nodded towards Wooten.

Wooten drew himself up in outrage. "*What* did you just call me?"

"A flittermouse." Dacian raised a brow. "It's a common name for bats."

"I am not common, nor am I a flying mouse!" huffed Wooten.

Judith bit back a smile. "His name is Wooten," she offered. "He also is your dear companion, a vampiri."

Dacian looked sceptical. "I seem to have sprouted a lot of dear companions rather quickly."

"We are both your friends," said Judith. "We are not conspiring against you, I swear."

"How did you come here, then?"

"Er." She hesitated. "I used your own Travel charm, actually: a ring. You slipped it onto my finger yourself."

"Show me."

Judith grimaced. "I don't have it; I gave it to someone else for sake-keeping."

Dacian's expression twisted into scorn. He backed away from the grate, obviously distrusting her assertions. Judith could not blame him: he had lost all his bearings and woken in a hostile environment that was clearly a prison, for all its soft furnishings. It was wise that he be suspicious. Only it hurt that he should narrow his eyes at her with such disdain.

"Even if you do not trust me," she said firmly, "I will still try to help you."

Their eyes met, and his gaze softened. It sent warmth running through her, and she felt sure that he must feel it too. But before he could respond, hasty footsteps sounded, descending the far stairwell.

Judith stood quickly, scrambling away from the grate, her fingers hastily adjusting her mobcap. She needed to cling to any authority her age and position gave her, as if this were a ball-room in London and not a military dungeon where women were decidedly unwelcome.

Seconds later, Captain Drumpellier burst through the archway with the guard at his heels. The captain looked even more rumpled and tired than at their last encounter, his sensitive brow heavily marked with consternation, while the soldier behind him looked wide-eyed with curiosity. Yvette and Marigold were nowhere to be seen.

"Lady Avely! What in damnation are you doing here?" Drumpellier drew to a halt and thrust out a hand. "Hand over your Travel charm at once, under orders of the Crown and Custos."

Judith stood her ground, glad at least that Drumpellier's accusations bore out her story to Dacian. "I will do so when I have your assurance that you will hear my testimony on the duke's behalf."

Drumpellier ground his teeth together. "The Custos have their own methods of justice, ma'am, which do not require your interference."

"Oh? Do you mean Truth Discernment?" enquired Judith calmly. "I am a Truth Discernor myself. Perhaps I may be of assistance."

"You may not! Now, hand over the charm!"

Dacian watched with interest. "Is this the charm that brought you here?"

"Yes, into the tower of Pendennis Castle," said Judith, gesturing to their surroundings, hoping that Dacian absorbed the information. "It is a Charm that *you* gave me, your grace, which you received as a gift from Lord Triskett."

Dacian frowned. "I do not know that name. Wait, did you say *your grace?*"

Drumpellier interrupted. "Enough of this. Ltn Greene, escort this woman to Custodian House. Under close watch!"

Ltn Greene shuffled forward nervously, his round face betraying discomfort. "To the guest quarters, sir?"

Drumpellier sighed. "Why not—but stand guard, and this time do not become distracted!"

Judith interrupted. "Can you at least tell me who will be presiding over his grace's trial?"

"No, I cannot!" Drumpellier glared at her, and she was taken aback, hearing the truth ringing in his voice. How could the captain not know who would pass judgement on Dacian if the trial was in three days' time?

"Well, whoever it is, they must know that his grace was fooled by a master Illusor and acted under duress when he flung his power at Lord Garvey; and moreover, that a young woman..."

Drumpellier interrupted her, his eyes narrowing. "Not another word, Lady Avely. If you insist on reminding the prisoner of anything *more*, I will have to renew the dose of Lethe, which I assure you is an outcome you do not want."

Judith's lips closed. Her eyes went to Dacian. He was leaning against the wall, peering through the iron bars with his arms folded.

"Who, me?" he said. "No memories here. Who is this young woman you speak of? Is she pretty? Does she wear a mobcap too?"

Judith patted her headgear. "Not one as respectable as mine."

"Not so much like a mushroom, you mean?"

Drumpellier did not go so far as to wrench Judith's arm, but it looked as if he wanted to do so. Instead, he put out a sharp hand, gesturing for her departure. With Ltn Greene mirroring it, she had no choice but to regally acquiesce, making her way over to the stairs that Yvette had mounted with Ltn Greene behind her. Before the cell was out of sight, however, she threw one more comment over her shoulder. "I hope to see you again soon, your grace. At your trial, if not before."

"The pleasure will be all mine," called Dacian. His tone was light, but his eyes were still narrowed.

She walked away, her heart aching.

Drumpellier crowded behind, hurrying her up the stairs. It was only two flights, she noted, before they pushed through another door and came out onto the main grounds of the fort, with grey walls encircling the core. She took a deep breath of the salt-laden air, cleansing after the dank closeness of the dungeon. The sound of the waves crashed close by. Soldiers stood at the ramparts, rifles at their sides, their red coats showing dully in the lantern light. They were well-trained, however, and did not turn to look at Judith as she passed, her skirts swishing over stone.

She was hurried through the archway, where two more

sentries guarded the entrance, and then down a long gravel path. In front of her was the impressive facade of the new barracks, the windows picked out in white, but Drumpellier led her to the left, where a low-slung stone building was set further back. It was modest compared to the fort and barracks, but sturdily built and covered by a slate roof. Drumpellier unlocked the front door and marched in, while Ltn Greene awkwardly waited for Judith to follow.

Inside, Custodian House was simply furnished but elegant, clearly set up for gentlemen officers. The foyer was decorated with a painting of a battle scene, in front of which Drumpellier swung around.

"Hand it over now," he snapped, "or it will be the worse for you."

In which a deal is made

As much as one would like to be without guile, sometimes deceit is necessary.

— from *Lady Avely's Guide to Guile and Peril*

JUDITH WIDENED HER EYES. "Hand over what?" She must not be seen to give in too easily.

"Do not trifle with me! The Travel charm!"

"Believe me, the charm has lost its power now," she replied airily. "I'm certain I used the last of it. And you heard me before: it was a gift to the duke from his dear friend, and it has great sentimental value. I would much rather keep it."

"I am sure you would," said Drumpellier grimly. He took a step closer, looming over her as Ltn Greene cleared his throat at her back. "But you will give it to me, or I will have you arrested for treason!"

"Treason! Goodness me! A slightly excessive reaction!" Judith fumbled with her fingers and made a show of reluctantly pulling off the diamond ring she had obtained from Yvette. Hesitantly, she held it out to Drumpellier, who took it with commendable restraint, not snatching at all.

"Thank you." He stepped back and managed a bow. "I apologise for my short manner, ma'am, but you must understand that this is a military fortification, and we are at war. I cannot have you disregarding my orders."

"Certainly not, Captain, but as a Truth Discernor, I cannot disregard the course of justice either." She leaned forward to murmur in his ear. "Please recall: I know that you are wearing a false name, and I will alert your superiors of the fact, if I must."

Drumpellier's expression hardened again. "Unfortunately for you, Lady Avely, my superiors are well aware of my false name. Indeed, they gave it to me."

She backed away, staring, and he continued with a trace of smugness as he tucked her ring out of sight. "As an agent of the Custos, I was given this position and a different name to hide my purpose. You will find that your attempt at blackmail will not work, and furthermore, that the Custos will not be patient with any indiscretions."

"But why, when we rode to Garvey House…" Judith trailed off. She had hinted at her knowledge then, and the captain had ceded a horse to her. She had thought that she might have a hold over him.

"Why did I allow you to dictate my actions? I did not want to give my game away, so I let you go ahead. Now, however, as Captain of this garrison, and as Head Custodian here, I command that you keep your silence regarding his grace *and* the presence of the Musor Custos."

Judith knew the Custos were law unto themselves; she had only hoped they would show some regard to due process. Yet she also knew that the whole point of the Custos was that they dealt their justice from the shadows, inspiring fear and compliance in the Musor community with their mysterious indictments. Pressing her lips together, she wondered how to proceed now that one of her cards had been taken away from her.

Drumpellier gentled his voice. "The Musor Custos have long been guardians of justice, and I admire your tenacity, Lady Avely. You must trust us to do as we see fit to curtail any misuse of power." He mustered a smile. "May I offer you a cup of tea? It appears that you have had a rather long night, and, whether we like it or not, you are now my guest."

Before she could respond, he turned on his heel and led the way into a neat sitting room. Judith followed crossly (with Ltn Greene right behind) and entered a room with a whitewashed ceiling upheld by dark wooden beams, and small paned windows looking onto the ocean. The sky was slowly lightening with the faint luminescence of predawn, the sea a murky grey. A pang of anxiety shot through her for Marigold and Yvette. As she took a seat on a hard-backed chair, she re-evaluated her tactics. It was clear Drumpellier was now trying to disarm her. Yet two could play that game.

Drumpellier sat facing the door and asked Ltn Greene to alert the housekeeper to their needs. The lieutenant rapped his heels sharply and withdrew.

"Well, Lady Avely," Drumpellier leaned forward with a rueful expression. "We have begun on a rather difficult footing, but allow me to remedy that. We are to be neighbours, if it is true that you are to take up residence in Castle Lanyon." He ended on a faint note of interrogation.

Judith adjusted her mobcap, tucking a curl of hair behind her ear. "Oh yes, I am the new Marchioness of Lanyon, by decree of His Majesty. To be entirely frank, that is partly why I used the Travel charm. It brought me much closer to my new home, which I am overdue to inspect."

Drumpellier did not seem unduly impressed. He said carefully, "I am afraid that you might find Castle Lanyon is not as salubrious as you might hope—it is, after all, situated on a tidal island, so it is difficult to maintain. The caretaker there, a fellow by name of Trebellow, does his best, but it is rundown. Moreover," he added, "it is reputed to be haunted with a desperate soul who casts a pall of dread over the place."

Judith raised her brows. "Haunted? Surely you don't believe that." She could hear a note of satire in his voice, but she did not want to test her Gift too much, else she would become Bemused. That her mind was still relatively clear meant that Marigold must be not too far away; the vampiri bond protected against Bemusement, especially when they were near to each other.

"No," admitted the captain, "but you will have to face down the rumours of ghosts if you are to find more servants. Currently, I think there are only about seven who live and work at the castle, though there are others who run the dairy."

"Ah yes, the creamery. I look forward to sampling the wares."

"A colony of puffins is also in residence, along with the cows. You will have your work cut out for you simply in managing the livestock."

She did not want to be distracted with such matters or cordiality, but just then, the housekeeper came in with a tea tray and plate of buttered buns.

At Drumpellier's nod, Judith mechanically began pouring the hot steaming liquid into delicate cups. As she passed him one, Drumpellier said, "I suspect that if you *are* a Truth Discernor, Lady Avely, you know how to lie."

She picked up her cup and took a sip, ignoring this slur. "As a Truth Discernor, I have a special regard for the truth. You must hear what I have to say in the duke's defence, informally at least." Hoping she could appeal to his sense of honour, Judith began describing the mitigating circumstances to Dacian's killing blow upon Lord Garvey. Captain Drumpellier's brow creased thoughtfully at intervals, but his face remained aloof.

At the end of her recitation, he absentmindedly pulled an oblong pebble out of his coat pocket. It was so deep blue as to be black, worn smooth by the passage of water. Judith recognised it as a Talisman Stone of schorl, the stone of Impactors. It seemed to soothe Drumpellier as he ran his fingers over it.

"Well?" she asked. "What say you? Are the circumstances not extenuating?"

He put the schorl down on the table with a click, a reminder of his power. "A fairly convoluted story, and it relies upon your own perception of the truth. Yet—if you are a Truth Discernor, you could prove your Gift to me."

"Pardon me?" The impertinence of the man, to question her Gift! Judith raised a hand to the gold chain on her neck, pulling out her own Talisman Stone; a large lapis lazuli given to her by no less than His Majesty himself. It was the stone of Discernors, and a small proof of her claim.

Drumpellier eyed the pendant. "Indeed. Well, I have a troubling matter on hand, and I could do with some help."

"Oh?" Judith took a buttered bun from the plate, and a large bite. It was accepting victuals from the enemy, but she hadn't had food for hours now. She stared at the captain as she chewed, in no mood to help him. He hadn't paid one jot of attention to her story! And Dacian was languishing in a cell without his memory.

Drumpellier leaned back. "Three days ago, one of my soldiers was found dead on the shore near Castle Lanyon. If you can discover the truth of his demise, I will allow you to tender a statement in the duke's defence."

Judith raised her brows. Was he simply trying to be rid of

her? Yet the captain looked rather intent, even as he made a show of leaning nonchalantly against his chair, his cup held idly in his hands. And his voice did not ring hollow.

"I cannot do much to investigate it myself," he added. "I am occupied here, facing the threat of invasion. I cannot waste more time with what appears simply to be death by drowning, despite my suspicions, when Bonaparte could start ferrying his troops into England any day now."

"Only if our navy fails us, which I doubt will prove to be the case."

"Nonetheless, I am fully occupied. Whereas you will be going to Lanyon Isle soon enough and can make discreet inquiries."

Judith weighed him; he took a sip of tea. She took another bite of her bun, feeling as if she ought to bide her time before she answered one way or the other. Did he really expect her to cooperate with him when he was keeping Dacian locked up in a cell? The bread was dry in her mouth.

"The matter is made more curious," he continued, "by the fact that Sgt Finlay's body appeared to be bruised and battered. The Pendennis surgeon assures me this could have been caused by the battering of waves and rocks shortly after he died, but the back of the head was injured in a way that provokes my suspicion."

"You think someone hit him on the head before he drowned?"

"The surgeon is of the opinion that Sgt Finlay simply hit himself on the rocks while swimming, but I have my doubts. And I can tell you who to question," he said, as if she had already agreed to investigate. "First, there is your caretaker butler, Trebellow, who has been sighted in various towns along this coast, away from his station, and possibly up to no good. I would dearly like some insight into the truth of his movements and whether he might have any reason to hit a soldier over the head. There is also Cador, the fisherman who found the body: a taciturn type. Then there are the twin footmen at Castle Lanyon, Kynver and Kade."

Judith grimaced. "I suppose you think the twins are suspicious just by virtue of being twins."

"Well, yes, for they are identical," replied Drumpellier, as if this needed no further explanation. "Like Trebellow and Cador, they are Cornishmen who keep to themselves. They do not trust officers of the Crown and did not take kindly to my questions."

It was true that Cornish people did not regard themselves as English (despite living in England), coming from Breton stock and having their own language as they did.

"They won't trust me, either," Judith pointed out, with another sip of tea.

"Yes, but that shouldn't matter, should it? You must simply question them and use your Gift to determine whether they are lying."

Judith knew it was not so simple. "People lie about all sorts of things, all the time."

He lifted a brow. "Oh, is that so? Is your Gift not always reliable?" He let that land. "If you can discover the truth behind Sgt Finlay's death, you will prove your Gift and your loyalty. Who knows? I might even offer you a position in the Custos if you show enough acumen."

Judith stiffened, not wanting anything to do with the power that now held Dacian captive. Wary of showing her disdain, she took another bite of bread. But she would be damned if she'd help this impertinent captain. Though if there *had* been a foul deed committed at her new castle, she might investigate privately anyway. Her family were due to visit, and she couldn't have any villains lurking about.

Drumpellier seemed to sense her hostility, for he tilted his head. "Lady Avely, let me be clear. You are not in a position to negotiate on this matter. You illegally entered my fort in the dead of night, yet you wish me to listen to your testimony as a Truth Discernor. How do I know I can trust you? You might be a French spy for all I know. You must understand that I will not countenance your interference with the duke's trial—unless you investigate this death for me."

She swallowed the claggy bread and took a sip of bitter tea. It appeared she wasn't going to be given a choice. However, as Drumpellier said, the investigation might prove a simple matter to her Discerning ear. At the very least, reporting her findings to the captain would give her an excuse to visit Pendennis Fort again and see Dacian.

"Very well," she said at last. With a belated attempt to assert authority, she added, "I will look into it, on the proviso that you will allow me to present my testimony."

"We have a deal." Drumpellier smiled and picked up the schorl, slipping it back into his pocket with an air of satisfaction. "You will have the help of Miss Onslow at Castle Lanyon: she is a scholar studying the extensive collection of books in the Lanyon library." Some private warmth glimmered in his eyes, and Judith wondered how well the captain knew this librarian. "I have already warned her to be on the lookout for anything untoward. There is also your housekeeper, Mrs Ulrich, though she is a rather melancholy type. And Baron Quarles might be visiting again soon; he declares the castle an ideal vantage point for stargazing. He was in residence when the soldier died."

"It seems the castle is well frequented by visitors."

"Oh, both Baron Quarles and Miss Onslow are there by standing royal invitation. They have been warned of your imminent occupancy, and if you wish them to leave, they will do so.

However, you might very well find that you are glad of the company in that draughty pile."

"Perhaps." Judith doubted it; she would have Marigold's companionship until her children arrived, and more important things to worry about, like how to rescue a duke who couldn't even remember his own name. Her own mind was starting to feel woolly at the edges, as the cost of her Gift began to take its toll.

Drumpellier stood, his posture once more resuming a military bearing. "Once you have eaten, you may sleep in the Custodian guest room. Ltn Greene can escort you to Castle Lanyon this afternoon. There is no point going now, as the tide currently covers the causeway." He gave a small bow. "I hope we can be of assistance to each other, Lady Avely."

"Indeed," she said dryly.

"One more thing." He turned at the door. "The ghost at Castle Lanyon—I confess I am intrigued. It might have something to do with Sgt Finlay's death. I suggest you find a discreet way to investigate it, without drawing attention to your interest. The last I heard of it, the ghost had established itself in the cellars, so you would do well to quietly inspect them. We wouldn't want anyone to have prior warning and hide the real reason for the rumours."

Judith bowed her head in acknowledgment. She didn't mention that the cellars were already of great interest to her, as they were intended to be the new residence of a roost of vampiri bats. These bats were, she hoped, currently on their way to England, escorted by her own children across the Channel, rescued from the isle of Sark.

It sounded like she would have her hands full in making the castle inhabitable. She let her shoulders droop in a show of tiredness which was all too real. "It sounds a fascinating mystery, but for now I will be glad to sleep."

Drumpellier gave a short nod. "The housekeeper will show you to your room."

THE GUEST ROOM was small and clean, with the same dark-beamed ceiling and whitewashed walls, and another window looking out to the wide vista of Falmouth Bay. The sky was a soft grey, tinged with pink, and Judith felt another flash of anxiety for Marigold.

As soon as the housekeeper shut the door, she went straight to the window and opened it, calling in a low whisper.

After a long moment, Marigold's brown creature shape flitted down to the sill and tumbled inside. Resolving into her human form, she vaulted onto the floor and stared up at Judith, twirling the topaz ring around one of her wrists. "Well? Are you under arrest?"

"Not yet." Judith smiled and took the ring back, slipping it into her pocket. "Thank you, my dear. Did you speak to Wooten? Yvette?"

Marigold shrugged. "Wooten is still trying to explain matters to the duke, who seems to be more than obtuse than usual. Yvette is still lurking about, as far as I know. Perhaps she is trying to seduce another soldier."

As if to refute this, another bat swooped into the room. The black arrow twisted into Yvette's shapely form and landed gracefully on the bedside table. "I was not seducing a soldier." Yvette wrapped her silk cloak around herself with a regal air. "My tastes run in a *different* direction." Her eyes slid in Marigold's direction.

Marigold harrumphed, even as a faint blush suffused her cheeks. "You were shameless, strolling up those steps, undulating your hips like that!"

Yvette smirked. "I'm glad you appreciated it."

Judith thought it odd that Marigold was suddenly objecting to nakedness, but she turned her attention to Yvette. "We were grateful for your intervention, Miss Belfleur. Did you return to the cell after you left?"

"No, I went to feed from a cow. I haven't supped in days."

Marigold snorted, and Judith started at the reminder. "Marigold, I must feed you now, quickly, before the sun rises!" She scooped her up and carried her to the bed. Rolling up her sleeve, she offered her wrist. While the vampiri gently sucked on her vein, Judith hurriedly recounted Drumpellier's blackmailing, and how she must now travel to Castle Lanyon and investigate a soldier's death. They also hastily arranged a way of sending messages to and from Pendennis and Castle Lanyon, determining that Wooten could fly halfway to Penrose Hill and meet Marigold with news, two nights from now.

"By then, I hope we will have solved the mystery of the death, or come up with some sort of plan," said Judith. "And while Wooten flies, perhaps you, Miss Belfleur, could keep watch over the duke."

Marigold pulled away from the vein to scowl in Yvette's direction. "I think not. How do we know if we can trust her, after all she did to me?"

Yvette folded her arms over her cloak. "Miss Cultor, would you not lie in Lady Avely's defence, or even lure someone into a trap if you thought it might assist her?"

Marigold's scowl deepened.

Judith cleared her throat. "Marigold and I have not been companions for very long. Nothing like the years of your bond, Miss Belfleur." She did not add that Marigold—to her knowledge—had never stayed with *any* companion for long, for she was an itinerant sort of bat. Perhaps Marigold was mistrustful in general and not just towards Miss Belfleur.

Marigold sniffed and wiped her lips, which were now a rosy colour. "Fine. While Wooten is away, you can make yourself useful," she snapped. "But now the sun is about to rise, so you'd better find a place to shelter."

"I didn't know you cared," said Yvette sweetly, and flapped off before Marigold could respond.

In which a sense of doom intrudes

Do not dismiss old tales. They often hold a skerrick of truth, and a warning for those who listen closely.
— from *Lady Avely's Guide to Guile and Peril*

JUDITH TUCKED Marigold under her bed, which was a rather unsafe sleeping place for a vampiri, but the circumstances demanded the risk. Then she fell into a heavy slumber despite the anxieties that cartwheeled through her mind. It had been a long night.

A few hours later, she was roused by the housekeeper returning with another tray of food: luncheon, to be hastily consumed before the journey. Harsh sunlight now slanted through the window, and the sea was a slate of blue as she ate the cold meat, bread, and cheese. Marigold continued to sleep in the shadowed dark under the bed, until Judith shut the curtains and carefully transferred her into a capacious pocket, wrapped in the flannel handkerchief.

Stepping out of Custodian House, a soft wind ruffled her

hair. The fort to her left was an impressive silhouette of grey stone, marked at intervals by the red figures of soldiers. She drew a breath, trying not to dwell on Dacian's imprisonment deep below the earth. Should she demand to see him again now?

But she wasn't given a chance. Captain Drumpellier hustled her onto a gig, with instructions for Ltn Greene to accompany her on the long journey across the bay. The lieutenant was clearly intended to keep a sharp eye on her and report her movements to Drumpellier.

"Now," said Drumpellier, looking up into the vehicle, where Judith sat, her hands tightly clasped. "Do not attempt to return and seek out his grace again; rather expend your energy to find out what you can about Sgt Finlay's death. I will send for you in three days' time."

Judith nodded, keeping her anger hidden under a veneer of matronly dignity. It was fortunate for Drumpellier that she had need to visit Castle Lanyon regardless. Otherwise, she had a good mind to tie herself to Dacian's dungeon door and see what they did about *that*.

The gig started up, and she sat back with a sigh (careful not to squash Marigold) and watched the green fields and blue ocean drift by. The sight of the vast sea turned her mind towards her children, who had set sail for Sark before she had left Devon, weeks ago. Had they accomplished their quest to find the missing French roost? Elinor's Gift for divining jewels would not have been much help in the task, though it was true that her Discernment had been slowly expanding into other facilities. Peregrine, with his ability to Travel, should have been useful. At the very least, he was able to smartly extricate himself from any trouble, and hopefully extricate Elinor too. Could he extricate a whole roost? That remained to be seen. And if they *had* succeeded, they would need the castle cellars, as they had planned together weeks ago. All before Elinor's wedding, which was fast approaching!

She had to take charge of the castle and sort out this haunting nonsense as soon as possible. And solve a murder. And rescue Dacian.

She needed a hot cup of chocolate.

Yet, despite the uneven roads, and the weight upon her mind, Judith managed a few more snatches of sleep, for the weariness of her exertions the night before still weighed upon her. Awful dreams plagued her, of Dacian turning away, his face blank, his wrists bound, and a door slamming shut between them. She woke up with tears in her eyes and dashed them away angrily.

Ltn Greene rode alongside the gig, keeping his distance, as was proper. When at last they came in sight of Lanyon Isle, she rubbed her cheeks and peered out at a fantastical sight.

In the distance, the castle rose up out of the water like something out of a fairy tale. Its stately towers and white gleaming stone emerged from the top of a dark green hill, which itself emerged from the teal blue of the sea. Yet she could see that one of the towers was collapsing and misshapen, so that the far right of the castle leaned brokenly, as if it were an old lady trying to stand up. Nonetheless, it was a beautiful sight, an otherworldly isle set apart from the rest of England.

The tide was receding, as Drumpellier had promised. It revealed a winding causeway that led from the mainland to the island. The cobbled path still glimmered with puddles, and the bay was strewn with dark brown splotches of seaweed.

It took some time to reach the causeway, but instead of rolling across it, the gig pulled to a halt by a stone cottage. Judith peered out to see that Ltn Greene had cantered ahead and tied up his horse. He was clearly waiting for her to dismount from the gig, his expression apologetic.

With a creak of her joints, she took his hand and clambered down, carefully arranging her skirts so that Marigold would not be too jostled. She resisted the urge to stomp her feet on the solid ground and took a deep breath of fresh air instead. "Why have we stopped here, Lieutenant?"

Ltn Greene bowed, his round face respectful. "This is Stonesthrow Cottage. The captain asked that you speak with the fisherman Cador, who lives here. He was the one who found Sgt Finlay's body."

She nodded reluctantly, and Ltn Greene turned and rapped smartly on the door.

It opened to reveal a sparse, wiry man with dark hair. He looked older than Judith, his face weathered and tanned. After his initial flash of surprise at seeing a soldier and a lady on his doorstep, his expression shuttered. Ltn Greene introduced her as the new owner of Castle Lanyon, and Cador's jaw tightened further.

"Ah," he said. "An English lady sent down by the king. We are blessed."

Judith's lips quirked at his ironic tone. Here was the scepticism that Drumpellier had mentioned: the Cornish distrust of the English. "It seems I am to be blessed too, with such a mighty burden." She gestured at the castle with its falling down ramparts and broken tower, and Cador raised a brow. She searched for a way to come to the point, for she did not have time to waste. "I believe that a body was found washed up on the shores recently. Is the causeway perilous to those who do not know how to swim?"

Cador nodded unwillingly. "Aye. The tide can come in quick. If you think to pop over to the isle and back you can be caught out."

"Is that what happened to this poor soldier?"

Cador's lips compressed. "It looks like it, doesn't it?"

Well, *that* was singularly unhelpful. She cast Ltn Greene a glance of frustration.

The lieutenant cleared his throat. "Cador, I believe you saw Sgt Finlay earlier that day, when he was still alive. We are interested in determining his movements."

Cador folded his wiry arms. "He came knocking at my door that morning, telling me some cock and bull story about smugglers. He reckoned there was going to be a drop that evening, or a fly, and told me to be on the lookout."

"Oh?" Judith tilted her head. Intriguing: here was a motive to kill the soldier, if he had indeed discovered a den of smugglers. "And was there a drop, or a…fly?"

"Not that I saw, though I went on patrol that evening," replied Cador dourly and truthfully.

"Did Sgt Finlay say how he came about his information?" she pressed.

"No, he did not. He was most clammy about it." Cador scowled. "Just told me to look out sharp, come moonrise, on the bay."

"So you went on patrol—by boat or foot?"

"Boat. The tide was in by then."

"And did you see anything at all suspicious that night?"

There was a pause. "No."

For the first time, Judith heard the hollow clang of a lie, making the fisherman's voice sound empty. She raised her brows. "Really? Nothing at all?"

"No," repeated Cador firmly, and just as untruthfully. "Only the gulls and the waves. No smugglers. And then the soldier, in the morning, by yonder rock." He pointed to a huge boulder that lay stranded by the tide, near the causeway, close to the shore.

Judith pursed her lips. He was lying, but how to force the matter? "I am enquiring about this on the request of Captain

Drumpellier," she urged. "Anything out of the ordinary must be reported, as a matter of military importance."

It was the wrong thing to say. Cador's expression became even more dour. "Captain Drumpellier has already questioned me, ma'am."

She bit back a sigh of impatience and glanced over the bay. "Can you at least show me where you found the body?"

Gloomily, Cador shut his door and led the way down the causeway. The smell of seaweed was pungent on the air, and gulls wheeled and called overhead. Judith lifted her skirts and followed, determined not to show any mincing airs of a London lady, despite her new title of marchioness. After all, she was a rector's daughter by birth, and well used to getting her hem dirty.

Cador walked about hundred yards along the cobbled path and halted. Nearby, at some distance from the causeway, but traversable over the wet sand, was an array of boulders, forming a little islet the size of a small house. When the tide was in, it would make a dark protrusion from the sea.

Grimly, Cador pointed to the rock. "That's Arloedhes Rock. Where the soldier lay, dead and sodden."

"Quite far from the shore then, when the tide is in," said Judith, with a flash of pity for the unfortunate soldier. The huge rocks were too sharply inclined to provide easy ascension, but he may have clung to them as support in his hour of need. Or had Sgt Finlay knocked his head on the bleak stone? Yet Captain Drumpellier had said the bruise was on the *back* of the head.

She turned to Ltn Greene. "The boulders are much closer to the mainland than the castle. Could he have swum most of the way, and then found himself in trouble?"

"It is possible," agreed Ltn Greene readily.

"And did Sgt Finlay have a particular reason for visiting the isle?"

"His platoon is on coastal patrol duty," said Ltn Greene.

Cador gave a scornful cough. "Patrol duties, I doubt it, with respect, ma'am. That solider were courting one of the dairy maids, Miss Isla, a pretty wench. Not that she would have him, I be bound."

Judith narrowed her eyes. "And was Sgt Finlay properly courting, or taking advantage? Speak plainly, I beg you."

"I couldn't say." Cador suddenly became wooden again, with a glance at Ltn Greene. "It is not for me to comment on the morals of an English soldier, ma'am."

Judith winced at the implication. "And this boulder? Does it have any significance, with its name?"

"Aye, it has a story to it." A glimmer of amusement returned to the fisherman's deep-set eyes. "A Lord Lanyon, far back, threw that boulder himself. He was trying to save his lady love from a giant that were chasing her, and threw it all the way from Castle Lanyon, if ye are to believe it, half a mile. But instead of saving her, it landed on her head and killed her dead." He finished on a note of dour triumph.

Judith blinked in dismay. "What a dreadful story."

"Ay, and it's said the lady still haunts the castle. The Crimson Lady of Lanyon, who stalks the corridors at night, both mourning and vengeful."

Judith pursed her lips sceptically, hearing Cador's tone distorted by the echo of exaggeration. Yet this was some confirmation of Drumpellier's warning of a ghost, though intriguingly *not* in the cellars. And she had some sympathy for the poor Lord Lanyon, who in trying to help his beloved had only condemned her.

She shook off the thought, her attention caught by something else: the power to throw a massive boulder sounded very much like the Gift of Impacting. Was Musing rife round these parts, or well known? How could she discreetly enquire? The new royal Edicts expressly forbade public mention of the magicks—a long tradition made explicit—but it was possible that Impact had killed the soldier before he fell in the water.

She shot a glance at Ltn Greene. He was in the confidence of Captain Drumpellier, and a lackey of the Custos, so he must know more. Politely, she thanked Cador for his information, and asked Ltn Greene to escort her in a walk across to the castle.

"Certainly, ma'am." He put out an arm, and she took it, stepping carefully over the wet cobblestones.

As they drew away from the fisherman, Judith lowered her voice. "Cador was covering something up."

Ltn Greene looked down at her in surprise. "Goodness, how do you know?"

"My Gift can hear it in his voice. He lied when he said he saw nothing suspicious. You can tell Drumpellier *that* when you see him."

Ltn Greene looked impressed, then doubtful. "Possibly Cador is merely in league with the smugglers himself," he suggested. "These Cornishmen don't understand the larger issues at stake; they are simply after the brandy."

"Well, that would give Cador himself a motive to dispatch a watchful soldier."

Ltn Greene nodded, then cleared his throat. "I do apologise, ma'am, that my captain has given you such a tawdry task. He comes from rather low beginnings and doesn't understand the proper order of things. A lady such as yourself should not be associated with such a sordid investigation."

She had begun to warm to the lieutenant, but this sentiment annoyed her. "I am perfectly able to look into the matter. It is the captain's attitude towards the Duke of Sargen that I find improper: not because of his rank, but because even a duke should be granted due process."

Ltn Greene looked away uncomfortably. "*In extremis*, I am afraid that due process is often neglected."

"*In extremis?*" she said sharply. "What *extremis?*"

He was silent, obviously regretting his words. She frowned. What could he mean? There was nothing urgent about the duke's impending trial, was there? But when she pressed him further, Ltn Greene clammed up, refusing to say anything more.

"And you?" she demanded, as they continued the walk along the causeway, the castle growing larger before them. "Are you a Musor? I assume you must be, for you are muddled up with the Custos."

"I am a Healor," he replied modestly. "Not much military use, except for when the wounded come in, but Drumpellier keeps me close, as a sort of runner."

"Oh good. If the duke is injured in his incarceration, you must Heal him." She thought also of Robert, most likely on his way to Cornwall now, who might need further Healing when he arrived. Ltn Greene might be a useful person to know, and she softened her tone towards him. "And do you know of any other Musors on Lanyon Isle?"

"Ah..." He shot her a sideways glance, with some amusement. "I thought it was good etiquette not to reveal someone else's Gift?"

"True, but in this case, we have a dead body to investigate."

He winced, the sea breeze blowing a brown lock over his brow. "If you are determined, then I can tell you that Miss Onslow is a Memor. As befits the Gift, she is very scholarly, concerned with cataloguing the castle's library."

Interesting. Captain Drumpellier had not thought to mention *that*. "And the servants?"

"I'm not sure," said Ltn Greene thoughtfully. "I suspect your butler, Trebellow, might be an Impactor."

"Why is that?"

"Wait 'til you see him," was all he would say, with a grin.

At that point, Judith became preoccupied with the view of the isle as they approached. It was, after all, intended as her new residence, and as she drew closer it sunk in properly that it was not simply a castle, but a whole island. To the right of the causeway loomed the staunch wall of a harbour, and beyond that the roofs of cottages. To the left, she could see the glimpse of green fields and cattle grazing. Above all loomed the massive fortification, grand and elegant, and she felt overwhelmed by the magnitude of it. How was she to be mistress of all this? Marchioness of Lanyon? She was a simple rector's daughter, not cut out for this sort of grandeur and responsibility.

As if hearing her thoughts, Ltn Greene spoke up. "The castle was originally a medieval monastery, built four hundred years ago. There is a lovely church in the middle of it all, though anyone might assume the dairy is the real heart of the island. The Lanyon cream is famous around these parts."

"Oh yes, so I've heard." Judith cheered up. Cream, jam, and chudleighs would be sufficient recompense and bolster her nerves. She could put dollops of cream in her drinking chocolate.

They reached the end of the causeway and Ltn Greene led her through the grey stone arch, lichened with age. Veering right, they began the climb to the castle. The narrow path was pretty, crowded by trees and foliage, hiding the battlements from view. It was steep, however, and when they came out on the first rampart, the wind was sharp.

Squaring his shoulders, Ltn Greene took her round to the front doors of Castle Lanyon. It was huge and imposing, and Judith felt quite oppressed as she stood in the shadow of the lintel, as if some sort of doom lay behind its facade, waiting. She took a step back, trying to shrug off the odd, gloomy feeling. This was not the sort of greeting one wanted from one's new residence! But before she could back further away, the doors creaked open.

In the dark of the frame, a large figure loomed: a mountain of a man, almost two feet taller than Judith. He was clad in the traditional garb of a butler: a black coat, white stockings, and a neat cravat, though his feet were like boats and his shoulders a wall.

"Good afternoon, ma'am." The mountain bowed, showing a shock of black hair lined with grey, over a craggy nose. "The new marchioness, I presume?"

In which a castle is in need of a new mistress

Ordinarily, one must trust one's senses. Yet sometimes they can be misleading, especially if the subtle enchantments of Diplomacy are employed.

— from *Lady Avely's Guide to Guile and Peril*

JUDITH INCLINED HER HEAD. "And you must be Trebellow?"

Trebellow rose from his bow, once more achieving his great height. "Indeed, I am Castle Lanyon's butler. Please, come this way to the Blue Drawing Room, ma'am, and I will command some refreshments for you. We are pleased to welcome you to your new abode."

Judith was glad to hear it, for she was growing hungry again after her long journey. The huge butler turned, revealing a high arched entryway with doors going off in every direction. He took the one in the far-right corner, and Judith followed, with Ltn Greene bringing up the rear.

Leading the way through long, dark corridors, Trebellow continued to speak in the softened vowels of a Cornishman.

"The Royal Steward wrote to say that you were coming a week ago—" he paused to let the reproof sink in "—so we have prepared a room for you. I hope you will find it satisfactory."

"I am certain I will," she said, though the warren of passage-ways was already confusing. At least the dreadful feeling at the front door had receded as she moved further away from it. Perhaps Trebellow had put a Defence spell on the anterior of the castle, which might account for the heavy feeling there. In the wake of the butler's wide shoulders and massive form, she could not wonder at Ltn Greene's hint that the fellow might be Gifted in Impacting. He looked as if he could throw a boulder even without the Gift.

Trebellow thrust a door open. As he stood aside, the close corridor opened up into what could only be the Blue Drawing Room. The walls were painted a lovely cool blue, set off with white accents and high ceilings that gave it a spacious feeling, and hung with heavy curtains in blue and gold. Yet the room felt cold, with the fire unlit. The windows, Judith observed in astonishment, were dirty, and the mantelpiece dusty. She care-fully sank onto one of the settees, mindful of Marigold in her pocket, while Ltn Greene stood nearby to attention.

Trebellow bowed again. "I will send the housekeeper in with a tray." His gaze weighed Judith's plain silk gown and simple mobcap, and something lightened in his regard. "I confess to a gladness in your arrival, ma'am. The castle has long been in need of a new mistress."

She nodded in acknowledgment, relieved that her butler did not show the same hostility as Cador had done. "I will rely upon your guidance as I go forward, Mr Trebellow."

"Of course." He paused. "With that in mind, please do not be put off by Mrs Ulrich, the housekeeper, with her gloomy air. She has been wasting away, with nothing to do. It will be well that you give her a direction for her energies."

Nothing to do? Surely the housekeeper would have plenty to occupy her in this extensive keep. Judith eyed the dusty mantlepiece. She could hear some sort of prevarication in the butler's voice, but she did not question him further. There was plenty of time to meet this Mrs Ulrich and ask the woman herself.

As Trebellow left, Ltn Greene widened his eyes in amusement. "Yes, you have a melancholic housekeeper! Your castle is complete! I warn you that she is suitably clad all in black, like a mournful crow." He grinned and gave a short bow. "Shall I leave you now, ma'am? Or do you wish me to assist you with your enquiries?"

Judith considered: it might be useful to have an extra pair of eyes and ears, but Ltn Greene's uniform would put the occupants on edge. And his offer was not as innocent as it seemed, for he was likely intending to spy on her for his captain.

"You may go. Thank you for your escort, and please tell Drumpellier that I will return in three days, whether he sends for me or not."

Ltn Greene bowed his head, a twinkle in his eye. "I will count it as a pleasure to come to fetch you."

"Thank you," she said gratefully. "Take some bread from the kitchen before you leave, now."

He clicked his heels together and left.

Half-expecting a gothic figure much like Ltn Greene had described, Judith was therefore surprised with Mrs Ulrich stalked into the room bearing a tea tray. The housekeeper was a stately, slender woman, clad in black, it was true, but more like an elegant heron than a crow. She had silver hair, gracefully pulled back in a bun, and green eyes that were nonetheless deeply shadowed. The contents of her tea tray matched her unfriendly expression: a pot of already cold tea, and a plate of old plum cake, dry and unappetising.

"Marchioness," she uttered, laying the tray down at Judith's side. "Welcome to Castle Lanyon."

The sentiment was a lie, but it wouldn't take a Gift to hear it. The housekeeper took a step back, put her hands behind her, and looked down her nose at Judith.

"Er, thank you." Judith eyed the stale cake, wishing she had the nerve to ask for some of the famous cream that abounded on the isle, or at least some butter. But she dared not under the scornful eye of her new housekeeper. Ulrich was a German name, wasn't it? This woman appeared to think she was descended from a royal line. In fact, Judith was starting to feel she ought to retreat from the castle, forsake any claims to it, and leave the field entirely. She wondered that Trebellow and the lieutenant had described this woman as gloomy: she didn't seem depressed, simply hostile.

She was suddenly disheartened. How could she possibly become the mistress to this pile? It was overweening pride to think that she, with her humble origins, could become a Marchioness: pure folly. The blue walls of the drawing room were abruptly icy.

Judith drew a steadying breath. Resolutely, she picked up the teapot and poured. Cold tea was still tea. She shook off her sudden plunge into gloom.

"Mrs Ulrich," she said firmly. "I hope we are to deal well together. Perhaps we can meet tomorrow, and you can explain to me how you run the place."

"Indeed, ma'am," said Mrs Ulrich austerely, while implying that such a thing was not in the realm of possibility.

Judith persevered, as she selected a piece of crumbling plum cake. "How many rooms do you keep open?"

"Four only, ma'am. Now including the master bedroom that you will occupy."

"And how many rooms are in the castle?"

"One hundred and twenty-one, ma'am."

Judith's mouth fell open, and she quickly snapped it shut again. "Good Lord. I can see why you keep them under covers. Does that include the fallen tower that I saw from the shore?"

"No, ma'am. Those rooms have long been abandoned, after a lightning storm many years ago. They are beyond help, well open to the elements."

"Indeed." Judith wondered if that tower was the location of the haunted cellars, but she did not want to betray her interest. Instead, she turned her questions to another urgent matter: the circumstances of Sgt Finlay's death. She needed to gather as much information as possible to present to Captain Drumpellier, even if she had the strong sense that Mrs Ulrich did not like answering questions.

"I wonder if you could tell me, Mrs Ulrich," she said carefully, "if you saw anything strange around the castle three nights ago. I've heard that a soldier died nearby that night."

Mrs Ulrich's green eyes hardened. "He was found on the mainland, ma'am."

"Yes, but he used to visit the castle, did he not?"

"I suppose so."

It was a strange answer, and Judith raised her brows. Mrs Ulrich pinned her gaze to the blue wallpaper and did not elaborate.

Judith ignored the feeling that she was treading on dangerous ground. "Were you on duty that afternoon?"

There was a pause. "Yes, ma'am."

A note of dissonance sounded in the aloof voice. Judith frowned. "Or perhaps you retired early?"

"No, ma'am. I was on duty, as I am every day."

The line was delivered with stinging condescension, but Judith could hear the hollow bell of untruth underneath. She sighed, taking another sip of cold tea. This was exactly the sort of thing she feared. Everyone she spoke to had some sort of secret, obscuring the real matter at hand. Looking at the straight shoulders and lifted nose of the housekeeper, however, she could not imagine the dignified Mrs Ulrich deigning to come to blows with a British soldier or having any reason to be rid of him. In fact, Judith was aware of some sympathy for the poor woman: in charge of this sprawling, ancient castle, with very little help, and no real purpose to it.

Well, all that was about to change.

"If you should hear anything, I would be grateful if you could inform me. I do not like to think there is any mystery about this soldier's death."

"No, ma'am."

"And we shall have to clean this castle up a bit, for I will be expecting guests before long."

"Guests, ma'am?"

"My son and daughter, at the very least." Perhaps better not to mention the prospect of bats just yet. Judith took another bite of stale plum cake. She was chewing it determinedly, and about to dismiss Mrs Ulrich, when a commotion came at the door.

A young woman hurried in. She wore green cambric, well-tailored in a modish style that suited her trim figure. Her brown hair was neatly tied back to show a rather striking face, with strong eyebrows and a firm, wide mouth. Her expression currently showed a degree of surprise and interest at Judith's arrival.

She came to a halt and dropped a low curtsy. "Marchioness! Is it indeed Lady Avely?"

Judith nodded, though the title was ill-fitting, especially under Mrs Ulrich's sceptical eye. "And who may I have the pleasure of addressing?"

The girl blushed. "I am sorry to thrust myself upon you like this. There is no one to introduce me properly, though I live here at the castle, you see. I am Miss Sophia Onslow. His Majesty kindly allows me to stay here and catalogue the library."

"Ah, the librarian! I was told of the circumstance," Judith admitted.

Miss Onslow smiled, then her eyes fell upon the tea tray. "Oh goodness, Mrs Ulrich! Why have you given her ladyship the last of that awful plum cake? You must fetch her some proper cream tea: it is traditional in Cornwall. And serve it in the Tea Tower Room, of course—you mustn't sit in this cold, dreary drawing room! Lady Avely, you are to be the mistress of the castle, after all! Come."

Judith was surprised to see Mrs Ulrich somewhat cowed by this performance, in that she inclined her head slightly and picked up the tray. Miss Onslow whirled around, gesturing, and after a moment Judith followed her.

Walking briskly, Miss Onslow led her through another winding passageway, and then up three flights of stairs, while chattering about the layout of the castle, and where the best views were to be found. Then she pushed open a heavy door and stood aside.

Judith stepped through, as if into a dream.

The Tea Tower Room was a large, circular room, with tall windows looking out in every direction onto wide vistas of the ocean. Ancient beams held up a high, pointed ceiling, and rich Turkish rugs crisscrossed the floor. The walls were hung with beautiful tapestries depicting the sea—sailing ships, islands, sunsets, mermaids—while couches stood comfortably beneath them. A curved bookshelf nestled sturdily into one third of the whole room, and opposite it, a large fire burned merrily. The whole of it hummed with a delightful feeling of soothing cheer and safety, as if here was the real sanctuary to be found.

Miss Onslow flung out a hand. "The Tower Tea Room! The true heart of this place! The Blue Drawing Room is all very proper and impressive for guests, but you aren't a guest, are you?"

"I suppose not." It was hard to imagine this all now belonged to her family. In awe, Judith walked over to one of the high windows. The sea stretched for miles out, a shimmering expanse that glittered in the setting sun. She could hear the wind whistling outside the tower, but it was a comforting sound. Down below, she could see waves breaking on the rocks of the isle, and the small white dots of puffins and gulls. Along the causeway, the red figure of Ltn Greene returned to the mainland.

Miss Onslow was waiting for her to take a seat, so Judith did so, sinking into one of the couches, under a painting of a sinuous siren. "What a delightful room!"

"Yes, I confess I have spent quite some time within it; I bring the books up from the library." Miss Onslow sat on a high-backed chair and gestured at a neat stack of books. "But I will return to my proper domain now that you are here, of course."

"Oh, well, I'm sure we can rub along well enough together," said Judith, a trifle uneasily, for she didn't want anyone disturbing her investigations or preparations. Then she remembered what Ltn Greene had told her: that Miss Onslow was a Musor. "I believe you are Gifted in Memory?"

Miss Onslow's gaze sharpened. "Who told you that?"

Judith winced. She did not feel it was fair to betray Ltn Greene's indiscretion, especially when it had been at her own insistence. "I was informed," she prevaricated, "because I too am a Musor: a Discernor."

"Oh, yes, of course!" Miss Onslow's shoulders relaxed. "I

suspected you might be some practitioner if the king granted you this place. You must have a powerful Gift."

"Oh, it was not for my efforts," Judith felt bound to say, "but those of my husband, who served and died for the Crown."

"Plenty do that,"—a note of bitterness sounded in the young voice—"without such recompense."

"True," said Judith, and saw her opportunity. "Indeed, a soldier died nearby, not three days ago, I believe?"

Miss Onslow pursed her lips. "Yes, Sgt Finlay." She seemed reluctant to say more.

"A tragedy?"

"Indeed."

The word was not quite true, and Judith cocked her head. "Did you know him?"

The young woman nodded. "I did." She paused. "Of course, any death is dreadful, but in fact, Lady Avely, he was quite an unpleasant man, and I cannot find it in myself to regret Sgt Finlay overmuch. He is not one who deserved reward for his service."

"Oh? Why is that?"

Miss Onslow hesitated, choosing her words carefully. "He paid far too much attention to the fairer sex, if you take my meaning."

Judith did. She remembered Cador's reference to the dairy-maid, Miss Isla. It sounded as if Sgt Finlay's attentions had indeed been more in the nature of a harassment than a courtship.

"I am sorry to hear that."

Miss Onslow shrugged it off. "He would neglect his duties as a result: a blot on the service. It is a shame they recruit all manner of men to the army."

"Yet Sgt Finlay dutifully reported rumours of smugglers on

the day he died," observed Judith. "Do you think *they* could have had something to do with his demise?"

"Oh goodness, Cornwall is rife with smugglers!" Miss Onslow's expression darkened further. "The locals think it is all fair game, but they don't realise that the boats take information across to France when they are fetching their brandy and lace. It ought to be stopped."

Judith raised her brows. "You think that Sgt Finlay tried to stop them?"

Miss Onslow's mouth twisted. But at that moment, Mrs Ulrich appeared in the doorway, carrying another tray with stately hostility and a grim expression. As she placed it on a table, Judith saw that this time the contents had improved, for it was laden with large bowls of cream and jam, a fresh pot of tea (this time covered in a woolly tea cosy), and a plate of round, fat chudleighs. She knew these particular delicacies from her stay in Devonshire: the yeast-leavened, buttery bread was soft and crumbly, and traditionally served with jam and cream.

"Wonderful!" said Miss Onslow. "A proper welcome for you!" She nodded in thanks to the housekeeper.

Mrs Ulrich's lips thinned, then she vanished down the stairs again.

Judith allowed the subject to change to the imperative topic of whether the cream or the jam was to be applied first. Miss Onslow informed her that in Cornwall, it was *definitively* the jam. Judith recalled that Devonians were of a different persuasion, but she politely did not mention it and dolloped the thick cream upon the rosy jelly.

"Mmm, strawberry?" she asked, after a delicious mouthful. "The cream *is* good, I must say."

"Lanyon Cream is the best in all of England," affirmed Miss Onslow. "In Bath we never had anything as good."

"You hie from Bath?"

"Yes." Miss Onslow licked her lips. "I was exiled here because of a minor scandal involving a rejected suitor. I didn't want to marry, you see: I'd much rather have my Gifts and my books. So, my mother sent me here, hoping to teach me a lesson. She thought that I would grow lonely." She looked around with a show of satisfaction. "Yet I am very happy at the edge of England, with the sea and solitude, in such a grand residence."

Judith heard the lie in her voice and wondered. It seemed unlikely that a young woman would not want the company of others, and suitors, and balls. Yet Memors were a different breed, content in the vast tracts of their minds, with mental resources of which others could not boast. And it *was* a lovely room, this Tea Tower.

A twitch of movement caught her eye, and she saw a new figure slink through the door: a cat. It was no ordinary cat, however, but a huge, magnificent creature, the largest she had ever seen. Its excessive fur was mostly black, but topped by a white face, which gave it an odd appearance. The large black and white ears currently twitched with curiosity.

The cat pretended to ignore her and stalked over to one of the windows. It proceeded to leap onto the sill and stare out as if surveying its realm with a faint air of disgust.

"That's Ghastagon," explained Miss Onslow, following her gaze. "Gorgeous creature, isn't he?"

"He looks as if he belongs to Trebellow."

Miss Onslow laughed. "He belongs to no one; indeed, he would have it that the castle belongs to him. He likes to give one a fright in the night, with that white face lurking in the darkness."

"I can imagine." Could that be the simple explanation for the haunted cellars? Ghastagon, hunting mice down there and curdling everyone's blood? Judith frowned, wondering if the cat was going to be a nuisance about Marigold. Traditionally, cats and vampiri did not rub along well together. But Miss Onslow's next words dispelled the worry.

"He is a special breed from Germany," she added. "Technically, he belongs to Mrs Ulrich, whose family brought over his ancestors. Apparently, the Zauberer breed is much more tolerant to vampiri than most cats. Not that I would know," she added, "as I do not have a vampiri."

Judith took a sip of tea, interested. "Why not? It would be most useful in your work, I imagine."

"There were not many in Bath," replied Miss Onslow, "and these Royal Edicts make it difficult to go about cultivating the acquaintance of one, when we are not allowed to be seen conversing together."

Judith was glad that Miss Onslow seemed to disapprove of the Edicts, for she planned on overturning them here in the confines of the castle. In fact, royal permission had been given to do so, though she wasn't going to mention that just yet. Perhaps Miss Onslow could befriend one of the roost. Another thought occurred to her. "Mrs Ulrich's family? Is she a Musor, too, then?"

"Ah, yes," said Miss Onslow. "A Diplomacor, I believe."

In which a butler is bashful

The guile of Diplomacy is insidious: sometimes, we are so taken by it that even when we know it is there, we do not object.
— from *Lady Avely's Guide to Guile and Peril*

"A DIPLOMACOR?" Judith put her cup down in surprise. "Mrs Ulrich didn't strike me as such." Diplomacors were usually charming sorts, able to finagle friendship out of anyone with their amenable air, while Mrs Ulrich had seemed closed and aloof. Perhaps that was why Judith had felt suddenly disheartened in the drawing room: the housekeeper had deliberately cast a pall over her!

"She's a miserable one, I grant you," agreed Miss Onslow. "I don't think she takes much joy in her Gift anymore."

Judith slathered another chudleigh with jam, both cross and thoughtful. Perhaps that was what Trebellow had meant when he implied that Mrs Ulrich was depressed: her magick had gone sour. It could explain why the front lintel of the castle cast such a heavy mantle over visitors: it was hung with a different sort of spell, to frighten people away. Diplomacy could influence the temper of a room, create a sentiment, and change a mind. Judith glanced around, suddenly perceiving another reason for the pervasive and soothing sense of ease. "Is there a Diplomacy enchantment on this parlour?"

Miss Onslow shrugged. "Possibly. You mean the sense of safety and comfort? It has always been like that, since I arrived. I suspect that it is an old, powerful spell, and not the doing of our delightful Mrs Ulrich."

With much to ponder, Judith soon excused herself from the Tea Tower, even though a part of her wished to simply curl up on the settee by the fire, open a book, and stay there until nightfall. The allure of the Diplomacy charm, perhaps, or simply her own fatigue. But she had Marigold to think of, who was no doubt rather squashed by now in her pocket, so she pulled the bell, and when Trebellow appeared, asked to be taken to her room.

Following him down the tower stairs, the thought of Dacian's plight also lurked painfully. How could she revel in cream tea while he was being kept captive and confused? Worse, Ltn Greene's words echoed in her mind. The lieutenant had implied there was some sort of *in extremis* to Dacian's capture, and she could not think what *that* could mean. After all, Dacian had been in exile for nine years on the continent. His crime had been committed long ago. Why the sense of urgency now to bring him to trial? Had someone else taken a hand in it, bringing the duke to the attention of the Custos? And why?

Trebellow led her in a confusing circuit, around and up again, and finally hesitated before a thick door. "Ma'am, I have placed you in the room traditionally occupied by the Lord or Lady of the castle. I thought that was the most appropriate course of action, given that you are now Marchioness of Lanyon, but you may find the accommodation rather eccentric."

Judith perceived that her butler seemed to be embarrassed for some reason. "Oh?"

"It's called the Captain's Cabin, ma'am. It was refurbished by a long-ago Lord Lanyon who had a fancy for the sea." Trebellow pushed the door open with a flourish. "You perceive."

Cautiously, Judith stepped past his extended arm and looked around in amazement. The room before her was certainly much larger than any cabin on a ship, but it was furnished in a similar fashion, with warm wooden panelling over the two opposing walls, complete with in-built shelves and dark-panelled cabinets. Rows of books were held in check by a narrow lip along the shelf, and an ornately carved sea-chest at the bottom of the bed depicted a ship sailing under a full moon.

The bed was enormous—quite the size of a boat itself—and covered in a dark green quilt. The sturdy headboard depicted dolphins paying court to Poseidon and Amphitrite, amid waving fronds of coral. Opposite this, the true glory of the room: ceiling-high windows facing the ocean, with an entrancing view of sea and sky. The windows were pleasingly rounded at the top, though the panes were dirtied and crusted with salt on the outside. A narrow rug of faded green and gold ran along the length of the windows, and an old telescope sat propped in the corner, next to a large silver bell.

She turned around slowly, taking it all in. A rope hung like a pulley across from the bell to the bed, and she wondered if it had served in the past as a perch for vampiri. It was certainly a very large bell, suitable for the captain of the castle, but she couldn't quite imagine pulling it herself.

Walking across to the furthest window, she admired the substantial writing desk placed to catch the light, set with brass fittings and a gimbal-mounted inkwell, now dry of ink. A ship's lantern hung above the desk, and old nautical maps were pinned across some of the wood panelling, showing faded, detailed renditions of the Cornwall coast and the Channel.

She did not think *this* room had a Diplomacy charm on it, despite its eccentric appearance. It felt strangely empty, as if it had been unoccupied for a long time. There was a faint smell of must, and the dark green curtains—currently gathered by a golden rope—were tattered and dusty.

"How charming." Privately, she thought it was rather masculine, and the olive-green bed-quilt could be changed to a lighter colour. She turned back to Trebellow. "I will need fresh ink and paper, if you will. For now, could I have some warm water to bathe in?" She eyed the massive sea-chest. "And I don't suppose there are any old gowns, in the far reaches of the castle? I am afraid I arrived in rather precipitous circumstances, and my luggage is a few days behind me."

Trebellow did not allow himself to express curiosity. "Certainly, ma'am. Are you happy to stay here, then?"

"Yes, indeed." If she was to be the new mistress of the castle, she might as well try out the Captain's Cabin, though it was rather large for one person. She would drown in that bed, by herself. A pang of longing for Dacian shot through her, and she repressed it. Beside the bed stood a large wooden wardrobe, which she hoped would soon be a suitable refuge for Marigold.

"Might you need a maid?" inquired Trebellow.

Judith knew this was a rebuke: she, as befit her new station, should have arrived with at least one servant, possibly three. "I will make do without, for the moment, and perhaps you can arrange one for the future." She paused, sighing, and sat on the chair, her allotted task ever present. "May I ask you what you were doing three nights ago, Trebellow? Were you on duty in the castle?"

The butler stiffened slightly. "I am always on duty, ma'am."

It was a resounding lie. Judith raised a brow. It seemed both the housekeeper and the butler had been otherwise occupied that night. Surely not *together*? How intriguing. "Yet you must have days off?"

Trebellow coughed. "Sundays, it is true, ma'am."

"But three days ago was Saturday."

"Precisely."

The implication was that he had been at his post. Yet Judith detected his unease. "Did you see anything unusual that night?"

His eyes narrowed. "Is this about the death of Sgt Finlay, ma'am?"

It was most trying when someone answered a question with a question. "Do you know anything about it?"

There was a pause. "I know he was discovered drowned near the causeway, by the mainland."

"So I have been told several times," she observed wryly.

"You suspect he was not drowned, ma'am?" Another careful question.

"I worry it. And so does Captain Drumpellier of Fort Pendennis. He asked me to look into the matter, so I am afraid that I must question all the servants here."

Trebellow's lips pursed. "Indeed, ma'am. Not the best way to begin your stewardship, if I may say so."

"I quite agree, but it is not proper of you to berate me thus." She must not let him grow too familiar too soon: butlers tended to think they were the true rulers of a household, though clearly Trebellow would have to fight Mrs Ulrich for that title. "Now I will ask you once more, what were you doing on the night of Sgt Finlay's death?"

The butler cast a look backwards. Then he ducked to step into the Captain's Room and shut the door behind him. For a moment, Judith was apprehensive, being closed in and alone with such a bulky specimen of masculinity. But the suddenly bashful look on his face stayed her anxiety. He shuffled on his large feet and hunched his shoulders.

"Ah, the truth, ma'am, is that I was at a wrasslin' match."

"A what?" she asked in astonishment.

"A wrasslin' match. The Londoners like to call it Cornish Hugg-Wrestling. I'm the local champion, see, but I must compete to defend my title."

"Oh." Judith stared at him blankly. "I suppose that you are built for it."

"Aye." Trebellow blushed.

"Where was this match?"

"In Marazion, ma'am. I crossed over the causeway early, when the tide was out at four o'clock, so I could be there for the evening." He paused. "The truth is that there was precious little for me to do here, as you had not yet arrived, and I thought to take advantage of the fact."

She highly doubted that, given the state of the castle, but she let it slide. "So you would not know if Sgt Finlay came to the island that night."

"No, ma'am. I'm sorry, ma'am."

She glanced at the closed door. "And tell me—is it true you are Gifted with Impacting?" At his nod, she tilted her head. "How does that fare in your wrestling? Surely it gives you an unfair advantage?"

Trebellow drew back his shoulders in affront. "Never, ma'am. We swear an oath in Cornish before every match: '*Sweet play is fair play.*' And each of us renounces the use of magick before any tournament, as is traditional."

"Oh? So the Musing is known round these parts?" Judith was surprised, for ordinarily it was kept well hidden.

"Well superstitioned, ma'am, but I keep to the oath." His head lowered, and his tone along with it. "Of course, I will give up the pastime now the castle is a proper residence once more."

Judith considered. "Well, I cannot see why you should *completely* curtail your wrassling ambitions now that I am here, but please be sure to ask for my permission before you attend the next tournament. Is there someone who can step into your duty while you are absent?"

"One of the twins, ma'am," said Trebellow eagerly. "Our footmen, Kynver and Kade. They are young, but Kynver could manage it for an evening."

"Ah, yes, the twins. Why have I not seen them yet?"

"They were helping at the dairy today, ma'am, for it is usually short of men."

Judith wondered if the twins flocked to the dairy for another reason: the famed Miss Isla. "I will need to speak to them soon. For now, I need a moment to myself. Please send both the footmen to fetch me for dinner, for I fear I will not be able to find my way without guidance."

"Yes, ma'am." Trebellow bowed, then met her eyes and grinned sheepishly. "Thank you, ma'am."

WHEN SHE WAS certain that Trebellow's footsteps had receded, Judith pulled the dark green curtains shut against the setting sun. The room became bathed in a dim green light, as if it were now under the sea, and gingerly she retrieved Marigold from her pocket. The little vampiri was still deeply asleep, curled up in a tiny ball in the flannel kerchief.

Judith did not want Trebellow, or anyone, to know of Marigold's existence just yet. Kept secret, she might prove to be an essential ally. She could spy, unperceived, on the inhabitants of the castle, and explore where Judith could not.

Carefully, she placed the vampiri in the top shelf of the large wardrobe, set in the back corner of the room. No one should think to look there that evening, and it was safe from any cat, should Ghastagon prove to betray his breeding. Then she lay down fully clothed on the huge bed, atop the dark quilt, and tried to order her thoughts.

She felt rather overwhelmed by the number of suspects she had been introduced to in short succession: Trebellow the butler, who seemed to have a reasonable explanation for his absence three nights ago; the hostile, stately Mrs Ulrich, who had also lied about being on duty and had yet to explain herself; Miss Onslow, who had expressed a dislike of Sgt Finlay; the twin footmen, whom she had not yet met; Cador, the taciturn fisherman; and the pretty dairymaid, Miss Isla. Or, she thought, some unknown smuggler who had not wanted the soldier interfering in a lucrative business.

It might very well be that one of those living at the castle was in league with the smugglers. Judith knew that smuggling was a common practice in Cornwall and Devon, often aided and abetted by locals who believed it was a just evasion of onerous war tariffs. And Castle Lanyon seemed an ideal place to land goods away from the mainland.

Miss Onslow had not doubted the existence of smugglers for a second; perhaps that was because she knew them all too well, though her disdain for them had been real. Could Sgt Finlay be the one who had been smuggling? Perhaps his direction to Cador to be on the lookout had been a feint. It was a pity Judith couldn't interrogate a dead man to see if *he* lied.

So far, Trebellow seemed to be the most likely candidate for violence, yet he would have no need to resort to a blow to the back of the head if he were an Impactor. Such a knock could have been administered by a woman just as easily. Judith was picturing a lovely dairymaid smacking a lecherous Sgt Finlay with a milk bucket, when a tap came at the door, heralding the arrival of her hot water.

It was borne in by two young men in footmen's livery: the twins. They were indeed identical, with handsome, narrow faces, sallow complexions, and dark mops of hair. Their lean figures were clad in matching livery of navy blue and gold, though one of them wore a red ribbon tucked in a top pocket. Judith wondered if this conceit was mandated by Trebellow in order to tell them apart. They were both looking around the Captain's Cabin as if they had never seen it before.

She sat up. "Thank you, and good evening. You must be Kynver and Kade?"

The two boys bowed low.

"Which one is which, if I may enquire?"

"I am Kynver," replied the footmen decorated with a ribbon, his voice low and pleasant, his smile charming.

The other said nothing. It was true that his name was thus implied, but still Judith found the silence a little insolent. "Trebellow tells me you have been helping in the dairy today."

"Yes, one of us," replied Kynver, his smile becoming a little roguish. Ah, perhaps it *was* the allure of Miss Isla that drew his generosity. She wondered if the two boys competed for the maid's affections, and if they would defend her from the inopportune attentions of a soldier. Perhaps one of *them* had wielded the milk bucket.

Behind them, Mrs Ulrich appeared, regally bearing a creamy gown that frothed with lace over her arms: old-fashioned and heavy skirted. "Will this do, ma'am?"

Judith did not wince. "Thank you, I suppose it will, for now. Kynver and Kade, please return for me in an hour, so you can guide me to dinner." She had not yet an opportunity to question them.

"I will fetch more gowns," announced Mrs Ulrich. She cast a

glance at the creamy pile in her arms. "We have several from the last century."

Judith sighed, but she bathed and dressed in the ridiculously frothy confection, feeling much like a character from a play, perhaps Lady Macbeth. What would Dacian say if he could see her in this monstrosity of lace? No doubt he would insist she take it off, even if he still couldn't remember her name.

She stared at herself in the mirror and wrung her fingers together to hold the fear at bay that he might never remember. Her last sight of him twisted at her heart: his jaw tense, arms folded, leaning against cold stone as he watched her leave. Would he manage to avoid further Lethe and recover his wits? But she must not dwell on his plight now, or it would erode her own courage, which she needed for the night's investigation.

Impatiently, she waited for the footmen to return, as per her instructions to take her to dinner, but when the door eventually opened it showed only one.

"Kynver?" she enquired, seeing the red ribbon tucked into the pocket.

"Yes, ma'am," came the response, but the voice echoed hollowly with the lie.

Judith stiffened, eying the servant. It must be Kade; but she bit back her quick retort. Perhaps it was better to pretend she was fooled by the charade and see whether she could gather the reason for it.

"Where is Kade?"

"Chopping wood." Another lie, of course, for Kade was standing before her. Was Kynver taking his place at the wood-pile, then, or somewhere else entirely? Judith repressed her huff.

"A shame he is not here, as I wished to ask you both some questions."

"Oh?" Faint unease sounded in his voice. Kade certainly did not have the assured charm of his brother.

"Yes, about what you may have seen three nights ago."

Kade did not blink, but his expression became fixed. "Three nights ago, ma'am?"

"The night Sgt Finlay died. Did you know him?"

"He visited the castle often, ma'am."

"Why?"

"As part of his patrol, I believe." A note of doubt sounded in his voice, or disbelief. And perhaps irritation.

"There was no other reason for his visits?" She paused then took a risky shot. "I heard he was courting a dairymaid on the isle."

A dark brow raised with scorn, and Kade's voice became certain. "Sgt Finlay might have tried, ma'am, but he would not have succeeded."

"Why is that?"

After a hesitation, the black eyes met hers again. "Because my brother Kade is courting her, with some success."

He was talking about himself, but Judith tried to parse the odd lie in his voice. Was the courtship *without* success? Or was it simply because he was referring to himself in the third person that made the words ring hollow? The determination in his gaze made it clear that at least one of the twins were pursuing the lovely Miss Isla.

She weighed his slight form and glittering eyes. Could Kade have been provoked by jealousy or chivalry into murder? Was he the wielder of the milk-bucket?

"Did you see Sgt Finlay that day?"

"I did." A pause. "I saw him crossing the causeway, around noon."

"To the castle, or away from it?"

"Towards the castle."

His words rung true. Judith frowned. "So the tide was out at noon. Did he manage to return in time? Perhaps he left it too late and drowned, as Cador suggested."

"Perhaps." The footman dared not shrug, but she felt his disdain nonetheless. "His body was found at the boulder near the end of the causeway. The one we call Arloedhes Karek, the Lady's Rock."

"Indeed. So, he made his way across somehow, whether by sea or foot. What time would the causeway next have been revealed?"

"Around midnight," admitted the footman, reluctantly.

"Sgt Finlay must have left long before that." This observation was met with silence, and a growl from Judith's stomach. She sighed. "Very well. Lead the way to dinner, please."

This time, the corridors were slightly more familiar, but still confusing. Judith wondered how on earth she was to find the cellars later and consoled herself that at least she could easily claim to be lost should anyone stumble across her escapade. Though, of course, as the new lady of the house, she shouldn't have to explain herself to anyone.

Dinner was a tepid affair in a rather odd dining room, which Trebellow informed her used to be the dining hall for the monks centuries ago. The table was a massive slab of wood, and the frieze near the ceiling depicted scenes of hunting. The food was uninspired: a cabbage soup, followed by braised chicken and a rice pot. Trebellow also awkwardly informed her that the cook was only young and new to the post, but he was sure that the fare would improve.

"What happened to the old cook?" Judith took a sip of the watery soup.

"She didn't like it here." Trebellow did not elaborate, and Judith wondered if the cook's dislike had something to do with the haunted cellars. But she did not want to alert the butler to her interest and plodded on with finishing the unappetising meal. Finally, she set her bowl aside and nodded to Trebellow. "I am weary; I shall retire now."

It was a lie, of course. She was still wide awake from all the sleeping she had done that morning at Pendennis, which seemed a lifetime ago now. It was a good thing too, as once everyone was asleep, she had cellars to inspect.

In which there are humbling reflections on the ducal character

✣

Dacian

Dacian knew he ought to be sleeping. The candles left by the guards were close to guttering. He had saved one of the wax sticks as a precaution, but it was next to useless having a spare light when there was no way out.

There was no point staying awake. He was trapped here, not merely behind an iron lock but also beneath weighty spells of Defence layered into the stone.

His hands flexed into fists. The little bat claimed that Dacian was ordinarily flush with power, but even if he had it now, he suspected he would not be able to break out of this cell. It was pointless to glare threateningly at the walls. There wasn't even a guard outside for him to rattle, that's how certain they were of his immobility.

Still, he did not trust sleep. He was starting to remember things. Just small flashes of knowledge, suddenly resolving in the dark corners of his mind. It was like finding something under a blanket: once you knew it was there, you couldn't forget it again. He had recollected his sister Agatha, a little termagant with dark colouring and a sharp tongue, and his father, a cold, hard duke. But he suspected they were old memories: his father might be dead by now, and his sister older than twelve. He had more memories to unfold, he knew it. Yet if he fell into a slumber, he might wake up back at the beginning, knowing nothing, in that awful place of emptiness and uncertainty.

Whoever he was, he knew that he was better than this. He would not allow some upstart captain to hold him here for long. There must be some way to turn the tables, if only he could remember what was going on.

So he sat in his throne of stone and red carpets, watching the shadows flickering on the wall. He had taken the bats' advice: both Wooten and another little French one (who had flown off for now) had told him not to eat or drink anything, and this advice had been echoed by the beautiful woman who had thrown herself down by the grate in the early hours of the morning. Judith, she had called herself. A stranger to him, but she swore she knew him well, her eyes filling with tears and her knuckles white on the bars.

He had wanted to believe her, but innate caution warned him not to trust anyone in this godforsaken place. It could have been a nice little piece of theatre when the captain had marched in and hauled her out, an attempt to convince him she was on Dacian's side. An old trick, sending in the gentle gaoler after the harsh. He wasn't going to play that game. He wasn't going to play any game. He wasn't going to eat or drink either, until he knew more of the pieces on the board, like his own goddamn memories.

So now he was hungry, and very thirsty.

Wooten had tested the last bottle of water himself, and had not died or lost his wits, but that was several hours ago.

Or perhaps he *had* lost his wits, because at the moment Wooten was blathering on about Dacian's state of attire.

"Absolutely abhorrent," he was muttering, "to leave a duke without recourse to his valet. The Custos should know better. You don't even have a coat. Though quite frankly," he added, "it was a mercy that they took your cravat, the state that it was in."

"I'm not cold, flittermouse."

Wooten fixed with him with a withering glare. "I'm not a flittermouse, as you very well know. And the point is that leaving you thus attired puts you at too much of a disadvantage. No wonder you don't know yourself."

Dacian sighed. "I doubt a coat would grant me self-knowledge."

"You'd be surprised what a good coat can achieve. And boots. And a decent cravat."

"What's a cravat?"

Wooten gasped in horror.

Dacian was only teasing. He knew cravats. His condition—or the drug—seemed to grant him general knowledge of the world while drawing an impenetrable veil over anything of a personal nature. He could tell Wooten about the war against France, but he didn't know if he had fought in it, or even his own title. Wooten had informed him that he'd done covert work while he was in exile from England. To Dacian's mind, that was even more reason to be suspicious of his current predicament. He flung a hand over his head, and felt it thud against cold rock.

His mind wandered to the woman again. Judith. *She* could be working covertly. Yet something in her eyes, as they rested on him, had seemed genuine. Though that could be his own wishful thinking. She had claimed to be an old friend, but he rather hoped that they had been lovers too. Surely he wouldn't have let a bosom like that pass him by? Especially when topped by such a face, and those pleading eyes.

Wooten was monologuing about the function and beauty of

cravats. Dacian interrupted. "That woman, Judith Avely." The name felt strange on his lips. "How well did I know her, exactly?"

Wooten paused. "Very well, I believe. I met her only upon our return to England, but you've known her since you were a young man. Or so you informed me."

"Carnally?"

Wooten coughed, displeased. "I believe not. Though I gather it was not for lack of trying on your part, your grace."

"You mean she refused me?" Dacian raised a brow, somehow not surprised.

"I believe so."

"Well, look at me. My attire leaves much to be desired."

Wooten sniffed. "You were better dressed on the occasions."

"In the plural? Even more humbling. Why did she rebuke my overtures?" Dacian could believe it, even putting aside his incarceration and evidently terrible temper. Even kneeling on the floor, she had seemed untouchable, contained within herself, resolute. What did she want with a reprobate like him? Though surely he was worth a second glance, at least. He had a feeling that he was quite handsome.

Wooten appeared to weigh his words. "Well, you lied to her, pushed her away, and also disappeared without a trace for several years."

Lord. A litany of sins. Dacian sighed. It seemed he was a right bastard. "So why, then, has she come back for me?"

Wooten did not answer. Instead, he stiffened and held up a warning finger. Then, in a blink, he disappeared under a pile of cushions, whisking under a particular richly patterned blue one with golden tassels. A few moments later, Dacian heard footsteps descending the stairwell.

He feigned sleep, tipping his head back and peering through closed lashes. It was most likely the captain again, bringing him another bottle of tampered wine, or a bowl of poisoned soup. Fortunately, Dacian had gone past hunger now, into a hard place of impervious denial. If only he wasn't so goddamn tired as well, and his mind so murky.

It was not Drumpellier. It was the lieutenant, Greene or something, his round face peering through the grate. Dacian watched, tense, as he scanned the room. What the hell was the lieutenant searching the room for? Wooten had better not twitch those cursed gold tassels. Suddenly, Dacian felt protective of the little creature. For all his lecturing, the bat was his only ally in this place (besides the mysterious Miss Belfleur), and he'd be damned if he'd let this soldier find him.

He kept his breathing even, and his eyes fixed on the lieutenant. To his astonishment, the man proceeded to kneel by the grate, a little like Judith had done, though without the same grace or charm. He held a bottle of water in his hand, and he waved it about, as if trying to gain Dacian's attention.

Dacian remained still. The lieutenant sighed and then made a great performance of drinking out of the bottle. Dacian saw his throat bob and heard the gulping swallows, and watched him wipe the liquid from his lips. He stayed quiet, regulating his breath. The soldier carefully set the bottle down on the ledge, and then pulled out a pie, mangled, from a napkin wrapped in his pocket. He enacted the same performance, taking a large bite and chewing solemnly before placing the pie next to the glass bottle.

He cleared his throat. Dacian continued to feign sleep, his senses acute. With a sigh, the lieutenant stood up and assumed his position of guard duty, facing out towards the passageway.

Dacian dared shift his gaze. He saw Wooten's eye peering up from under a tassel, wide and startled. He had obviously witnessed the pantomime too. The vampiri gave a jerk of his head, encouraging.

Suddenly, Dacian did not feel so impervious. With the possibility of real, untainted food before him, he was abruptly ravenous. Still, he waited another twenty long minutes, his eyes fixed to the grate, watching, reluctant, and fearing a trick.

When he felt his eyelids begin to droop, he made a decision. Better to eat it now, than fall asleep and have it whisked away or ruined. He shook himself and gave a theatrical yawn. Two could play at charades. Clearing his throat and groaning a little, he ambled over to the grate, his bare feet kicking a cushion out of the way.

The lieutenant was still standing there, his shadow long against the ground. He stared straight ahead, and did not turn, though he must have heard Dacian approach. Quietly, Dacian took the food and drink, and retreated.

Then he sat cross-legged on a rug like a sultan and wolfed it down.

In which a cellar is foreboding

I have often thought that it is a great pity that vampiri can only sense the casting of magick, and not the Charm itself.
— from *Lady Avely's Guide to Guile and Peril*

AFTER THE LACKLUSTRE DINNER, Trebellow guided Judith back to her room. Dismissing him with thanks, she locked the door after him and waited quietly.

In a few moments, she crossed to her cupboard. Peering in, she saw that Marigold was awake. She yawned largely for such a small creature and asked if Judith had solved the murder yet.

"Not yet," Judith carried her to the long windowsill, while Marigold looked around the room curiously. "Welcome to the Captain's Cabin. I'm now, rather uncomfortably, the Captain of Castle Lanyon. Moreover, it seems that my crew is a little mutinous."

Marigold eyed the massive bell with the rope pulley. "Just ring that, and it should make them all jump."

"I dare not." Judith laughed, then sobered. "You know,

Marigold, you are free to leave now if you wish and end our bond. It was always intended to be a temporary measure, and here I am dragging you into yet more peril."

"Ha! As if I would miss out on the adventure!"

"Are you certain?" At Marigold's nod, Judith sighed and pulled back the sleeve of her gown, and while Marigold fed, she described her encounters thus far, using it as an opportunity to order her suspicions. "So Trebellow left at noon, and Sgt Finlay arrived around the same time. On the face of it, that excuses Trebellow from guilt, for he tells me he was at his wrassling matches all afternoon."

"Good. Better not to have a murderous butler, if one can."

"Yes, nor a vengeful ghost, but it sounds like the Crimson Lady is quite the fixture at the castle. Cador said she walks the corridors, not the cellars, but I haven't run into her yet."

"Well, let us hunt her out," said Marigold cheerfully.

Judith scanned her with misgiving. "You have no clothes with you." The flannel kerchief inadequately shielded Marigold's modesty, and furthermore it was starting to look rather grimy.

"I shan't need them as a bat."

That did not resolve the question should they need to converse, but Judith reasoned to herself that they should not run into anyone in the cellars at night, so Marigold might avoid too much of a scandal. For one night, at least.

Hoping that the castle's inhabitants retired early, she cautiously opened the door. The empty corridor beckoned, and they emerged. Marigold hovered at Judith's shoulders and both of them kept a sharp eye out for any Crimson Lady.

"You go ahead," whispered Judith, holding a brass candle aloft. "See if your nose can find the kitchens."

She trod slowly after, and sure enough, Marigold soon returned with a direction, leading Judith down in a spiral through the castle. The passageways of stone and carpet helped muffle her steps, and she kept her ears pricked. Only the pounding of the waves met her perception, seemingly upon the very walls of the keep. The tide must be in again, the causeway covered.

For some reason, the thought made her shiver: they were stuck here, unable to leave until the waters receded again. Fortunately, the corridors showed no trace of any lady, Crimson or otherwise, though Judith once felt the breath of air upon her neck. She whipped around sharply but saw nothing; it must have simply been the draught from the old walls.

Eventually, they reached the kitchen. It was empty, though awash with the smell of chicken, cabbage, and fat. Judith circuited around it, noting that it was neat and ordered: the new young cook had that much to recommend her, even if her cabbage soup left much to be desired. The larder looked a little sparse, but at the back of it was a heavy door: the entry to the cellars.

Drawing a breath, she wrenched it open and descended down a broad sweep of steps, holding her candle before her. Marigold fluttered at her shoulder, her wings sending faint rushes of air against Judith's cheeks.

The circle of light showed the dim expanse of a large room, stacked with barrels and wooden boxes, and hung with produce. Pushing past the sprigs of lavender and rosemary, and the dangling chains of onions, Judith pressed further in. It grew colder as she went deeper, and she suspected by the smell of it that there were ice blocks placed at intervals, wrapped in hay to keep them cool. At the far wall, she saw two archways, one leading to further rooms, and one cresting stairs to an even deeper cellar.

Pausing, she wrinkled her nose. It was not the smell of hay or meat that bothered her, but rather the sense of something *sad* just outside her perception, like tears ignored. Was this the pall of dread that Drumpellier had mentioned? It seemed to emanate from the stairs lower down, rather than the other archway. Resolutely she breasted them, gesturing for Marigold to follow, and trod downward.

Halfway down, she paused, startled. The room below was *huge*, much larger than the well-stocked cellar above. The walls stretched out so deep and far that she could barely make out the other end. She marvelled at the construction of it, even as she saw that it was mostly empty, except for a wheelbarrow, a spade, and broom propped up against a wall, and a bevy of round-bellied kegs crowded in the back. Uneasily, she was aware that the whole castle pressed down upon her. The pounding of the waves was now louder, a great murmuring thunder.

Judith descended the rest of the stairs cautiously, lifting her candle. The massive room was strangely barren apart from the kegs. Perhaps it was too large to keep cold, and indeed it was oddly warm, moderated in its bower of earth. Judith looked around in satisfaction: here indeed was a suitable hall for a queen's roost. She could transform this into something elegant and welcoming, given time. She could just imagine the walls softened by hangings, and the floor carpeted a warm red. The long wooden beams across the high ceiling were perfect for bats, and she could affix ropes and landings.

Rectangles of darkness interspersed the left-hand wall, hinting at further storerooms, or possible guest vampiri rooms. She peered into the dark archways as she passed, seeing cells of varying size and cleanliness. As she strolled along, she noted with interest that the feeling of sorrow was intensifying. In fact, it seemed to be coming in waves from the far corner where the kegs sat.

It was now mixed with an insidious fear, suggesting to any visitor that they should leave *right now*.

Judith paused and braced herself against the enchantment, for that was surely what it was. Grimly, she noted that she had felt an echo of it earlier in the day when Mrs Ulrich had served her plum cake. *That* had been an exercise of Diplomacy, subtle yet effective, persuading Judith that she was unwise to stay. This was a similar weaving, she was certain, but increased manifold times and mixed with a dreadful grief.

She had a moment to wonder if the gloomy housekeeper had fashioned this experience too. Almost, she began to feel sorry for her, to be able to evince such sorrow. Then a glimpse of movement caught her eye. She spun around, her candle flickering wildly.

A shape of woman hovered against the far wall. Her face was dim and indistinct, her dark hair piled upon her head, bare of any cap. Judith had half-expected to see Mrs Ulrich, but this woman wore an ornate gown from a bygone age, glowing deep red in the fluctuating light.

Judith stared, disbelieving. After a long, tense moment, the figure vanished, leaving darkness in her place.

"Did you see that?" she hissed to Marigold.

Marigold dived down, becoming human and clinging to Judith's skirts. "Yes!" she squeaked.

"She seemed strangely far away. As if she were beyond the wall."

"Uh huh," said Marigold nervously.

"It is a trick, of course."

"Uh huh."

"A crimson gown, I note."

Marigold was silent. Then the red figure suddenly flickered into sight again.

Judith tried to master her nerves, despite the fear and dread that now overwhelmed her. This was *not* a ghost, she told herself. For one thing, the sense of despair was emanating from the far-left corner with the kegs, not the wall where the Crimson Lady hovered to her right. There must be two different charms working together in unison. Ordinarily, someone treated to the chorus of them would be too unnerved to think closely on it, but Judith was not an ordinary observer. She was accustomed to parsing truth from lies.

The lady vanished again, leaving darkness in her wake. Bracing herself, Judith turned her back on the spectre and trod towards the awful feeling that came from the kegs, stoutly disregarding the instinct that told her to flee. Whatever it was, it didn't want anyone near it, which was enough to pique her curiosity.

Really, it was quite understandable that the last cook had left her position. Who would want to fetch the potatoes with *this* lurking below? It simply *must* be hiding something.

She reached the kegs, and stopped, assailed now with the scent of brandy, fruit, and spices. It was the heady smell of ratafia: peach, citrus, cinnamon, and cloves, mixed with brandy. The sweetened liquor was commonly drunk by ladies of the ton, and it took months to ferment. Someone had set up quite the operation here, for there were at least a dozen kegs slowly fermenting in their dark nursery.

A smugglers' stash? Judith wondered. It was doubtful that smugglers would trade in ratafia, but the brandy could be a smuggled ingredient. Could this be the reason for the theatrical ghost, to hide this secret brewery? It seemed an excessive performance for what could be claimed as lawful goods.

Then she saw it: another door, shadowed and easy to miss. It was set deep into the corner behind the kegs.

"Aha," she murmured. "A secret door!"

"Excellent," said Marigold, with some irony. "Only...it seems to be a door of doom."

Judith had to agree, gritting her teeth at the sense that

welled from the door. It was a cry of dread, of deep, dark despair, and she felt as if she might suffocate with the horror, or drop into never-ending sadness. She had to hold herself firmly as she gripped the handle, repressing the notion that the Crimson Lady had only appeared to warn her. Was this another more dire admonition? Might she find a mouldering skeleton beyond?

Carefully, she opened the door.

But rather than a skeleton, her dim candlelight showed a broad passage, with an archway at the end. She stepped through into the welling anguish, narrowing her eyes, searching for the charm that must hold this awful Dread Spell. Spinning in a slow circle, she held herself stiff. Marigold clung to her pocket, eyes slitted, her body hunched and rigid.

Above the lintel they had just crossed, Judith saw it. A wine cork, unassuming but oddly placed. It lay flat, just visible, its shadow flung larger by the flickering light. She stepped towards it, reaching as high as she could, but it remained frustratingly out of reach. She wished she had Dacian with her right now, and not just because he was tall.

"Marigold," she whispered. "The cork above the lintel. Can you fetch it for me? I suspect it might hold the charm."

She held her light up. Marigold lifted into the air, wings sweeping out. She flapped past Judith's shoulder, and in the sudden draft of her flight, the candle went out.

The darkness was abrupt and complete.

Judith bit back a curse, her heart thudding loudly. Wing beats fluttered against her face, and a moment later, her skirts twitched slightly again.

"I'm sorry," Marigold whispered. "I was unnerved."

Judith couldn't blame her. She tried not to dwell on the fact that they were deep within the bowels of the castle, a dreadful sense of horror all around, and a red spectre in the next room.

"Never mind," she replied calmly, despite the constriction in her throat. "Did you get the cork?"

"It seems to be stuck. But it certainly felt like the source of it all. Like imminent death by despair."

Judith considered. "Perhaps it is best to leave it." She took a wary breath. "Is anyone around?"

"No. Other than the Crimson Lady next door." The skirts twitched again.

"Such an ostentatious ghost." The sense of terror clawed at her throat, and she told herself firmly that it was false. "Marigold, you are going to have to tug me in the right direction, for I can see nothing. But first I would much appreciate it if you could fly through that arch and tell me what lies beyond."

"Are you mad?"

"Please, Marigold. I cannot see, so you must look. We cannot abandon the opportunity now. This is obviously what the Crimson Lady is trying to hide."

Marigold heaved a sigh and detached herself from Judith's skirts, presumably twisting into her bat form again.

Judith was given plenty of time to regret her instruction, as she was left sitting right under the Cork of Doom in the black darkness, with only the company of a ghost in the next room. She swallowed and felt her way back through the door—holding her breath as she passed under the lintel—and edged into the large cellar, creeping along the wall until she felt the reassuring bump of a keg of ratafia. Closing her eyes, she clenched her fingers on the solid wood and focused on the smell, identifying the fragrances in a bid to distract her thoughts. Cloves. Cinnamon. Orange. The scent of fortified brandy reminded her, oddly, of Almacks and her last outing there with her daughter. Nothing could be further from this stark cellar than the famous assembly rooms, bright with dancing and laughter. Though, of course, the ratafia at Almacks was famously watered down, unlike the rich smell that wafted from the kegs.

Long minutes later, a brush of air heralded the return of Marigold. The weight of her human form landed on Judith's shoulder.

"There's another small cellar," she whispered in her ear. "With a table, two chairs, two glasses, and a decanter of brandy, by the smell of it. And less dread."

"A meeting place," Judith speculated. "And smuggled brandy, I'll wager."

"Looks like it."

"Anything else?"

"Beyond, another passageway. I didn't want to go too far down and leave you here in the dark. Regardless, I came to another door and couldn't turn the handle myself, curse it."

That was the problem with vampiri: even in their human form, their tiny fingers could not manage to turn large doorknobs.

"Curse it, indeed," said Judith. "How intriguing, another passageway. We'll have to come back in daylight, with another lantern."

"Yes, but can we leave now?" asked Marigold plaintively. "Let's hie away from this awful miasma. I'll tug you in the right direction. Better close the door first."

Judith felt a scrap of lace tug at her bodice, and she edged obligingly along, pulling the door shut with a soft thud, with much relief to put a barrier between her and the Cork of Doom. Then she had the unnerving task of traversing into the huge empty blackness of the underground hall. At least she was inching away from the despair, though she did not like to think of the Crimson Lady watching her progress. Soon, thankfully, they had left the nest of kegs far behind. Marigold whispered a warning, guiding Judith around the wheelbarrow and spade, until they reached the stairs to the upper cellar.

Judith had managed two faltering steps up the stairs when suddenly Marigold swooped up to her ear again.

"Footsteps," she hissed.

Judith froze on the stairs. Ears straining, she could hear nothing over the pounding of the sea. Then she made it out: soft footsteps, and the swishing of skirts.

It seemed to come from just above her head. Or behind her, or below her. Judith shook herself sharply, her skin prickling. It must be Mrs Ulrich, coming to check on her ratafia, walking through the cellar above, or the kitchen. Judith grimaced, for she would be in plain sight to any candle, standing like a startled rabbit on the steps. And Mrs Ulrich surely would not believe her excuse of being 'lost', so far from her room.

Yet the footsteps did not pause at the cellar door above. They continued and faded, in what direction Judith could not fathom, slow and deliberate.

Judith felt Marigold lift off her shoulder without a word. She did not need to be told to flit high and unseen, to track the hidden walker.

After an interminably long time, she returned, settling next to Judith's ear again with a huff. Her voice was low and baffled. "I couldn't see her anywhere. Do you think it *was* a ghost?"

Judith frowned. "Nonsense. It must have been the housekeeper. Perhaps she went behind a door where you could not follow."

"I didn't hear any door." Marigold was silent for a moment. "I'm starting to doubt anyone was there in the first place."

Judith shook her head in the darkness. "The atmosphere of the place is impeding your judgment."

At that moment, Marigold gave a tiny scream. It was rather loud in Judith's ear and made her start.

"What?!"

"A creature! An enormous creature! With a white face and glowing eyes!" Marigold gulped. "It's coming down the steps!"

After a horrified moment, Judith's shoulders sank in relief. "That must be Ghastagon, the castle cat."

"A cat!" If anything, Marigold's voice lifted higher. "It's enormous!"

Judith felt the push of a large body against her skirts and heard a loud rumble. Ghastagon was purring.

"He wants a pat."

"Don't pat him! He's a monster!"

She recalled that Marigold had experienced violent encounters with a feline previously at the inn where they had met. "He won't eat you. Miss Onslow told me that he is a Zauberer breed, who tolerate vampiri." Cautiously, Judith bent slightly to run her hand over the massive furry body. The purr intensified.

"Well, *I* don't tolerate *him*!" Marigold scrambled onto the top of Judith's head, to move farther away from the lethal jaws.

Ghastagon purred even more loudly, pushing himself against Judith's legs. "I think he might want some food."

"Yes, me!"

"Come now, Marigold. He hasn't tried to leap at you, despite all your squawking."

"Squawking!"

"And I still can't see, so you must lead on."

"Not I!" Marigold continued to cling to Judith's mobcap.

Sighing, Judith put her hand against the wall of the stairs, using it to guide her. It was even more difficult trying to navigate steps in the dark with a monstrous feline underfoot and a vampiri on her head, but she doggedly managed it, while Marigold kept up a stream of invective from her vantage point. When they reached the well-stocked cellar, however, the vampiri condescended to drag Judith forward by the ribbons of her mobcap, in the direction of the final steps to the kitchen.

They had left the door open, so a faint light came through as Judith grew closer. As she crested the steps, she was extremely glad to see the glow of coals in the hearth. She quickly set about lighting her candle again. Ghastagon's white face peered up at her, oddly amusing in the sudden relief of tension.

"Let's see what I can find for you," she murmured, and after a short hunt around the kitchen, presented him with a couple of herring, stolen from a string drying above the fireplace. "I hope the cook won't miss them."

Marigold perched on a high wooden beam. "Don't encourage him!"

Judith smiled down at the cat, who was wolfing down the herring with a pleasing enthusiasm. Poor creature, he must be hungry. She would have to ensure he was properly cared for now that she was mistress of the castle. Then he looked up and let out an ear-splitting miaow, much like the keening of a goat.

Her smile dropped. "Shhh!"

"Miaaaooow!" repeated Ghastagon, now like a large goat giving birth.

Judith snatched another herring and thrust it at him. Then she picked up her candle and skirts and ran out the kitchen.

Of course, they became hopelessly lost on the return journey, for this time Marigold didn't have the scent of the kitchens to guide her. Yet they eventually managed to scout out a path back to the Captain's Cabin, and Judith collapsed gratefully onto the huge bed.

"Good work, Marigold. Could you have a hunt around, while I sleep? See if there is anything else nefarious lurking around."

"You mean apart from the cat?"

Ghastagon had followed Judith up to her room, perhaps hoping that she would produce more herring. He now leapt onto the bed and clawed at the blankets, purring loudly again. At least he had stopped keening. Perhaps his wails explained the myth of the Crimson Lady, suggesting desperate despair to the unwary listener.

Marigold eyed him in disgust, though with less alarm, for it was true that he seemed uninterested in eating her. "I don't know if I should be offended or not. Cats are usually *eager* to snack on me."

"Perhaps you can be friends instead." Judith kicked off her slippers, absently stroking Ghastagon. Marigold huffed and leapt into the air, becoming a bat once more, and vanished out the door, leaving it open a crack.

Judith stared at the large feline. A belated thought had arisen: the memory of Miss Onslow saying that Ghastagon could be quite frightening with his white face showing in the dark. The observation had proven true, but now Judith wondered how Miss Onslow had cause to make it. Had she been the one creeping around the castle so late?

Or if, as was far more likely, Mrs Ulrich had been the prowler, what was the housekeeper up to? And if she was hiding something in the bowels of the earth, why, then, didn't she come down the stairs?

Firmly, Judith put aside the foolish thought that the footsteps might truly belong to a perambulating ghost. Marigold must have simply—in the strain of the moment—missed the sound of a door opening. It was quite unnecessary to postulate the existence of a lady who could pass through walls.

In which a letter is written

Beware the peril of an insubordinate housekeeper. It is essential that there is no ill-feeling between the two mistresses of any household.
    — from *Lady Avely's Guide to Guile and Peril*

JUDITH WAS WOKEN before dawn by Marigold tugging on her ear.

Blearily, she opened her eyes to see that Ghastagon had disappeared. Marigold was sitting stark naked in his place, with a disgruntled expression.

"Open the cupboard, please. The sun rises soon."

Judith sat up and carried Marigold over, unlatching the cupboard door. "Did you see anything interesting on your gallivant?"

Marigold shrugged as she clambered onto the upper shelf. "Cows, puffins, cottages, a dairy, a hundred rooms to this castle, and lots of locked doors impervious to my determined assault." She brightened. "But it does seem to me that there are some rooms without windows, which may be ideal for vampiri, away from sunlight."

Judith reflected it might be a good thing they needn't rely upon the cellars, if she couldn't detach the Cork of Doom. She shuddered at the memory. "What about attics?"

"Also locked." Wearily, Marigold crawled further into the cupboard.

"No sign of others like yourself?"

Marigold shook her head. "Not that I saw."

Judith sighed, fetched a new linen handkerchief (courtesy of Trebellow), and tucked her in. "Sleep well, my dear. Don't forget: tonight, you must fly halfway to Pendennis to meet Wooten for news."

"I'm sure the duke is fine." Marigold yawned. "Don't fret too much. You still have two days to find your answer and bargain for his freedom."

But with Marigold safely shut away, Judith found it difficult to fall asleep again. Now she wasn't preoccupied with investigating a haunted cellar, thoughts of Dacian's plight plagued her. Yet—she told herself—he was safe enough in his gaol. Wooten was watching over him, and Yvette too. Marigold was right, they had time. Two days should be enough for a Truth Discernor to discover a murderer.

It was frustrating that she didn't already have the answer, but at least she had some news to report to Drumpellier about the 'ghost'. It seemed clear to her that the Cork of Doom had been infused with a Diplomacy enchantment, to keep people away from a secret meeting place. Was it a smugglers' lair? If that was the case, maybe Sgt Finlay had discovered it and been killed for his pains.

Judith frowned. That would make Mrs Ulrich the smuggler and the villain, for surely she was the one casting the Dread Spell, with her uniquely powerful Diplomacy. Yet even if the housekeeper was mixed up with smuggling, it did not necessarily follow that she killed the soldier. A chat with the Mrs Ulrich was imperative, and Judith's Discerning ear could clarify the matter. Then she could return triumphant to Fort Pendennis and demand Dacian's release.

First, however, she must write a letter for Marigold to carry at nightfall. Trebellow had delivered foolscap and refreshed the gimbal-mounted inkwell as requested. Judith sat down at the captain's table by the window, to compose a letter by lanternlight and the faint luminescence of dawn.

It took some thought to know where to start.

Dearest Dacian,

I have high hopes that you are slowly recovering your memory by now. In case you have not, I remind you that I am your dear friend, Judith. At least, I hope I am dear to you, for you are such to me.

She paused here and pressed her lips firmly together. It would be much better if she could say that in person, while winding her hands around his neck and pressing against him, breathing in his smell. She *would* have the chance to do so, she was determined.

But some history, in case you do not recall—I married your good friend, Nicholas Avely, when I was young. Suffice to say, I would have married you instead, but you turned me away with a lie, out of some sort of misguided sense of honour.

The anger that had once overtaken her when she had realised his duplicity now turned to sorrow. If only she had realised the lie at the time. If only...

Nicholas died twelve years ago. Perhaps I would have renewed our friendship then, but I did not know that you had lied, and I was angry that you had kept a secret of Nicholas' from me. Then you fled to the continent, after your fatal encounter with Lord Garvey, and stayed away for nine years without a word.

While we are on the vexed topic of Lord Garvey, please understand *this: your Impact killed him, but only with the help of another. And you were under the Illusion that Lord Garvey held <u>me</u> in his arms, so you were unfairly provoked. I have explained this to Captain Drumpellier, but I will endeavour to make it heard at your trial.*

In the meanwhile, it is <u>imperative</u> that you do not allow your captors to muddle your wits any further. Play the fool, pretend to drink and eat what they give you, and let Wooten take it away. And continue to act your forgetfulness, so they do not suspect. I have a lowering suspicion that there is some other force at play. I suspect there is someone eager to prevent your pardon, despite my testimony. If that is the case, we will have to take other measures to gain your freedom. I beg you to be on the lookout for any interventions I may have to stage.

Judith paused here, knowing that she should not write more than one page, for Marigold had to carry the weight of it a long distance. What more could she say, regardless? She did not want her first words of love to him to be cold and black on a page, easily disbelieved, and perhaps meaningless. Yet what if she should not have any other chance?

Beloved, I pray for your safety and your memory. I hope that we shall converse once again as dear friends, or something rather more.

Yours always,

Judith Avely

Marchioness of Lanyon

P.S. That last title is a new one to me, should you find it confusing. You first knew me as Miss Judith Horis, picking blackberries on your estate...

With that duty done—though unsatisfactorily—she sighed and blew the candle out. She ought to sleep more, but as she tossed and turned on the huge, quilted bed, visions of the Crimson Lady flickered in her mind, along with an unnerving sense of lurking doom. Damn Mrs Ulrich and her Diplomacy; it was all too effective.

SHE WAS WOKEN HOURS LATER, the curtains glowing deep green with sunlight and muffling the sound of gulls crying outside. A tap came at the door, and when she called for entry, Trebellow appeared, holding a breakfast tray.

He set the tray down on her lap, presenting a pitiful breakfast: cold tea again, dry toast, and a spotted pear, brown and soft. There was not a chocolate molinet in sight.

Too hungry to confront the butler immediately with any of these crimes, Judith poured herself a cup of tea and swore to herself that she would sort out the chocolate situation as soon as she had sorted out the mystery of Sgt Finlay's death. If not sooner. She had to keep her strength up, after all, if she was to continue feeding Marigold.

Trebellow opened the curtains, allowing sunlight to pour into the room, brightening the wood-panelled walls and gleaming on the silver bell. "A lovely day, ma'am."

"Indeed." Judith nibbled on the browning pear. "A good day for a spring clean, don't you think? Perhaps today we should clear out some of the dust and grime and prepare the castle for guests."

"Guests, ma'am?"

"Yes, I am expecting... a young friend to join me soon, with my luggage. And the rest of my family will eventually arrive, too. I hope you don't mind me remarking, but some of the windows could do with a clean."

He shifted uncomfortably. "Yes, ma'am. I will inform Mrs Ulrich."

"Don't look so worried, Trebellow. Clean windows might cheer Mrs Ulrich's spirits too."

"Indeed, ma'am." Trebellow coughed. "Mrs Ulrich's blood is already mixed with spirits, if you take my meaning."

"Oh?" Judith raised her brows.

The butler looked as if he regretted his lapse. "Shall we say —she finds comfort in brandy. But don't we all, ma'am?"

"Ah."

Brandy mixed with fruit and spices, no doubt. Judith contemplated the remains of her pear. Could this be why Mrs Ulrich guarded the lower cellar with her Dread Diplomacy, simply to protect a vice? It would explain why the housekeeper had been so disagreeable. Being mastered by brandy did not make for joyful days.

"Is there some reason that Mrs Ulrich turns to the drink, Trebellow? I find it is usually to escape an unpleasant reality."

He cleared his throat. "Ah, ever since she lost her husband a few years back, ma'am. It wore away all her courtesies, I'm afraid. She is rather grim to be around now."

Judith's heart sank with pity. No wonder Mrs Ulrich's Diplomacy had descended into dreariness. Was the Cork of Doom simply an outlet for her despair, stuffed down out of sight below the castle? She frowned. Perhaps it had nothing to do with Sgt Finlay, after all.

"Well, we must try to give Mrs Ulrich something other than brandy to enjoy," she said firmly. "Send her into me, please, and I will discuss the matter with her."

Doubt flitted across Trebellow's face, but he bowed and withdrew. Judith set about finishing her cold toast and was pouring another cup of bitter tea when Mrs Ulrich herself came in.

The housekeeper was as stately and sour as yesterday, and yet, in the fresh light of the morning, Judith could see that her green eyes were bloodshot and tired. It was a hint that Trebellow's disclosure was correct, and that Mrs Ulrich did not have full mastery of herself. Judith was aware of a sharp sympathy, but she put it aside. The housekeeper's weary appearance could also be further proof that she had been prowling around late at night, up to no good.

Judith paused with the cup at her lips, thoughtful. If it *had* been her footsteps, then why hadn't Mrs Ulrich come down to the kegs and secret room? Had she somehow known that Judith was there, petrified on the steps? If that was the case, it would be fruitless to try to keep watch for any smugglers and catch them in the act.

It might be better to try and shock them into action and betray their hand. Then Judith could take a whole party of villains to Drumpellier, and he would be forced to demonstrate his gratitude.

"You requested my presence, ma'am?" The housekeeper stood with her hand on the doorknob, quite as if *she* were the mistress of the household.

The sight annoyed Judith, provoking her into bluntness. "Yes, I have a question for you, Mrs Ulrich: is the castle haunted?"

The housekeeper's hand fell from the doorknob, a sight which pleased Judith immensely. After a moment, Mrs Ulrich said, "Yes, ma'am. There are many accounts of the Crimson Lady of Lanyon."

Judith's brows went up. Strangely, Mrs Ulrich's words did not ring hollow. True, she was speaking of 'many accounts', which could well be hearsay, and a clever evasion. But her initial affirmative had sounded honest.

"And why does she walk, do you know?"

Mrs Ulrich hesitated again. "Some say she was Lord Lanyon's lady love, the one he killed with a boulder, the Arloedhes Karek."

"Then surely she would walk by the causeway?"

"Ghosts are not rational creatures, ma'am. They remain human in that way."

Judith let that pass. "And where does she frequent, if not the causeway?"

"She is most often seen in the long northern corridor, but who's to know where else she wanders?"

Judith heard the bell of truth and frowned. It seemed that Mrs Ulrich *did* believe in the ghost. Had Judith been wrong about the Cork of Doom, after all?

Then Mrs Ulrich leaned forward slightly, as if to convey a confidence, gripping her pale hands tightly together. "Best to keep away from the cellars too, if you can, ma'am. It's true there's a dreadful feeling down there in the dark."

Judith narrowed her eyes at this blatant attempt to dupe her, even though the words did not ring empty. Well, it certainly *was* true that there was a dreadful feeling down there in the dark. She began to feel cross. Did Mrs Ulrich think she was stupid?

She linked her fingers together. "And what is the Crimson's Lady's purpose, I wonder? To chase off the unwanted, perhaps?"

Mrs Ulrich did not seem to register Judith's sardonic tone, for she remained impassive. "It is said, ma'am, that she doesn't like those who have the Gift of Impacting. It was that which killed her, and some say that she will curse any Impactor in her path. But I don't believe that myself. It is men who like to paint her as a weak woman crushed by a rock."

Judith stared, taken aback. This was loquacity—and truthfulness—that she had not expected. "Then how *did* she die, by your reckoning?"

"She sacrificed herself," said Mrs Ulrich. "She carried the rocks of Arloedhes Karek herself to the end of the causeway to block the marauders. It is my belief she fought to the end, holding them at bay, until she died in the Northern Corridor at the hands of the new lord."

Judith blinked. The housekeeper was not lying. Only pity

coloured her voice, though her face remained aloof. And this was a very different version of events: the Crimson Lady not as a tragic lover, but a strong woman defeated. Typical if the tale had been distorted to enshrine male power instead of womanly fierceness. Judith pursed her lips, aware of some fellow feeling with Mrs Ulrich.

Then she became aware of another sensation: a subtle weaving of grief laying over her.

She shook her head briskly, annoyed. "A terrible story. Nonetheless, Mrs Ulrich, even if it were true, we cannot have her disturbing the cellars. What say you that we clear them out today, and put the Crimson Lady to rest?"

The housekeeper's eyes widened, and the weaving of sorrow fell away. Judith continued inexorably. "Kynver and Kade can help with the heavy lifting, if necessary. Even I will roll up my sleeves and lend a hand with a broom." The thought of some solid, practical work was quite appealing, after all this poking around in the dark. "We can all help you."

"The cellars are already cleared," replied Mrs Ulrich, after a tense moment. "Do not concern yourself with them, ma'am. You need never go down there at all. It's not a place for a lady."

"And yet the Crimson Lady seems to be quite at home there! I feel as if I need to establish myself, Mrs Ulrich, as the only Lady of Lanyon. I do not like having a ghost competing with me or casting a pall of gloom about."

This time, the housekeeper seemed to hear the underlying meaning, and she lowered her eyes. "No, ma'am. Indeed not, ma'am. But you must not humble yourself to help; it would be unseemly in a marchioness."

"Before I was a marchioness, I was a rector's daughter, and well used to being my father's housekeeper," said Judith bluntly. "I shall not balk at some cleaning."

A flash of surprise crossed Mrs Ulrich's face, quickly hidden.

Judith tipped her head. She was aware of a desire to be frank, and it was not—if she was honest with herself—just to provoke a reaction. She wanted to see if it was possible that they could work together, after all. "The truth is, Mrs Ulrich, that I shall have need of those cellars. My children are on their way to Castle Lanyon, escorting a lost roost of French vampiri. We need to prepare some appropriate quarters for them, well out of the sun. And we cannot have the Crimson Lady disturbing their nights."

"A whole roost, ma'am?" Mrs Ulrich stared. "What of the Royal Edicts?"

"Precisely my point: the vampiri must be kept well out of sight. And I should mention that they may have been hibernating for many years and therefore be a little wild. However, they are accompanied by their queen."

This news succeeded in shocking the dour housekeeper. She drew a quick breath that might almost be called a gasp. "Ma'am...! A French queen? The cellars won't do for that. We have other rooms, far more salubrious—" She caught herself and continued in more measured tones. "Castle Lanyon is well accustomed to receiving royalty, after all."

Judith was glad to see a chink in the stately armour, and finally a hint of housewifely pride. "The French queen might be well pleased with the cellars and feel safer there. I will visit them later this morning and see for myself." She paused and took the plunge. "I expect any trace of the Crimson Lady to be quite vanquished by then. I hope you understand me? We cannot have such enchantments disturbing the peace."

Mrs Ulrich's eyes narrowed at her significant tone. There was a silence. Judith took a sip of her cold tea, meeting her gaze over the rim.

"Yes, ma'am." Mrs Ulrich looked away. "I will do my best. I

must also prepare a room for Baron Quarles, as he is due to arrive this afternoon—if you are still happy to permit his visit?"

Judith allowed the change of subject. "Has the baron not been informed of the castle's change in ownership?"

"It seems not, ma'am."

Or the baron was trying to push his luck. Yet she would need to question him. He had, after all, been staying at the castle when Sgt Finlay had died. It was intriguing that he was returning so soon—to the scene of his crime? Judith sighed. "I suppose he may, if he has a standing royal invitation. Give him a room situated far from me, and please ask Trebellow to meet me in the Blue Drawing Room in an hour, so I can further confer with him."

"Yes, ma'am."

After further discussion, canvassing the state of the windows in the drawing room, among other matters, Judith dismissed Mrs Ulrich. She curtsied and left with a return of her austere mien. Yet Judith dared to hope that she had made a slightly better impression upon her redoubtable housekeeper, and that they might find some way towards conciliation.

In which a visitor arrives early

Traditionally, enchantments of Diplomacy are used to create peace, soothe troubled souls, and broker congeniality. However, in their darker manifestations, they can be used as a defence or an attack.
— from *Lady Avely's Guide to Guile and Peril*

JUDITH's blue silk gown had been cleaned, and she donned it with a sense of triumph, along with an uneasy doubt. She hoped she hadn't been too hasty in confronting Mrs Ulrich and forcing the issue of the ghost. Yet the cellars must be swept and cleaned, and any spells removed. The housekeeper could not be allowed to wallow in her grief. And if dismantling the Crimson Lady caused the smuggler—or murderer—to show their hand, then all to the good.

She doubted, now, that Mrs Ulrich was a villain. She rather hoped not. The housekeeper clearly believed in the Crimson Lady and had amplified the rumours to guard her kegs of ratafia. But that did not mean she had killed Sgt Finlay just to protect her stash.

Baron Quarles's visit at this point was an interesting development. Was *he* a smuggler? Or had he some other quarrel with Sgt Finlay? Was he returning to the scene of his crime? Judith decided she would be quite interested to meet this baron.

She tied on her matching mobcap, wishing she had her Norwich shawl to throw over her shoulders. Robert was bringing her trunks and accoutrements, but she could not reasonably expect him till the morrow, for he would be travelling slowly with his injury. She rather looked forward to showing him the castle: it was a grand old dame, and impressive with its beautiful views and skirts of green and blue. And his Gift of Illusion might prove useful in her investigation.

The rest of the morning passed quickly. Trebellow proved most helpful when she listed her requirements: a room to be prepared immediately for Robert; several rooms to be aired in preparation for the possible arrival of her children and the Earl of Beresford in the future; drinking chocolate to be sourced; another gown to be found; and Baron Quarles to be informed that this was sadly to be his last visit. When questioned about his lordship's activities, Trebellow was dismissive.

"Oh, the baron is harmless enough; he potters around on the upper terraces at night with his telescope."

"You've never seen him belowstairs?"

Trebellow paused. "Once, yes, ma'am. He was talking to the old cook, the one who left. I'm not certain what they discussed. It might have been about his lordship's possets, which he liked to have at night."

Judith sighed. A pity she couldn't question the old cook. And a posset might be nice too, if she couldn't have drinking chocolate.

Having put Kade to work on scrubbing the windows (at least, she *thought* it was Kade, for he was not adorned with the red ribbon), Judith spent some time going through the list of staff with Trebellow and arranging for more help to be employed to assist Mrs Ulrich. It was ridiculous that a castle this large should be barely staffed, and from a close inspection of the books it seemed that the income from the dairy should allow for more expenditure. Eventually, weary from parsing the accounts, she asked the butler to send luncheon to the Tea Tower. She was feeling hungry after her inadequate breakfast, and the Tea Tower Room's pleasant, cheerful air was a balm.

Outside, the sea was no longer such a bright blue, with clouds sweeping in from the north. The piling, soft blankets in the sky made their own sort of beauty. She ate slowly, enjoying the warmth of the cheery fire and the comforting presence of books and Ghastagon, who was stretched out showing his stomach in a rather indecorous manner.

There was no sign of Miss Onslow, who must have retreated to her library as she had promised. Judith had just drunk the last sip of her tea—still no chocolate, unfortunately—when Trebellow appeared in the doorway, puffing slightly.

"Ma'am, your first visitor has arrived."

"Robert?" She put down her cup eagerly. "Already?"

"I assume it is he: a hired coach is crossing the causeway as we speak. Baron Quarles usually arrives in his own carriage."

Judith crossed to the window and saw the small shape of a coach trundling across the thin, curving line of the causeway. It was pulled by two horses: Robert must have travelled recklessly fast to reach Cornwall so soon. Pleased satisfaction rose in Judith, though it warred with anxiety for his wound.

"Goodness, take me down to greet him at once!"

Trebellow bowed and led her down the stairs and passage-ways. It was most provoking that she still didn't quite know the way around the castle, but soon she stood in the arched entryway with its multitude of doors. The butler pressed open the heavy leaf of the entrance, and she stepped out.

At once, she felt the pervading sense of doom she had felt upon her arrival. She shook her head crossly, trying to shrug off the grim feeling. She had forgotten to tell Mrs Ulrich to dismantle this charm as well. Or perhaps this one wasn't Mrs Ulrich's.

"Trebellow, have you put a Defence charm upon this lintel?"

He looked surprised, and stepped after her, tilting his head. He frowned. "Ah. I see what you mean. It is not simply my Defences, ma'am." He paused. "I will speak to Mrs Ulrich."

"Please do." She looked at him curiously. "Have you never noticed it before?"

Oddly, he flushed. "No, ma'am. I apologise, ma'am."

She wondered how he could have missed it: perhaps he left the castle at a run, being so eager to reach his wrassling matches. Or, more likely, he left by the servants' entrance.

Rubbing her arms, she shivered, for a brisk breeze was blowing, cutting through the silk of her gown, and the sea was growing choppy with surging white tips. "We must walk to meet Robert. He is injured and you may need to carry him."

They met Robert about halfway down the path, under the tunnel of trees. He was limping, but valiantly working his way up the steep avenue, his brow furrowed, leaning heavily upon a walking stick while also carrying a portmanteau. The coachman walked behind him, labouring under two more valises, which must be hers and the duke's.

"Robert!" she called. "How on earth did you arrive so quickly?"

He stopped, leaning upon his stick, and smiled at the sight of her. "I'm afraid I called upon the duke's resources and changed horses several times. I reasoned that his grace would want me to join you as soon as possible."

She tutted. "What of your injury?" Gaining his side, she kissed his cheek, patting his arm in affection. His blue eyes did look rather heavy with fatigue, and his clothes wrinkled. Judith was inordinately pleased to see that he had decided not to wear his old livery and instead adopted the clothes of a gentleman. He was wearing one of the duke's coats, with an inexpertly tied (and rather bedraggled) cravat.

He answered her anxious question. "Miss Garvey employed her nursing talents on me. My leg is much improved already."

"Hm," said Judith sceptically. "Do you want my butler to carry you for the remainder of the climb?"

"Certainly not!" Robert's expression was affronted. Then he took in the sight of Trebellow, a small mountain blocking the path, and he grinned. "It looks like you could carry both me and Lady Avely at once."

Trebellow bowed. "If it were so required, sir."

"Not at the moment." Robert staunchly continued walking, while Trebellow took his portmanteau. "What's news of the duke?"

She shot him a warning look. "Oh, he is all right enough, I dare say. I'll tell you about it later."

He nodded and obediently changed the subject, glancing around. "I must say, Castle Lanyon is beyond anything I imagined. It has its own island!"

"It's rather grand, isn't it?" Judith took his arm, hoping he would lean on it. "The housekeeper informs me it has one hundred and twenty-one rooms, so I assure you there is plenty of space for you. And there are delightful landscapes to paint, if you wish to do so."

They chattered on about such trivial matters, although she sensed Robert's impatience for news. Then, when they came in view of the entrance, they saw Miss Onslow coming round the corner of the ramparts, dressed in a fetching gown of dark apricot with green trimmings. She drew up in surprise at the sight of them.

Judith smiled. "Ah, Miss Onslow! Out for some fresh air?"

"Indeed, before the rain comes." Her curious gaze took in Robert's tall form and chestnut hair, the blue eyes and clefted chin, and she blinked.

Judith introduced them. "This is Mr Robert Steer," she added, remembering with a pang that Robert wished to continue under his mother's name. She hesitated, unsure how to describe her relation to him, but Robert came to her rescue after an awkward pause.

"I am a distant cousin of Lady Avely's," he said quickly, "on her husband's side."

Judith tried to hide her surprise. Her feelings were mixed: displeasure that he would not admit to a more immediate family connection, but relief that he was prepared, at least, to claim some sort of relation. She saw Trebellow cast her a curious glance, for she had not described Robert as family. "He has come to stay with me while he recovers from an injury," she explained.

Miss Onslow curtsied. "Were you injured while fighting Bonaparte's troops, sir?" she said, with marked interest.

Robert flushed. "Er, no, nothing of the sort, I'm afraid." He looked very embarrassed. Perhaps he was also conscious that until a day ago, he had been in the lowly position of a footman. Ordinarily he would not have been permitted to address a gentlewoman as an equal, despite his schooling at Taunton.

"Oh, I do apologise." Miss Onslow also looked embarrassed. "It is simply that my brother is missing in action, and I fear for his life. I'm afraid my eagerness to hear any news of him led me to jump to a hasty conclusion."

Robert looked at the ground, red still staining his cheeks. "Unfortunately, I cannot tell you anything about the front."

Judith intervened hastily. "The truth is that Robert leapt in front of a bullet for me: that is how he was injured. I am extremely grateful for his bravery." At Miss Onslow's look of astonishment, Judith continued. "Perhaps we can tell you about it, if you join us in the Blue Drawing Room for refreshments. I suspect that Robert will not manage the climb all the way to the Tea Tower."

Miss Onslow admitted to being most intrigued, and she led them to the Blue Drawing Room, while Trebellow was sent to fetch cream tea. Soon they were all settled in the elegant chaises, and Judith was entertaining Miss Onslow with their tale of how a master Illusor had confronted them at gunpoint.

"Goodness," said Miss Onslow, smothering cream over another chudleigh, with an admiring glance at Robert. "You are both so courageous. I cannot imagine facing such peril."

Robert took refuge in a sip of tea and said nothing. Perhaps he did not want to mention that both Judith and Dacian had been closer to the danger in question, and that he had been concerned with conjuring a yew hedge at the time.

Miss Onslow continued. "And you say that, despite all this, his grace is now incarcerated at Fort Pendennis?"

"Yes," said Judith firmly, ignoring Captain Drumpellier's warning not to mention the presence of the Musor Custos. "Awaiting trial." Seeing Robert's anxious look, she added, "He is safe enough for now, and I intend to visit him again soon."

At this moment, Trebellow, who had been standing back (as unobtrusively as a man of his size could manage) spoke up. "Do you mean his grace, the Duke of Sargen?" He had missed the first part of the story, in his quest for refreshments.

"Indeed."

Trebellow's eyes lit up with interest, but he did not say anything more, recalling his place and pressing his lips together. Judith eyed him, for there was an air of repressed excitement about him now, rather like a mountain showing faint signs of being a volcano.

"What is it, Trebellow? Do you know the Duke of Sargen?"

His eyes gleamed. "Aye, if he's the one who's been abroad for nigh on ten years?" At Judith's nod, he continued. "He's a verra good wrassler, that man."

Judith stared. "Cornish wrassler?"

"Aye, he used to come up to Cornwall for a match when he were younger."

Somehow, Judith wasn't surprised. Dacian tended towards recklessness and stupid masculine displays of virility.

"Perhaps he'd like to see the next tournament," continued Trebellow, his enthusiasm causing him to forget the reticence proper to a butler. "We'd be honoured to have him, ma'am, and even more so if he would fight."

"Well, that is impossible at the moment," said Judith tartly, "for he is imprisoned."

Trebellow pursed his lips in disgust, obviously feeling that anyone who favoured Cornish wrassling should immediately be granted a general pardon.

Miss Onslow, chudleigh at the ready, cocked her head. "Do you mean under Captain Drumpellier's command? I know the captain quite well. He visits Castle Lanyon often, so perhaps I can add my entreaties on behalf of his grace." She cast her eyes down demurely and took a delicate nibble and licked the cream off her lips. Robert watched, mesmerised.

Judith was distracted by another matter: Captain Drumpellier often visited Castle Lanyon, did he? "Does the captain have much business to attend to here?"

"He has to check on the platoon stationed in Marazion," Miss Onslow offered, somewhat evasively. That, however, did not quite explain why he visited the isle. Yet if he was courting Miss Onslow, all the better, for she could add her voice to Dacian's defence. Judith recalled Drumpellier's look of wry amusement when he had mentioned Miss Onslow, and hoped it was one of fondness.

All this talk of Dacian was also making Judith rather tense with worry. While they chatted over cream tea, he was trapped in that dank dungeon with only half his wits. She worried her blue silk between her fingers, wishing she could transport him into the Tea Tower, sit him before the fire, and brush the hair from his eyes. Then maybe she would sit on his lap and kiss him soundly, even if he couldn't remember her just yet. Judith rather suspected that he would welcome her overtures enthusiastically, even if she remained a stranger to him. You could take a man's memory and leave his lust intact—especially if it were Dacian's lust.

Judith sighed. There was no point daydreaming. She put down her tea. "Robert, I insist that you rest now. You are looking rather peaked. And I must inspect the cellars! I have a ghost to oust."

In which brooms are deployed

Oddly enough, it is in the realms of courtship and affection that many deploy excessive guile, perhaps out of a desire to guard their hearts. This, of course, can be a bar to genuine affection.

— from *Lady Avely's Guide to Guile and Peril*

JUDITH LEFT Robert still sitting with Miss Onslow, finishing the last of the chudleighs under Trebellow's benevolent eye. Did Miss Onslow require a chaperone now that a young man was staying at the castle? Quite possibly, yes. With any luck, she already had a maid to perform that function. Judith didn't have time to worry about such trivial matters, for she had to attend to Mrs Ulrich.

It was with some trepidation that she went down to the cellars to see how the cleaning had progressed. She lit a candle from the kitchen fires again, nodding to the plain young woman who was cutting up potatoes, and asked to borrow an apron. The cook nodded, wide-eyed, and Judith unhooked one from behind the door and descended the first set of stairs.

The cellars were better lit today, by the light coming from the door and several lit lanterns, but she could see it was in *more* disarray than her last visit. There was no sign of Mrs Ulrich, but Kynver (or was it Kade?) came lurching out of the far archway, holding a large bin of produce, his livery dusty.

At his awkward bow, Judith nodded at him, then sidled past into the room he had exited. It was large and fairly empty, except for Mrs Ulrich, who was aggressively sweeping in a back corner, her skirts swishing angrily. Judith winced, aware that she had promised to help before she had been distracted by the accounts and Robert's arrival. Hastily, she tied the apron on. There was another broom propped against the wall, so she picked it up and began to sweep.

Mrs Ulrich glanced up once, then ignored her with icy disdain. Scorn wafted through the room, a prickly coldness. Judith did her best to disregard it in turn.

After a while, she wiped the sweat from her brow. "Mrs Ulrich, may I enquire why we are concentrating our efforts in this room?"

The housekeeper looked up, her jaw hardening. "We are preparing a cellar for the vampiri roost—as you requested, ma'am."

Judith coughed at the dust. "I do appreciate your work here, but I had hoped you would clean out the cellar below."

"This one would be better, ma'am."

"Why do you say that?"

"The little vampiri will be dwarfed by the large cellar below, ma'am."

"Nonsense, they will need space to fly about." Judith began sweeping again, though in a milder fashion than Mrs Ulrich's vigorous strokes. "And it has a grandeur suitable for a queen."

"It echoes, ma'am. In a desolate way."

"It won't if we put furniture and rugs in it." Judith looked over. "Have you managed to chase out the Crimson Lady yet?"

Mrs Ulrich pressed her lips together and stood her broom straight. "The Crimson Lady will not be chased, ma'am. She simply vanishes into the wall."

Judith could hear this was the truth, and indeed she had seen it for herself. She let her broom rest. "Shall we face her down together then?"

There was a long silence. "If you insist, ma'am."

"I do." Judith led the way to the descending stairs, obtaining a lantern on the way. Mrs Ulrich followed behind reluctantly.

As they descended to the lower cellar, the sense of sorrow welled up, and Judith pursed her lips. Mrs Ulrich had certainly not dismantled her Diplomacy charm. If anything, it had been strengthened in a bid to frighten her away. Or perhaps the Cork of Doom had been moved to more prominence. Sadness washed over them like a soft wave of despair, suffocating. Behind her, Mrs Ulrich's silence was pregnant.

Judith stalked to the centre of the hall. She could see no sign of the cork, but it was difficult to see in the dim expanse. The vanishing lady did not deign to make her flickering appearance, and Judith did not wait to give her the chance. She turned, ignoring the urge to weep or run, and spoke calmly. "Mrs Ulrich, you must undo the Diplomacy in here at once."

The housekeeper stared, her hand still clenched around the broom, as if she were about to deploy it as a sword. "Excuse me, ma'am?"

Judith clutched at her lantern firmly. "The charm that spreads sorrow and fear down here. It is your doing, is it not?"

"I don't know what you're talking about, ma'am."

It was a lie. Judith was almost relieved. "I think you *do* know. And I want no more of it, do you hear? If we are to deal well together, we can have no more subterfuge. And you must obey my orders, for I am mistress of this castle now."

"Yes, ma'am." Mrs Ulrich's lips compressed, but at the same time her shoulders straightened, and she glared back.

Judith swept a hand up to indicate the high ceiling. "This underground hall is ideal for the French queen, and well you know it. Please turn your mind as to how we can make it more habitable." She paused. "You have my permission to take rugs and hangings from other rooms in the castle, if it would help. Whatever furnishings you think best. We can make it quite the palace down here, if we put our minds to it."

A gleam of reluctant interest crossed the housekeeper's face. "If you say so, ma'am."

"And vanquish the Crimson Lady's melancholy, I beg you, and I will not ask you again. You can keep your ratafia kegs, if you must, but the ghost must go."

"Indeed, ma'am," Mrs Ulrich said, with a flash of surprise followed by a glimmer of respect. "I will see to it."

JUDITH RETREATED to order cleaning rags, and when she returned, she was glad to feel that the Cork of Doom had been removed or dismantled. She made no comment, however, and simply set to work.

After another two hours of cleaning, she stumbled out of the cellars with relief and undid her apron. Mrs Ulrich was ordering Trebellow and one of the footmen (Kynver? Kade? they were too dusty to tell) to beat some heavy rugs outside before laying them down on the newly swept floor. She didn't want to compete with Mrs Ulrich's directions, and she needed fresh air.

It seemed that the housekeeper had reluctantly accepted

her orders. Judith felt more certain now that the Crimson Lady hid nothing more than the woman's grief. Yet if she *did* connive at smuggling, then tonight would be the night to watch for any reaction.

In the meanwhile, there was still one suspect that she had not interviewed about the death of Sgt Finlay: the famous Miss Isla, the dairymaid.

Exiting through the scullery door, Judith circled round the keep, brushing down her skirts and sneezing a little in the sunlight. Retracing the steep path, she trod through the leafy avenues. When she came to a split in the path, she took the left rather than the one direct to the causeway. The precipitous stone steps soon flattened out, opening to views of the harbour and green paddocks.

A quaint building in grey stone stood right near the path. It was hexagonal, with its own pointed turret. Cows munched on the grass close by, and a pungent smell of butter wafted on the air. This must be the dairy, and it was time for the buttermilk to be churned, after it had sufficiently fermented.

Judith approached cautiously, trying to keep her footsteps quiet, and peered into a low window. It was dim inside, yet she could see the shape of stalls, a bench, and a row of elongated kegs; the butter churns with their long handles protruding.

A young woman worked one of them, her sturdy arms lifting and plunging steadily. She was dark-haired and full-bosomed, with curves that put even Judith's to shame, accentuated by the tightly waisted apron. Her face was obscured, but even her figure was enough to draw appreciative attention.

She was not alone. Working another churn was one of the twin footmen. The cursed boys, they seemed to be everywhere. Judith could not tell if it was Kade or Kynver, for his coat was off, hanging on one of the stalls, and he also had adopted an apron. His thin, wiry arms plunged another churning paddle, as he smiled and said something to the maid.

Judith heard a laugh, and the conversation continued, though she could not make out the low words above the sounds of slurping paddles.

She decided to make her presence known. Finding the door, she pushed it open, stepping into the faintly warm atmosphere and the scent of rancid milk.

The two labourers looked across in surprise, but they did not stop their work immediately, so accustomed as they were to maintaining the consistent rhythm. But then the footman's face showed dismay. He released his paddle and bowed, brushing his hands against his yellow apron.

"Lady Avely. How may I help you?"

Guiltily, the girl also let go of her paddle, dropping into a curtsy. "Ma'am." She was indeed pretty, a lovely Cornish lass with deep blue eyes, dark brows, and rosebud lips.

"Good afternoon," said Judith cheerily. "You two look busy. Is this task done every day?"

Miss Isla—for it must be she—said, "Yes, ma'am. We sell the butter on the mainland, and the cream, as well as the milk, of course." She gave a charming smile. "Have you tried the cream yet? It is most delicious."

"Indeed, quite superb. And may I enquire as to your name?"

"Miss Isla Trebellow," was the reply.

Judith raised a brow in surprise. "A relation of the butler?"

The girl dropped another curtsy. 'His niece, ma'am."

No wonder Trebellow was happy to allow his staff to assist in the dairy, if it were to help his pretty niece. "I'm surprised you do not have others working with you." Judith looked at the footman (she suspected it was Kade, from his silence; it had been Kynver with the roguish glint, and Kade the serious one who had lied.)

Miss Isla stood straight. "Please don't be angry with Kade, ma'am. He was only trying to help. I can hire a lad from the village if you prefer it." She gave a bright smile again, but Judith was distracted by a faint note of dissonance in her voice.

"He was only trying to help?" she repeated.

Miss Isla's creamy skin became slightly pink. "Yes, ma'am."

Kade shuffled and looked at his feet.

Judith frowned, for the odd note had gone from the girl's voice. Perhaps Miss Isla herself doubted the real reason for Kade's presence. "Do you have other visitors, perhaps? Did Sgt Finlay ever come by the dairy?"

"Once or twice, ma'am," she replied airily, confident of *that* attention, at least.

"Did you see the soldier on the day he died?"

The girl nodded, and her gaze darted to Kade.

"What time was that?" asked Judith. "I'm afraid that I must ask, for I am concerned that Sgt Finlay's death was no accident."

Miss Isla stared. "No accident? But he drowned, everybody says so."

"I've been told on good authority that he could swim," explained Judith. "Did you see him before or after the tide was in?"

The girl's airy smile had now vanished. "Not long after noon, I think," she said slowly. "While the tide was out. I was sweeping out the stalls when he came knocking."

"Were you alone?"

Miss Isla hesitated. "No, Kade was helping me." Involuntarily, her eyes shot again to the footman. His jaw tightened.

"Oh, so you *both* saw Sgt Finlay?"

Kade spoke at last, his voice low. "Yes, ma'am. He often popped into the dairy."

The dairymaid looked anxiously at Kade again, opened her mouth to speak, then shut it again.

"Did he, perhaps, have some hope of your affection, Miss Trebellow?" asked Judith.

"Ah, no, ma'am," the maid replied cautiously. "My affections are engaged elsewhere." She blushed, and a smug look flickered across Kade's face, quickly wiped away.

Judith looked from one to the other. "Kade, your brother told me that he saw Sgt Finlay crossing the causeway at noon towards the castle." Which, of course, had been Kade himself. "Did you see him leave later, when the tide was coming in?"

Kade shook his head, and it was Miss Isla's turn to stare at the floor.

"Miss Isla?" pressed Judith. "Did you see Sgt Finlay later that day?"

"No, ma'am." It was the truth. But the girl's hands were pressed tightly together, and she seemed determined not to look at Kade again.

Judith pursed her lips. "Did Sgt Finlay seem troubled by anything when you saw him?"

"Not troubled, no," said Miss Isla. Then she added, "If anything, he seemed rather more cocksure than usual." She gave a faint echo of her earlier smile, but Judith could see the doubt lurking beneath.

Kade scowled, but Judith had a hard time believing that Sgt Finlay's arrogance had been enough to incite him to murder, when the dairymaid had declared her affections to be engaged. Yet Miss Isla was anxious. Did she know of something else that could have provoked Kade into violence?

"Cocksure?" she enquired. "Why was the sergeant cocksure on that day in particular, I wonder?"

There was a silence. Then the boy spoke up, deliberately. "Sgt Finlay did say something about sniffing out secrets in the castle, ma'am." He paused. "He seemed very pleased with himself that day, like the cat with the canary. I think he had discovered something."

Miss Isla went white. Judith looked between them with interest. Why was Kade suddenly volunteering this information? His voice rang true, and yet she suspected he was creating a diversion, especially when Miss Isla looked so anxious. Kade, however, ignored the dairymaid and stared defiantly at Judith.

"Oh?" she said. "What secrets might he have discovered? You seem to have some idea."

"I suspect it is to do with Mrs Ulrich, ma'am." Kade jutted his chin out. "I've seen her on the southern side of the island, lighting a lamp at night, down behind the castle. You may draw your own conclusions, and no doubt Sgt Finlay did too."

The implication was obvious, but Judith was shocked. "Mrs Ulrich guides the local smugglers in?" It was one thing to suspect the possibility, and quite another to have it confirmed. Judith was aware of a sinking sensation of dismay. She had started to like Mrs Ulrich, despite her prickliness, and she had thought they had come to some sort of understanding. This disclosure, however, meant she was once more a prime suspect for Sgt Finlay's death.

"Indeed, ma'am." Kade pursed his lips. "You should ask her about it. But now we must keep churning, or the mixture will lose its consistency." He gave a pointed look towards the butter kegs.

Judith felt the reproof: she was interrupting the serious work of the castle. She backed away reluctantly, closing the door behind her on the two young people, her brow heavy with consternation. Her housekeeper was aiding and abetting smugglers after all.

And Kade and Miss Isla were undoubtedly trying to hide something too.

In which Marigold is a carrier pigeon

Marigold

For once, Marigold was glad to wake to a tightly closed cupboard door. If it had been open, she feared that the monstrous feline might somehow manage to leap up to the top shelf and eat her while she slept.

She rolled over in the linen handkerchief and stretched lazily, listening to see if Judith was in the room. Ah yes, she could hear footsteps—but they did not sound quite like Judith's.

Marigold sat up swiftly, ears pricked. The steps were lighter, stealthier. They were not the heavy tread of the butler, so perhaps a footman? But why would a footman skulk around Judith's room?

She listened for several long moments, tracking the movement. It sounded as if the intruder was looking for something, opening the multitude of drawers in the panelling and cabinets, and even lifting the blankets off the bed, of all things. Did they think Judith was hiding something? Marigold stiffened, for she well knew that the cupboard would be next.

Hastily, she shuffled back to the deepest corner, clutching

the kerchief around her. Would the searcher bother to look under a handkerchief? She feared so, and pressed up against the wood, fluffing the cloth around her. Then she felt something dig into the back of her ribs.

It was a wooden protrusion from the wall, almost like a doorknob. Marigold stared at it, then gingerly twisted it.

A panel opened in the back of the cupboard.

Eyes wide, she peered in. There was a whole other compartment behind the panel and it was furnished for a vampiri, with a soft rug, a small bed, and a chair. Without further hesitation, she hustled in and quietly shut the panel behind her.

Mere moments later, she heard the main cupboard door open. Keeping utterly still, she waited, seeing the faint glow of light as someone peered in. Would the searcher know about the secret compartment?

It seemed not. After an unbearably long pause, the door shut again, taking the light with it. Marigold slumped on the floor with relief. Then she heard the bedroom door click softly, as the intruder left.

She looked around. The private cupboard room was really quite pleasant, with a delicate pattern carved into the ceiling. There was even a small rod across the far side, with room underneath for a bat to hang. The air smelled dusty, however, and the bed was bare of any blankets. Marigold flounced over to it with her handkerchief and waited.

At least a quarter of an hour passed before Judith returned. Hearing the familiar tread, Marigold let herself out of the vampiri compartment and banged on the front door.

Judith opened it at once. Marigold stepped onto her hands, rapidly explaining what had happened.

"Goodness," said Judith, astonished. "Who could it have been?"

"Someone with light feet, and maybe light fingers."

"But I don't have anything to steal." Judith had arrived at Castle Lanyon with nothing, except for the clothes she wore, and the topaz ring of the duke's, which she kept in her pocket. Then Marigold saw that a valise rested on the sea-chest at the bottom of the bed, still locked.

"How did that arrive?" Marigold pointed. "Is Robert here already?"

"Yes!" said Judith, examining the trussed valise. "It seems untouched."

"I would have heard them tussling with it, had they tried to open it."

Suddenly, Judith stiffened. "My letter!"

Tipping Marigold onto the bed, she hurried over to the captain's desk and fumbled in the drawer. She pulled out a small roll of foolscap, tied with string, staring at it.

"I can't tell if it has been tampered with."

"I think we must assume it was. What does it say?"

"It is addressed to Dacian, reminding him of our past, and instructing him...I mention the Custos, I think, and the Lethe. Surely no one here has any interest in such matters?" Her tone was doubtful.

Marigold folded her arms. "If they killed Sgt Finlay with magick, they might."

Judith slumped back down on the bed. "Curse it. This matter is more obscure than I hoped. It can't have been Kade who was tiptoeing around in here, as I was just speaking to him in the dairy. But perhaps it was his brother? I thought he was in the cellars with Mrs Ulrich." She sighed. "I had hoped Sgt Finlay's death was simply a matter of jealous rivalry, but there doesn't seem to be a strong enough case for that. The footman Kade seems confident in his courtship, not threatened. However, they both appeared to be hiding something, and Miss Isla seemed afraid, somehow."

Marigold frowned. "Who is Miss Isla again?"

Judith reported her encounters from the day, while Marigold fed from her wrist. "So, it seems clear that Mrs Ulrich is our primary suspect now," she finished. "The Dread Spell was to protect the smugglers' den, and the housekeeper must have killed Sgt Finlay when he discovered it." Her voice sounded dubious, however. "It doesn't explain, however, why Kade disguises himself as his brother, or why someone went through my room."

Marigold pulled away from the vein. "Well, at least you have something to report to the captain." She eyed the letter warily. "Do you want me to fly that to the duke tonight?"

"Would you?" begged Judith. "I want to send my own words, to reiterate what Wooten has told him."

"I'm not a carrier pigeon!"

"Certainly not. You are a military runner, essential in our campaign."

Grudgingly, Marigold became a bat in order for Judith to tie the letter to her leg, so that she would not drop it in the sea.

Once the missive was safely attached, Judith bent to place a kiss upon her head. "Fly safe, my dear. Remember, only to Penrose Hill, and gather the news from Wooten, then return."

Marigold nodded. Judith opened the paned window, and a gust of fresh sea air flowed in.

Marigold flapped out into the night.

IT WAS a long way to Penrose Hill, even as the bat flies. Marigold soon left Lanyon Bay behind, but kept close to the coast, cutting over the headlands and tracking a straight path towards the dim glow of Falmouth. Fortunately, the wind was behind her, pushing her along, but she wasn't looking forward to the return journey.

Still, it was lovely to be buffeted by the cool breeze, and stretch her wings against the wide, dark sky. The waning moon was rising, light gleaming upon the waves.

She had arranged to meet Wooten an hour before midnight, so she stopped to rest in a pine tree, the letter awkwardly hanging by her side. She was not wearing any cape, which would no doubt cause Wooten a mild heart seizure. Marigold pushed away a passing thought that it might be Yvette who would meet her instead. The scheming hussy should know to stay well away. Why was she meddling in Judith's concerns? With any luck, the conniving creature had left Pendennis by now and flown back to France.

Marigold repressed a pang of disappointment at the thought. It was simply that she enjoyed bantering with another female vampiri who wasn't as prudish as Wooten.

Following Judith's instructions, Marigold flew to Falmouth, then turned up the Porthleven inlet as far as she could, then headed directly east until she saw Penrose Hill. Nearing the crest, she saw an old house set back from the road. That would do. Becoming human, she landed on the slate roof at its highest point, nudging the letter out of her way as she balanced on the peak.

She took in the mottled pattern of moss on the tiles, sleepy fields beyond, and the sea in the distance. Then, reminiscent of their first meeting, Yvette stepped out from behind a chimney.

Yvette *was* wearing a cape, the midnight blue one she had worn at Garvey House. It was held tightly in front, but when she saw that Marigold had no such assistance to modesty, she let the cloth part. Marigold saw a narrow prism of pale, womanly flesh, including the tantalising dip between Yvette's breasts.

Marigold huffed, folding her arms across her less impressive bosom. "You again!" Then her gaze narrowed, taking in Yvette's sombre expression. "Where's Wooten? What's wrong?"

"Wooten has forgot himself." Yvette walked forward, cape swishing. "He drank the potion intended for the duke."

"What?" Marigold stared in horror.

A dose of Lethe intended for a hefty man like the duke would be enough to wipe Wooten's little brain off the face of the earth. Suddenly, Marigold was aware of a strangling fondness for the uptight fop. The stupid bat! If he hadn't killed himself, she might well do it for him.

"Not all of it," Yvette hastened to add. "I saw what happened."

She told the story, carefully and without much inflection. Apparently, the duke had started to remember himself, and with it, his temper. Wooten kept removing any food or drink left in the prison, carrying it out the tower and dumping it far away. So his grace (Yvette said) was no doubt hungry, as well as worried, and furious at his captivity. He tried to hide his returning knowledge, but his worsening mood had made his captors suspicious. In the evening, Captain Drumpellier had come in with a drink of wine and offered the duke a glass and a cigar.

That, of course, was a difficult moment. If Dacian refused to drink it, he showed his awareness of what they were doing, and he risked them forcing it down his throat again. Yet if he drank it, he would lose his memory again, already patchy.

He left the glass standing on the table, biding for time, smoking the cigar and talking to Drumpellier, and demanding to know more about the war and Napoleon.

"Napoleon?" interrupted Marigold. "Why would he mention that? It would reveal that he recalled something!"

Yvette shook her head. "Drumpellier has been telling him all the latest news from the front."

"Why?" Marigold sat down on the shingle, with a heavy feeling. "I suppose it must be some ploy to gain his sympathy." She looked up. "Never mind that. What happened next?"

"Wooten was hiding under the table, clinging to the leg. When Drumpellier turned away to trim a candle wick, Wooten grabbed the chance. He flew out and tipped half the cup's contents down his throat, almost knocking the glass over. The duke grabbed it, Wooten hid, and when Drumpellier turned around, it looked like his grace had drunk of the potion."

"And then?"

"The duke drank the rest. To save his companion, I think, from drinking any more. Though Wooten rapidly became in no state to carry out any more heroic consumption. He collapsed into an unresponsive heap on the floor, and the duke hid him with his foot. Fortunately, Drumpellier left soon afterwards, after his grace finished the wine."

"Steaming sunlight," muttered Marigold, her heart wrenching for Wooten. "What a disaster. And the duke? Did he become stupid again?"

"Fear not, his grace thew up the wine straight away," continued Yvette. "Under my instruction. He vomited into a pillowcase, and I took it away and dumped it behind the barracks."

"That was good of you," admitted Marigold, for it would have been an unpleasant task. "I have this for him." She stuck her leg out, bending to untie the letter. "It is from Lady Avely, explaining things."

Yvette watched with interest. "An interesting use of such a neatly turned ankle. I am not sure that I approve."

Marigold hid her blush. "I don't need your approval. And your ankle is going to have to bear the same burden."

"Will you tie it on for me, please?" Yvette sat down beside Marigold, stretching out a long leg from under her cape. Her ankle, Marigold noted, was very elegant indeed. In fact, she didn't know if she'd seen such a fascinating ankle in the whole of her existence.

"I shall not!"

Yvette fluttered her long lashes. "Miss Cultor, I wish to know that you trust me with this task. And that *I* trust *you*. Tie it on, please, as a demonstration of our alliance."

Marigold gulped. Then she reasoned to herself that this way she could assure Judith that the precious letter had been tightly secured. She bent and wound the string around Yvette's ankle, her fingers brushing against skin. Yvette was pale but warm, and Marigold felt her whole body flush with the intimacy of it.

"Still feeding on cows, are you?" she demanded, to hide her reaction.

Yvette suddenly looked away. "Ah, not exactly."

"What do you mean?" Marigold tied a complicated knot to stay bound, but not too tight. She wouldn't want Miss Frenchy to have her circulation restricted.

There was a pause. "I fed from the duke before I left."

Marigold started back, glaring with accusation. "Are you trying to steal him from Wooten?"

There was a flash of hurt in Yvette's eyes. "No. I was trying to *help* his grace. If the duke is to use his Gift again, he must guard against Bemusement." She paused. "And I needed strength for the flight."

Marigold folded her arms, wishing again that she had brought a cape. It was more difficult to deliver a scolding when one was stark naked. "The duke could *continue* to feed Wooten."

"He has. But we cannot be sure that the bond will still provide its usual benefits, when Wooten's mind is so addled. And the last thing his grace needs now is more addlement."

Marigold paced along the shingle of the roof, away from the infuriating creature. "Has Wooten regained consciousness?"

"For a little while. He was like a child, completely confused." Yvette shivered. "He was courageous to make such a sacrifice."

Marigold shuddered also. It had been a brave act, certainly. And foolish. She wondered if she could have done the same for Judith. She thought not—but she had only been Judith's companion for a short while, unlike Wooten, who had been with the duke for years. The Musor bond seemed to have unfortunate side effects. The longer it lasted, the more likely a vampiri would do idiotic things for their companion.

She eyed Yvette thoughtfully. Perhaps she also had been coerced into villainy.

"Was Wooten unfairly driven by his blood bond?" she asked abruptly. "Were you, with your companion?"

Yvette regarded her steadily. "I am afraid not, Miss Cultor. Both Wooten and I were acting of our own volition and in defence of someone we loved." She paused. "My companion rescued me after I left France, years ago. I was grateful. I was not seeing clearly, not because of the bond, but because I wished to keep my friend."

Marigold found she had nothing to say to that, so she hunched her shoulder away. After a moment, she muttered, "Is there any other news that I must report to Judith?"

"Yes," said Yvette. "I'm afraid that they have moved his grace to a different cell, looking onto a training courtyard. I can draw a map for you."

"But why have they moved him?" Marigold suspected that Judith would not like this news.

"He is being tested now; his strength and fighting skill pitted against soldiers. They say it is to give him an outlet for his aggression, but to me it looks very much like they are training him."

"Training him?" Marigold repeated. "For what?"

"I think they are planning to put him to use," said Yvette coolly. "For what, I do not know. But it is for some sort of violence, that is clear."

In which the sea quietens

The dark magnifies our fears.
— from *Lady Avely's Guide to Guile and Peril*

AFTER MARIGOLD LEFT on her journey to Penrose Hill, Judith went to find Robert.

Trebellow had put him in a large room furnished in cream and brown, with spectacular views of the moon rising over Lanyon Bay. Robert was marvelling at the window when she came in.

He turned impetuously. "I wish I could paint it."

"Why don't you?" she replied. "How do you feel?"

"I had a long sleep this afternoon, so I am full of vitality." He sat down on the windowsill. "Now, please, tell me how the duke fares. I have been in a fever of impatience to know his plight."

She took a high-backed chair and told him all the grimmer details, those she had left out before Miss Onslow: Dacian's loss of memory, Drumpellier's ultimatum, and the conversations she had conducted with those at Castle Lanyon.

Robert listened attentively and made astute observations, the last of which was, "You seem to be reluctant to suspect Mrs Ulrich, even now. Why is that?"

Judith sighed. "No, I agree she is our most likely culprit. I suppose I want some proof first, that she went as far as murder." She paused. "The truth is that I feel some sympathy for her. I am a widow too, after all, and I was greatly shaken by your father's death when he passed—before I discovered how he had lied to me. I know what it is like to feel overpowering sorrow."

Robert looked uncomfortable. "But then your sorrow turned to anger."

"That is quite expected, I believe. Anger feels preferable, somehow. So, I can understand that Mrs Ulrich wanted to find a vent for her feelings, and a distraction. That does not mean, however, that she killed a man for it." She paused. "And you must know that I am no longer angry with your father. I am glad to have met you, and that you have consented to be part of the family, however distantly."

"It is only a provisional measure," he said awkwardly, "while we sort this mess out. Then I'll be off."

Judith tried not to show her hurt. She knew that Robert felt a strong loyalty towards his dead mother, who had not liked Judith. Therefore, his own feelings towards Judith were very conflicted: sometimes amenable and friendly, then sometimes withdrawing into aloofness. She let the matter pass for now, hoping that their common quest would bring them closer together. "Well, I have a strong suspicion that the twins are hiding something. There is more going on in this castle than meets the eye." She considered Robert, noting that his cheeks had more colour. "Perhaps you can accompany me tonight. Now that the haunted cellar has been cleared out, I'm curious to see if it provokes any response. Perhaps we can gain the evidence we need to indict Mrs Ulrich."

"Ghost hunting? You must be good at that by now," he observed, leaning back in his chair, clearly glad of the change of subject. "Are you sure it is safe? I suspect the duke would not approve."

Judith scoffed. "Currently, his grace is not in a position to concern himself with our conduct. If you are worried, come with me—though you must promise not to leap in front of any bullets again."

"Only if you promise not to *incite* bullets." He grinned reluctantly, and it reminded her suddenly of her son, Peregrine. There was a resemblance there, sometimes, in the way the two boys smiled, similar to their father.

She wondered if she should remark upon it. But she did not want to undo the returning ease between them, so instead she asked, "Can you be quiet, with your stick?"

Robert nodded, and barely winced as he stood, leaning on the walking cane.

They crept out of the room, and Judith did her best to lead the way down to the kitchen. Without Marigold's nose to guide her, she made a few wrong turns but eventually found the doors.

The kitchen was as empty and tidy as before, with no sign of Ghastagon or the young cook. Judith led the way through the larder and down the first steps, holding her candle aloft. It was different this time, without Marigold. One would assume she'd feel safer accompanied by a young man with a hefty stick, but Judith was oddly more worried for *his* safety, and she missed having Marigold's eyes and ears in the dark.

She paused midway down the second stairs, hearing Robert gasp at the size of the vast underground cellar. It was now luxuriously carpeted in glowing reds and golds, with exotic patterns swirling beneath their feet. The wheelbarrow and spade were no longer in evidence, but the kegs still stood in the far corner. Treading down, she gestured to her right.

"That's where we saw the Crimson Lady," she murmured, "on the far wall."

They both stared hard at the stone. Nothing flickered there, not even a rat's tail. The high ceiling stretched away above them, with the sound of waves pounding in the distance. Judith could smell the scent of brandy drifting on the air again and made her way towards the ratafia kegs.

As before, the door behind them was hidden in shadows, but the Dread Spell was now absent. A faint trace of it lingered, perhaps: a distant sense of sorrow, like homesickness, but the onslaught was gone. Briefly, she wondered where Mrs Ulrich had put the cork that held the charm and devoutly hoped that it wouldn't find its way into a wine bottle.

She pushed through the door, carefully shielding her candle, and saw the passageway as before. It looked less mysterious and secretive now that the Cork of Doom no longer held sway over it. Cautiously, she went through the next arch and saw the little room that Marigold had described. Intriguingly, the table, chairs, and whisky were no longer to be seen: just a newly swept floor. Now it looked like a small dungeon, cold and bare. Judith thought of Dacian and was glad that he at least had rugs, pillows, and whisky.

The bare room posed another problem: there was nowhere to hide as they lay in wait for their quarry. She had a sudden thought. "If necessary, can you disguise me as a keg?" she asked, leading the way back to the little brewery. "If I sit on the ground next to the others?"

Robert's lips quirked. "It's below your dignity, of course. But if you're willing, I can give it a try."

"Nonsense. Ratafia is very ladylike."

Judith settled herself on the cold stone, sitting with her legs pulled up, which was quite improper but necessary to bring them in line with the kegs. Robert spent a few minutes eyeing the other casks, then stared at her fixedly.

She felt the faint warmth of Illusion spring up around her, though she could not see it. Hastily, she blew out her candle so it wouldn't ruin the effect.

Robert considered his handiwork with satisfaction. "It will do, I suppose."

"And you? Can you camouflage yourself against the wall?"

Robert examined the stones next to the door. Then he put down his own candle, stepped up to the wall and proceeded to melt into it. Judith could, if she strained her imagination, make out his form, but anyone walking by would not look too closely.

"Very good," she said with approval. "Drop it now; we don't want you becoming Bemused."

Robert's tall form appeared again, but he was looking down, into the corner. "There's something here."

"Oh? A dead rat?" She grimaced. "Or a cork?"

"Neither." He bent and pulled out a loosely rolled canvas from behind the kegs. "It's not dusty."

"Oh?" she said with more interest and stood to have a better look.

Slowly, he unrolled it, stretching it out so they could see. Oddly, the corners had been trimmed to make it into an oval shape, meaning that he had to hold the very top of the canvas. It was so large that Judith had to hold the other end, to stretch it out.

At first, it seemed like it was just a blank sheet, empty. Yet as they stared at it, something flickered into view.

It was a portrait of a woman in a red dress, her hair bound

up, floating on a dark background: an oil painting, dim with age, the expression of the lady neutral and aristocratic.

The painting vanished again, leaving the canvas blank once more.

"Well!" said Judith, immensely pleased. "I think we found our ghost!"

"An Illusionary painting? Worn down?" Robert squinted at it. "She's coming back."

The woman appeared, rested her aloof gaze upon them, then disappeared again.

"It might have been framed once," observed Judith, "until someone took it out and nailed it to that far wall." She pointed to the rusty marks of nail piercings in the canvas. "Clever to soften the corners, so it looks like she was emerging from a dark pool."

"I can imagine the effect was quite theatrical."

"Yes, Marigold was rent speechless."

Robert laughed. "*That* is hard to imagine." He rolled it up again. "Should we keep it?"

"Best leave it and see if someone fetches it. Mrs Ulrich might have an accomplice." Judith considered. "But now I think we should explore the next passageway, which Marigold could not. There's a mysterious door, apparently."

She admitted to herself that she was glad the sight of the Crimson Lady was now explained and pondered their discovery as she led the way through the first passageway into the little cell. It was clear that someone was either playing a prank or deliberately attempting to scare people away from this meeting place. Had it been Mrs Ulrich, with her smuggling friends, or had someone else sought to take advantage of her Dread Diplomacy?

Could this room be a place for Kade and Miss Isla to meet, far from the disapproving eyes of her uncle? Judith stared around. She rather doubted it was a suitable scene for romantic trysts: too damp and dark. A den for gambling, maybe? Or had Marigold missed something?

She lit her candle again from Robert's, and with some trepidation searched for the passageway that Marigold had mentioned. There was an arch, set at right angles to the cell, tucked in the corner, and Judith gestured for Robert to follow.

One by one, they breached the arch. It led into a long, narrow passageway. The very narrowness of it hinted that it would not take them to another storage place under the castle, for it would be difficult to carry anything through, let alone two men carrying wide chests or barrels. The path curved round slowly, and Judith saw another low door, the one that had balked Marigold.

The lintel bore a heavy weight of stone, at the height of Judith's shoulders. Old then, perhaps built by the monks. It was wooden and barred with iron.

Fearing it was locked, Judith bent and turned the handle with all her might. It swung open with a groaning creak. She ducked under the lintel, Robert at her heels, his stick lightly tapping behind her.

Fortunately, the ceiling rose again, so they could walk straight. But the roof was oddly curved, the passageway shaped like an oval, much like the painting had been. It was built of a different type of stone, too, lighter than the heavy grey rock of the cellars. Certainly, it must have been built by earlier inhabitants of the castle, centuries ago. Judith wondered if it had been a private passageway for the monks. The stone walls were close, the floor uneven. Her heart beat with excitement. Of *course* this castle had a secret underground passageway. How could she have doubted it? *This* was the secret that the Crimson Lady guarded.

Gradually, the path turned north, and she realised suddenly

that the pounding of the waves had quietened. The truth dawned on her. They were now under the sea itself, past the reaches of the island: they could no longer hear the ceaseless thunder of breaking waves.

She cast a look back at Robert to see that his eyes were wide in the lamplight.

"Are we heading towards the shore?" he whispered.

"I suspect so." It was hard to maintain a sense of direction underground, but it felt as if the passage was curving in a similar direction as the causeway. Could it even be *under* the causeway? Could this explain how Sgt Finlay had escaped the island after the tide came in?

Her excitement was abruptly interrupted, for the pale limestone suddenly flattened into a dead end. She stared at in consternation, then saw a yawning dark mouth before her feet. Holding her candle above it, she could see the space of another tunnel, lower down, with shallow steps cut into the plunging hole.

Robert peered over her shoulder. "Should we press on?"

"How will you manage, with your leg?"

He scowled. "You can't go without me. The duke would have my hide."

She was pleased at this sign of protectiveness, and his confidence that Dacian would recover his opinions. "Surely no one else is down there."

At the thought, they both stilled to listen. And that was when they heard the whistling.

It was an eerie sound, echoing up through the hole, bouncing on stone. The tune was jaunty, faint, and distant. But possibly drawing closer; it was hard to tell. This must be their conspirator!

And possibly a murderer.

"Quick!" hissed Judith. "Blow out the candles." She put her

own out in a gust of breath. Light would be seen long before anything else. Her pulse accelerated.

Robert's face stared at her, aghast. "Really?"

"We can walk back in the dark, feeling the walls. We'll wait by the kegs, like we planned. Can you manage it?"

"I suppose." He grimaced. "You go first."

He let her step past him. Then darkness descended, utter and absolute.

Grimly, she retraced her steps, walking with careful haste. The side of the tunnel was rough under her gloves, and the scent of dry, old earth filled her nostrils. In the blackness, the sound of Robert's breathing and the scraping of his stick seemed overloud. Judith felt guilty that this reckless retreat would not be good for his injury. But it would have been foolish to come alone, she reasoned. She only hoped they wouldn't both be trapped and killed together by a desperate smuggler.

The whistling was bizarrely out of place in the nightmarish dark, but it did not evoke a sense of desperation. Whoever it was did not seem to have anything on their conscience. Yet a remorseless wrongdoer would be even more dangerous.

Beyond Robert's erratic progress, the jaunty sound grew closer. Judith dared not hurry too much, fearing they might trip on the uneven floor. She heard what might have been a scramble and imagined their faceless pursuer crawling up into the very tunnel that they were now traversing.

Finally, she felt the wall taper and barely stopped herself from crashing into the low door. Fumbling, she opened it, whispering to Robert to be careful of the lintel. Ducking through and away, she waited until she heard him shut it quietly again, then inched forward. Soon she was under the next arch into the secret cell, and creeping along the wall to the final door.

It was with relief she breathed in the sweet smell of fermenting ratafia. She pushed the hidden door open and slipped out into the shadow of the kegs. Close behind her, Robert carefully shut it behind them.

At least they had two doors between the whistler now. The flat granite was hard beneath her feet, and the sound of the waves had returned, beating against the cliffs of the island and reverberating through the foundations of the castle.

"Quick," she whispered. "I'll sit by the kegs, as before."

Blindly, she bumped into the reassuring solidity of wood. Fingers clutching at the keg, she edged along to the end, then collapsed into the nook, drawing her legs up.

It seemed a very long wait for the unseen whistler, though they had sounded so close behind. Judith sat in the cold dark, listening with all her might. The cheerful tune grew nearer, muffled. Then the walker came through the low door, and the whistling ceased.

She could hear footsteps now, slow and cautious. They drew closer, entering the secret cell, and then the last passageway.

The hidden door opened.

Light leaked over the kegs, glimmering softly.

Judith widened her eyes at Robert. He was pressed up against the wall on the other side of the door, but as she watched, he melted into it, becoming stone. At the same moment, she felt the warmth of Illusion spring up around her.

A careful tread came into the room. Lantern light glowed, and behind it, a figure loomed in the archway.

In which an unsuspected passion reveals itself

Pay attention to omissions and evasions.
    — from *Lady Avely's Guide to Guile and Peril*

JUDITH NARROWED HER EYES. She could make out the weathered features of Cador, the fisherman from Stonesthrow Cottage. The angle of the lantern light made him look even more craggy and threatening.

He stepped into the underground hall, his brow furrowing as he took in the newly laid carpets, soft underfoot. He wore corduroy trousers and a thick brown coat. His eyes widened, as he took in the absence of the Crimson Lady's grief.

Oddly, he smiled.

Judith frowned. Why would Cador smile? His lurking indicated that *he* was the smuggler, not the coastguard he pretended to be, in which case he should require the Cork of Doom to hide his presence.

Her heart in her throat, she looked on. Cador trod gingerly over the new carpets, as if afraid to dirty them with his boots, and stared hard at where the Illusory painting had once hung. After a moment, he looked around suspiciously, as if he could feel the presence of hidden watchers. Judith stayed frozen, but when he crossed to the upper stairs to leave, she made a decision. She stood up, quietly twisting her hand at Robert to dispel her Illusion.

"Cador," she said sharply. "What are you doing down here?"

The fisherman spun around. The lantern swung wild shadows across the walls. "Ma'am!" he growled. "You gave me a fright."

"I could say the same of you. And I must enquire again: what are you doing?"

"Ah." He lowered the lantern and assumed his most wooden expression. "I was inspecting the cellars for smugglers, ma'am. As part of my patrol."

She raised her brows, for surprisingly he was telling the truth. "But I heard you approaching from a long way off, with your charming whistle." She did not mention that she had been in the tunnel herself. She gestured. "Where does that passage go?"

His inscrutable look flickered. "To, uh, other storerooms, ma'am."

This time the lie rung hollowly. She shook her head in reproof. "Don't mislead me, Cador. Otherwise, I will have to follow the passage myself."

He twitched slightly. "Oh no, ma'am, that won't be necessary." At her hard look, he pursed his lips reluctantly. "If you must know, the passage leads to the mainland and comes out at my cottage on t'other side of the causeway. 'Tis a secret tunnel away from the island, but not many know of it, though I suppose you have the right of it now that you are Marchioness of Lanyon. The Cadors have long been guardians of it, and I beg that you won't tell anyone."

Judith carefully did not let her eyes stray to where Robert still pressed against the wall. "I suppose you come and go from Castle Lanyon as you please, then?"

"Yes, ma'am, but not very often, I swear. I'm only concerned now that smugglers have come to know about the passage too, which goes right against the grain, I can tell ye."

Judith remembered suddenly that Sgt Finlay had told Cador to look for smugglers on the bay on the night he died. What if that had been a story to *distract* Cador? Perhaps Sgt Finlay himself had known of the tunnel and wanted Cador out of the way so he could use it to return from the island, late at night.

She stared narrowly. "You saw something, on the night Sgt Finlay died, didn't you? I remember when I asked you, you hesitated." Actually, he hadn't hesitated, he had lied to her with a straight face, but she didn't want to reveal her Gift.

Cador seemed taken aback. "Aye, I did see something, as it happens, early the next morning." He paused thoughtfully. "I suppose you might as well know about it now, seeing as you know about the passage."

"Well?"

"I found the body of the soldier himself, stuffed down the drop in the tunnel." Cador seemed to take a contrary pleasure in her shocked expression. "It gave me a start, you can imagine, lying all awkwardly like a broken scarecrow, his red coat gleaming by my candle. But I couldn't leave him there. He'd start to smell for one. He'd already been dead a few hours by the time I found him, by my reckoning."

Judith blinked, horrified. "*You* took him to the shore?"

"Aye, and left him on Arloedhes Rock, all obvious-like, so the authorities could find him. But I couldn't tell Captain Drumpellier about the passageway and betray the secret of the castle."

"But..." Judith stuttered. "How was the captain going to discover the real cause of his death, if you moved the body?"

"At least this way, he *found* the body. Whoever left it in the passage probably never meant it to be found at all."

She swallowed. "And who do you think left it there?"

There was a long silence, and she was aware of Robert listening intently, pinned to the wall. Finally, Cador said, "I don't know, ma'am."

It was the truth, but Judith doubted it, nonetheless. "Mrs Ulrich?" she asked sharply. "I have it on good authority that my housekeeper assists the smugglers by guiding in their boats. You must know something about *that*."

Cador looked down. "It wouldn't have been Mrs Ulrich, ma'am."

"Oh, really? How can you be sure?"

He hesitated. "I saw her light in her window," he muttered, "when I was out keeping watch on the bay. It was shining late into the night."

"So? Mrs Ulrich might have left it there as a decoy."

Cador shook his head. "Mrs Ulrich would never have left a candle unattended in her room, for fear of fire. And she wouldn't have liked the tallow smoke permeating her quarters if there were no need for it. Besides," he paused reluctantly. "I saw her profile at the window, looking over the sea."

Judith tipped her head to the side, remembering Cador's smile when he realised that the Crimson Lady's grief had abated. Was it possible that the fisherman had a spot of tenderness for her housekeeper? She contemplated the image of him in his boat, floating on the waves, wistfully looking up at Mrs Ulrich's patrician profile like a lovelorn Romeo.

She was also aware of sensation of relief. Mrs Ulrich had an alibi for the night Sgt Finlay died. Judith's instincts had been correct: her housekeeper was not a killer, despite her entanglement with smugglers. And Cador's testimony was the proof.

It might be interesting to press the coastguard a little more. "Hmm," Judith murmured. "I would like to believe you, Cador, but the fact remains that the Crimson Lady has been casting quite the pall over this cellar. That must be Mrs Ulrich's doing, at least."

Cador shuffled and looked at his feet. "That rigamarole only started a year ago, ma'am. She said it was to keep people away from the passageway, so I allowed it. I thought it might soothe her tumult, if you take my meaning, to put her feelings into such a task. But I confess it's a relief she's undone it today." He looked around the hall, admiring the new carpets. "What on earth is she doing to the cellars now? It looks as if she is expecting royalty. Are you moving down here, ma'am?"

Judith contemplated him silently and did not tell him about the bats. His voice sounded as if he were speaking the truth—as he knew it. But she couldn't help feeling that there was a piece missing. She twisted to stare down the dark passage. She rather liked having a secret escape from the island, one she could use even when the tide was up. Best not to board it up then. But she *didn't* like the idea that anyone could come and go as they pleased, unseen, despite Cador's protestations at its secrecy. Perhaps that was another reason why Mrs Ulrich had instated her Cork of Doom.

"I think it is time to put a lock on that low door beyond," she announced.

Cador tipped his head. "You've seen that door, have you, ma'am?"

She did not deign to answer. "I want you to put a lock on it and deliver one of the keys to me. It is my duty to secure this castle, Cador, especially when a soldier was found dead in it last week. There has clearly been a breach of secrecy."

He bowed in silent acquiescence, his face closing into its usual inscrutability. Judith thrust out her candle, to be lit from his lantern, and he obliged.

"Right," she said. "As you see, there are no smugglers here tonight. You may return to your cottage, while I retire to bed." She did not want to reveal Robert, or his Gift, nor leave him alone here with Cador.

But Cador shook his head. "No, ma'am, I must finish my patrol. I'll walk around the castle now, while it is dark."

She nodded in acquiescence, and when Cador turned his back to her, she discreetly gestured a staying hand at the wall, then followed the fisherman up the cellar stairs. She parted ways with Cador outside the kitchen, trusting that Robert would be able to manage his own way back. As she watched Cador's burly figure recede, she wondered if he would stare wistfully across to Mrs Ulrich's room from the ramparts.

She made her way up to her room, thinking of Dacian. He would receive her letter soon and, she dared to hope, read it with gladness.

IT WAS STILL DARK when Marigold woke her.

Judith had left the window open, so the room was chilly. Marigold was sitting on the bed next to her, poking her side with sharp jabs.

Blinking, Judith sat up. The waning moon had long vanished, and she could barely make out Marigold's face.

"What is it?" She groped for a tinderbox blearily and lit a candle.

"I delivered your letter." Marigold hunched a corner of the quilt over herself, huddling glumly. She seemed tired after her long flight. "I handed it to Yvette."

"Why?" Judith's hand quivered a little with the flame, as fear swept through her. "Where was Wooten?"

Grimly, Marigold told her what had happened. "And now he's barely conscious, by the sounds of it."

Judith was aghast. "Wooten is lucky to be alive."

Marigold nodded sombrely. "Stupid bat. Yet his sacrifice was effective, I'll give him that."

"Dacian is *compos mentis*?"

"He remembers enough to be chafing against his imprisonment." Marigold paused, and Judith could see she was reluctant to speak. "Yvette says they have moved him to a different cell, and they are training him with other soldiers."

"*What?*"

Marigold winced. "It might be a good sign. Maybe they intend him to serve a conscription as punishment instead?"

Judith stared frowningly at the wall. "I don't like it." She ought to be glad, as it indicated that the Custos at least didn't intend to execute him. They might even rescind the punishment of Lethe and Obruo if he was to be useful to them, but she was filled with disquiet. Did they have a particular use for Dacian? Was there some other purpose for his capture that she did not yet understand? Or were they simply short of men?

"We must force a visit on Drumpellier," she said firmly. "Yet I am still not certain who killed the soldier. I *did* make an interesting discovery, but I don't know if I ought to share it with the captain."

She told Marigold about the secret passageway, adding her theory that Sgt Finlay might have known about it and found his way back to the mainland *under* the causeway. And yet someone had intercepted him and dispatched him swiftly, leaving his body to be found by Cador the next morning.

"Or," said Marigold thoughtfully, "perhaps Finlay was killed in the castle, and dragged through the passage."

Judith sighed. "Yes, but that means it is even more likely that the killer is someone in the castle." She frowned. One of the twins? She was determined to question them both, together, and sniff out what they were hiding. If she could haul one of them before Drumpellier, all to the good. He would accept the idea of their guilt. Not that she would accuse an innocent man, but if it could just give her an excuse to return to Dacian's side... No, she told herself firmly. She must find the real culprit and deliver them to justice. Then she could in good conscience ask the same for Dacian.

Outside, dawn teased at the horizon. Thoughtfully, Judith selected a soft, black woollen shawl from her valise, so that Marigold would be more comfortable in her new secret compartment in the wardrobe. Intriguingly, the Captain's Room clearly made provision for a vampiri residence; the previous Lanyons must have been Musors too.

Marigold retired sleepily, with one last injunction for Judith to be careful with smugglers and murderers lurking about. Judith waited another hour before quietly making her way to Robert's room, reluctant to disturb him but anxious to discuss the matter.

She tapped on the door a few times before his sleepy voice bade her enter. She consoled herself with the thought that once Ltn Greene returned to the castle, he could administer some of his Healing. For now, they needed to talk, before the servants started prowling around.

She swept in and Robert blinked at her in astonishment. Ignoring his huff of protest, she pulled the curtains back, though it was still dim outside.

"I see you found your way back." She turned and tossed him a blanket from the end of his bed, so he could tuck it around his shoulders. She almost offered to tuck it herself, but then recalled that he didn't *want* to be her son and was barely conde-scending to be her relative.

"What are you doing here?" he struggled to sit, ignoring the blanket. "This is my room! It is vastly inappropriate that you storm in here like a...like a mother!"

Judith took an involuntary step back. Her heart winced inside her, like a pillow being deflated by an axe. "I apologise," she said stiffly. "I can meet you later in the breakfast room, if you like."

He glared at the blanket accusingly, then sighed as she turned to go. "Wait. What is it? Has something happened?"

Folding her hands tightly in front of her, she recounted Marigold's sobering news about Wooten and Dacian's change of cell. Robert sank back against the pillows, frowning.

"So you see," she concluded awkwardly, "as soon as I have spoken to Miss Onslow, I must set out for Pendennis. I came to ask if you could take charge of the castle in my absence."

Robert blinked. "Me?"

"Why not?"

He cleared his throat and tried to cover up his confusion. "Oh, just that I'll have to fight Mrs Ulrich for that position."

"Well, I dare not leave her unsupervised."

"That fisherman seemed convinced of her innocence."

Judith gave a wry smile. "Yes, but I suspect he may be less than objective on the matter."

There was a pause, and the tension seemed to lessen a little. Robert sat up, theatrically rubbing sleep from his eyes, giving her a rather furtive look. "Actually...I got a bit lost on the way back to my room last night, and I bumped into someone else in the northern corridor."

"Oh?"

With a hint of reluctance, he said: "Miss Onslow."

Judith tipped her head, intrigued. "Did she see you?"

"Yes." His cheeks reddened slightly. "When I heard her footsteps, I cast myself as part of the scenery—some pretty green wallpaper—but she noticed something was off and brushed her hand against me."

Judith contemplated this tableau. "Oh dear. She must have been startled when you appeared."

"A little. She took it remarkably well." The spots of colour in his face deepened, and Judith wondered if Miss Onslow had taken advantage of him, pressed against the wallpaper. She raised her brows, and Robert looked away, fiddling with his blankets. But she was glad he had chosen to confide this much in her, perhaps as a peace offering.

"And did she explain why she was wandering about?" The northern corridor, Judith recalled, was the one that the Crimson Lady was said to frequent.

"She claimed she was fetching some warm milk, and she asked me to accompany her to the kitchen." Robert hesitated again. "She did seem nervous."

"Hm," said Judith. "A little improper for you both to be wandering around together after dark without a chaperone. Perhaps she was simply aware of the delicacy of her situation."

There was a flash of something eager in Robert's eyes, then he gave a shrug of nonchalance. "Well, I don't know if we *were* entirely alone. I heard footsteps behind us." He paused. "Or perhaps they were in front of us. There was no carpet, and I could hear the floorboards creaking. Yet I couldn't see anyone when I looked around. It might have been one of those sneaky footmen."

Judith leaned forward with interest. "Or the Crimson Lady making another appearance! Did Miss Onslow say anything about it?"

"No, she hurried us on to the kitchen, but she did look rather unnerved. It almost felt, at one point, as if something brushed against me." He shivered. "It felt like a ghostly touch, and it made the hairs on the back of my hand stand up."

Judith sat back sceptically. "A door must have opened further down the hall. It would be easy to become over-imaginative in the dark, after our little adventure below."

Robert looked unconvinced. "Perhaps. It really felt as if someone else was there."

"Well," said Judith dryly, "a ghost was scarcely a sufficient chaperone. I hope you did not dawdle so late at night with an unmarried lady."

Robert's jaw tightened. "I am well aware of the rules of gentility, and that I would be an unacceptable suitor."

He was referring to his illegitimacy, and his childhood as a son of a blacksmith. Judith lifted her chin crossly, for she knew that there was some truth in his words, as much as it irked her. "No person of true nobility would turn you away simply for the circumstances of your birth," she said sharply. "Besides, you are a gentleman's son, whether you like it or not. I would be happy to claim you as my own too, and then you would have no trouble wooing *any* lady, least of all Miss Onslow." She caught herself. "Though, of course, you are posing as my nephew for now," she added. "And Miss Onslow obviously enjoys your company."

Robert chewed on his lip. "Hm. And yet."

"And yet?"

"I can't help but feel she was hiding something last night." He met Judith's eyes. "You should ask her yourself, with your Gift. It would have been too easy for her to lie to me."

Especially if Miss Onslow was wielding her charms, with those wide brown eyes and generous mouth. Judith nodded slowly. "Very well. I will seek her out this morning."

Robert tried, and failed, to sound nonchalant. "I could accompany you."

"Certainly. She might confide in *you* more than *me*, in the end."

At his scowl, she cleared her throat and hastily left the room before she was tempted to give him advice on how to woo a young woman, which no doubt would be poorly received.

JUDITH LEFT Robert to dress and went down to the breakfast room. It was a lovely, sunny room facing the rolling hills of Cornwall. The tide was in again, covering the causeway with a swathe of blue, and the clouds from the previous evening had now cleared. She repressed another stab of anxiety as to what Dacian might be undergoing at the moment and sat down to a cold plate of bacon and eggs.

The fat had congealed. She sighed. They needed to install some sort of Travelling charm to transport food from the bowels of the kitchen to the far reaches of the castle, before it froze over in the draughty passageways.

Nonetheless, despite its temperature, the breakfast was nourishing, and she realised she was quite hungry after her night's adventures. Miss Onslow arrived shortly afterwards, which gave Judith the opportunity to question her immediately.

First, she dismissed Trebellow from his post by the door. She did not want the butler to know that Robert had been roaming around at night too. Indeed, it seemed like half the castle's occupants had been roaming around. In a residence this large, she wouldn't know if the twins or Mrs Ulrich had been skulking around in a different wing to her own perambulations.

"Miss Onslow," she began without preamble, "Robert tells me that he met you in the corridors late last night."

The young woman looked up, startled. Then she quickly smoothed her expression. "Yes, I was fetching some milk." Her voice clanged unpleasantly. Then her brows twitched, as some unwelcome thought occurred to her. "Er, that is, um..."

Judith watched her with interest. "Yes?"

Miss Onslow swallowed. "I cannot tell you the reason I was in the corridor, I am sorry."

"Can it be," said Judith slowly, "that you know I am a Truth Discernor?"

Miss Onslow bit her lip as she realised the bind she was in. "Er...yes?"

Judith, abandoning the eggs, sat back and folded her hands on the table. "Who told you?"

"Probably the same person who told you about *my* Gift." Miss Onslow busied herself with slathering a piece of bread with butter, avoiding her gaze.

"Captain Drumpellier." Judith tilted her head. "What I cannot fathom is *why* he would tell you this."

Miss Onslow munched on her bread with a studied air of unconcern and did not answer.

"I insist that you be frank with me, Miss Onslow." Judith leaned forward. "This is my castle now, and I want to know what goes on under its roof. Is Captain Drumpellier courting you?" She paused. "But that would not explain why you were creeping around at night. I am afraid that if you do not tell me, I will assume the worst, which in this case is that you were somehow involved in Sgt Finlay's demise."

Miss Onslow straightened, almost choking on her mouthful. She coughed and spluttered, then took a long gulp of cold tea. Then she looked across at Judith.

"Fine," she said resolutely. "I'll tell you. But you must tell the captain that you coerced the matter out of me."

"What matter?" Robert's voice came from the door. "How are you coercing Miss Onslow, Judith?"

Judith turned, pleased that he was back to using her name,

though amused to see that he was wearing one of the duke's jackets, hanging a little large on his more slender frame. She raised a brow, for it also looked like his boots had been Illused to hug his calves, in the style of a gentleman.

"I am just asking a few pointed questions, my dear. Miss Onslow was just about to explain herself."

Robert seated himself with an apologetic smile. Miss Onslow sighed, putting down her teacup with an air of resignation.

"Very well," she said. "If you must know, I am a spy for the Crown."

In which a confession is forced

Do not be fooled by the guileless appearance of the young.
— from *Lady Avely's Guide to Guile and Peril*

"A SPY?" Judith repeated with incredulity.

Miss Onslow nodded. "I work for the Musor Custos, under Captain Drumpellier's command. It was he who arranged for me to live here, as he knew of my prodigious Gift." She said the last without any arrogance, just stating the matter frankly.

"Your Memory?" asked Judith.

"Yes, it is most useful in remembering codes and translating them." She shot a glance at Robert, whose mouth (it must be said) was hanging open. Judith suddenly recalled the strange codes she had seen in the papers at Drumpellier's desk: no doubt Miss Onslow had authored some of them.

"But why here?" Judith demanded. "Why Castle Lanyon?"

"It is closer to the Isle of Jersey," explained Miss Onslow, "where the English have another bastion of intelligence.

Drumpellier's men take a ship out of Jersey to a point in the Channel where they are able to Travel to England."

Judith narrowed her eyes. "Travel by the Gift, you mean? To this castle?"

Miss Onslow smiled, embarrassed. "Yes. Travel is limited to a certain distance, and we find they cannot manage the whole jump from France to England. So instead, they Travel from their ship to Lanyon's Blue Drawing Room, which is easy to depict for their reference, and simple to imagine. I meet them there and receive their dispatches in code. They do not have to constrain their messages to paper, as no matter how lengthy, it is easy for me to recall. Then I relay them to Drumpellier, verbatim."

She seemed quite proud, and almost relieved, to be able to tell them all this. Judith stared at her, hearing the incontrovertible truth in her voice. So that was why Miss Onslow had been sneaking round at night and seen Ghastagon's startling visage. Perhaps it had been *her* skirts swishing in the kitchen two nights ago.

"*That* is why the captain visits?" asked Robert, alighting on a rather irrelevant point, Judith thought.

Miss Onslow nodded.

Judith recalled how eager the girl had been to hurry her out of the Blue Drawing Room and into the Tea Tower Room. Had she been expecting a covert caller even then? "And does Trebellow know of your...visitors?"

"Not exactly," admitted Miss Onslow. "The meetings are usually at night, when he is asleep, or...away."

"I know about Trebellow's wrassling," said Judith irritably. "It seems that he hasn't paid enough attention to his duties."

Unless Trebellow knew very well what was going on. Were his wrassling forays also a cover for another undertaking? She did not like to think of it and frowned, wondering who else might know of Miss Onslow's real task at the castle. Could someone be trying to intercept the Crown's messages? Could Sgt Finlay have seen someone spying on Miss Onslow, and then been killed before he could warn her? She ran through the possibilities: Trebellow, Mrs Ulrich, the twins, Miss Isla, the baron...

Before she could ask more, Trebellow himself reappeared at the door of the breakfast room. He looked rather uneasy, his jaw tight. "Ma'am, Captain Drumpellier is in the Blue Drawing Room."

Everyone's heads snapped towards him.

"*Now?*" said Judith. "Where did he come from?" The causeway was still covered: she could see the uninterrupted teal of Lanyon Bay.

Miss Onslow coughed politely. "He may, in fact, have come to see me." She raised an enquiring brow at the butler, but Trebellow shook his head.

"No, the captain informed me that he wishes to speak to Lady Avely at once."

Judith stood, aware of a rising anger. "Did the captain arrive by boat?" she asked, in a clipped tone.

"No, ma'am," said Trebellow woodenly. "The first I knew of him was the bell ringing from the Blue Drawing Room."

That meant one of two things: either the captain knew of the secret passageway under the causeway already and had not deigned to tell her about it, or he had arrived at the castle by way of a Travel charm. Grimly, Judith thought she knew the answer.

She pushed out her chair. "Take me to him immediately."

The butler bowed and led her through the warren of corridors. "I add," he murmured, "that he also brought with him Ltn Greene."

Her teeth unclenched slightly. Ltn Greene might provide a

tempering influence on his captain, and moreover, might be able to look at Robert's leg while he was here.

She marched into the Blue Drawing Room, ignoring its elegant, cool splendour. The captain's red coat stood out starkly against the blue walls. He stared out a window, his hands clasped behind his back, a deep frown on his face. By the unlit fire, Ltn Greene smiled tentatively at Judith as she burst in.

"How did you arrive here, Captain?" she demanded, without preamble. "The tide is in, and I saw no boat crossing the waters."

He turned and gave an ironic bow. "I have my ways, Lady Avely." He gave a pointed nod of dismissal to the butler, which Judith saw with irritation. *She* was mistress of this house now, despite Drumpellier using it for his own purposes.

Trebellow slid backwards out of the drawing room and the door shut with a click.

"A Travel Charm?" she snapped.

"Why, yes." Drumpellier looked smug. "You're not the only one who has a prodigiously useful one. We have both trespassed equally now, shall we say."

She was incensed. "You made me drive all that way in a gig!"

"Unfortunately, I cannot waste resources of the Crown on a matron's convenience. And I was very preoccupied that day, otherwise I might have escorted you myself." A smile quirked at his lips. "Though I know his grace didn't like it the last time we Travelled together."

Judith fumed. "You wanted me out of the way." She crossed her arms. "You must have to hold Ltn Greene rather closely, too."

Ltn Greene cleared his throat awkwardly and looked at the floor, his cheeks staining red.

Drumpellier shifted. "It couldn't be avoided. Lieutenant, check on the platoon. You have two hours to do your patrol."

Ltn Greene clicked his heels and saluted. "Yes, sir."

"Now, Lady Avely," said Drumpellier, once they were alone. "I gave you an important enquiry. Have you had any success with it?"

She ground her teeth together. "I have discovered a few things going on in this castle, some of which you could have warned me about."

"What can you mean?"

"Miss Onslow's secret dispatches." She felt a flash of annoyance at his look of amused surprise. "Were you waiting for me to discover it?"

"I did wonder how long it would take," he admitted. "If you are indeed a Truth Discernor. A good little test for Miss Onslow, which I see she failed. And did you discover anything else?"

She eyed him with hostility. She ought to tell him how the body had been moved, but somehow, she did not want to mention the hidden tunnel under the causeway just yet. He might not know of it. And Cador had stressed its secrecy. Why betray it when she might have need of it later? Captain Drumpellier had done nothing to deserve her confidences, and he had left the investigation in her hands. "I have been questioning the servants," she said stiffly, "and finding my way closer to the answer."

"And...?"

"Regardless of my success there, you now have proof of my ability through my discovery of Miss Onslow's secret role. I insist that you take me back to Pendennis now, so that I may see the duke."

Drumpellier bowed his head. "If you wish it."

She stared at him, suspicious. "Excuse me?" This was a change from his threatening manner a few days ago.

He turned to look out the window again. "I'm afraid that your duke is in a rather...unfortunate state."

Her pulse spasmed in sudden fear. "What have you done to him?" Had they damaged him, hurt him, with their new training regime? She wanted to shout accusations, but realised that she could not reveal her knowledge, in case it should betray Wooten and Yvette's presence in the fort.

Drumpellier continued to avoid her gaze, which made her all the more uneasy. "His grace has descended into a confused anger. Early this morning, he became extremely uncooperative and lashed out at his keepers."

Judith gave a short, humourless laugh. "I am not surprised. Forgive me if I am unsympathetic."

The captain turned his head to give her a hard look. "You should be sympathetic, for I suspect our interests align on this matter."

"How so?"

"I find that I do not want to give him many more doses of Lethe, in case his grace becomes a simpleton. Yet that is what I shall be required to do, if he doesn't calm down."

Her throat was suddenly tight. "What do you want me to do?"

"I will take you to him. See if you can soothe the savage beast, as it were. I recall that he was quite chatty with you. A woman's presence might reassure him."

She could hear the faintest echo in his voice, the smallest hint of a lie. Drumpellier was telling the truth, but it wasn't the whole truth. He would also be watching closely, to see if Dacian remembered her, to gauge the duke's state of mind. He must be suspicious of Dacian's erratic behaviour. He wanted to test the duke's response to Judith.

Judith knew she must lend credence to Dacian's performance.

She drew her shoulders back and fixed the captain with a glare. "Can you be surprised that this has happened? His grace is an Impactor. Those with that Gift are well known for their excessive energy, and, dare I say it, their aggression. If you insisted on meddling with his mind, you must expect him to become wild."

"That may be so," agreed Drumpellier mildly, "a strong will is typical of the breed." He paused. "Yet may I remind you that I am also an Impactor. I know we *also* harbour the desire to control our own impulses. *You* must give him a reason to curb himself."

She digested this in silence, her mind working quickly. "Am I allowed to talk of our past?"

"Yes, I suppose," he allowed, "but you must not talk of his crimes, or his punishment. Your task is simply to soothe him and remind him that he is a subject of the Crown."

Judith bit back a retort. She said calmly, "Very well. Take me to him at once."

Drumpellier stepped away from the window. His face showed the first signs of discomfort. "You will have to wrap your arms around me, Lady Avely, so that the charm can carry us both."

"Where will we arrive?" She devoutly hoped it was not in Dacian's cell, where the sight might provoke him to tear off Drumpellier's head off on the spot. On the other hand, that might be an excellent outcome.

"The tower room where we first met," replied Drumpellier, and now he smiled. "It seems that our acquaintance is destined to be rather improper, Lady Avely."

She froze him with a glare. "A matron is never improper."

He lowered his eyes. "Of course not." Then he held out an arm. "Shall we depart?"

Judith gritted her teeth. "Give me one moment." She hastened to the door, and found Trebellow just outside, where he had clearly been listening, for he leapt backwards, eyes wide.

She ignored it. It was probably for the best that Trebellow knew everything. "Please tell Robert that I am going to Fort Pendennis. I leave the castle in his charge, and I should return by nightfall."

"Certainly, ma'am."

She shut the door again and marched up to Drumpellier. She grasped him around the waist and pulled him flush up against her, shutting her eyes. "Let us go."

THE SENSE of being a sheet shaken in the wind soon passed. Judith opened her eyes to find herself in the centre of the Pendennis tower room, surrounded by the imposing circle of grey stone. It had none of the comfort of the Tea Tower Room. As before, it was furnished only with Drumpellier's large desk and one small rug, upon which they now stood.

Hastily, Judith detached herself. "Lead the way."

Drumpellier brushed himself down and turned abruptly. They descended three flights, but instead of progressing further to the dungeon cell, he cut across to a different passage.

"This way."

"You've moved him?" Judith felt it incumbent upon her to express surprise. "Why?"

"We thought he could do with some exercise."

Again, she heard the faint dissonance of a lie. That certainly wasn't the primary purpose of Dacian's new regime. Judith began to suspect that they had intended to use him as a weapon all along. Why, after all, let a good Impactor go to waste? Especially one whose memory had gone and who would be a biddable soldier.

Except Dacian was not proving biddable. No surprise there.

She chewed her lip. How was she to play this? How would Dacian greet her? Fear touched her that he might have actually lost his mind, and that it was no performance. What if they had managed to force more Lethe down his throat after Wooten's brave sacrifice? What if he was truly lost to her? She dared not think on it and instead wondered feverishly what she might communicate to him now.

They approached another deep-set door, and Judith drew a breath. This time it was guarded by two broad-chested infantrymen, both with rifles and grim expressions. No complacency this time in how they had assigned guard duty. Drumpellier stopped and exchanged low words with one of them.

"Is he improved?"

"No, sir. Still raving."

"Has he said anything...different?"

"No, sir, unless you count bawling for cognac."

"Did you give it to him?"

"One glass, sir. We have tried to be amiable, as you suggested, sir, but to no avail. He threatened to disembowel us."

Drumpellier sighed and cast a glance back at Judith. "Prepare yourself, ma'am, for a difficult meeting."

She glared back. "I blame you for that, Captain."

"You must tell him that he must learn to behave as an English gentleman and a loyal subject."

Judith did not deign to answer.

"I am serious," Drumpellier threatened in a low voice. "You must obtain his cooperation, or it will be the worse for both of you."

Reluctantly, she gave a tight nod.

Drumpellier stepped up to the door and shouted through it. "Sir, I have a visitor for you."

Judith bridled at his lack of proper address, and perhaps Dacian was equally disgusted, for silence came from within.

"Sir!" shouted Drumpellier. "A friend of yours is here to see you. I am going to open this door and enter, but if you respond badly, *both* of you will suffer."

Judith grimaced. Too late, she realised that Drumpellier might use her as a hostage for Dacian's compliance. Assuming that Dacian even recognised her.

A growl finally emerged from the cell. "Who is it?"

"You will see when we enter." Clearly, Drumpellier didn't want to give away Judith's identity: he wanted to see Dacian's reaction for himself. He pulled a heavy key from his pocket and slipped it into the thick padlock. "Are you away from the door?"

"Yes, Goddammit." It was a bellow. "This better be good, or I'll wrench your head from your shoulders."

"You can try," the captain gritted out, "and if you succeed, you'll be shot on the spot."

There was silence again, as if Dacian was contemplating the benefits of such a bargain.

"Right." Subtly, Drumpellier squared his shoulders. "You first," he nodded at Judith, "and you behind me, Corporal Threadbow, with gun at the ready."

Despicable coward, sending a woman in first. Judith felt her spine stiffen with fear as the corporal drew out a pistol and cocked it. She stepped forward, Drumpellier breathing down her neck.

He reached past her and slid back the heavy lock. Cautiously, he shoved the door open and gestured for Judith to enter.

In which a prisoner is contrary

It is hardest to be guileful when under the sway of strong emotion. Keep a calm head and you will do better at deceiving.
— from *Lady Avely's Guide to Guile and Peril*

COMPARED to Dacian's first cell, this one was empty of comfort —no rugs, cushions, or food. It was simply a hard, square room of stone.

The duke stood in the middle of the room. His black hair was in wild disarray, his cheeks shadowed, his eyes hooded. Only a pair of brown half-trousers covered him, leaving his chest and feet bare. His fists were loosely clenched before him and bound in manacles.

Judith let out an involuntary gasp of horror.

Dacian stared, impassive, his jaw etched in rock. Then his expression warped into anger.

"Who is this lady?" he growled. "What trickery now?"

Judith kept herself firmly in hand. She must not throw herself on him and weep upon his chest, as much as she may wish to do so. And she didn't know what to think of this ferocious anger. It was difficult to parse a lie from the questions he threw at her. Should she be relieved that his acting passed muster? Or afraid that he had forgotten her completely?

"I am Mrs Judith Avely," she said quietly, leaving her new title out of it. "I am your friend."

Dacian snarled. "Oh, really? Like the rest of them here?"

She wondered what Drumpellier had told him. Behind her, the captain watched. She could feel his attention, as sharp as a hawk's.

"You have forgotten me," she said slowly, "but I remember you well. And I do not recall a beast."

Dacian took a threatening step forward. "I do not recall anything, so why not a beast?"

Her shoulders almost sagged with relief, hearing the echo of a lie in his voice. He did remember something. Her? She kept her posture ramrod straight.

"Because you are an English gentleman," she replied, mindful of Drumpellier's instructions. She turned to the captain haughtily, stepping away from him slightly. "I must ask, sir, why have you bound his hands?"

Drumpellier's lips thinned. "To keep him contained. Those are wristbreakers, so I do not have to constantly exert myself."

She frowned at the implication. "You have imbued them with an Impacting charm?"

He nodded.

"You mean they cannot be broken?" She wanted to know what Dacian was dealing with; wanted him to hear it too.

Drumpellier seemed to guess her intent, for he gave a mirthless smile. "Worse, I'm afraid." He gestured at a chain that hung in a loop through his crossbelt. "If I pull at this loop, the manacles will tighten unbearably. You can imagine the result, should I tighten it completely."

Judith swallowed down bile. "It will break his wrists."

"I assure you, I do not wish for that, any more than you do."

Dacian growled, "Coward." He lurched forward threateningly, but Corporal Threadbow raised his gun in a pointed manner.

Dacian stilled.

Judith licked her lips, turning to face him again. "Dacian, I beg you to calm yourself. I am certain that no one here wishes to break your arms." Especially if Drumpellier intended to use him as a soldier. "You must show yourself to be reasonable, otherwise they will sedate your further."

She widened her eyes meaningfully, hoping he would understand the threat of Lethe that still hung over him.

"They don't want me sedated," he snarled. "They were using me as a plaything yesterday, and I want no part of it."

Judith glanced at Drumpellier accusingly. "What were you doing?"

Drumpellier remained wooden. "As I told you, we were allowing him some exercise. He partook in some wrassling matches against the other soldiers—without weapons, or power, you understand. It is a popular sport around here, and I thought it a good opportunity to see if he might follow the rules."

"And did he?"

Drumpellier became dry. "Almost. He threw someone from a supine position, which is not permitted. Though he *did* seem familiar with the finer points of the sport."

Judith nodded. "Indeed, his grace has undertaken wrassling before. Or so my butler, Trebellow, informed me. Perhaps those sorts of things are a visceral memory."

Dacian raised his manacled hands. "Are you talking about *me*? I do not recall wrassling with any butler."

"Not *with* my butler," she assured him. "Though Trebellow

would welcome the opportunity." Dacian stared at her in growing confusion, and she hurried on. "I should think you would *enjoy* exerting your strength again, your grace. You might need it in the future." That was as much as she could say, to hint that he must be ready to act. For an idea had begun to take seed in her mind, inspired by everything she had learned that day.

"Not if I am to be kept in this godforsaken keep for the rest of my life." Dacian snapped.

Uneasily, she realised that there had been no talk of Dacian's crimes or hearing. She remembered Drumpellier's injunction not to mention it. What game was the captain playing? She looked over her shoulder, frowning at Drumpellier. "What have you told him?" she demanded, then she turned to Dacian. "What do you know?"

Dacian scowled. "Merely that I am a murderer, and that I must serve my punishment. You can forgive me for doubting it, when I cannot remember anything of the sort."

Again, it was a lie. Judith bit her lip, trying to stay impassive. She might, after all, still be a stranger to him. And she was starting to feel Bemused, from the intense exertion of her Gift.

"You will continue to remember nothing," snapped Drumpellier, "if you refuse to cooperate."

Cooperate with what, exactly? And Drumpellier's voice also clanged hollowly. Anger rose in Judith, like a fire suddenly doused with brandy. "How dare you! His grace has not even been tried, and already you are punishing him!"

Drumpellier gave her a warning look. "I am giving him a chance to prove his character, before it comes before the court." He folded his arms across his chest, brushing the iron chain that hung on his cross-belt, and directed his next words to Dacian. "Might I add that if you prove yourself compliant, I will remove those cuffs. Furthermore, I shall even allow the return of your power. Then you can try fighting with your Gift. There is a form of wrassling, not so well known, that indulges in more difficult manoeuvres."

Judith heard truth in these declarations, but she narrowed her eyes in suspicion. "I suppose *you* are a practitioner of the art."

Drumpellier nodded shortly. "And if our prisoner should prove himself worthy, I will face him as an opponent."

A gleam came into Dacian's eyes, but Judith was unimpressed.

"No doubt you will ensure that your power is the greater," she snapped, through gathering Bemusement. "I beg leave to suggest, sir, that it will not be a fair fight."

"You go too far, ma'am." Drumpellier's jaw tightened.

Dacian bared his teeth. "You are the one hiding behind a bracelet, instead of fighting like a man."

"If you can give me your word of honour," said Drumpellier rigidly, "that you will obey orders of the Crown and Custos, then I will consider releasing you, and allowing you the freedom to fight."

Dacian stared at Drumpellier for a long, hard moment. Then he shrugged his broad shoulders, took a few steps back, and threw himself upon a stone seat. "I will think on it." He turned his hooded eyes upon Judith. "And you, ma'am, what is your relation to me? Are you some infernal cousin or sister, trying to rescue me?"

Judith almost choked. "Certainly not! We are much closer than...you have..." Then she realised what might be his intent: to protect her, and that she should not reveal their intimacies. "You have flirted with me, your grace, on more than one occasion," she said coldly, in her best approximation of outraged dignity.

His gaze became sardonic. "Flirted? Really?"

"Yes."

"Did I ask for your hand?"

"No," she said icily.

"Perhaps you already have a husband?" he suggested. "A lucky man, no doubt." He gave a leer.

Judith drew herself up haughtily. "I am a widow."

His eyes lit up. "Oh, a widow! Now I understand!"

Judith saw his gaze travel to her bosom, and she drew a heaving breath. "Please do not insult me, your grace. I am a friend, trying to help you."

He laughed, but it was a bitter sound, and he leant his head against stone. "Yet you come before me with soldiers at your back."

She could not deny it, and she had to go along with his performance. Desperately, she hoped that it *was* a performance. What could she say or do to help him? She was aware that Drumpellier was closely scrutinising every word.

"There is no point dwelling on your indignities," she said stiffly. "If the captain is offering you a way forward, you must take it. Have patience and reticence, and I am certain all will be well."

Dacian scowled over her shoulder at Drumpellier. "You ask a woman to speak your piece."

Yet Judith hoped he had somehow heard her warning, and her reassurance, even as he avoided her eyes. She tilted her head. "Are you sleeping well? I find that if I don't have a proper sleep, I am quite unbearable." It was another clue, she hoped, for him to be alert that night, if he could read between the lines.

She ignored the faint doubt at the back of her mind, which was now rather clouded. Dacian had given her no real sign of recognition, no hidden clue or word to show that he remembered her. Yet she ought to retreat before she said anything foolish. She turned to Drumpellier. "Are you satisfied now, Captain? Your prisoner seems calmer. I hope that you may now count on his cooperation."

Out of the corner of her eye, she saw Dacian's fists clench.

Drumpellier looked between them, unreadable. "I am glad of it. Lady Avely. Perhaps you can join me for some tea, now that your duty is done?"

She inclined her head, gracious.

The duke let his head thunk against the wall. "The tea is terrible. Much better to have drinking chocolate, ma'am, if you can find it."

Judith tried to remain expressionless, even as her heart leapt within her. He *did* remember her. Their eyes met for a charged instant.

"Indeed." She dropped a shallow curtsy. "Good day, your grace."

His gaze dropped. His lips twisted. "Good day, ma'am."

She turned and walked away. Every fibre of her being revolted against it, but she had to leave him behind.

Drumpellier followed her and opened the door. Corporal Threadbow kept his face to Dacian, gun still primed and backed out after them.

As the heavy door slammed into place, she turned ferociously. "You should take better care of him, Captain. He is not even properly clothed!"

Drumpellier strode past her. "He has refused other shirts. And we discovered an Illusion charm on his livery. I don't suppose you know anything about that?"

"No," she lied baldly.

"Speaking of charms," said Drumpellier coldly, as he began up the stairs, "that diamond ring you gave me does not appear to work as a Travel charm."

"I warned you," said Judith, trying for an equally cool tone. "Its magick has been exhausted."

"That may be so, but I warn you: if I find you Travelling into my domain again, I shall have no choice but to arrest you for treason. This is a military fort, and unauthorised trespass must be treated with the utmost severity."

"My dear Captain," replied Judith, "I have no wish to trespass upon your dreadful fort. Besides, even if I should do so, what good would it do? His grace does not remember me."

Abruptly, Drumpellier spun round to face her on the landing. "On the contrary, I think he *did* recognise you."

She hoped her shocked pause was not telling and drew herself up. "I certainly saw no sign of it."

"That's because you didn't witness his behaviour this morning. He was a raging beast, a veritable demon possessed. Yet that little performance fell away as soon as you arrived on the scene."

Judith was silent for a dreadful moment. Then she rallied. "No doubt it was the natural civility of a gentleman in the presence of a lady," she said austerely. "I am glad to hear that his breeding showed through, despite your ill treatment."

Drumpellier scoffed. "Rather, his grace didn't want *you* to see him like that, because you know a very different man. He softened before you; I saw it. He recognised you," he repeated, with more certainty. "Which means he has more of his memory than I thought. I wonder how he is doing it."

"Nonsense," said Judith sharply. "Just because *you* have no notion how to treat a respectable widow does not mean that his grace is devoid of all proper feeling, even without his memories."

"Hmm," Drumpellier said sceptically. He began walking again through the cold stone entryway of the keep.

Judith hastened after him. "Regardless, I think it is a very good thing if his grace recalls himself. I just heard you promise him the return of his power and freedom, which I am glad to hear. It seems as if you intend to drop the charges against him."

They had reached the gate, and he gestured for her to follow the same path of three nights ago, through the portico and towards the barracks.

"Do not misunderstand me," said Drumpellier, his hardness returning. "His grace must still be tried and punished. We are merely trying to establish some compliance, for his own good."

She heard the lie and lifted her chin with scorn. "I suspect it is more for your good," she snapped. "I wonder what you truly want from him?"

Drumpellier did not answer. His silence was all the confirmation she needed. He intended to use Dacian for his own purposes.

She was determined it would not happen.

In which shots are fired

As I'm sure you know by now, Bemusement offers its own peril.
— from *Lady Avely's Guide to Guile and Peril*

SHE REFUSED the cup of tea at Custodian House. She was starting to feel excessively Bemused from exerting her Gift so constantly, and her head was slightly dizzy. And she didn't trust tea from the captain.

"I must hurry back to the castle," she said, as forcefully as she could manage. "And I will *not* go by carriage. I insist that you transport me back *immediately*."

Drumpellier acquiesced, perhaps because he needed to fetch Ltn Greene. Awkwardly, they embraced, Judith fuming that she must compromise her dignity thus, to clasp such a villain in her arms. Yet she was relieved to arrive back in the Blue Drawing Room, where its cool elegance felt almost like a return home.

Trebellow stood by the open door, eyes wide.

Judith hastily disengaged from the captain. "What is it, Trebellow? Why are you lurking around?"

"Apologies, ma'am. Baron Quarles has arrived." Nervously, Trebellow extended a meaty hand, in the manner of one presenting a witness in the box.

In consternation, Judith turned to see a tall, thin man. He was sitting in one of the wooden chairs, gingerly holding a cup of tea. He had narrow, aristocratic features under a receding hairline, an expensively tailored coat, threadbare upon his shoulders, and a bewildered smile upon his face.

The baron put down his cup and manoeuvred his long limbs out of the chair, standing with a bow. "Lady Avely. I proffer my deepest gratitude for your hospitality."

Damnation. Judith dropped a perfunctory curtsy. "Any friend of the king is welcome here," she muttered, and gestured. "This is Captain Drumpellier, of the -nth Regiment at Fort Pendennis." Belatedly, she recalled that she wanted to ask the baron some pointed questions. He had been around when Sgt Finlay had died, and he had been seen lurking around the castle in odd corners.

Baron Quarles bowed again. "We are well acquainted. Greetings, Captain."

Drumpellier canted his head slightly and straightened his coat. "Baron. What brings you to Castle Lanyon again?"

"The stars, of course!" Baron Quarles's tone was light. "The view is brilliant from the ramparts. I have great hopes of seeing Venus tonight."

Judith, however, heard the hollow clunk of a lie through her gathering Bemusement. "Just the stars, Baron?" she enquired.

The baron smiled. "Indeed, what more could there be?"

He smiled at her kindly, but again the lie echoed. Her head ached, and she glared, wondering if she could just throw him out of the house forthwith. She had enough on her plate without a devious baron thrown into the mix.

Drumpellier cast a glance at her, perhaps sensing the reason for her doubt. He raised a brow at the baron. "Surely the moon is still too full for stargazing tonight, my lord?"

"Ah, but the moon is a transient creature," Baron Quarles said genially. "I can outwit her, for the sake of my beauties."

"I wish you joy of it," snapped Judith crossly. "I may not see you at dinner, however."

"Please, do not let me inconvenience you." Baron Quarles tipped his head, considering. "I swear, I did not hear you come in through the door—it quite seemed as if you appeared out of nowhere."

Judith stared at him. His tone rang false. He must have seen them Travel in. Was his comment simply meant to be teasing? Or was it an oblique warning for them to abide by the Edicts? For the baron was a close friend of the king, who had instigated the Edicts. Perhaps he did not know how His Majesty had recently granted an exemption for Castle Lanyon. But before she could parry the question, footsteps came pounding outside the corridor.

They all turned. Ltn Greene burst through it, his face flushed, his breathing ragged, his red uniform disordered.

"Someone shot at me!" he cried. "From the castle walls!"

JUDITH STARTED and turned to the lieutenant.

Ltn Greene looked around wildly. Then his gaze landed on Baron Quarles. "You! Who are you? Where were you a quarter hour ago?"

The baron drew up his thin form in hauteur. "I am Baron

Quarles, and I was sitting in this Drawing Room, as the butler can attest."

Trebellow began to nod, then cleared his throat instead. "I left you here, it is true, my lord."

"While you fetched the tea," stated Baron Quarles haughtily. "What is it that you imagine I did in your absence? Leap out with a gun?" He turned in irritation to Ltn Greene. "Explain yourself, young man."

"Yes, Lieutenant," said Drumpellier grimly. "What happened?"

Ltn Greene took a deep breath and pulled his lapels straight. "I was exiting the castle, sir, as you instructed, on my way to inspect the platoon," he said in a calmer manner. "When I came out near the rampart terrace, I heard the crack of a pistol shot, and a bullet whistled past my ear. I spun around, and another shot came soon after. It came—I think—from the direction of the broken tower. I ducked down and crawled my way back inside. Since then, I have been searching for the culprit, pelting through the corridors."

Judith, listening, heard that the lieutenant only spoke the truth. She sat down on a settee, rubbing her forehead. What new villainy was this? It must be connected with Sgt Finlay's death: another attempt on a British soldier. But why? And why must her wits abandon her now?

Drumpellier frowned. "And did you find anyone skulking around with a pistol?"

"No, but it is easily hid," replied Ltn Greene. He glared at the baron. "I suggest that we search this room."

Baron Quarles sniffed dismissively. "Be my guest." Then he glanced apologetically at Judith. "If Lady Avely will permit it."

Judith tried to gather her thoughts. After a moment, she said, "Unless he is very stupid, the baron would be unlikely to hide the weapon in this room." She was quite pleased at this logic.

"Why, thank you," bowed the baron, with some irony.

"However," she continued, "the baron might well be very stupid, and we should look."

Baron Quarles raised his brows.

Drumpellier coughed. "Are you feeling quite all right, Lady Avely?"

"Perfectly fine," she lied. Everyone else lied, so why not she? She waved a hand airily. "Go on—search the drawing room, and the whole castle if you must."

Ltn Greene needed no further encouragement. He leapt into action, looking under and behind the settees, sweeping the curtains up, and even poking in the fireplace.

But no gun was to be found.

He turned grimly to his captain, his nose now smudged with coal. "May I have your permission to continue the search elsewhere, sir?"

Drumpellier pursed his lips, suddenly seeming reluctant. "Even if we should find the weapon, it will not tell us who fired it." He looked at Judith. "Do you have any idea who it may be, Lady Avely? You have been questioning the occupants of the castle, have you not?"

Baron Quarles's eyes widened with curiosity. Judith examined her new guest through the haze of her Bemusement. Just minutes ago, the baron had lied to her about his stargazing being the sole reason for his visit. Perhaps he *had* tried to shoot the lieutenant. In her befuddled state she couldn't quite garner the reason.

"Baron, *did* you shoot at the lieutenant?"

The baron drew himself up again. "How dare you suggest such a thing!"

"Answer the question!" she snapped. Drumpellier's eyes narrowed, and he turned to stare at the baron.

"I most certainly did not." The baron's thin cheeks now had two spots of angry colour.

Judith's shoulders sagged in disappointment, for he was telling the truth. Curse it. The baron would have made a nice villain. He had even been around to bump Sgt Finlay on the head...

The baron, oblivious to his lost leading role, continued to bluster. "What is going on? Is it not safe to stargaze anymore? Is the castle under siege?"

"You recall that one of my soldiers drowned last week," said Drumpellier shortly. "This latest violence might have something to do with that misadventure."

Judith tried to think. She turned to Ltn Greene, where he stood at attention by the fireplace. "Lieutenant, do *you* know something about Sgt Finlay, or the night he was killed?"

Ltn Greene's expression became alarmed. "I swear I did not kill him, ma'am!"

It was the truth. "Yes, but do you know something about that night, some clue which might point to the killer, and explain why a gun has now been turned upon you?"

A frown settled on the lieutenant's brow. His gaze lowered, to stare unseeingly at the carpet. There was a long pause.

"Well, Lieutenant?" pressed Drumpellier.

Ltn Greene spoke slowly, "I couldn't say, sir."

"Your life might be in danger," said Drumpellier sharply. "If you know something, you must tell us."

Ltn Greene remained silent. Judith sighed. She *really* desired a cup of chocolate right now. Or a nap. Or both. Perhaps *then* she would see and hear more clearly. For it seemed to her that Ltn Greene did know something, which he was reluctant to speak aloud.

Drumpellier cast a glance at her and appeared to guess that she had reached the end of her resources. "Well, Lieutenant, let us depart now, and whisk you to safety. You can think about it back in the shelter of the Pendennis barracks and let me know if you have any sudden insights."

"Yes, sir," said Ltn Greene woodenly.

"Lady Avely," continued Drumpellier, his tone sharpening. "You had better find out what is going on here, or you will lose any right to intervene in any *other* matters. This is the second soldier of mine to come under threat, and the issue must be resolved speedily. I trust you will expend all your effort."

Judith said nothing. She was too busy imagining a molinet of chocolate in the Tea Tower Room, and whether Ghastagon might like a pat.

"But first," said Drumpellier, "I must speak to Miss Onslow. May I see her in the Blue Drawing Room now?"

Judith blinked. Was the man actually commandeering her drawing room? She was aware of a distant sense of outrage but then gave an unladylike shrug. "You may. Trebellow, please fetch Miss Onslow."

Trebellow bowed and left. Baron Quarles coughed and excused himself, following close after the butler.

There was a silence. Drumpellier cleared his throat. "Perhaps you wish to retire as well, Lady Avely, so that I may speak with Miss Onslow in private. Ltn Greene will stand watch at the door."

Judith gave him an icy glare. "You go too far, Captain. This is *my* castle, and I will continue to host in the drawing room."

"As you very well know, I have secret matters of the Crown and Custos to discuss with Miss Onslow. Your presence cannot be permitted."

Judith sniffed and stood. She was uneasily aware that she could not throw a spoke in the wheel of English intelligence.

"Very well," she uttered, "I shall cede the ground to you this time, Drumpellier, but only because I want a nap."

His lips quirked, and he bowed. "Thank you, Lady Avely."

She swept from the room.

Halfway down one of the corridors, she saw Miss Onslow. Her face was pale as she hurriedly reported for duty. Judith gave her a reassuring smile, but for some reason the girl looked even more worried. Shrugging it off, Judith made her way up to her room, only becoming a little bit lost in the process. When she finally collapsed on her bed, she fell straight into sleep.

In which blackmail and whisky are persuasive

Dacian

Dacian was angry.

Not only had he been forced to fight like a cock in the ring this morning—against inferior combatants—he was still hungry. He had drunk deeply from the carafe that his opponents had shared, but he was avoiding the food, for good reason. Pretending to eat was difficult with so many eyes on him, so he had resorted to the surly paranoia of the mentally addled, lashing out at his keepers, and tipping over plates of food in orchestrated fits of rage.

His pretence was close enough to the truth. His anger was a simmering furnace, ready to erupt. He had been taken here against his will, drugged, locked up, and manacled, and he was beginning to suspect that the stated grounds—his duelling crimes— weren't the real reason. Why had Drumpellier started him on a training regime, otherwise? Of course, the captain thought he was witless, without any memory, and that he would accept his allotted role as a brainless weapon.

More fool him. Dacian was trying to convince him that the

weapon might explode in his hands. And it seemed to be working.

It had been an hour since the captain escorted Judith out and agreed to undo the wristbreakers. Dacian had to watch her go without saying a word. He'd had to stare at her like she was a stranger, and snarl like an animal, while she stood white-faced and afraid. If only he could have blasted everyone else to oblivion and swept her into his arms and kissed her thoroughly enough to make her confusion vanish. He remembered now the taste of her lips, the softness of her body against his, her confiding smile and mocking eyes. He had experienced such a small taste, after so many years longing for it, and now heaven had been snatched away from him again.

Maintaining the act of scornful ignorance had been worth it, for Drumpellier had offered a compromise in her presence. Did he mean it? Rewards for good behaviour made Dacian grit his teeth, but he was in no position to negotiate. His fits of wildness were an attempt to gain leverage, but they could equally land him back where he had started. He had not expected these damn manacles, thrumming with power and chafing against his skin.

He paced around the small cell, his bare feet cold on the stone. Then he heard boots approaching, at least three men. Quickly, he arranged himself against the back wall, sprawling, his cuffed hands nonchalantly resting on his knees. He did not want to show uncertainty. Better to bargain from a position of authority, even like this.

Drumpellier's voice came from behind the door. "Your grace?"

Dacian said nothing for a moment. Your grace? This was a turnabout. A trick, surely. He growled, "What did you call me?"

Drumpellier sighed heavily. "Don't pretend anymore. I know you have regained yourself. I have come to talk to you about how we should proceed. A discussion—not between a duke and gentry, or captain and prisoner, but man to man."

"Show me a man first, and I'll think about it."

"I'm opening the door."

Dacian said nothing. It was not as if he could do anything to stop him.

The lock clicked loudly and the lever swung. Drumpellier stepped into the room, backed by his two thugs. Ltn Greene hung back, watching anxiously. The lieutenant had not risked another delivery of untainted food, and Dacian was careful not to meet his eyes. He didn't understand what game the lieutenant was playing, but he was willing to take his help if he needed it. Indeed, it may have been the lieutenant who had convinced the captain to try this new tactic of compliance.

Drumpellier strode up to him, fearless. Dacian narrowed his eyes, wishing that just one ounce of his power remained. Then Drumpellier sat down next to him and leaned against the wall. Dacian blinked and turned his head to look at him.

The captain smiled grimly. "Lowering myself to your level, your grace. So we can talk properly." He jerked his head at the other soldiers. "Leave us."

Threadbow and Ltn Greene looked uncertain, but they backed out of the room, leaving the door open. Dacian knew they could hear everything, but he found himself appreciating at least the appearance of privacy. Though of course Drumpellier still had the advantage, with these damned wristbreakers confining him.

Briefly, Dacian wondered if he should throw another fit of rage and pin the captain to the wall. Then caution and curiosity got the better of him. "What do you want?"

"I want your help."

"You have a strange way of asking for it."

Captain Drumpellier's lips twisted. "I underestimated you,

certainly. I don't know how you are resisting the drug and avoiding food for so long, but I do know that you are not abiding by my plans."

Dacian did not deny it. "I don't like being a pawn."

"In times of war, we must all concede to be moved on the board."

"Not blindly."

"Yes, I concede the point. Which is why I will tell you now that I need a weapon to send into Austria. To commit an assassination."

Dacian was silent for a long, shocked minute. He knew enough about the front to know what was implied. "You want me to assassinate Bonaparte?"

The captain simply nodded. "There is no other way."

"I beg to differ." Dacian began to feel angry again.

"Bonaparte is unstoppable. It is only a matter of time before he makes his move. And then England will fall."

"You have too little faith."

"I prefer the virtue of wisdom over faith. And wisdom tells me that we have a chance now, which we must grab with both hands. Your hands."

Dacian stayed uncompromisingly silent, though he had an inkling of how Drumpellier had reasoned himself into madness.

Drumpellier sighed. "I had cousins in France, you know. They were Chouans, Musors. They were summarily executed by Bonaparte without a proper trial. That same ruthlessness guided him to power, and now he has crowned himself emperor." He paused. "If we are to stop him, we must be equally merciless."

No doubt these Chouan cousins had been fighting with underhanded methods and had not been granted honourable treatment. Yet Dacian was aware of some sympathy, as well as curiosity as to what Drumpellier proposed. Such an insane plan might give him a way to escape. And he wondered what authority was the captain was acting under. His own? Had his zealousness led him astray, into paranoid fancies? Or was he under someone's command? Either way, a journey into Austria could shift the board.

The captain continued, his voice dry. "Before you start plotting, your grace, I think you should remember that I now possess a valuable card. Now I know of your true relation to Lady Avely."

"That woman earlier?" Dacian tried for insolent surprise, but he feared it was unconvincing. Fear curled in his gut. "And, pray tell, what is she to me, exactly? I would like to know it myself."

"She is dear to you. Very dear, I suspect."

This time Dacian's silence was damning. His heart twisted.

Drumpellier continued. "And I think you will do as I ask, on the condition that she is left in peace, rather than arrested for treason."

Dacian scoffed through gritted teeth. "She is a lady, not a soldier. You cannot arrest her for treason."

"Lady Avely has entered this fort unlawfully twice, by means of Travel. At the very least, it is trespassing on military ground. Furthermore, she rifled through strictly confidential communications in my headquarters. I can argue a very convincing case that she is working for the enemy. Unless," he paused, "you prove both your loyalty and hers, by taking on this task. You have the nerve and the brains to do it, as well as the Gift. And you will be saving England single-handedly from a monster."

Dacian wet his lips. The iron was heavy against his wrists, and his heart even heavier. "If I agree, you must leave her alone entirely."

"I suspect it is more a matter of her leaving *me* alone," Drumpellier muttered. "If I can show her that you are collaborating with full awareness, she might back off and leave me be." He paused. "And I confess that her convoluted tale of your innocence was marginally persuasive. If what she told me was true, you've been a pawn before this."

Dacian stonily let that pass. "If I am to do this, you cannot cast me as a witless fool anymore."

"No, this will be a new arrangement. Once I have your word of honour that you will cooperate fully, I will grant you immunity from the Custos charges and release you." Drumpellier put a hand to his pocket and pulled out an oblong, deep blue stone, dark and polished. He put it on the ground between him and Dacian. "I will even give you this schorl to help temper your Gift. It is one of my own, and I hope you will take it as a gesture of trust."

Dacian stared down at the Talisman Stone. "You will pardon me? Forgo the charges against me?"

Drumpellier nodded. "Full immunity. It is not uncommon in the workings of justice, if there is enough reason to grant it."

Dacian felt a swoop of relief but did not let it show. "We will work together as equals."

"I swear."

He wished he had Judith's talent for Discerning lies. Drumpellier's tone sounded sincere, but how could he trust the man? Yet what choice did he have? At least this new approach gave him room to manoeuvre. And he could not allow Judith to be dragged into this nightmare fort on some trumped-up allegations of treason.

After a long silence, Dacian said with a sigh, "Only if you bring me food and share it with me now."

"I can do better than that. I can take you to the barracks, where the cook is preparing food for the troops. You can eat it hot from the pan, and I will taste any mouthful you want."

Dacian tried to tell himself this was not a more convincing

argument than Judith's safety. "Fine. And I want whisky straight from the keg."

"You will have it."

Drumpellier pushed himself up from the wall and held out a hand to Dacian. Disgusted, Dacian took it and was pulled to standing.

"Right. First, let us dispense with these." The captain gingerly extracted the silver chain from his pocket and slipped a long flat key into the wristbreakers. The weight fell off Dacian's hands as if they weighed ten times their size. Perhaps they did, with the hefty spells ensorcelled into the metal.

The captain held out his hand again, this time to shake Dacian's. Grimly, he complied, though not without a private doubt that he was walking into another trap. And this time the gun to his head was far more persuasive: Judith's safety, rather than his own.

In which a butler proves evasive

In times of great peril, one must act with cunning and decisiveness. Obviously, this is better done when not Bemused.
— from *Lady Avely's Guide to Guile and Peril*

AFTER HER IGNOMINIOUS retreat and a fitful sleep, Judith awoke an hour later, groggy and hungry. Her first thought was for Dacian. He remembered her. And he was cuffed and trapped, a pawn in some game she didn't understand. And poor Wooten was in danger too, laid low by his attempt to save his companion.

The curtains were open, showing a cloudy sky. A soft breeze floated into the room. It was not that which had woken her, however, but a tapping at the door.

"Yes?" she called blearily, sitting up. "Come in!"

The door opened a few inches, showing the anxious face of Miss Onslow. "My apologies, Lady Avely. I didn't mean to wake you."

"No matter," said Judith, though she could hear the bell of

untruth in that declaration. "What is it? Have the captain and lieutenant left?"

"They have." Miss Onslow edged into the room and shut the door, her usual ease of manner markedly absent, her shoulders tense. She didn't even cast a curious glance around the Captain's Room. "I have come to speak to you about something rather concerning."

"Oh?" Judith rubbed her eyes. Wasn't there enough to concern her already? "What is it now?"

"It regards the Duke of Sargen."

Judith's sleepiness vanished. "What about him?"

Miss Onslow gave a portentous pause. "His grace was in the latest dispatch that Captain Drumpellier wished me to memorise."

"Sargen? In the dispatch to France? What does it say?"

Miss Onslow tentatively sat down on the wooden chair next to the bed. "Brace yourself, Lady Avely. I am afraid to tell you that Captain Drumpellier intends to send the duke into Austria. He has intelligence of Bonaparte's whereabouts, and he means to send his grace to try an assassination."

Judith's draw dropped. "*What?*"

Miss Onslow nodded sombrely. "Apparently, Drumpellier thinks he has obtained a level of compliance from the duke, alongside a dosing of Lethe, and that makes him an ideal candidate to send into enemy territory. They intend for his grace to use raw Impact to kill Bonaparte. The reasoning is that even if he should be captured, his lack of memory should guard against any intelligence being lost."

Rage clutched at Judith's throat, making it difficult to breathe. "They are sending him on a suicide mission!"

"Yes," agreed Miss Onslow. "They want someone who cannot be tortured for information, but I have little doubt that his grace will be captured and executed." Her mouth turned down bitterly. "Like my brother."

"Your brother?" Judith stared. "Was he an Impactor?"

"No, but he was sent on a similar mission by Drumpellier."

Judith was quiet for a moment, in sympathy. "But how is the captain ferrying soldiers into Austria?"

"By Travel, of course," Miss Onslow explained. "In stages—first from here to Jersey, and then to safe houses in France, across to Germany, and then into Austria. Though they may well use mundane forms of travel for some of it."

Judith clenched her hands so tightly that her nails bit into her palms. They probably had never intended a trial: this had been Drumpellier's plan all along. No wonder he had not known who was to preside over the court, for there was to be no trial! That was why he had been so eager to ignore her evidence and hustle Dacian into captivity. He was desperate to snuff Bonaparte out in a dishonourable, cowardly attack.

Miss Onslow bowed her head in sympathy. "I'm sorry. You cannot know how much I empathise."

Judith threw her blankets aside and paced the room. "Yet surely this is all strictly confidential. Drumpellier would be furious if he knew you had told me." She paused. "Why did you?"

Miss Onslow folded her hands in her lap rather nervously. "I found your letter," she said. "The one you wrote to the duke."

"*You* were the one sneaking around my room?"

Miss Onslow's eyes widened in surprise. "You knew of it? How?"

"Never mind," snapped Judith. "What gave you the right to snoop through my things?"

"I am a spy," Miss Onslow reminded her. "I thought it wise to find out more about you. I thought the captain would like to know anything I could discover. But instead, what I read turned my sympathies to you." She drew a deep breath. "Also, I find that I am rather tired of Drumpellier's disregard for mercy. He sent my brother off to his death without a second thought. I could not bear the same to happen to your friend."

Judith squeezed her eyes shut, trying to ward off the images that rushed through her mind: Dacian thrust into the icy Austrian landscape, alone and exposed, and expected to somehow exert his Gift in fatal violence. Whether or not he managed to kill Bonaparte, he would be captured, tortured, and executed by the French.

But Dacian was not as witless as Drumpellier might suppose. Judith opened her eyes. Would he somehow go along with the plan, reach the safety of Jersey, and then escape?

She chewed on her lip. He would be well guarded and continually monitored for signs of insubordination. Drumpellier could feed him Lethe at any point. Dacian might well lose the ground he had gained.

An even worse thought occurred to her: that Dacian might *want* to serve the Crown in this manner. God knew that Bonaparte threatened English sovereignty, and the very safety of its people. Dacian might decide that the risk was worth it, even though an assassination would not appeal to his sense of honour and a fair fight between nations. Especially if his mind was compromised and he didn't truly understand what was being proposed.

She must rescue him before it came to that, before he could make that awful choice. She must remove him from Pendennis before Drumpellier could force the issue. And she must think more on her mad plan, the first inklings which had occurred to her this morning.

Judith looked at Miss Onslow, who sat pale and downcast. "Do you know when Captain Drumpellier intends to enact this plot?"

"He must wait for confirmation from Jersey, but I think he intends to move the duke in two days' time."

"So soon!" Prickling panic ran along Judith's arms. "I need time to think! Please go tell Robert what you have told me—he will need to know."

Miss Onslow nodded. At Judith's impatient look, she stood hastily and withdrew. The door clicked shut behind her, and Judith sank onto the bed. Her mind was working feverishly.

She had an idea: a preposterous one, but the circumstances might require it. It had first occurred to her earlier that morning, when hearing of Miss Onslow's arrangement with the ships out of Jersey. Miss Onslow met secretly with British officers who had Travelled from a ship far out in the English Channel. Officers who somehow managed the jump all the way from mid-sea to Castle Lanyon.

Judith also knew of a ship that was currently, *possibly*, also traversing the English Channel. A ship that was returning from Sark, another island near Jersey. And on that ship was another Travellor: her very own son, Peregrine.

If she could somehow reach Perry and gain his assistance, they might have a chance to rescue Dacian.

She strode to the window. It was past midday, and the sun was infuriatingly high in the sky, the water sparkling to the west. It would be many long hours before Marigold could wake and attempt to find the *Crescent*, Lord Beresford's ship, upon which Elinor and Peregrine sailed.

In the meanwhile, Judith could set other things in motion. Her stomach growled. She could eat, and gather her strength, and scheme with Robert. Dacian might be within her grasp, after all. At all costs, she must save him from Drumpellier's mad plot. She eyed the big silver bell, wondering if this was the occasion to use it: a moment of emergency. Placing her hand on the thick rope, she gave an experimental tug. The bell barely moved. Losing her nerve, she rang the little servant bell set in the wall and waited impatiently for Trebellow to respond.

When the butler finally ducked through the door, she was pleased to see that he had anticipated her needs. He bore a tray of luncheon, piled high with cold meats, thick bread, cheese, and even a slice of a jam tart. The crowning glory was a teapot, this time ensconced in a woollen cosy of warm yellow, a dainty teacup at its side.

Judith sat down by the windows and poured the tea immediately. Trebellow began edging out of the room.

"Wait a moment," she said.

Trebellow stopped, looking uneasy. Judith took a long sip and sighed. She looked at her butler, remembering the circumstances in which she had last seen him. Fortunately, her Bemusement had now completely subsided.

"Is Baron Quarles well settled, Trebellow?"

"Yes, ma'am. I carried his telescopes and luggage to his room and served him further refreshments."

"Tell me, Trebellow, do you know what Gift the baron possesses? For it seems to me that he is quite cognisant of the Musing."

Trebellow shifted. "He has not seen fit to inform me of his Gift, ma'am."

His voice rang true. "Indeed," said Judith. "And have you found out who fired upon poor Ltn Greene?"

Trebellow straightened. "No, ma'am. But I discovered that a pistol is absent from the gunroom."

Judith took another sip and layered some butter onto her bread, thoughtful. "And do you have any idea how someone could have taken the gun?"

"Any one of the castle inhabitants might have entered the gun room, ma'am, for it was unlocked," Trebellow confessed.

"And do you have a suspicion as to whom it might have

been?" Judith took a large bite of chewy bread and stared at her butler. He appeared to be sweating slightly.

"No, ma'am."

She finished her mouthful slowly. "I should tell you now, dear sir, that I am a Truth Discernor."

He went slightly pale. "Really, ma'am?"

"Yes."

He said nothing.

"Which means that I know you just lied to me."

Trebellow opened his mouth, shut it, then said, "If I have my suspicions, ma'am, you must allow me to keep them to myself."

"Why is that?"

"Loyalty, ma'am?"

She took another bite, this time of a morsel of beef. The food was certainly helping. When she finished, she said, "Loyalty to yourself, a friend, or a niece?"

A muscle ticked in his jaw. "A friend, of course."

It was the truth. The whole truth? Was he protecting Miss Isla? Or Mrs Ulrich? Or Miss Isla's beau, Kade?

"You cannot," she said, "want to protect a *friend* who is a killer."

The butler swallowed. "Perhaps this friend only meant to frighten Ltn Greene."

"Two shots?" Judith raised her brows sceptically. "I somehow doubt it."

"Perhaps this friend now realises the error of such an attempt," he persevered.

"I wish I could believe that." She took another sip of tea. "But we must also account for Sgt Finlay's demise. That is not a failed attempt, but a very dead body."

Trebellow again said nothing.

Judith sighed. She wanted to believe that her butler had a

good reason for his silence. Perhaps Sgt Finlay had been a villain and forced himself upon Trebellow's niece. That might very well explain his reluctance to reveal his killer. But then why had someone shot at Ltn Greene? She examined another slice of bread, this time with ham and cheese, letting Trebellow stew a little. Perhaps he was protecting Cador, believing it possible the fisherman was involved. Yet Cador had only moved the body, not dealt the killing blow.

Then she tutted to herself. Drumpellier had asked her to investigate with a false promise. She found it hard to care much now about Sgt Finlay's death, though she hoped that Ltn Greene would manage to keep himself out of harm's way.

"Quite frankly," she said eventually, "I confess that I am not as concerned as I ought to be about the matter right now. We can discuss it later, if needs be." She put down the slice of bread and made a decision. "Call Mrs Ulrich," she told Trebellow. "I have something important to say to both of you."

In which the household pulls together

Three heads are better than one.
— from *Lady Avely's Guide to Guile and Peril*

AFTER TREBELLOW LEFT, Judith hastily drunk the rest of her tea and stood by the captain's desk. There were some useful maps on the wall, showing the stretch of ocean between England and France, and she was examining them when Trebellow returned with her housekeeper.

Judith turned. Mrs Ulrich wore her usual veneer of cool detachment, but Judith sensed some uneasiness in the way her fingers were clasped.

"Well," said Judith, "I must be rather blunt now. Please forgive me for this reprimand."

Both Mrs Ulrich and Trebellow remained deferential. Yet a faint miasma of innocence began wafting over the room.

Judith ignored the enchantment and continued. "I'm afraid that the castle can no longer be used as a smuggler's port. Mrs Ulrich, I am aware that you have been guiding the boats in and keeping goods in the cellar. I am also aware that local senti-ments about smuggling are quite lax, and that perhaps you did not realise the wrong you were doing. Quite apart from breaking the law, it is possible that in helping the smugglers you were also helping French spies take information in and out of England."

Abruptly, the weaving of innocence fell away. Mrs Ulrich's eyes widened but she said nothing. Trebellow slid an anxious glance towards her.

"I will not turn you over," said Judith. "I don't believe you meant any real harm. However, now that the castle is properly inhabited, all such activities much cease."

Mrs Ulrich gave a tiny, short nod of acquiescence. Then she added reluctantly, "Thank you for your reticence, ma'am."

Trebellow gnawed on his lip nervously. Seeing it, Judith realised what still troubled him. He was worried that Mrs Ulrich had done the fatal deed, the poor dear.

"However, despite your untoward behaviour, Mrs Ulrich, I do not suspect you of Sgt Finlay's death," she pronounced. "I have every reason to believe in your innocence on this matter."

Trebellow looked relieved. Mrs Ulrich nodded stiffly. "Of course I did not kill him," she said, and her words rung true.

Judith smiled. She did not tell them of Cador's evidence on the housekeeper's behalf: let them think that she merely trusted both of them. And, in fact, she found that she did.

"Let us leave all of that in the past," she said. "Right now, I require your help in a rather particular manner. It will require the use of your esteemable Gifts."

Trebellow's brows shot up. "You need us to frighten someone off?" he asked, with surprising acuteness.

"Well, yes," admitted Judith, "and I need a place to hide a duke."

Mrs Ulrich blinked.

Trebellow, however, straightened. "The Duke of Sargen needs our help, ma'am?"

"Indeed. At the present moment, he is bound and manacled under false pretences. If I manage to fetch him to the castle, I need a safe place for him to rest."

Trebellow bristled. "Manacled? The wrasslin champion of 1792? That's a crime, that is!"

"Yes," agreed Judith. She added, "They won't let him wrassle anymore, with his wrists bound."

Trebellow's eyes bulged. "Whatever you need us to do, ma'am, I will be happy to assist."

Mrs Ulrich cleared her throat, slightly less enthusiastically. "What do you have in mind, ma'am?"

Judith leaned forward. "I need a hidey-hole, and a distraction. And I think you will be useful for both, Mrs Ulrich."

AFTER SHE HAD SET her retainers to work, Judith sought out Robert.

She found him eventually in the library. She had avoided this room thus far, not wanting to intrude upon Miss Onslow's domain, but now she stepped inside, looking around with interest. The library, after all, would be an important facility if Castle Lanyon became a school for Musors.

It was pleasingly large, and situated at the back of the castle, with windows overlooking the endless blue ocean towards France. Bookshelves covered all the remaining walls to the ceiling (leaving space only for a hearth), with wooden ladders propped to reach the higher tomes. An upper gallery, reached by a winding staircase on the eastern side showed yet another level. Brown, blue, and green bindings glowed in orderly lines, as well as in neat piles on the floor. Sturdy square tables were set in each corner of the room, giving it a sense of solid stability.

At one of these tables, Robert sat with his head bent next to Miss Onslow's. The afternoon sun slanted through the window, casting a glow over them both. They looked up guiltily, rustling a map between them.

Robert stood, pushing the paper aside and leaning on his stick. "Sophia told me the news. She is showing me the route that Drumpellier might send the duke on to reach Austria."

Judith noted his use of Miss Onslow's Christian name with interest. It seemed that the young woman was allowing Robert some familiarity, her cheeks a faint pink as she also surged to her feet.

"Good," said Judith kindly. "I want to have a look at those maps." She eyed Miss Onslow. The girl was a spy: could she be trusted with the knowledge of Judith's plans? Yes, she decided, for she had been the one to warn of Dacian's fate.

Judith sat down at their table and gestured for the scroll. "Miss Onslow, do you know how far out into the Channel we might spot a ship?"

Miss Onslow sat down hurriedly and pushed the map across. "I am not a sailor. However, I do know that we can see further from the Tea Tower or the northern ramparts. Perhaps twenty miles?"

"What are you thinking?" asked Robert, leaving Miss Onslow's side to look over Judith's shoulder.

Distractedly, Judith noticed that he had abandoned the duke's dark coat. However, the waistcoat below, which she recalled as a plain oak colour, was now embroidered with wine-red flourishes, giving it an air of distinction and faint dandyism that Dacian wouldn't ordinarily countenance. She raised a brow. Was that *Illusionary* embroidery? Was Robert trying to impress Miss Onslow again? It would be interesting to hear Wooten's pronouncements upon the matter. Perhaps he might even approve of wine-red flourishes. Judith bit her lip, and smoothed the map out. It would be a gladdening relief to have Wooten safe again after his noble sacrifice.

"This all depends on a rather large contingency," she said, "which is whether my children are on their way back from Sark or not. I have high hopes that they are not too far away, heading towards Devon."

"In a ship?" asked Miss Onslow. "Why are your children sailing from Sark?" She had removed her cap, and her burnished hair glinted in the sunlight.

"Never mind that for now," replied Judith. She didn't want to mention *all* her business to a spy. "The crucial point is that they might be within Travel distance from Castle Lanyon—and my son is a Traveller."

She looked up. They both stared at her, Robert with a measure of consternation. Hurriedly, she continued, gesturing to the ocean outside. "If we can find their ship, we can send a message with Marigold—she is my vampiri companion," she explained to Miss Onslow. "Marigold can fly out there with a sketch of the Blue Drawing Room, just like the one you send to English officers. Then Peregrine, my son, can visualise it and Travel here. He can help us rescue the duke, I'm sure of it."

Miss Onslow's mouth dropped open. "What an audacious plan, marchioness!"

Robert, however, took a step backward. "I doubt that you'll manage to find your son. His ship could be anywhere."

"It will be tracking towards Devon." Judith traced the path on the map with her finger. "We know where to look; it is just whether we can see that far."

"Oh!" exclaimed Miss Onslow in excitement. "The baron's telescope! That will increase our range!"

Judith smiled in approval. "What an excellent suggestion!

Do you think you could ask him for the loan of it to the Tea Tower Room? Tell him that I will appropriate it tonight, as payment for his visit."

Miss Onslow nodded and rushed from the room. Robert watched her go with a frown between his brows.

Judith stood and took the map over to a window. "We might even be able to spot the ship with our bare eyes, if we are lucky."

Robert did not move. "What will your son say when he sees *me*?"

She turned, lowering the scroll. This was something she had not dwelt on, in all the extremis of the circumstances.

"I have no doubt he will be very pleased to make your acquaintance," she said firmly, and told herself that this was true. Peregrine was a sanguine young man, happy to make friends with most. He would soon regard Robert as a friend, especially once he knew they were half-brothers.

"Have you told him about our relation?"

Her throat suddenly clammed up. "Ah, no. In fact, I have not." She floundered at Robert's closed expression. "Please forgive me! When I first discovered your existence, I was hurt and...angry, and I didn't confide in my children. That was before I knew you so well."

There was a taut silence. Robert folded his arms across his chest, suddenly hostile. "Well, I don't think you should tell him now."

Judith's fingers tightened on the map. "Very well, if that is what you wish. You can simply be Mr Steer for the meanwhile."

This didn't seem to satisfy him, and he limped restlessly towards a far window, leaning on his stick. "Perhaps I should leave before he arrives." He cast her a brooding look. "When I came to Castle Lanyon, I never expected to meet *him* too. I think I should leave."

"Don't be ridiculous." Judith was suddenly cross. "We might need you! The duke needs you! You can't run off now."

His lips twisted. "I can't run anywhere with this leg, curse it. I won't be much good to you, anyway."

"Nonsense," she said sharply. "We may well need an Illusion or two. I haven't told you yet what Mrs Ulrich plans to do. Please stay, Robert."

He heaved a sigh. "All right. But allow me to say that your plan is completely mad, and criminal besides."

"I am long past considerations of criminality," she retorted, "when Drumpellier's conduct has proven to be so base."

In which Marigold is a homing pigeon

Marigold

Marigold awoke abruptly just after sundown. Loud knocking came at the wardrobe door. Blearily, she unfolded herself from the vampiri bed in the secret compartment and pulled her linen handkerchief around her shoulders. She could sense the sun had not long gone from the sky, its heat still radiating from the horizon.

"What is it?" she muttered, making her way to the front of the cupboard. The insistent rapping continued. "What's the hurry?" Had Judith discovered Sgt Finlay's murderer? Was there some danger? What events had she missed in the long hours of the day?

Judith peered in through a crack in the door, haloed by dim, green light. "Oh good, you're awake," she said, as if it was at all possible that Marigold was still asleep. "I need your help, my dear. Do you think you can fly over the ocean for about twenty-four miles? I know it is a lot to ask, but all our hopes rest upon you."

Marigold blinked at her. "I thought I was flying to Penrose Hill again. What if the duke should send a letter with Yvette?"

A flash of pain showed on Judith's face. "I wish you could—oh, how I wish for word from him. However, we have a new plan." She put out a hand, and Marigold stepped onto it, to be borne over to the bed.

Judith stripped off her glove as she explained. "We have, with the use of the baron's telescope, spotted a ship which I hope is Lord Beresford's—you remember that he is travelling with my son and daughter back from Sark. I want you to fly there and make contact with Peregrine, my son, and convince him to Travel back to the Blue Drawing Room. We need his Gift to help rescue Dacian."

Marigold stared. "Your son is a Travellor?"

"Yes," said Judith impatiently. "He only recently came into his power, so he is still learning how to manage it. Yet I think he could manage a jump to Pendennis Castle and back, if we gave him time."

"You mean to break the duke out of prison?" Marigold pursed her lips. "I hate to be the voice of reason, but isn't your plan rather...illegal?"

Judith squared her shoulders. "Oh, I have not told you the whole of it. I'll explain while you have your supper."

Marigold obligingly sank her fangs into Judith's wrist, but then almost choked when she heard how his grace was going to be thrown into Austria on an assassination attempt. She could hear the anxiety in Judith's voice and feel it in the rapid beat of her heart. It was clear that Judith feared the worst: if she did not intervene, she would never see Dacian again.

Withdrawing her head from the vein, Marigold said, "I'm certain the duke has more of his wits about him than Drumpellier knows. He might well have his own plan to escape."

"Yes, but what if he should decide to go to Austria, out of

some stupid logic wheedled in his head by Drumpellier?" Judith's voice was strained. "I must at least have a chance to talk to Dacian properly, or—" she swallowed, "—say goodbye."

Marigold wiped her mouth with the back of her hand. "It won't come to that," she said bracingly. "Let us focus on how to fetch him, first, before we conjure more problems. Where is this ship?"

Hastily, Judith put her gloves on again, and found a fresh kerchief—a pretty, pale lavender one—from her valise. Marigold wrapped herself up and deigned to be moved to Judith's pocket, listening to how Miss Onslow had found a telescope to aid their efforts and Robert thought he had found the right ship. Still talking, Judith strode up to the Tea Tower Room, her step hasty.

When they reached it, Marigold peeped out. She saw, to her disgust, that the awful feline was stretched out on one of the windowsills, his eyes closed. His ears twitched above his odd white face as Judith swept in.

Marigold was plucked out of the pocket without ceremony. She darted her gaze around the room, for although she liked to scoff about the Edicts, she was still accustomed to abiding by them when it came to strangers. She saw a young woman sitting with a straight back by the bookshelf, clothed in a neat, apricot gown. She must be Miss Onslow, the Memor who was (Judith had told her) a spy for the Custos. A massive man who could only be the butler stood by the door, his demeanour full of suppressed excitement. Robert had his eye bent to a telescope, which was pointed out an open window. He was intent upon the horizon, where the sky was still a faint, diminishing gold above the dark blue sea. The evening cacophony of gull cries were fading as the birds settled down to sleep.

"Miss Onslow, may I introduce you to Miss Marigold Cultor." Judith placed Marigold on the windowsill under the telescope. Without waiting for Miss Onslow's nod of acknowledgment, she turned anxiously to Robert. "Is it still there?"

"Yes." Robert did not remove his gaze. "Tracking slowly to the east. It should halt soon; surely they can't sail at night."

"Let us pray Lord Beresford lights some lamps, for else it will be difficult for Marigold to stay a course towards him."

Miss Onslow twisted her hands nervously. "But how can you be sure that it is the ship you want?"

"We can't. It is a gamble. But even if it is not, Marigold can rest upon the rigging and then look again." Judith turned, biting her lip. "Is it too risky, Marigold? Will you have the strength to return, should you not find them? I hope it will be a journey in one direction only, and that Perry can carry you back if you are tired. And on the way there, you can rest on the ships closer to land."

"I will be fine," Marigold replied stoutly. "If the wind is the same as last night, it will carry me out. And if I have to fly back, I can hide belowdecks for a day and return tomorrow."

Judith looked pained, but she did not disagree. "Right. Miss Onslow, do you have the sketch of the drawing room?"

The young woman carried over a scroll of paper and showed it to Marigold. It was a neat rendering of a room, filled in with blue and brown watercolour paint in the appropriate places. Marigold recognised it from her investigations the previous evening: the Blue Drawing Room, with its long blue curtains and pale blue walls bordered in white.

"A good likeness," she allowed, and Miss Onslow smiled, though she continued to stare at Marigold in rather a rude manner. Marigold supposed she must not be familiar with vampiri. Or perhaps it was because Marigold was naked under her pale lavender kerchief. But this was no time for prudishness!

Judith explained again what Marigold was supposed to do

once she reached the ship: find Peregrine Avely and convince him to Travel to Lanyon Castle, using the sketch as guidance. Marigold nodded and became a bat, and the sketch was tied to her leg, much like the letter had been the night before. Robert showed her where the ship sat upon the distant horizon, and where another boat sat in a similar trajectory. Finally, Judith carried her to the sill, and Marigold (without her human tongue) dipped her head in farewell.

Then she dropped away from the tower, swooping into the cool, sea air.

It was a relief to fly away from the tense atmosphere of the Tea Tower Room. Below her, the waves swelled and heaved, a mesmerising sight. The sky was turning grey, the golden colour leaching out of it. Pinpricks of stars appeared overhead. Fortunately, just as she had surmised, the wind coming from the north-west filled her wings.

Also fortunately, lanterns soon showed on the distant ship, making her navigation easier. Still, it was a very long flight over a monotonous landscape. After a long hour of persistent effort, she landed on the first stopover ship, a little to the west of where she would like it, but a welcome rest. She hung from the topmost mast for almost half an hour, conserving her resources, allowing her supernatural strength to renew. Then it was into the night again, skimming high on the wind.

It was easy to wander off course or become distracted by the sight of strange creatures moving through wave tops. Were those dolphins? Or seals? Marigold flapped valiantly onwards, trying to remain fixed upon her destination. Another hour passed, the rolled foolscap at her ankle growing heavier and heavier.

The last miles were very tiring, and she felt the first inkling of fear creep into her heart. If she *was* to become exhausted, there was nowhere to land now. Just the endless, rolling water.

She would sink like a rock, and the sketch would become ruined. Or would she float? She had never tried to swim before and suddenly regretted that omission. Her wings would be unwieldy in water, but her human limbs could manage, couldn't they? Or, far more likely, a huge fish would snap her up as a morsel of dinner.

Crossly, she put such thoughts out of her mind and focused on the ship. It was much clearer now, and a beautiful sight. The waning moon was up, and pale light picked out the elegant lines of the masts. The sails were rolled up, and the anchor thrown, thank God. Lanterns glowed at either end and in the cabin on the quarterdeck. Her acute hearing made out snatches of voices, blurred by the wind. It seemed that the occupants kept late hours.

Finally, she drew close enough to make out the name on the side of the hull: the *Crescent*. It was Lord Beresford's ship. Relief flooded through her, her wings faltering now that she was almost there. Squinting, she saw odd black shapes hanging from the rigging. Then she realised, with a flash of surprise, that they were bats.

A *lot* of bats.

Judith had mentioned that her children might be escorting a roost back from Sark. There were indeed many vampiri hanging on the ropes, and as Marigold approached, she saw them swooping through the night air, somersaulting, vaulting, and looping, like children let free.

She panted heavily now, too tired to care much how she made her entrance. She feared she might even fail at the last moment and slip under the waves by the hull. Her wings ached with the strain. Quivering, she collapsed onto the wooden deck in a heap, just shy of the bow on the port side, gasping for breath. The foolscap was crinkled under her, but she couldn't bring herself to mind.

Nobody noticed her at first. Perhaps all the other vampiri assumed that she was one of them, doing foolish tricks and needing rest. Then she heard the light patter of someone landing right next to her. She turned her head.

A vampiri stood a foot away from her: a young boy, in his human form, stark naked and rather skinny. He had curly brown hair, and his expression was filled with curiosity.

"You're not one of us." He tipped his head to his shoulder to stare at her. He spoke in a French accent rather similar to Yvette's. "Who are you?"

Marigold kept heaving deep breaths, pitifully.

"I'm Raddle," he added. "Do you need some help, mademoiselle?"

With a groan, she made the effort to transform. "I'm all right," she croaked with her human voice, then sat up. "I need to find Mr Peregrine Avely. His mother sent me."

Raddle's eyes widened. "His mother? Lord Avely's?" He hesitated. "Oh yes, he's not really a lord, is he? I think he's in the cabin. Do you want me to fetch him?"

"Wait," she said huskily. "Can you do it quietly, without telling everyone else? This is a private matter."

The truth was that she didn't feel like having several gazes upon her while she explained, or any arguments about it. There was some urgency, after all, to return to Judith with her son that very night.

Raddle looked intrigued. "Certainly, mademoiselle." He glanced about. "If you want privacy, maybe I can show you to his room. It's close by, as he sleeps in one of the crew cabins with Jaq. Quicker to fly, though," he added, looking in concern at Marigold's limp form sprawled on the deck.

Moaning, Marigold became a bat again and heaved herself into the air. Raddle did likewise and led her around the booms to a hatch in the deck, ignoring the wheeling forms of bats overhead. He swooped down into the dark vent, and she followed.

The drop opened out into a narrow room. Two bed slats bracketed it, covered with blankets. In one of them lay an extremely handsome young man, with high cheekbones and thick dark hair. He was lolling, one hand flung out, long lashes against his cheek. He was fast asleep.

In the other bed was another young man: blond and awake. Hazel eyes, much like Judith's, blinked at Raddle and Marigold as they hovered mid-air.

It was Peregrine Avely, sitting covered from the waist down with blankets, his chest bare. Marigold landed on the bed with a bump. At least she didn't need to worry about her own nudity if *he* wasn't wearing clothes. She became human.

"Good God." Peregrine lifted a hand to cover his eyes. "Not another one! I thought I'd be safe from them down here! Raddle, what game are you playing, bringing a lady bat into a gentleman's private chamber?"

"Oy!" said Marigold crossly. "You're naked too."

Peregrine looked down at his chest and snatched his blanket higher. "I'm not prancing around on the bed! You French vampiri have no sense of decency!"

"I'm not French," she said indignantly.

Raddle also landed in his human form. "Mademoiselle is not one of the roost. She says she comes with a message from your mother."

Perry sat up straighter, blinking in surprise. "My mother?" he hissed. "Is she all right?"

"She is fine," said Marigold. "But she is...worried."

Perry rolled his eyes and sank back against his pillows. "You can tell her that I'm all right."

"She's not worried about *you*."

"Elinor's fine too."

It was Marigold's turn to roll her eyes. "Judith is concerned about a more distinguished fellow than either of you. The Duke of Sargen is in grave danger—imprisoned. She wants your help to rescue him."

There was a silence, as Perry gaped at her. "I don't believe you."

"It's true!"

"But it doesn't sound like my mother at all," objected Perry. "She doesn't even *know* the Duke of Sargen." He glanced over to the other bed, where his friend continued to sleep deeply and obliviously.

Marigold put her hands on her hips. "I think you will find that she knows the duke quite well," she said dryly. "She's been frolicking around with him for the last two weeks."

"*Frolicking*? My mother doesn't *frolic*," said Perry in outrage.

"I think you will find that she does." Marigold turned to Raddle. "Perhaps if you leave us now, Raddle, I can explain matters properly to Mr Avely?"

Raddle looked mutinous, but he obliged, flapping out of the room in a huff.

Perry stared after him, then narrowly examined Marigold. "Prove to me that you know my mother. I don't believe it for a minute."

Marigold considered. "She's a Truth Discernor, and she loves drinking chocolate. She is overly fond of mobcaps. And she has a red paisley shawl with a pocket sewn into it."

Perry grimaced in acknowledgement. Then he sighed and set about extricating himself from the bed. Marigold was soon treated to the sight of Judith's son naked before her, hunting for a dressing gown. If she was a human that way inclined, she might have found him to be quite an attractive specimen, lean with muscles, his blond hair thick with dried salt, his forearms tanned from the sun.

"Come," he whispered at last, once he was decently clad. He held out a hand. "Let's go to the next room to talk."

With one last fond look at the slumbering, dark beauty in his bed, he eased a door open in the wall. Soon they were in another narrow, close cabin.

He set her down on one slatted bed and sat on the other. "Explain yourself."

Marigold began. She had to deal with Perry's various interruptions and exclamations of disbelief, but when she untied the sketch of the drawing room, he fell silent. He stared at it, as if it somehow lent more credence to her story.

"So this is the drawing room at Lanyon Castle?" he asked eventually.

"The Blue Drawing Room, yes."

"And Mother wants me to catapult into it, now?"

"Yes. She'll be waiting there for you, all night, sitting in that chair." Marigold pointed. "You must land in front of the window here, if you can."

"Of course I can," he said, though she heard a sliver of doubt in his voice.

"Will anyone miss you?" She cocked her head, still hearing the sound of activity resonating from the quarterdeck. "I would have thought everyone should be sleeping now."

"We keep odd hours here, so that the bats have some company. Elinor won't notice; she's too seasick to care where I might be. But I'll be needed tomorrow to help crew the ship. And Jaq might notice that I'm gone tonight."

"The sleeping beauty? He's unconscious."

"Yes." Perry bit his lip and seemed to come to a decision. "He might try to stop me if he knew. Very well. Let's do it quickly then. It must be several hours before dawn still."

"That's the spirit." Marigold paused, then added, "I don't

know why I am saying this, but you might need something more than a dressing gown."

Perry looked down. "Ah yes. I'm about to break into a military fort, after all. Not the right attire for the occasion."

"And do you have a gun or some sort of weapon?" she added hesitantly. Judith hadn't mentioned anything like that, but Marigold could be sensible for the three of them.

Perry began to shake his head. The suddenly he snapped it up instead. "By George, I *do* have something that might be useful. Wait here, while I fetch it."

In which several persons behave oddly

I have found that the hardest thing to endure is not my own suffering, but the suffering of others when I can do nothing to help.
— from *Lady Avely's Guide to Guile and Peril*

JUDITH TRIED to snatch some sleep when Marigold would be making her dangerous crossing, but it was impossible. Her nerves were too stretched, her mind too anxious with all that could go wrong. Eventually, she flung her legs over the side of the bed, put her cloak on, and slipped out of her room.

First, she made her way outside, to the eastern ramparts. Somehow, irrationally, she hoped she might still be able to see the distant mast of the *Crescent*, in the dark without the telescope. But leaning over the thick grey stone, she could see nothing. Just endless ocean, the waves a constant roar.

The sky was hung with stars; the night was clear, at least, the misshapen moon casting silvery beams upon the water. Judith stayed there a long time staring into the darkness, allowing the cool breeze and the rumble of the waves to soothe her.

She must not allow herself to think how Dacian could be snatched away to Austria. Instead, she must imagine what she would do with him once she had him safe in the castle. How she will bundle him into her bed—any bed—and lay her body right up against his. How she will ply him with drinking chocolate and cream, and how they will talk for hours and make up for lost time and become thoroughly entangled, his hair in her hands, his warm lips on hers, his laughing eyes...

Lost in these pleasant fantasies, she was almost frozen in place when she caught sight of movement below. Beneath the ramparts were steeply terraced garden beds, clinging to the cliffside, overgrown and neglected. A woman hurried up one of the zigzagging paths, her shoulders hunched.

Judith narrowed her eyes. It was too short to be Mrs Ulrich. In fact, it looked very much like the neat figure of Miss Onslow.

She was carrying something in her hand, curled up before her, and glancing around nervously. She even gave a penetrating look in the direction of the ramparts, and Judith felt sure she must be discovered. But her own figure must have been indistinguishable against the bulky stone, for Miss Onslow looked down again, continuing her furtive scurry along the tangled path.

What was she doing? Judith wished for the telescope again, for Miss Onslow was too far away to make out what she carried. As she watched, the young woman reached a particularly stony wall, a steep face of the terrace. She put down her burden and proceeded to heave a large rock out of the cliff wall. Placing it on the floor, she put her parcel into the cavity and returned the rock with some difficulty. Then she dusted her hands off, casting another searching glance above her.

Judith stayed utterly still. Miss Onslow turned away again and hurried back down through the gardens. Her steps seemed lighter, her posture relieved.

How intriguing. Was this part of Miss Onslow's intelligence activities? Was she leaving a message for someone? Yet why would she need to do that, if she met regularly with Captain Drumpellier in the Blue Drawing Room?

Judith frowned down at the cliff wall, wondering if she had time to investigate herself. She chewed on her lip, indecisive. She didn't really like the idea of scrambling along the steep path in the dark, but that made it even more curious that Miss Onslow had attempted it.

Robert's voice came behind her. "Can't sleep?"

Judith swung around, startled. "Goodness me. Not at all." She saw he was carrying his stick under his arm, rather than leaning upon it. His leg must be improving. "You neither?"

He shook his head and came to lean against the rampart. He stared out at the heaving ocean. "It's a long way for a little bat."

She felt a flash of guilt. "Do you think I should not have asked it of her?"

Robert shrugged. "We don't have any alternative, as far as I can see."

Judith was glad he had said 'we'; there was a sense of camaraderie between them again, conjured by their shared anxiety for the duke. She ran her eyes over him and saw that he wore the same coat as earlier in the day, but the red embroidery had faded. Teasingly, she gestured at the sleeve. "I see you are not trying to impress *me*, at least."

Robert gave a rueful grimace. "I am conscious that Miss Onslow must be accustomed to much grander company than mine."

"Nonsense. You should simply present yourself as you are,

without any subterfuge. After all, if you wish to court her, it must be as yourself."

Robert said nothing, just looked out to sea. With a start, Judith remembered she had just seen Miss Onslow below and debated if she should inform him of the fact. He wouldn't like the idea that Miss Onslow was devious. Or worse, he might try to investigate the cliff-face himself, with his injured leg.

As she debated, Robert cleared his throat.

"I saw something odd just now," he said.

"Oh?" Had *he* seen Miss Onslow?

"One of the footmen—he was carrying water up to his room."

Judith took a moment to digest this. "Is that odd?" Of course, Robert would know. Up until recently, he had been a footman himself.

"Ordinarily, male servants wash behind the stables. So why would he carry a bucket of hot water up to his quarters?"

Judith frowned in thought. "I hope he is not entertaining Miss Isla in there." Another thought occurred to her. "Could he be sheltering someone in his room, do you think? A smuggler?"

"I did, as a matter of fact, quietly follow, and listen at his door," confessed Robert. "Given that you mentioned your suspicions about the fellow. But I couldn't hear any other voices, just the sound of sloshing water."

"So what was he doing?" Judith was perplexed, and belatedly remembered the murder she was supposed to be investigating. "Laundering bloodstains, perhaps?"

Robert huffed a laugh. "I confess, I had the same thought. Perhaps he was the one to drag the soldier's body through the tunnel, and his clothes became stained as a result."

Such a theory fit with Kade's hostile reaction to Judith's enquiries. It also explained Miss Isla's nervousness, but Judith wondered again at the motive.

"But why? Why would Kade dispatch him, when it seemed clear that Miss Isla was uninterested in the soldier?"

"Perhaps Sgt Finlay threatened him in some other way," mused Robert.

"Mm," agreed Judith. "Could he be the hypothetical French spy, spying on Miss Onslow? Passing on her communications to the wrong people?"

It seemed unlikely. Cornishmen, like Kade and Kynver, didn't like the English. Yet they were still staunchly patriotic to Britain, and they wouldn't cede anything to the French either.

Judith sighed. "I know I should be more concerned about the possibility that Kade is up to no good with his bucket of water, but I'm afraid that all my attention is taken up by our rescue attempt."

Robert hunched a shoulder in agreement. "I'll keep an eye on the footmen, if you like. There's something that strikes me as not quite right about them."

"Kade? Or Kynver?"

"I don't know; they seem to keep changing places," said Robert, "which is suspicious enough in itself. And I saw one of them talking to the baron too, in a way that seemed to go beyond an ordinary functional exchange."

"Hmm," said Judith. "It is not the first time the baron has been seen deep in conversation with the servants. What could he be about?" She pushed away from the wall, suddenly worried about the time. "But I must wait for Perry in the Blue Drawing Room now. Do you want to wait with me?"

"No," Robert said shortly.

She eyed his stiff figure. "Perry will like you, you know." Even as she said it, she realised that wasn't the problem. It was that Robert was determined not to like Perry. "If you wish to stay away, I understand. But don't linger too long in the cold."

Robert nodded, avoiding her eyes. Damnation, she had been

too motherly again. Judith left, quite feeling as if she were abandoning one child for another.

IT WAS ALMOST midnight by the clock in the Blue Drawing Room. Judith took up her place on the settee next to the fire, pleased to see that one of her retainers had kindly lit the hearth. Warmth filled the room, softening the cool tones. Candles had been left aglow by a plate of chudleighs and cream. Her housekeeper had attempted to ease her vigil, a gesture of support that Judith was glad to observe.

She nibbled on the bread, trying not to become anxious as the minutes ticked by. It would be a long flight for Marigold, who also had the arduous task of finding Perry and explaining everything. Judith couldn't reasonably expect them until well after midnight. She settled back in her chair, wishing she had the foresight to bring her embroidery with her: she had already finished knitting the creamy wool stockings for Elinor's wedding, but she wanted to embroider some handkerchiefs with her daughter's new initials. Elinor would need extra kerchiefs, after all, with Miss Zooth as her companion. 'EB' could be done in quite a flowing style, or perhaps in a black-letter font...

After some time, Mrs Ulrich herself glided into the room, careful to stay by the door, out of the way of any materialising young relatives.

"I have done as you asked, ma'am," the housekeeper said. Her customarily morose voice now held a note of excitement. "Is there anything else you require?"

Judith resolutely put aside any thoughts of embroidery. "There *is* something you could do. I saw Miss Onslow creeping along the garden terraces an hour ago, and she hid something in one of the walls. Do you know of any secret cavities in the cliff-face in the gardens?"

Mrs Ulrich nodded slowly. "Yes, ma'am. On the steep south-eastern terraces? Shall I inspect the contents?"

"If you would be so kind."

The housekeeper inclined her head and vanished again. Judith sighed and sat back, letting her mind stew over the puzzle of Sgt Finlay's death as a distraction from her vigil. She felt as if she should be able to put the pieces together by now, if she were not so taken up by Dacian's plight.

On the one hand, she had discovered how Sgt Finlay had returned to the mainland through the underground tunnel, dragged part of the way by Cador. Who had left the soldier there in the passageway? Considering how battered his body had been, he might have been dragged there shortly after his death. Who had the strength to do that, except Trebellow? Perhaps Kynver and Kade together could manage it, though they were individually slight—but they would have to move single file through that narrow tunnel. The baron was not bulky, but he was tall and might manage it.

Then she had another thought: the wheelbarrow she had seen in the upper cellar that first night. Could someone have hauled Sgt Finlay's body into it, and then pushed it along the tunnel? This would work up until the drop-off into the lower passageway. If the killer had tipped the body down the hatch, that would explain the dirtied clothes.

Such a feat could be managed by even a woman, straining. Miss Onslow, then, or Miss Isla. Or the slender baron. Judith was considering these unlikely suspects when her son abruptly appeared in the drawing room.

He materialised by the far window, just as she had asked, and stumbled slightly. As he righted himself, she examined him with a rush of affection and relief. His face was browner than at her last sight of him, and a faint bristle adorned his cheeks, giving him an unkempt look. His sailing clothes consisted of white pantaloons, a linen shirt, and a loosely knotted blue cloth posing as a cravat. He looked round, blinking, then his eyes lit upon her.

"Mother! What's all this now?"

She crossed over and clasped him close, tears starting in her own eyes. "Perry, my dear boy. How are you?" She held him at arm's length. "How is your arm? Is it healed?"

He patiently allowed her embrace. "Oh, God, yes. My ankle is more of a bother lately—I twisted it on those dashed cliffs at Sark, though I've had some Healing to sort it out. We've had all kinds of adventures, I tell you!"

Judith wanted to hear all about it, but first there was a more important question. "Where's Marigold? Is she all right?"

Perry plucked a bat out of his pocket. "Here she is. Right as rain. Bossy little thing, isn't she? Almost as bad as Miss Zooth."

Judith put her hand out for the precious burden and then stroked Marigold's furry bat head. "Thank you so much, dear Marigold. Such a Herculean task." She looked up at Perry. "How is Elinor? Did you find the roost?"

"Yes, all found. Elinor is safe, though she is not suited to the sea, I'm afraid. Always moaning and groaning about the waves." Then he added, "Beresford almost died, but he has recovered now. Luckily, Elinor is such a queasy-guts, otherwise Miss Zooth would have her hands full chaperoning them."

Judith pursed her lips. "It sounds as if you have lots to tell me."

Perry spotted the plate of food and stalked over to help himself to a chudleigh. "Mmm, I've missed these. But tell me *your* news first." Munching, he threw himself into the chair that Judith had occupied. "Your bat told me a garbled account of some duke being in prison, but I want to hear it from you."

Marigold transformed in Judith's hand, irate and naked. "It was not garbled!" she said indignantly. "I explained the matter quite succinctly."

Perry averted his eyes and ladled a spoonful of cream onto his food. "Yes, but you said that Mother wants to conduct a prison break."

Judith winced. "That is, in fact, what I intend to do." She avoided his gaze, busying herself with tucking the lavender kerchief around Marigold.

Perry stared. "But who is this precious duke?" he demanded, around a mouthful. "I mean, I've heard of Sargen, but I thought he was abroad. Isn't he the one who duels all the time? The confirmed rake? Wouldn't think you'd approve of him, Mother."

Judith sat down opposite Perry and began the difficult task of explaining. It took a while, as it required an overview of the whole Garvey affair, and Perry was slightly Bemused from his big jump. Judith did not delve too much into her own history with Dacian, simply stating that she had thought the worst of him and been proven wrong, and now owed it to him to conduct a rescue, given how he had been manipulated into violence.

"If you say so," said Perry doubtfully. "But to go against the carriage of justice doesn't sound like you, Mother."

"I am not obstructing justice! Quite the contrary. They are not giving him a fair trial, or indeed any trial! They intend to send him on a suicide mission to Austria."

"Austria?" Perry tutted. "It will be freezing there. And Frenchmen everywhere. Not safe at all."

Judith, not wanting to dwell upon the possibility, pulled out the topaz ring that she had been keeping in her skirt pocket. The dull blue stone seemed almost black, the gold tarnished. Dacian had worn it the whole time he had been in exile: a gift from his old schoolfellow, from a family of Travellors. Now it would be the first step to his freedom.

"This ring," she said resolutely, "will Travel right into Captain Drumpellier's office in the Pendennis Tower. All you need to do, Perry, is go there and spy the lay of the land, so you can Travel back at will." He would not be able to Travel into it, sight unseen. "Best to do it now, while it is so late, and unlikely that the captain will be at his desk."

Marigold sniffed. "He might have put a guard on it. He's not stupid, old Drumpy."

"Yes, you must be very quiet," replied Judith. "Ltn Greene could be on watch outside the door—I doubt Drumpellier would let him stay inside his private office, as it is full of coded messages. Or someone else could be on guard. We must hope they are drowsy by now, but Perry, you mustn't leave the room —simply look out the window and learn the lay of the fort and barracks. That way you can Travel in again later, to somewhere Drumpellier *doesn't* expect." Judith leaned forward with entreaty. "Don't take any risks. Just gather information. When we make our proper attempt, I will come too, with the ring, and distract the guards."

Perry grimaced. "Mother, really? Let me do it without you."

"No, you couldn't," she said sharply. "It's crawling with soldiers. We shall have to be very clever to even have a *hope* of succeeding."

An odd smile came onto his face. "Ah, but I have a secret weapon." He reached into his trouser pocket and pulled out an object, triumphantly holding it aloft.

In which coats are disguised

Guile is preferable to violence.
— from *Lady Avely's Guide to Guile and Peril*

PERRY HELD UP A GREY STONE: round, smooth, and unremarkable.

"A rock?" said Marigold dubiously. "You're going to throw a rock at Drumpy? He is not Humpty-Dumpty."

"It's not just a rock," explained Perry, with some annoyance. "It's a shatterstone. We found a bag of them on Sark. They're imbued with Impact and explode with great force. This little pebble should be able to blow up a prison wall easily." Carefully, he placed it on the mantelpiece.

Judith drew a breath. "We can break Dacian out of his cell!"

"Whoa, wait a minute!" Marigold put her hands up. "I can't believe I'm the voice of reason here, but are you suggesting we blow up a part of Fort Pendennis? Are you mad? Do you want to lose your mind, and your power too, Judith, like Dacian? Because that is what the Custos will do, if they catch you at it."

Judith lowered her gaze. She could not say that with Dacian wrenched from her, it would be almost preferable to forget. Anyway, that would be a lie. She could not allow her spirit to be broken. She had her children to care for, Robert, the castle—even Marigold, if she would stay.

"No," she admitted. "But how will they know it is me, if I blow up a wall? Drumpellier will not suspect a dignified matron, and even if he does, recall that it is an Impacting spell. We can say that it was Dacian. Perhaps in his confused state, wild and not himself, he allowed his power to explode. That would only be Drumpellier's fault."

Marigold looked unimpressed. "Well, I think it better if we just use Mr Avely to Travel inside the cell, snatch the duke up, and return. Why do we need to throw bombs around?"

"It would be fun." Perry grinned. "But I take your point. Why don't you draw me the duke's cell, Mother, and I can try Travelling there?"

"Because we haven't seen his new quarters," said Judith. "They've moved him again, or so Yvette told Marigold. We need to find Yvette again, and hope that she can tell us where he is now."

Marigold's nose wrinkled. "*If* she's still hanging about."

"Who's Yvette?" demanded Perry. "Another bat?"

"Yes, and she has been invaluable," said Judith. "She carried my letter to the duke, and I have high hopes that she continues to watch over him and Wooten."

"Wooten? Who's that now?"

"Yet another bat," said Marigold, her bare shoulders showing as her handkerchief sagged. "You'll probably like him. He's quite particular about clothing."

"As he should be." Pointedly, Perry looked away. "Right, then, it sounds like we have an army of bats on our side."

Marigold cleared her throat. "Wooten is a man down, actually. He drank the Lethe and fainted. He might have recovered by now, but we cannot count on it. *I'll* come, though."

Perry did not look thrilled at the prospect, and he was starting to argue about the potential use of the shatterstone again when there was a tap at the drawing room door.

"Yes?" called Judith. Could that be Mrs Ulrich, back already from her investigation of the cliff-face?

But it was Miss Onslow herself who came through the door, her expression alight with curiosity. And she dragged in Robert at her side, firmly tucked into her arm.

His expression was extremely reluctant.

"Oh!" cried Miss Onslow. "You succeeded in your quest, Miss Cultor! How wonderful." She hesitated at their rather blank reception. "We were in the library, but the baron wandered in from his stargazing. He was asking all sorts of questions, so we thought it best to leave him. Then we heard voices in the drawing room! We could not resist coming to see if Marigold had succeeded."

Marigold preened a little, but Judith frowned. The baron was rather underfoot lately. She was tempted to lock him in his room, to keep him out the way.

Miss Onslow ducked a curtsy, glowing at Perry. "You must be Mr Peregrine Avely! I am so glad to meet you!"

Perry nodded, rather taken aback.

Judith, through force of habit—and being forced by Miss Onslow's misconduct—uttered an introduction. "This is Miss Sophia Onslow, a Memor who is cataloguing the castle's library. Miss Onslow, my son."

Perry managed a perfunctory bow, then his eyes moved on to Robert. Robert stood like a statue, pinned next to Miss Onslow, his face blank.

"And who's this?" asked Perry.

Judith floundered wordlessly. "Ah..."

Miss Onslow laughed. "Surely you must remember your own cousin? It's Robert, of course."

Perry stared. "My cousin? I can't remember any cousin by name of Robert."

"Ahem," said Judith desperately. "On your father's side. Um, Uncle Gerald's son."

Gerald had been her husband Nicholas's youngest brother, and a bit of a dissolute rake. He had (handily) died the year before from heart failure. Judith hoped that a proper respect for mourning would dispel further questions, but in fact landing on Gerald had another effect.

Perry widened his eyes in sudden understanding. "Oh! I see! One of Gerald's by-blows, are you?" He thrust out a hand to shake Robert's. "A nice surprise, to have a new cousin emerge from the woodwork!"

Robert took it awkwardly. "Yes," he said stiffly. "Indeed."

Miss Onslow dropped her hand from Robert's arm and took a step back, her eyes darting from one boy to the other. Robert's jaw tightened, but he did not look at her. He was appraising Perry with a narrowed gaze.

Perry chuckled. "Uncle Gerry was always a bit of a rake and troublemaker. Are you like him, then?"

"Er, no." Robert's eyes slid to Judith, and he seemed to take some satisfaction in her expression. "I don't believe so."

"More's the pity," said Perry. "*My* father was a noble sort, which is a bore, you know, trying to live up to it all the time."

Judith's innards twisted in mortification. Perry did not know that his 'noble' father had sired the illegitimate son before him. Hastily, she waved her hands, desperate to change the subject.

"Well!" she said brightly. "Perry is here, yet now he must depart again! Are you ready to try the ring, Perry?"

"Aye, aye, Captain," said Perry. "Hand it over. Let's trot it out."

Judith shook her head but dropped the ring into his palm. "Just be careful, won't you? Reconnoitre only. No foolish risks."

"Seems to me, Mother, that you have only one leg to stand on, and it is wobbling," said Perry. Then he slipped the ring on his finger, twisted it, and vanished.

There was sudden silence in the drawing room.

Robert stared at the empty space. "He didn't even say *Veho*."

"He doesn't need to; it's his own Gift." Judith suddenly felt a bit overwrought, seeing Perry disappear into thin air. Had she really just sent her son into an enemy military fort? What had she been *thinking*? Perry would do something foolish, and be shot, and then she would never see him again, and...

Robert stepped up to her and grasped one of her shoulders with a firm shake. "He'll be back. Give him at least five minutes before you start panicking."

She took a deep breath and turned her eyes to the clock next to the shatterstone. "Yes, you're right. Five minutes, *then* I panic."

It was ten minutes before Perry returned. By then Judith was pacing, wringing her hands. She was not even able to curse out loud, for Miss Onslow sat primly on one of the settees, her own hands folded neatly. Judith wished the stupid girl would just go away. She didn't need strangers lurking around in this time of family crisis—except that Robert was sitting next to Miss Onslow and he seemed happy to have her there.

They were quietly talking. At least Miss Onslow wasn't giving Robert the cut direct, now that she knew he was illegitimate. The atmosphere of high tension must be serving to undermine the usual rules of society. Marigold, who never had much regard for society, was reclining on the mantlepiece with an unseemly amount of leg showing beneath her lavender silk kerchief. Really, Judith must sew her a new gown as soon as possible. At least, she was pleased to note, the mantlepiece had been dusted now that Mrs Ulrich was finally playing her part. Though what use was a clean mantlepiece if one's son disappeared forever?

When Perry reappeared, Judith almost fell upon him.

"Thank God," she said fervently, clasping his hands. "I've changed my mind: Perry, you can't go back in there *ever* again."

Perry blinked around at them. "Nonsense, Mother, I'm going back in ten minutes. One of your bats caught me."

Judith fell back a step. "Who? Which one?"

"Miss Belfleur, apparently. Black-haired little Frenchy."

"Of course." Judith sagged in relief. "Sensible girl, to suspect I might show up in that tower again. I wonder if Dacian told her to keep a look out for me."

"Hmm," said Marigold, twitching her handkerchief.

"Yes, well," said Perry, "The delightful Miss Belfleur leapt into my hair and hissed at me to duck behind the table, which I did. Then she almost ripped my ear off, until I explained why I was there, and that you sent me, Mother. Then she announced that she would fetch another bat—Wooten, I believe?—for me to take back. She flapped off again, leaving me crouched behind the desk."

Judith looked at his empty hands. "But you haven't got Wooten."

"No. I crept out from the desk and tiptoed over to the windows, like you told me. Got a good eyeful of the courtyards below, and the barracks. I was committing it to memory, when I heard footsteps on the stairs."

Miss Onslow gasped.

Perry glanced at her. "So, I thought it best to disappear for a bit, and here I am. But I need to go back to fetch this Wooten fellow. From what Miss Belfleur told me, he's in a bit of a bad way."

Judith gnawed on her lip. Of course they must help Wooten

—poor, brave Wooten—but she didn't have to like it. "You heard footsteps! There might be someone in the tower now!"

"Yes," said Perry patiently, "and they'll look around, see nothing, and go away again. I'll give it ten minutes. Probably best if I wait a bit, anyway, otherwise I'll get too Bemused."

Judith almost rolled her eyes. She was the one who had taught Perry that, back in London, soon after he discovered his Gift. "Yes, my dear," she said. "But it's too dangerous. We need some other contingency. Otherwise, I'll have heart failure, if you leave me behind again. How about *I* go, with the ring, and fetch Wooten myself."

"Mother!" said Perry. "You can't drag me out here and then make me sit in an armchair. Besides, how will you get back? That ring Travels one way only, from what you told me."

Judith wanted to gnash her teeth. "I can't let you die at the end of a gun!"

There was a taut silence. Miss Onslow looked from one to the other, eyes wide.

Robert spoke up, his voice gruff. "I could disguise Peregrine as a soldier. It might confound them enough to give him a moment to escape."

Judith turned, hope sparking in her heart. "That might work. They won't shoot someone in their own uniform."

Perry raised his brows at Robert. "Oh, and you have a spare uniform, do you?"

"No," said Robert, expressionless. "I'm an Illusor."

Perry's eyes lit up. "Oh, brilliant. Can you do me a red coat then?"

Robert shrugged. "I can try." He got up and stood in the middle of the room. After a moment of staring at Perry, he closed his eyes. When he opened them next, Perry's disreputable coat vanished under a veneer of jolly red, with round brass buttons and white cross-belts. His loose pantaloons neatened, becoming tighter and (it must be said) cleaner, and his boots lengthened and blackened.

Miss Onslow gasped again. Perry looked down at himself, then strode to the window, pulling the curtain open so he could examine his reflection in the dark glass.

"Very smart." He admired his buttons, then glanced over at Robert. "Does that mean you'll have to come with me?"

"Not if I do it in a charm," said Robert. "But that will take a while to set. I gather you have to go back soon for Wooten?"

"Miss Belfleur said ten minutes."

Robert grimaced. "Not enough time."

"I'll go then," said Judith. "I don't need a uniform."

"Mother, you can't return," said Perry patiently, "Robert can come with me." He turned to Robert again. "You can make a coat for yourself, can't you? Two soldiers are better than one. Then they *really* won't know what to do with us."

Judith's mouth fell open in horror. "Certainly not! Robert, I don't want *both* of you going in there, for God's sake!"

Robert gave her an inscrutable look. "If Peregrine takes too long, Miss Belfleur and Wooten might be seen. Especially if Wooten is behaving erratically. Then the whole game might be up."

"Oh yes," agreed Perry. "They might torture Miss Belfleur for information. Can't have that."

Marigold gave an involuntary squeak of protest.

Judith squeezed her eyes shut. "Curse it. Perry, why did I ever allow you to become involved?"

"I don't know," he said cheerfully. "Because you had no other choice, I imagine. Now, Robert, let's dress ourselves up. Officers Avely and Avely!"

Miss Onslow's eyes moved from one boy to the other, but she wisely did not say anything about Robert's last name being Steer. A stain came onto Robert's cheeks, but he also kept quiet. Instead, he focused on conjuring the uniforms, casting both of them into a semblance of military order.

Perry straightened his shoulders as he looked down at himself. "I always wanted to be a navy man, myself. But this is good for a lark. Wait 'til I tell Elinor. She's going to be so vexed to be missing out on the fun!" He paused moodily. "Except I've a good mind not to tell her anything."

Judith examined them both critically. "Well done, Robert. You should both pass muster in a crisis." She paused. "But not a literal muster! Don't attempt to pass yourselves off as part of the garrison and go marching round the fort."

Perry puffed out his chest. "I don't know. Maybe we could just stride down to the prison cell and demand the duke's release."

Marigold rolled her eyes. "Anyone looking at you for more than ten seconds will fall over in a fit. Especially Wooten. Your hair is atrocious, and neither of you have proper military bearing."

Perry pulled his chin in sharply. "Fine." He glowered at Marigold. "Luckily, all I need is two seconds to fetch us out of there."

Marigold sniffed. "Take me with you, so I can find Wooten."

Perry's posture drooped again. "Dash it, do I have to? I'm always ferrying bats around."

"You might need me." Marigold folded her arms.

"Fine," said Perry ungraciously. "Hop aboard. At least I'm not herding sheep this time."

Judith raised her brows at this cryptic remark, but Marigold tossed her lavender kerchief aside and became a bat, swooping over to Perry. He winced as she landed on his shoulder, then he glanced at the clock.

"I think it's time," he announced. "Wooten awaits. Hold on to my ear, Miss Cultor."

Judith sighed. "Be careful, please. All of you. And be quick."

"Yes, Mother." Perry jerked his head at Robert. "Come here, cousin. We need to have a bit of a cuddle while I Travel us in."

Slowly, Robert walked over, his face a picture of reluctance. A slightly hysterical laugh burbled up inside Judith's chest, but she swallowed it. Poor Robert, being forced to embrace his half-brother, when he was so determined to hold him at a distance.

Sanguine and oblivious, Perry held out his arms. Robert shuffled into them and stood stiffly while Perry clasped him round the middle, grinning at his mother.

"See you soon," he said, and they vanished.

There was a stark, empty silence in the drawing room.

"Damnation," said Judith, with great feeling. She found that she was now careless of any gently bred ears. "Hellfire and devil's testicles!"

Miss Onslow's eyes almost popped out of her head. She cleared her throat. "I'm...sure they will be fine."

"You don't know my son," snapped Judith. "Even in your five minutes' acquaintance with him, you must see that he is reckless and stupid. I say that as a loving mother." She began to pace again, swishing her skirts furiously. "And he's taken Robert *and* Marigold with him."

"They will provide a sensible influence," Miss Onslow suggested cautiously, though she did not deny the maternal charges. "They will simply pop in and out. I think it is all rather exciting! They'll be back soon, I'm certain of it."

In which a letter is received

Words on a page can be full of guile. And they are impervious to Truth Discernment.

— from *Lady Avely's Guide to Guile and Peril*

THEY WERE INDEED BACK SOON. Only five minutes later— thank God—Perry and Robert appeared once more by the window, stumbling apart. The red coats vanished, showing their rumpled clothes beneath. Robert's face was startled, Perry's triumphant.

Perry thrust out his hand, uncurling his fingers. In his palm was the crumpled form of a brown bat. Wooten blinked blearily up at them.

Judith sank down on the settee closest to the fire and spread her skirts out, gesturing for Perry to lay Wooten down upon them. As he did so, she tenderly laid Marigold's lavender silk over the top of the furry body.

"Wooten Willoughby!" said Judith. "My dear bat, are you all right?"

Wooten's eyes bulged at her.

"Do you remember me?" she added anxiously. "It's Judith. Lady Judith Avely."

Under the handkerchief, Wooten transformed, his bat head becoming human and protruding from the top. Black locks tangled around his long face, and his dark eyes were shadowed. His usually swarthy skin had a sickly undertone to it.

"Lady Avely," he said dreamily. "I think I do, indeed, recall..."

Then he did something truly shocking. He cast the kerchief aside, stood up, and bowed to her, stark naked.

Judith drew a horrified breath. This was not the Wooten she knew. Hastily, she grabbed the silk again and draped it over his shoulders. "There, there. I apologise that we do not have your cape handy."

"What cape?" said Wooten. "I do not need a cape."

"Sunbeams!" uttered Marigold.

Wooten turned to look down his nose at Marigold. This he managed even though she was on the mantlepiece above him, so at least some of his character remained. "And who are you? I do not believe I have the pleasure of your acquaintance."

"Um. I'm Miss Marigold Cultor." She dropped a curtsy, also naked, and Judith momentarily closed her eyes in mortification.

"Good God." Perry was aghast. "Mother, who *are* these vampiri? They're worse than the French."

"The French?" snapped Marigold, offended. "Are you comparing me to Yvette? I might abhor clothes, but at least I don't tell bald-faced *lies*."

Perry's brow furrowed. "I would have thought my mother would have instilled better manners in you both by now."

Wooten tossed the kerchief off and strolled off Judith's leg. "I hardly think she can instill manners in me if I don't know her."

"You *do* know me," Judith put a hand to her head. "I am a friend of the duke, who is your blood companion. And, may I say, you are ordinarily better dressed than this."

"Ah, this duke!" said Wooten, ignoring her reproof. "Miss Belfleur also chattered endlessly about him. Apparently, I saved his life, or his mind? Hard to believe when I don't even *know* the fellow." Suddenly he sat down at the end of the settee. "Oh, my head hurts." He clutched at it and groaned. Perry, nearby, hastily thrust his own handkerchief to cover the vampiri's lap, a garish red one that looked as if it had been borrowed from a sailor. Wooten did not even blink at it.

Marigold leaned forward, concerned. "When was the last time you fed?"

"I'm not sure." Wooten moaned again. "Miss Belfleur suggested I must feed from the duke, which I scarcely thought proper, and then she proffered a cow instead, which was hardly much better."

Marigold snorted a laugh. "I hope you told the duke he was no better than a cow." Then her expression sobered, and she glanced at Judith. "Wooten needs Musor blood. Then he might return to his usual insufferable self."

Judith nodded and began rolling up her sleeves. "Do you mind if I...?" Then she stopped herself and turned to Perry. "Perry, be a good boy now, and feed Wooten."

"Uh huh." Perry crossed his arms. "I've been feeding half the roost, back on the *Crescent*. I've got nothing left to give." At her shocked expression, he added, "Fine, not half. A few. And I'll need to do so again when I return."

Judith's gaze shifted. "Robert? How about you?"

Robert had been standing behind Perry, looking rather betwattled himself. At this, he shook himself and asked, "Is it good etiquette? To feed a duke's companion? Won't I bond with him?"

"Perhaps a little," allowed Judith, "but we are long past considerations of etiquette now."

"Excuse me," said Wooten grumpily. "Are you going to ask for *my* opinion on the matter? I think I'd rather a cow."

Marigold snorted again, and Robert tried to look offended, but instead just looked relieved.

Perry let out a crack of laughter. "Well, there's plenty of cows on Lanyon Isle, aren't there, Mother?"

"Yes, but Wooten needs Musor blood, not bovine blood!"

Miss Onslow had been watching proceedings, agog. Now she spoke up, her voice firm. "May I offer myself? If that is not too forward of me?"

Judith turned to her in relief. "What a splendid idea. Wooten, surely you can bring yourself to bond with this lovely young lady, temporarily...?"

Wooten gave Miss Onslow a considering look. Everyone waited with bated breath for his judgment. Marigold held up a hand to forestall it. "For the love of God, don't say that you'd prefer a cow, Wooten."

Wooten sniffed, but appeared to concede the point, for he nodded. "Very well. She will do."

"Miss Onslow will more than suffice with her gracious offer," Judith corrected him hastily. "Thank you, Miss Onslow, that is very kind. Would you rather take him to a more private spot? Marigold can accompany you and give you some guidance on how the transaction is managed."

"Yes, of course." Miss Onslow stood up. "I'll take him up to my room and see if I can make him a little nest."

"An excellent idea."

With no small measure of gratitude, Judith watched as Miss Onslow gathered up Wooten in the handkerchief and bore him from the room, with Marigold flapping reluctantly after them.

"Phew." Perry leaned on the mantlepiece. "Thought you

were going to foist him onto me." Then he pushed himself off again and felt inside his coat. "Oh! I almost forgot! Miss Belfleur gave me a letter for you, Mother. It's from the duke."

"*What?!*" Judith leapt to her feet. "Give it to me at once, you dreadful boy!"

Perry held out a neatly rolled foolscap. She snatched it from him and hastily spread it out. It was crossed with a bold scrawl and signed with Dacian's name at the end.

Heart in her mouth, she read it. The opening address made her shoulders droop with relief, but by the time she reached the end, she was blinking back tears and gritting her teeth.

DEAR JUDITH,

Of course I remember you. I'm unlikely to forget someone seared on my memory at the age of twenty-two, when you condescended to dance with me at the Plunnow ball. I remember how you arched your brows at the effrontery of a duke who dared to approach you. You will say that I condescended to dance with you, but you know very well it was the other way around.

You must know by now that you have never been long out of my heart since then. Even abroad, even after what I thought had happened, I could not help but wish for your company again, and to lay my heart at your feet.

But, Judith, that does __not__ mean I want you to rescue me now. Please, I beg of you, do not entertain any foolish plans to somehow breach the walls of this fort. I do not want you locked up in here with me. Or I would like that very much—to have you alone with me, here—but we would not be alone, and the stone benches are not very comfortable. I'd much rather wait until we have a castle at our disposal, then I may treat you properly as the circumstances require.

In the meantime, I will find a way out of here myself, so please do not risk your own neck, or any further allegations of treason. I will come to Lanyon Castle when I can, after I have done what I must, for this grimly determined captain. And I have an unexpected ally, who might yet lend me further help.

It is true, perhaps, that I owe the Crown a recompense for the wrong I have committed. I would think that you'd be the first to say that my station does not excuse me; indeed it condemns me further. And the captain has offered me a bargain: he will not tamper with my mind anymore if I will do this one thing for him, as much as I abhor it.

It will be like killing an eagle with a rock, but the captain seems convinced that it is necessary, and he is better informed than I.

You shall just have to wait, my dear. I know we have waited long enough—God, don't I know it—but what is one more month after all these years?

Judith, if—when—I return, please marry me. Please forgive all my stupid mistakes and accept my hand, for I am already entirely yours.

I must only add that I am worried for Wooten. He is not himself. If you do visit Pendennis again, please convince him to go home with you. Yvette has custody of him to keep him safe, and they sleep in the barracks, but he remains rather confused.

Judith, my love, ~~I may not see you again~~ I will see you again, I swear it. I will return as soon as I possibly can. Please guard your own safety in the meanwhile, while I am unable to do it for you.

Yours, always,

Dacian.

Her heart seemed to be suspended within her. Marry him? She had not even considered the possibility, despite all her longing for him. How could he ask it of her now? And there was the rest of the missive, which quite undermined his declaration.

"Guard *my* safety?" she stuttered. "What about *his* safety? Does he *really* think I'm going to knit in a corner while he sails off to his death? *I don't think so.*"

There was a silence. She looked up, belatedly remembering that she had an audience.

Robert shifted uncomfortably. Perry stared at her, open-mouthed.

"Good God, Mother, what's come over you? How well do you know this duke, exactly?"

Robert coughed.

Judith glared. "I have known him for years and years," she said sharply. "He was a good friend of your father's."

"Oh, was he?" Perry looked doubtful. "Isn't the Duke of Sargen a dreadful rake? Always seducing ladies and fighting duels? He doesn't seem like Father's sort of man."

Robert raised a brow.

"Your father knew him as a boy," replied Judith stiffly.

"But I've never even heard you speak of his grace before."

Judith lowered her gaze to the blue rug. She couldn't really tell Perry that Dacian had broken her heart, twice. She couldn't announce that she might have married Dacian instead of Perry's own father, and that the duke had just made her an offer of marriage. She couldn't say that if Dacian died in Austria, she would sink into a black despair and possibly never emerge from it ever again.

"He needs our help." She looked up. "Even if he doesn't want it." She shook the letter angrily. "The foolish man thinks he should do as Drumpellier directs."

Robert frowned. "He wants to go to Austria to assassinate Bonaparte?"

She nodded, unable to voice it.

Robert drew a breath, opened his mouth to speak, then thought the better of it and closed his lips.

Perry glanced at him, and said, "But Mother, if he wants to serve England in the war, you can't *stop* him."

Judith brought a hand to cover her face. Tears leaked from her eyes as the truth of Perry's words sunk in. *She couldn't stop him.* Dacian wouldn't want her to, and he might not forgive her if she did. Her plan was moot. She couldn't do anything at all.

JUDITH RUSHED from the drawing room, still clutching the letter. Tears blurred her vision, and she could not bear to stay and send Perry on his return journey just yet. He would have to wait and make polite talk with Robert for a minute while she collected herself. She stumbled away, instinctively making her way to the Tea Tower Room. Sobbing as she walked, she allowed all the pent-up emotions of the last few days to erupt and pour down her cheeks.

The steep climb up the Tea Tower forced her to stop crying, and by the time she reached the top step, she had regained some of her composure. Still heartsore, she pushed the door open with relief, stepping into the soft welcome of the room.

Despite its gentle soothing, the Tea Tower Room was in darkness. Curtains, open from their activities earlier, allowed starlight in, casting a pale glow. The telescope was still propped up near the easternmost window, maps strewn around it.

She set about lighting the candles and reinvigorating the coals in the fireplace. When a tidy flame burned on a new pile of sticks, she sank onto the nearest couch, drained and empty. Yet the cheerful comfort of the room worked its magic upon her, gradually easing the frown from her brow. And Ghastagon came to sit on her lap, purring loudly, like a huge pillow filled with vibrating rocks.

She read the letter again, and then again. There might be a chance that Dacian would survive, she told herself. He was used to living in exile, using his wits to survive. Though clearly, he had lost his mind now! Yet Drumpellier would want to keep the duke alive and sane, after all, as a valuable weapon. Between the two of them, and all the resources of the Custos, Dacian might just manage to jump into Austria, do the deed, and escape.

She dared not dwell on any other possibility. She could not.

She was not sure how long she sat, staring at the middle of the circular room, absentmindedly patting Ghastagon while her mind became curiously blank. The fire warmed her skin, and the Tea Tower Room soothed her spirits, but her heart ached inside her. Even as it ached, it exulted, for Dacian's letter laid out his affection for her in no uncertain terms.

...lay my heart at your feet...please marry me.

He was hers. If only she could give herself to him in return. Even just see him one more time, before he left. Could she ask Perry to do it, to take her back to the fort one more time?

Perry. She sat up and shook herself out of her stupor. Had Perry gone back to the *Crescent* already? She must say goodbye and give him a message for Elinor, if he could not be convinced to stay and Travel her into the fort.

Before she could stand, however, she heard footsteps on the stairs, in the quiet of the night. She tensed, then looked up to see Mrs Ulrich's head appear around the edge of the door. Slowly, the rest of the housekeeper's body followed, and she darted a look around the room in a pantomime of caution.

Judith stared. The housekeeper was holding something in her hands, wrapped in cloth. What task had she given Mrs Ulrich? And why was her expression so grim?

The housekeeper presented the bundle, as if holding a funeral shroud. "Ma'am, I found this hidden in eastern cliff-face."

"Oh?" Judith sat up, intrigued. Miss Onslow's secretive stash!

With great ceremony, Mrs Ulrich swept the cloth aside.

Underneath was a gun.

In which a friend proves false

One's perception does not always match reality, even if one is a Truth Discernor.

— from *Lady Avely's Guide to Guile and Peril*

JUDITH GAPED. She could be forgiven this unladylike response because she could barely believe the evidence of her eyes and ears.

"Miss Onslow hid the gun?" she uttered. "*Miss Onslow* shot at Ltn Greene?"

"It appears so." Mrs Ulrich's lips pursed. "Shall I throw her out of the castle, ma'am, or lock her up?"

"What? No!" Judith rubbed her forehead. She couldn't understand it: Miss Onslow had helped her and befriended Robert and Wooten. "Could she have hidden it for someone else? Or are we to understand that she was taking potshots at the lieutenant?" Judith looked up. "Maybe she was hiding it for one of the twins. Is she friendly with either of them?"

At this juncture, Ghastagon, unhappy with no longer being

the recipient of devoted attention, leapt off her lap. He stalked over to the window to claw at the telescope, clearly unimpressed that it occupied one of his daises.

Judith watched him, frowning. "Or Baron Quarles? Is Miss Onslow shielding the baron? I must say, I am confounded. I thought Miss Onslow was our *friend*: she has been helping us make plans to rescue the duke."

Mrs Ulrich carefully wrapped up the gun again. Her expression was impassive. "You are a Truth Discernor, ma'am. Why don't you ask her about it?"

This was an eminently reasonable suggestion. "I will," said Judith with determination, then she recalled that Miss Onslow was currently tasked with feeding and caring for Wooten. Her shoulders caved again. "We shouldn't disturb her at the moment. She is looking after an injured vampiri and setting up a new bed for him. They might both be fast asleep by now."

"What about the footmen, then?" suggested Mrs Ulrich. "I can pull them from their beds, and you can question them instead."

Judith sighed. "It would be unfair to wake them."

"With all due respect, ma'am," said her housekeeper austerely, "there was an attempted murder today, and we've just discovered the weapon. I think you would be justified in asking some questions, no matter the hour of the day."

Judith stared at the shrouded gun and sighed. "Very well. Bring them here. But return that to the gunroom first and lock it away. And stay close by. I don't fancy a violent confrontation."

Mrs Ulrich obliged, regally bearing the weapon away as if she held a platter of tea cakes.

When she returned twenty minutes later, she had only one footman thrust in front of her. It was Kade, Judith fancied, by the ferocious scowl on his face. Mrs Ulrich's escort, it was clear, was forcible, with a firm hand on the boy's shoulder. Kade's long black hair was loose around his shoulders, and he was dressed in only a long nightshirt, which was white.

In fact, Judith realised with dawning surprise, Kade was not a boy at all. Kade was quite clearly female, her curves apparent under the pale shirt. She made an effort to fold her arms across her chest, but it did nothing to disguise what must ordinarily be bound underneath her footman's livery.

Mrs Ulrich's face was equally forbidding. "Ma'am," she said grimly. "It appears that Kade is not who we thought he was. I found *her* like this. The other one was dead asleep, so I left him."

The young woman in her grasp blinked back an angry tear, and Judith became aware that the housekeeper was also holding her in a Diplomacor spell, evocative of awful guilt. It clawed at her own throat, a sense of utter remorse, but she could see Kade was fighting it with all her might, her jaw tight.

"Good Lord, Mrs Ulrich! Release her at once, in all ways!"

The housekeeper's hand came off the girl's shoulder, and with it, the guilt spell. Kade stumbled forward and righted herself. She stared defiantly at Judith, dashing the tear from her eye, shrugging the Diplomacy off angrily.

"Explain yourself, Kade," said Judith calmly. "Or should I call you Kadee?"

"Kadee is my real name," the girl replied sullenly. "But there's nothing to explain. Why shouldn't I be a footman? I might be a girl, but I'm just as capable as my brother."

"I'm sure you are, but it is scarcely proper. Do your parents know about this charade?"

"My mother and father are dead. I have no place to live, so I applied for this position with Kynver. I am just as good as him. Please don't send me away, ma'am." Her expression was now pleading, under the mess of dark hair. "It is not easy to be a woman without protection or family."

Judith bit her lip, sympathetic despite her annoyance at being deceived. "It is a risky secret. You might come into harm's way if anyone discovered it." She paused thoughtfully. "Did Sgt Finlay, perhaps, find it out?"

"No," said Kadee sulkily. "He bragged about his acumen, but he didn't know my secret. I swear it."

"How can you be so sure?"

"He treated me the same as he ever did, with thoughtless condescension." Kadee scowled. "If he knew I was a woman, he would have tried something. He was that sort."

"That is exactly my point!"

"And my point is that he *didn't* discover it."

Judith trusted the truth in her voice. So Kadee had not killed Sgt Finlay to keep her secret. But perhaps someone else had. "And Miss Isla?" she asked, after a moment. "Does she know that you are a woman?"

Kadee dropped her gaze. "She does."

That explained the dairymaid's nervousness, and the odd lie in her voice when she spoke of Kade. "And," Judith enquired delicately, "she still accepts your courtship?"

Kadee flushed pink. "That's my concern, not yours."

That seemed to be an answer in the affirmative. Judith forbore to press the matter. Such relations were generally frowned upon, though she could not fault them herself. It *was* their concern, not hers. Yet if Miss Isla had feared Kadee's exposure—or the exposure of their relationship—she might have bashed Sgt Finlay on the head with a milk pail, after all.

Seeing Kadee's pale face, however, Judith did not voice her suspicion about the girl's lover. "Well, I am glad that I know the truth now." She tapped her finger against her chin. "I suppose you may continue as you are for the moment, despite it being so unorthodox. We will discuss it again in a week, when I've dealt with some other more pressing matters."

Kadee's head drooped in relief. "Thank you, ma'am. I'll show that I'm fit for the position, I promise you. I am sorry to have deceived you. I felt I had no choice."

Judith smiled and wearily nodded her dismissal. Kadee gave a short bow, then turned on her heel and strode out the room with a manly stride.

Mrs Ulrich watched her go with a disapproving frown. Judith sighed and sank back into her chair. "Goodness me, that certainly explains why she was washing in her room."

The she shot up again. "Robert! Is he still with Perry? I must go to them!"

"I believe they are in the kitchen." Mrs Ulrich paused wryly. "Mr Avely informed me that he was hungry."

Judith stood, hastily retying the ribbons on her mobcap. "Goodness, my wits have gone begging. Please take me there at once." She paused and drew a breath. "By the way, Mrs Ulrich, we have decided to abandon the plans for rescuing the duke tonight. It turns out that he *wants* to remain captured," she finished bitterly and ignored the faint hint of sympathy that tweaked Mrs Ulrich's brow. Then, as they walked down the stairs, she irritably brushed off the tentative sense of calm that emanated from her housekeeper's back. It wasn't a very good spell anyway. Mrs Ulrich was clearly out of practice with the gentler manifestations of her Gift. She was far better at conjuring horrific doom and remorse.

This time, Judith was almost sure she could have found the way herself. The labyrinthian corridors were starting to become familiar, and she had marked out various landmarks (a painting, a statue, a broken cornice) as clues for direction. They made a quick journey down and found Perry and Robert sitting around the massive kitchen table. Mrs Ulrich vanished into the cellars beyond, perhaps to pour herself a much-needed glass of ratafia, and to dismantle the spell she had reinstated there, now that it was no longer needed to distract Captain Drumpellier.

The two boys were ploughing through a bowl of peaches and plums, the stones littered around them. Judith spared a thought for the young cook who would find her stores decimated.

"Hello, Mother," said Perry, once he had finished a juicy mouthful. "Robert went to Taunton! I didn't know that Uncle Gerry had connections there."

"Neither did I," said Judith truthfully, and quickly changed the subject, for it had been the duke who placed Robert at Taunton. "You boys are going to give yourselves a stomachache."

"Oh, but it's delicious."

She was surprised to see Robert still with Perry. "And what's your excuse?" she queried, then answered herself. "I suppose young men don't need an excuse to eat."

Robert looked as if he was surprised to find himself there too. "The baron wandered into the Blue Drawing Room, so we thought we would leave. Perry dragged me down here."

Perry grinned. "We needed refuelling after our military incursion."

Judith frowned. "What was the baron doing lurking around so late at night?" It was well into the early hours by now. Though, she reflected, that may well be the best time to see planetary movements.

Perry shrugged. "He said something about Pollux and Castor. Bit of an odd fellow."

Ah, the stars in the Gemini constellation. Judith sighed. She was too tired to worry further. "Well, it's time for you to go back to your ship," she said. "It is very late, and we all need to sleep." She paused and drew a breath. "Can you return tomorrow night? Please, Perry?"

Perry eyed her, wiping juice from his chin. "Why?"

"Just in case."

"In case you wish to Travel inside the fort?" he said with deplorable acuteness. "I thought you acknowledged that this Captain Drumpellier has won the match."

Robert's brow creased at this insensitive summation. "It galls me too, Judith," he said abruptly. "How can we be sure the duke is in his right mind? Or that he truly knows what Drumpellier intends? Maybe we should satisfy ourselves on that point."

"Yes!" said Judith, grateful for this unlooked-for support. "Exactly! All we have is a letter, and that could have been written at gunpoint, for all we know." Though she doubted it, given its intimate tone. "Perry, you simply *must* return this evening, as soon as you can. Otherwise, I might Travel back with the ring, without you. Return it to me now, please."

Perry handed the ring over with a long-suffering sigh. "Fine. I'll come back. But only if you let me take some of these peaches with me." He gathered up an armful and winked at them. "Bye, Mother. See you soon, cousin." Then he vanished.

Judith glanced over to Robert. He was staring at the empty table—and pile of peach stones—with a Bemused expression, as if he had been casting a particularly complex Illusion.

"Well," she said, "*that* is your half-brother. Did you dislike him, after all?"

Robert looked over and did not answer the question. "He looks like me."

"He does," she agreed.

"With an added easy confidence."

"I suppose so." Born of Perry's position as a gentleman was the unspoken rejoinder. Judith knew, acutely, that Robert was thinking how different his life might have been had their places been exchanged. "Born of foolishness, you might say."

"He has a reckless bravado." As if to contrast between them, Robert pushed his chair back and mechanically set about tidying the kitchen table, like a footman. Judith helped, and tactfully changed the subject by telling him about Kadee's revelation. Robert was intrigued, but then as they walked up to their rooms, Judith decided to tell him of Mrs Ulrich's *other* discovery.

"I saw Miss Onslow below the ramparts this evening," she said quietly. "I watched as she hid something in the terrace gardens."

Robert's head twisted towards her as he walked, his hands thrust into his pockets. "Oh?"

"I sent Mrs Ulrich to see what it was." She hesitated. "It turns out that Miss Onslow was hiding a pistol."

Robert came to a startled halt. "*The* pistol?"

"We must assume so." She put her hand on his arm, adding hastily, "I do not assume, however, that she is the one who shot it. I find it hard to believe when she has proven herself to be our ally. She might have been hiding it for someone else, either the baron or Miss Isla. I am going to ask her first thing tomorrow. But I thought you should know."

Robert did not look reassured. If anything, his face became more grim. "Why would she protect the baron? He must have a hold over her. All his nonsense about stars must be hiding something else."

Judith set off again, dragging him along with her. "We will find out soon enough. For now, I will allow her to sleep, for she fed Wooten tonight. And she was the one who warned me about Dacian's fate; I am indebted to her, after all. I just hope that she can explain herself to us in the morning."

DESPITE EVERYTHING, and despite the knowledge that Dacian had turned away from her to his fate, Judith slept late the next morning after her storm of tears. It was almost midday when she awoke, a bright bar of sunlight lying across her bed from the gap in the curtains. The wardrobe was shut, she saw sleepily, though she had left it ajar last night. Marigold must be safely tucked inside. Judith rolled over, then lurched upwards, as the events of the previous evening crashed back into her consciousness.

Dacian. Dacian was choosing to go to Austria in two days' time, as part of Drumpellier's insane scheme. Judith *must* see him once more before he left. And in the meanwhile, Miss Onslow had hidden a gun on the terrace, which was still incomprehensible. Who was she protecting? Well, her odd behaviour could occupy Judith until nightfall, when she could visit Dacian one last time with Perry's help.

She dressed, and rather than ring the bell for a tray, she made her way to the breakfast room, feeling pleased that she only got lost once on the way. But when she reached the door, she found Mrs Ulrich guarding it, in the manner of a Valkyrie presiding over a coffin.

"Ma'am." The housekeeper's tones were heavy with portent. "I am glad you have risen. I have locked Miss Onslow up."

"Oh?" Judith blinked. "Was that really necessary, Mrs Ulrich?"

"Yes, ma'am." She gave a pregnant pause. "I followed her to the cellars in the early hours of this morning."

"To the cellars?" Judith's heart sank.

"Yes, and," —her tone lowered— "I heard her speaking French."

"*French?*"

Mrs Ulrich gave her a pitying look. "I did not see her interlocutor, as they were hidden from me. However, a man replied, also in French."

Judith gaped. "Miss Onslow is meeting with the *enemy*?"

"It appears so."

There was a long silence as Judith grappled with this new information on an empty stomach.

"Good God," she said weakly. "She's a double agent."

In which plans are amended

Be wary when you rely on someone's guile to serve you: it can be turned against you.

— from *Lady Avely's Guide to Guile and Peril*

MRS ULRICH LED the way down the hall. Judith gave a longing glance at the breakfast room and then followed. Of course, apprehending a traitor to the Crown was more important than coffee and toast. She only wished she could apprehend the traitor *after* coffee and toast. She shook her head sharply: Miss Onslow had fooled her utterly with her charming demeanour. And poor Robert, what would he say?

Belatedly, it occurred to her to wonder if Miss Onslow had misled her about the assassination plot, if she was such a conniving wretch. But no, Judith would have heard the lie in her voice. For some reason, the girl had decided to disclose it, probably to gain Judith's trust. And it aligned with her other betrayal of Drumpellier, and most likely suited her own purposes.

"We must assume," said Mrs Ulrich, as she stalked down the

corridor, "that Miss Onslow has been meeting French agents for some time."

Judith grimaced. "Yes, she must have sought to take advantage of your Dread Spell to hide her activities."

Mrs Ulrich came to a halt and turned to face her, her expression severe. "I apologise, ma'am. In fact, Miss Onslow asked me to cast the Dread Spell."

"She did?" Judith stared, offended. "Why didn't you tell me?"

The housekeeper hesitated. "She claimed to have a great fear that smugglers might use the cellars, and she wanted me to lay the spell to frighten them away."

"Oh." Judith contemplated the housekeeper's grim expression. "She was blackmailing you, wasn't she? She knew that you were helping the smugglers, and that was the price of her silence."

Mrs Ulrich nodded shortly, then spun on her heel again and marched down the corridor. "I apologise, ma'am. I should have enquired more closely as to why. I assumed she wished to meet a lover in private; it never crossed my mind she was a French spy."

"Never mind," said Judith, trailing after her again. "You weren't to know that she was a traitor. And now you've locked her up. Er, how *did* you lock her up?"

"I employed Trebellow's assistance."

"How?" asked Judith, with some trepidation.

"I bade him wait in the corridor. Then when Miss Onslow came by, he gently expelled his Impact to push her into the open door of a storeroom. I was waiting behind the door, slammed it shut, and locked it. There is no window, so she has no way to escape."

"Oh," said Judith faintly. Her retainers were proving to be a redoubtable team. "Why not lock her in her room?"

"I was aware that she had a vampiri in there. I did not want her to have a hostage."

"Oh, Wooten, of course." Judith rubbed her forehead. "Very clever, Mrs Ulrich. I am indebted to you."

They reached the door, a sturdy wooden thing with a brass knob, set in the yellowing wallpaper of the hall. Mrs Ulrich pulled up her chatelaine, holding up a large iron key. "I don't recommend you open it, ma'am."

There was the sound of something banging within the room, then Miss Onslow's voice on the other side of the door. "Mrs Ulrich? Is that you? Let me out at once, you madwoman!"

"I have brought Lady Avely," said Mrs Ulrich, in triumphant and sepulchral tones.

Miss Onslow gasped and spoke loudly through the door. "Marchioness! Please make your dreadful housekeeper release me! This is outrageous!"

Judith cleared her throat. "I believe that Mrs Ulrich has good reason for imprisoning you, Miss Onslow. She claims to have heard you consorting with French spies in the cellars."

There was a pause, then Miss Onslow rallied. "Yes, she has decided that I am some sort of villain, when you know very well that I have been helping you! I told you about the duke! You must trust me!"

Judith grimaced at this clever evasion. Miss Onslow made a rather good spy, it seemed. "I'm afraid that I saw you hiding the gun in the terrace gardens last night, Miss Onslow."

There was a silence. Then came the sound of a body sliding against the door, and Miss Onslow's voice, subdued and lower down, as she leaned against the wood. "Oh." She sounded suddenly very weary.

"You killed Sgt Finlay, didn't you?" There was a silence. "Did he discover your meetings?"

Miss Onslow's reply was barely audible. "Yes."

"How did he find out?"

"He followed me into the cellars." Her tone grew stronger, indignant. "Then he had the gall to ask for my favours—my body—in return for his silence. You cannot blame me for killing him, Lady Avely. I simply could not submit to him."

Judith frowned at the door, her heart plummeting with sympathy. Then she hardened her voice. "So you lured him down there again, I suppose, and hit him over the head with a spade. Did you drag him through the tunnels with the wheelbarrow?"

"How did you know that?" Miss Onslow sounded surprised.

"I made it my business to know," snapped Judith. She gnawed on her lip, suspecting that it had been Miss Onslow, after all, who had told Sgt Finlay the cock and bull story about the smugglers to feed to Cador. She would have wanted the fisherman far from his cottage that night so she could drag the body into the tunnel. So in fact her crime was coldly premeditated and not just a matter of self-defence. "I also know about the tunnel you used to dispose of him."

"Goodness me." Miss Onslow was subdued. "You do know rather a lot. I suppose that is the advantage of being a Truth Discernor."

"What I do not know is *why*. I thought you were happy using your Gift to serve your country. Why sink to treason and murder?"

"My country betrayed *me*! Drumpellier sent my brother to his capture!"

Ah, perhaps the brother lost in battle was not dead after all, as Judith had assumed. She leaned her head against the door. "Is he being held as a prisoner of war?"

"Yes, and Drumpellier doesn't care a jot. *I* had to help him instead."

"You bargained your knowledge for his safety?" Again,

Judith repressed her unwilling sympathy, mixed as it was with her outrage. "Is he safe now? At what cost to other British soldiers? Who knows what damage you have done!"

"I didn't like it," said Miss Onslow, her voice low. "But I had to do it. I could not allow my brother to be executed. You should know how I feel, Lady Avely, when your beloved is sailing into the same trap."

Judith bit her lip. She could well understand the desire to rail against the price of war. But the alternative was worse: England under the heel of Bonaparte. "It is very hard," she said softly. "Yet it was your brother's choice to fight."

"And it was my choice to save him," Miss Onslow gritted out. "And save myself from that lecher."

Judith rested her forehead against the door jamb, thinking. After a moment, she asked, "Do you have a minder over here? Some other traitor, to whom you report?"

Miss Onslow was silent. Judith gritted her teeth crossly; it was too much to hope the wretch would willingly divulge such information. But she thought she knew who Miss Onslow's minder was: Baron Quarles. Even aside from that suspicion, she had enough proof to indict the girl, and *here* was her ticket for Dacian's safety. She could bargain with Drumpellier and offer him a traitor in return for his weapon.

Then another thought occurred to her, and abruptly she lifted her head. "Wait. This morning—did you tell your informant about Drumpellier's plans for the duke?"

Silence came from within. Judith banged on the door with her flat palm, angrily. "Did you?" she demanded, panic rising in her throat like bile. "Tell me!"

The ensuing quiet was confirmation enough. To her right, Mrs Ulrich cleared her throat. "I did hear the name Sargen mentioned, ma'am, in the flurry of French."

"You *told* the French about the assassination plot?" Judith shouted at the door, suddenly losing all sense of compassion. "*You* are the one closing the trap!"

A muffled sob came from within. "I had to do it. I didn't want to, but they promised me my brother."

Unmoved, Judith pushed away from the jamb. "You can look forward a long acquaintance with that room, Miss Onslow," she said furiously. "And you'd better hope that I can save his grace—otherwise I'll strangle you with my own bare hands."

"LOCK BARON QUARLES IN HIS ROOM!" Judith instructed Mrs Ulrich, who hurried away at once. Judith stormed down the corridor in the opposite direction. But by the time she had reached the breakfast room, her pace had slowed to something more thoughtful.

She had realised that Miss Onslow's traitorous snivelling could actually work to Dacian's advantage. Judith simply had to tell Drumpellier that the assassination plot was already revealed to the French, and he would have to abandon it. And he *would* return Dacian to her, if she had to hold a shatterstone to his head herself.

She clenched her fists angrily, then reluctantly sat down for a much-needed breakfast of coffee, eggs, and ham. As she sipped her coffee, she pondered what metaphorical shatterstone she could hold to Drumpellier's head. The more she considered it, the more she began to suspect that Drumpellier was operating on his own. It was quite possible that he had gone rogue, obsessed with his own cleverness, with this idea to assassinate Bonaparte. Who was his higher command? Could she go to his superiors?

She sighed. She very much feared that his superiors wouldn't give a damn. Most likely, they had handed him *carte blanche* to do as he willed, quietly, on the side, as long as it served the country. The king couldn't publicly endorse an assassination, but he would look the other way while it was orchestrated.

She pushed her cup away and wandered through the castle, restless. Twisting the topaz ring in her pocket, she contemplating using it now: Travel to Pendennis, confront Drumpellier, and attempt to negotiate with him, holding this new card. Yet if he refused to listen, she'd be trapped there in his power, unable to escape. She would probably end up locked in a cell and proffered a cup full of Lethe.

No, it might be better to go directly to Dacian and speak to him. He would be more open to reason, she was sure. And they had to be prepared to snatch him away in the moment, if necessary.

Yes, as much as it galled her to wait, she must hold fire until Perry arrived. Nightfall would also bring Marigold and Yvette's help, if anything went wrong. Even Wooten might be useful, if he would just put some clothes on. She had to wait. In the meanwhile, she could renew the preparations, ready the castle and the staff.

But first, she had to break the news to Robert.

It took a good half hour to find him. She tracked him down finally in a dusty room with windows looking out across the rugged coastline of Cornwall. He had leaned a sketchbook against the window fame, and he was drawing with frowning concentration. Judith caught a glimpse of the sketched battlements framing the ocean and hills, with a woman standing against the stone, her gown a graceful line, her head tilted in thought.

Oh dear. Before she could lose her courage, in the manner of one quickly dousing a wound with spirits, Judith told him what she had discovered about Miss Onslow: that she was a spy for France and had killed Sgt Finlay.

Robert stared at her in consternation, his charcoal now lax in his fingers. "That's preposterous. I don't believe it. You must be mistaken."

Judith hunched her shoulders. "I could hear the truth in her voice."

His expression darkened, and he turned away. Judith felt he blamed her for the news. It was another reason for him to dislike her Gift, now that it condemned his newfound friendship and nascent courtship.

She swallowed. "I am sorry, Robert. It was a terrible shock to me too. I refused to believe it at first, even when I knew she had hidden the gun. I know you must be deeply hurt." She nodded at his sketch. "You trusted her, and liked her, and I do not blame you. She was very charming."

Angrily, he tipped the paper off the ledge, hiding it from her. "I was simply flattered by her interest in me. I should have known it was false."

"That might not be true!" Judith objected. "She might still have admired you, even as she lied to you. She is a young woman of many motivations, some honourable and some deeply flawed."

"I *didn't* trust her, remember," averred Robert. A gull wheeled outside with a melancholic cry. "She was prowling around at night, and I *told* you it was odd."

Judith allowed him the defence. She sighed. "Well, Mrs Ulrich has locked her up, and you must see that this gives us something to take to Drumpellier. Our new knowledge is a real coup, in fact, and we must focus on how we can take advantage of it."

Robert's jaw ticked. "You want to swap them over. Give him Miss Onslow in return for the duke."

When he said it like that, it did sound rather cold. Judith

straightened her shoulders. "It might be our only chance, and I won't let it slip. And she is a traitor, after all."

Robert was silent for a moment. "So Perry returns tonight?"

"Yes." She paused. "I'm sorry, I know you find this all rather awkward."

"Not awkward," he said coldly. "Damn difficult when I imagine what my mother would say if she could see me cosying up to you lot."

Judith pressed her lips together, hiding her pain. Obviously, Robert regretted the companionable intermission in the kitchen with Perry. And he was reeling from the news about Miss Onslow, so she must try to forgive him his moodiness. After all, she had put up with sulky behaviour from her other children in the past. It was part and parcel of being so young. Had she been so moody when she was twenty?

"Indeed, your mother would not like it," she said carefully. "But can you put aside *her* feelings for a moment, and examine your own? After all, Perry knows nothing of the trespasses against you. So you are visiting the sins of the father..."

Robert gave her a scathing glance. "It was I who suffered the sins of the father. Not Perry."

She nodded hastily. "Indeed, you are right. I am so sorry, Robert. Once we have managed this crisis, you can leave us far behind, if you wish."

He turned his face away, staring out over the coast. "I do wish it."

Tears rose in Judith's eyes, but she left the room before he could see them.

In which plans go awry

Distrust a strong sensation of boredom. Often it is disguising something else.

— from *Lady Avely's Guide to Guile and Peril*

WHEN THEY REASSEMBLED the council of war, Mrs Ulrich had some unsettling news: Baron Quarles had left early that morning for Exeter. He had taken his valise, but left his telescope, and had not informed Kynver when he would return.

"Never mind," said Judith. "We must be ready to apprehend him as soon as he reappears. Trebellow, I shall rely on you for that."

Trebellow puffed out his chest manfully, and Judith turned her mind to overseeing the resurrection of her old plans, with some modifications.

The long, warm hours of the afternoon were filled with activity, primarily with establishing a safe hidey-hole for the duke. It was to be out of sight and barricaded by Illusion, Defence, and Diplomacy: all the magicks at her disposal.

Mrs Ulrich helped Judith to select a small sitting room adjoining a large bedroom in the east wing. Robert, putting aside his ire, cast an Illusion charm over the communing door so it now showed a seamless continuation of the bedroom's striped wallpaper. Then Trebellow spent hours casting Defences into the same door and surrounding walls, so that not even an army might break into it. And Mrs Ulrich wove an enchantment over the whole bedroom, which Judith had taken to calling the Humdrum Spell, for as soon as one walked into the room one began yawning and feeling utterly uninterested in everything, especially the incredibly boring striped wallpaper.

"Don't cast it so powerfully," she advised Mrs Ulrich. "Otherwise, someone might be overcome with apathy and fall asleep on the bed, right in our way."

Still, she was pleased with the end result: an unremarkable (vastly boring) master bedroom that hid a secret retreat. Drumpellier might search the castle from top to bottom and not discover it at all. And of course, Mrs Ulrich had employed her other talents in doom and gloom in another part of the house, as a decoy.

When night finally fell, the Baron still had not reappeared. Trying not to worry, Judith took her place in the Blue Drawing Room. Did the Baron know that they had captured Miss Onslow? But he had not made it back to Lanyon Castle, and now the tide was in, so he could not disrupt their plans tonight.

Impatiently, she waited for Perry. He finally arrived an hour after sundown. When he materialised by the window, she marched forward and grabbed his arm, dragging him to a seat.

"Right," she pronounced. "Eat now. You will need your strength, and you must rest for a quarter of an hour before you Travel again."

Perry looked around, weaving slightly on his feet. Robert stood uncomfortably by the fireplace and nodded a greeting.

Marigold waved from the back of the armchair, wearing a hastily constructed cape of black cotton, tied with string and fortunately covering all of her. Wooten, fetched by Judith earlier from Miss Onslow's room, was tucked up in the lavender silk kerchief, with a whole settee to himself. He ignored Perry entirely, a dreamy expression on his face.

"Oh hoh," said Perry. "You've marshalled the troops, I see."

"Yes," said Judith with dignity. "We are going to rescue the duke tonight."

"Pardon me, Mother?" said Perry in disbelief. "I thought we were going to let him sacrifice himself on the altar of duty?"

"We cannot be sure he is in his right mind," replied Judith, putting aside the thought of the very lucid letter she had received from Dacian yesterday. "And we have new information to leverage for his freedom." Briefly she explained the matter of Miss Onslow, which Perry took with a suitable expression of shocked horror.

"The charming young lady who fed Wooten?" he exclaimed. "Good Lord, Wooten, I hope you didn't pick up any treasonous inclinations."

Wooten merely yawned, showing his tiny fangs. "I *said* a cow would be preferable."

Perry chuckled, then cast a rather acute look at Robert, who was staring stonily at the carpet. "Still, I never suspect such depths to her. She's just a girl, after all."

This irritated Judith, perhaps because she had fallen prey to the same prejudice. "Yes, well, young women can be extremely resourceful. Consider your sister, for example."

"Yes, but that's *Elinor*," said her brother dismissively. "She's different to most girls. Clearly, she inherited her streak of reck-lessness from you, Mother," he added, with some disapproval. "What is that you want us to do now? Blow up a wall of the fort with the shatterstone?"

The smooth grey rock remained on the mantlepiece, somehow ominous in its simplicity. Judith hadn't wanted to touch it, wary of how it might detonate. "No, but I want you to explain how it works, in case we should need it."

Perry blithely told her that she must simply lob it like an orange at her intended target, whereby it would violently explode upon impact.

"I can throw better than you," he added with great condescension. "I'll carry it. We wouldn't want you to miss at a critical juncture."

Robert repressed a grin, which, frankly, Judith was glad to see as a sign of brotherly feeling.

"Certainly not," she said crossly. "We leave it here, safely out of the matter."

"But why did I bother to fetch it, then?"

"Be sensible, Perry." Carefully, she rolled the shatterstone further back away from the edge of the mantlepiece, hiding it behind the clock. "We shall not need it. The plan is to move with stealth, not loud explosions."

"Pity." Perry sighed, then cocked his head. "I thought you wanted to negotiate with Drumpellier now. What's the call for stealth?"

She put her chin in the air. "I've decided that it is better, in this instance, to take first, then ask later. I don't trust Drumpellier to be reasonable. And I want to explain matters properly to his grace."

Perry raised his brows. "So you are going to snatch the duke instead?"

"If necessary," said Marigold, from the armchair. "And we're all going to help."

The look of dismay on Perry's face was comical. "*All* of you?"

"Not Wooten," put in Robert stiffly. "He's staying behind.

But you'll need me to cast your disguise, and Marigold will find Yvette, who should tell us where the duke is being kept. Judith plans to use the ring, so Marigold can go with her."

"What are *you* going to do, Mother?" demanded Perry, with great suspicion.

"I'm going to distract Drumpellier, or whatever guards he has on the fort tower. While I'm kicking up a fuss, you're going to find Miss Belfleur and the duke and whisk them out of there. That way, I have an alibi for when the duke vanishes. Drumpellier can scarcely blame me if I was talking to him at the time."

"I don't know," said Perry sceptically. "Sounds to me like Drumpellier will certainly blame you."

"Which is why you need to hide his grace." Judith rang the bell at her elbow, and Mrs Ulrich and Trebellow stepped into the room. She introduced them to Perry and explained how they would assist. Perry eyed the massive bulk of Trebellow, and the martial glint in Mrs Ulrich's eye, and swallowed any objection he might have made.

"All right then," he said. "Let's get this over with." Then he grinned. "A snatch and stash job, I like it. Not sure his grace will, though."

TWENTY MINUTES LATER, Judith reeled against the stone wall in the tower of Fort Pendennis.

The ring was warm under her fingers, and hastily she slipped it back into her pocket. Marigold climbed out of the other one, already in her bat form, and took off without a word through one of the deep-set windows.

Alone, Judith looked around the tower room, relieved despite herself that Drumpellier was not lying in wait for her. The small square of carpet, she realised, was obviously a Travel landing pad. Drumpellier must have a Travel charm that brought him here just as promptly as hers did. Well, she needed to give him a good reason to use it.

She marched over to the desk and pulled the drawers open loudly, rattling the contents. What a delightful wad of coded messages! She resisted the urge to shove them all into her pockets. However, she was currently playing the role of a respectable, righteous widow, not one who pilfered military dispatches.

Her banging and stomping soon worked. Within minutes, the tower door swung open—but more tentatively than she had expected. And rather than Drumpellier's furious face, she saw Ltn Greene peering anxiously around the door.

"Lady Avely!" he said, in a shocked voice. "What are you doing here?"

She slammed the drawer shut. "I need to speak with your captain immediately."

Ltn Greene gaped. "Oh? What about? I am afraid that the captain is absent at the moment."

"I can see that!" She paused, and then the meaning of his words sunk in. "You mean he is not at Fort Pendennis at all?"

"Yes, he's off on some Custos business. Top secret stuff in Ireland. He left this morning, and I don't know when he'll be back."

Judith heard the truth in his words, and her shoulders sank at this unexpected intelligence. "Curse the man!" She drew a breath, reevaluating her options, then narrowed her eyes at Ltn Greene. "Well, you may escort me to Custodian House, and I will wait for him there. I insist on seeing him as soon as possible."

The lieutenant swung the door open and smiled at her. "I have a better idea than that. You want to speak to your duke, don't you? I can take you to him right now."

"What?" she said inelegantly. This was all wrong: she couldn't be seen anywhere near the duke. How could she conceivably refuse the invitation? Ltn Greene would grow suspicious immediately.

But he was giving her a reassuring smile. "His grace is on guard duty by the inner gates. Not the outer ones, of course; Drumpellier isn't completely stupid."

"The *duke* is on guard duty?" Judith repeated stupidly. Her mind reeled. "How...?"

Ltn Greene held the door open, gesturing. "He has agreed to Drumpellier's terms. The guard duty is to see if he can be trusted to follow orders."

"And can he?" Judith numbly walked out of the tower room, watching as the lieutenant locked it again, then trailed after him down the stairs.

"Seems so," said Ltn Greene cheerfully. "Though his memory regressed a little today. But it should be easy enough for you to speak with him." He glanced back. "Might be good for him, poor fellow."

Judith's fists clenched in her skirts. She could not bring herself to refuse the opportunity: she must just hope that she reached Dacian before Perry and Robert did. Please God, let Yvette be supping on a cow or something, and keep them waiting.

And what if Dacian refused to go? What if he were content with his lot, happy to serve as a puppet of the Custos? Her heart's blood felt as if it were slowly draining away at the possibility that she might have to say goodbye, there with Ltn Greene watching. But no: she had discussed this with Perry. She wasn't going to take no for answer. Dacian was coming with her, whether he liked it or not. He could chastise her for it later.

Ltn Greene led her down the cold tower stairs and out the main fortification. The portcullis gleamed wickedly over her head, and the air was damp with sea mist. Her eyes searched desperately for Dacian, racing over the soldiers posted at intervals around the circling ramparts, one at each deep crenel. Then her gaze travelled back, disbelieving, to one of them: a tall, familiar figure.

It was Dacian, dressed in an infantryman's uniform. His broad shoulders filled out the red coat, and the white cross-belts strained across his chest. The black hat made him seem even taller than usual, and his face was blank, his eyes fixed between the crenel gap. His profile faced her, the grooves in his cheek hidden by the strap of his helmet, but the grim angle of his chin was apparent.

A little nervously, Ltn Greene led her to him. Judith also slowed her steps, unsure of her reception. She thought of the letter he had written and tried to feel encouraged, but the man before her seemed utterly a stranger.

Ltn Greene cleared his throat. "Corporal, a lady to see you."

Dacian moved his head slightly and saw Judith. His gaze remained blank, without a flicker of recognition.

"Ma'am." He gave a short bow. "May I serve you?"

Judith stared speechlessly. It was so odd to see him in uniform, and obedient. "Dacian, how are you? Do you remember me?"

"I do not." His eyes shuttered. "My apologies, ma'am."

It took Judith a moment to realise that his words rang true.

Her heart plummeted like a stone. It felt like the line that joined their two souls had snapped: rent by his disavowal, or no longer finding purchase in the emptiness that now dwelt in his eyes. It was as if the ground under her was tilting. She felt ill.

She gulped down her wave of nausea. "We spoke yesterday. Do you remember?" It was only yesterday that he had thrown that quip about chocolate at her and met her gaze with a secret warmth. There was no sign of that today.

'No, ma'am.' Dacian glanced at Ltn Greene. "I woke up this morning in the barracks with no recollection of how I came to be there. The lieutenant here explained to me that I have a rare condition of memory lapses, but it should return in time. He advised me to continue in my duties as an aid to recollection."

Judith turned to stare at Ltn Greene with incredulity. His shoulders rose defensively and he widened his eyes: *what else was I supposed to say?*

"What happened?" she said coldly. "Did Drumpellier dose him up again?"

"No. It must be a regression from earlier doses." Ltn Greene's voice carried so little conviction that it sounded very much like a lie. Judith stared at him narrowly.

"What dose?" Dacian's voice sharpened. "Dose of what?"

Ltn Greene backed away a step and held up his hands placatingly.

Judith hesitated. "A dose of Lethe. It is a drug of forgetfulness, and it is administered as a punishment."

"Punishment?" Dacian jaw tightened. His hand went to the sword at his hip, the other one clenching into a fist. His large form was even more intimidating in a soldier's uniform, and Ltn Greene took another hasty step back.

At that moment, however, Judith saw—to her horror—Perry and Robert coming around the side of the fortification. A black shape darted before the boys, leading them towards the gate. They marched side by side, in unison, just as they had practiced, though their posture looked ludicrously upright, their arms overly rigid.

Their gazes were fixed on the duke. Then Perry's eyes flicked towards Judith and widened in alarm. After a heart-thumping moment, she discreetly gestured for them to proceed. She might need their help even more than she realised.

For she could feel a swell of power gathering in Dacian. His fist was still clenched, conjuring Impact as his impatience grew.

"Punishment for what?" he repeated, and the words were like rocks falling on ice.

Hastily, she put a hand out and closed it over his own. He blinked, startled, and the swirling power faltered.

"I can explain," she said urgently. "You must not lash out. Please, Dacian. Wait."

In which brothers are in arms

Guile does not always seek to disarm with pleasant allure: sometimes it seeks to enrage, provoke fear, or convey guilt, and thus manipulate.
— from *Lady Avely's Guide to Guile and Peril*

SHE DROPPED HER HAND. Before he could answer, Perry and Robert were upon them. The two boys pulled to a halt, standing straight as two pins on either side of Dacian. Just as they had planned.

The duke's head turned, looking at each of them. A frown marred his brow, but he showed no sign of recognition, which was *not* part of the plan. Robert doggedly stared ahead, while Perry blinked innocently at Ltn Greene.

Ltn Greene looked taken aback, though also rather relieved at the sudden drop in tension. "Who are you?" He frowned at Perry. "I don't know you. Do I?"

Perry executed a sharp salute. "New recruits! Sir! The captain put us on roster. To share the guard here. Sir!"

Ltn Greene's frown deepened. "Really? I do not recollect such an order being given."

Dacian was staring at Judith, eyes hard. She willed him to be silent and patient, even as she debated internally how to proceed. Could they still snatch Dacian back to Castle Lanyon when he no longer knew or trusted her? He might very well react violently and suspiciously. Yet the alternative was to leave him here in the clutches of the Custos, with his memory gone and subject to whatever plan Drumpellier concocted.

She might never see him again if she left him here now. She couldn't bear the thought.

"Well?" said Ltn Greene suspiciously to Perry. "Explain yourselves. Captain Drumpellier is not here, so how could he have given you such an order?"

Perry's chest was puffed out, but it seemed like he was holding his breath with the effort of it. As he was bereft of words, Robert spoke up. "The captain gave the order before he left. As an extra precaution. Sir!"

"Oh." Ltn Greene nodded thoughtfully and then looked between them again. Perry stood even straighter, if that was possible, tucking his chin in like a turkey. Robert had fixed his eyes on Ltn Greene's helmet, and Judith was fairly certain that Robert's own hat was slowly growing in size to match it.

Between them, Dacian said grimly, "I do not require assistance in my duty. But I do require explanations, ma'am, and you have promised to give them to me."

"And I will." She put as much meaning as she could into the words, holding his gaze with all the warmth and reassurance she could manage. Yet his face closed even further. Judith hastened on. "You were being kept as a prisoner here after killing a man with your Gift. But you struck a bargain with the captain of this regiment, agreeing to help him if he would allow the return of your memories. It seems he has failed to keep his side of the terms."

"No, no," said Ltn Greene weakly. "No such thing. Please, Lady Avely, I must protest."

Dacian ignored him, staring at Judith. "I killed a man?" he said slowly. "I believe that, somehow. Is that why they took my memory?"

"So they claim."

"Then why are you defending me?"

Judith swallowed. "The matter is not so clear-cut. I believe you are being unfairly detained."

Ltn Greene coughed violently. "Not at all. An overstatement! Best to wait for the captain and we can discuss it together, as men." He coughed again. "Er, as sensible people."

Perry looked very worried, though perhaps that was because his chin was tucked into his throat. Judith knew that she had to clear the scene so that Perry could work his magic and whisk Dacian away, and she clenched her teeth together, wondering how she could manage it.

Fortunately, the lieutenant was equally anxious to remove her. He shifted from foot to foot and cast nervous glances between Dacian and the front gates of the fort. He was clearly concerned that the duke would make a dash for it with his newfound knowledge.

"Come, come, Lady Avely," he said anxiously. "Let us repair to Custodian House and leave this soldier to his duty."

She nodded with a show of reluctance. As they turned to go, she took his arm and loudly complained so that Dacian could hear, "Ltn Greene, you are not in possession of all the facts. I am afraid there is a matter of treason that needs to be brought to the attention of your captain."

"Treason?" said Greene, in disbelief. "What can you mean? Come, ma'am, let me take you to Custodian House and you can tell me all about it." He cast one more look back at Perry and Robert and apparently decided that they would be sufficient to guard the duke. "It sounds as if you have news that should not be bandied about in a courtyard."

She allowed herself to be chivvied along. But she turned her head and glared at Perry with all the threat she could muster. Then she gave a tiny jerk of her free hand, pointing at the duke.

Perry visibly paled. Robert gulped.

She marched off beside Ltn Greene. When they reached the central gate, she looked back once, just before she passed through.

Perry had his hand on Dacian's shoulder. The duke was shaking his head vehemently, and Robert said something, his expression urgent. They were frozen in dispute, three red soldiers triangled towards each other in postures of aggression. Then suddenly Perry threw himself forward, putting his arms around Dacian, with Robert following close behind. Under Judith's anxious gaze, they squirmed around in a strange silent embrace, then vanished into thin air.

The whole thing took about five seconds to enact.

She saw another solider look around, perhaps alerted by the sounds of a faint scuffle. All that met his gaze was the quiet, empty yard. He turned back to his crenel.

Breathing a sigh of relief, she turned her head forwards, allowing Ltn Greene to escort her out the gates.

Once out of the fort, the lieutenant ushered her towards Custodian House and led her into the sitting room that she had previously occupied with Drumpellier. She sat down with a thump, her heart beating hard. Her imagination followed Dacian to the castle. How would he react? She feared it would not be with equanimity.

Again, she was plied with tea and bread, and Ltn Greene poured out eager questions. She forced herself to address them and give her men a chance to sort themselves out before she returned.

"Yes," she acknowledged to Ltn Greene, once she had finished half a cup. "I have discovered who killed Sgt Finlay. It is not someone you might expect, I'm afraid: Miss Onslow."

The lieutenant did not look as taken aback as she might have expected. His shoulders bowed a little, and he lowered his head to stare at the floor. "I feared as much."

"You did?" Judith choked on her tea, startled. "Why?"

Ltn Greene paused. "Sgt Finlay told me he was going to meet Miss Onslow on the day he died."

Judith stared; this was pertinent information indeed. "But why didn't you tell me?"

"I didn't want to compromise her reputation." Ltn Greene looked abashed. "I know it was wrong."

Judith sighed. "Well, it is bad enough that you protected a murderer. I'm afraid I must tell you that Miss Onslow is also a French spy, and we've locked her up."

Ltn Greene's eyes widened to a comical degree. "A French spy?"

"Yes, and she has compromised your captain's plans. I intend to tell him that myself."

The lieutenant looked shocked. "Certainly! And where have you locked Miss Onslow up?"

"In one of the parlours. She is being closely watched, do not worry."

Ltn Greene nodded, eyes like saucers. Then he hesitated. "But, ma'am, the captain might not return for days. Do you want to stay at the fort for all that time? Won't you let me escort you back to Castle Lanyon, instead? Not by gig," he added hastily. "I'm in charge for the moment, and I can extend you the courtesy of a Travel charm back to the island, though it will require us to, uh, embrace for a moment."

Judith chewed on her lip. She desperately wanted to rush home, to examine Dacian's mind and every other part of him, and calm him down if needed—which, she suspected, would be greatly the case. And if she *did* stay here, she would be left alone, unguarded at Custodian House, and therefore become open to suspicion when the lieutenant discovered Dacian's absence. That would defeat her whole purpose in coming here in the first place.

Ltn Greene sensed her weakening. "I can send Captain Drumpellier to you as soon as he returns. Really, I don't think it is wise for you to stay here alone, ma'am."

Judith could not bring herself to refuse. She had done her duty, after all, and distracted the command while Dacian vanished. Ltn Greene could honourably testify that she had been with him the whole time, especially if he himself escorted her back to Lanyon Castle. She only hoped that Dacian, Perry, and Robert had by now removed themselves from the Blue Drawing Room, as per her strict instructions.

"Very well," she said, putting down her cup of tea. "Let us go."

JUDITH HASTILY DISENTANGLED herself from Ltn Greene's arms. To her surprise, they had not arrived in the Blue Drawing Room, but instead stood on the western ramparts, near the broken-down tower. A breeze whistled through her hair, and she could hear the waves crashing loudly on the rocks.

She directed a look of enquiry at the lieutenant, but he simply shrugged it off. "I apologise for the second-rate landing pad, ma'am; I don't have the same Travel Charm as the captain," he explained. "Now, I shall bid you adieu. I ought not to leave my post unattended for long."

"Certainly, and thank you," she said, grateful for his help.

He winked at her, then bent to twist a buckle on his boot, and disappeared. She was to think back on that wink later.

For now, she was simply glad that he had gone. She was home, and Dacian was nearby. She hurried along the sloping, uneven stones, anxiously making her way into the castle. The Blue Drawing Room was closest to her, so she rushed to it first, in the fear that Dacian might still be there, recalcitrant.

He was not there, but the drawing room looked like a whole troop of soldiers had Travelled into it and then undertaken a mock battle. A table had been splintered and lay twisted on its side, the rug was askew, a settee bumped out of place, and the shards of smashed porcelain was swept into a pile by the fire.

"Good Lord." Judith pulled up short. "What happened here?"

Trebellow was sweeping the porcelain, looking rather askew himself, and sporting the beginnings of a large bruise on his left eye. He started guiltily. "Ma'am! We did not expect you so soon." He cleared his throat. "There was a bit of a skirmish when his grace arrived."

"He resisted his rescue?"

"Aye, and I couldn't really tell what was going on," said Trebellow apologetically, "so I leapt into the fray myself."

"Oh dear." That explained the general scene of disaster, if Trebellow had been rolling around with the duke, wrassling Cornish-style through the drawing room. "You couldn't pass up the opportunity to wrassle his grace?"

"Indeed, ma'am." Trebellow straightened his shoulders. "He's a right strong one, and real twisty too. I had to use my Gift to restrain him, which I didn't like to do, being against the usual rules, as I told you. But I also had to contend with your boy, Perry, and the other one, Robert, who were also in the tussle."

Judith grimaced. "And how did it all end? Were you strong enough?"

"No," confessed the butler, ashamed. "His grace responded in like, and it all...escalated, you could say. But then Mrs Ulrich cast a dampening spell. It is hard to keep brawling when icy despair and doom fall upon your head, ma'am. It took the fight out of all of us, and I snatched at the opportunity to restrain his grace properly. I'm a bit more accustomed than his grace to Mrs Ulrich's melancholic moods, you could say."

Judith nodded, grateful for her housekeeper's intervention, for otherwise she might not have a drawing room anymore. "And? Where are they all now?"

"I escorted the duke to his hidey-hole—he was a bit reluctant, so I had to force the matter. I wouldn't have done it," said Trebellow apologetically, "except that I thought that your villainous captain might be here any minute. Between my strength, Mrs Ulrich's imprecations, and Mr Robert's explanations, we managed to corral his grace into the secret room. And I've reversed the Defence spells on it, in case his grace decided that he didn't like it there anymore." He paused. "The boys have gone to the breakfast room, as you ordered."

Judith sighed. "Thank you, Trebellow."

She turned on her heel and left the Blue Drawing Room. Her steps were quick, but when she arrived at the eastern bedroom, she pushed the door open slowly and quietly, trying to gather her resolution.

The last time she had been alone with Dacian had been in the master bedroom at Garvey House. There he had kissed her, with a passionate enthusiasm for her presence.

She well remembered that kiss, even if he had now forgotten it. It had become very heated, only to be dampened by the necessity of Dacian emitting snores like a drunken donkey at regular intervals. They hadn't even been able to talk properly with the fear of being heard. This time, however, there was no such fear or necessity. She finally had him all to herself.

Except that he was not himself.

Creeping inside, she heard no sound emanating from the secret sitting room. The stripes of the wall were neatly in place, the hidden door invisible. She could even believe that she had come into the wrong room. As she stood there, the Humdrum Spell calmed her nerves, and she let her shoulders drop. He was safe now. It would only be a matter of time before his memory returned. She must have patience and offer him the same. Really, it was quite an ordinary matter, so very ordinary it was quite boring...she didn't even know why she should bother with it after all.

She shook herself sharply. Damn Mrs Ulrich, with her powerful Diplomacy. Crossing the room, Judith tapped softly.

"Dacian? May I enter?"

"If you can open the damn door." His voice was harsh.

She winced, remembering that Trebellow had locked him in with Defence spells. Yet at her touch, the door handle became visible and turned easily. She pushed through, stepping into the sitting room, and out of the Humdrum Spell. All her emotions crashed back: relief, joy, and fear at the sight of him.

He stood with his back to the window, his face grim, his hair disordered. His posture was tense, and he still wore half of that dreadful uniform: a loose white shirt and tan breeches, but the red jacket had been discarded, and the black hat flung on the floor. His arms were folded across his broad chest, his stance wide.

"Who the hell are you?" he demanded. "And where in damnation am I?"

In which a matron goes to extraordinary lengths

In the face of aggression, follow the example of Diplomacy, and meet it with softness and openness. You will be surprised at how kindness can undo hostility.

— from *Lady Avely's Guide to Guile and Peril*

JUDITH'S HEART sank like a rock. She had, foolishly, hoped that he might have improved in the short time she had been absent.

She drew a breath. "The better question might be: who are you? Do you remember anything at all?"

"I've already told you," he bit out, "that I do not."

"Not even your name?"

He scowled. "I'd rather you tell me yours again, and what right your butler had to manhandle me into this prison."

She edged further into the room, while he watched her stonily.

"I am a very old friend of yours. If you were in your right mind, I promise that you would be here gladly. I am the Marchioness of Lanyon, Judith Avely, but you first knew me as

Miss Judith Horis, a long time ago." She smoothed her skirts down nervously. "A few days ago, you and I were together at Garvey House, when you were snatched away by Captain Drumpellier. I followed you to the fort, and tried to speak in your defence, but no one would listen to me."

"What makes you so convinced of my innocence?" His arms were still rigidly folded, but she saw one hand flex against his bicep. "Right now, I feel as if I am quite capable of violent retribution."

She nodded carefully. "That is your Gift, your forceful Impact. It has been hard for you to control, especially when you were younger. Someone knew this and used it to frame you for murder."

He was silent for a long moment. "An appealing story, to absolve me of any guilt. And yet you hustle me into this gentle cage, and do not give me my freedom."

"Captain Drumpellier will come after you and search this castle high and low. I am trying to keep you safe."

"So you kidnapped me?" He raised a brow, something of his old amusement stirring. "A bold move for a lady."

"The matter is complex," she said defensively. "The captain isn't planning a fair trial for you. He intends to use you for another purpose."

"What other purpose?" His eyes narrowed.

"He wants you to assassinate Napoleon Bonaparte."

Dacian frowned. "The French general? That hardly seems fair play."

Judith resisted the urge to sweep the hair from his brow. She let her hands drop to her side. "Interesting that you retain notions of fair play and European politics and yet cannot remember anything else."

He shrugged. "It is a strange half-light in which I dwell. I remember many things that have nothing to do with me. Yet whenever I turn my mind to my own concerns, it remains frustratingly blank. I have dim memories of places, but no faces. And I can't remember anything of the last few days."

She reflected angrily that Drumpellier had taken advantage of this: freely made promises that Dacian would not remember. Fumbling in her bodice, she withdrew the letter that Dacian had written to her. "Read this. It is in your own hand: you wrote it to me yesterday."

He did not seem inclined to come closer and stared sceptically at the paper. Judith walked forward, holding it out. Reluctantly, he took it gingerly, as if it might be a shatterstone.

"It explains much," she pleaded. "And if you doubt it is your hand, you can try writing yourself and see how it matches." She nodded to the small writing desk in the corner.

He sank into the window seat. Unfolding the paper, he read it once, then again, and then a third time. A deep frown marred his brow.

Judith watched with her heart in her mouth. She well remembered the contents of that letter: *'Dear Judith, Of course I remember you...you have never been long out of my heart since then...lay my heart at your feet...I will find a way out of here myself, so please do not risk your own neck... I will come to Lanyon Castle when I can, after I have done what I must, for this grimly determined captain...'*

At long last, Dacian looked up and met her eyes. "It seems, from this, that I'm quite fond of you."

"Yes," said Judith, rather numbly, for he spoke with clinical detachment.

"It says *years*." He paused. "Have I indeed been courting you for years?"

"You could say that, yes. Though you were in exile abroad for nine of them."

Abruptly, he stood, casting the letter aside. Suddenly he seemed rather large in the small sitting room, towering over her. "And why didn't you accept my courtship? I am a duke, am I not?"

"You are, indeed." Judith swallowed. "But you lied to me, and pushed me away when I came to you, twenty years ago. You thought I was promised to your friend."

"And were you?" He took a step closer, eyes narrowed.

"Well...yes and no."

He raised his brows. "It sounds as if I behaved rather nobly."

"Nobly and stupidly," she retorted. "You lost us twenty years."

"Hm." His gaze remained hooded. "Perhaps you should remind me. Have we engaged in any intimate embraces?"

She swallowed. "We have kissed." He raised a brow and she hurried on. "Once when we were young...and then again, recently."

There was a longer pause. He tilted his head, suddenly thoughtful. "Perhaps we should try it again? It might trigger a memory in me."

Judith drew a breath, relieved to see the teasing gleam in his eye, and his hostile suspicion receding a little. She licked her bottom lip and saw how his gaze followed the movement. "I am not certain that is a good idea...However, it *is* true that our sense of smell can be very evocative." She hesitated. "Perhaps the smell of my hair might work instead...?"

He let out a huff of laughter. "If that is all you will offer me, I will take it." He smiled, and the arrogant charm in it suggested he was confident of further.

Tentatively, she undid the ribbons to her mobcap. Fascinated, his eyes followed her fingers, and she made slow work of it, pulling the cap off her head. She let it drop, holding his gaze. Then she pulled her hair looser, extracting pins and placing them on the dresser. His eyes were intent, and slightly amused.

"That's better, I must say. Can you undo your bodice as well?"

"Your grace! One thing at a time."

"Oh? So there's hope?" He took a step closer. Suddenly he was only two handspans away. "Well then. Come here, *my love*. Give me the scent of your hair."

She stepped into his arms willingly and put her head against his chest. She would have done anything for him, and she had been waiting to do this for a long time.

It was coming home. The glorious strength of his arms around her, and yes, the smell of him: smoke, leather, and some other indefinable masculine scent that was Dacian. He bent his head to the top of her head and drew a deep breath. His arms tightened around her.

"Mmmm," he said dazedly. "Very nice."

She blushed, nuzzling against his chest. "Any memories?"

"Not yet." He paused. "I think I might need to try further methods."

She turned her face up to his, caution melting away. "Very well."

He looked down, examining every inch of her face, and lifting a finger to trace along her cheek. "I do feel some sense of belonging. As if you are mine. Even though I don't even know who you are."

She nodded, wordless for a moment. "Yes. I am yours."

He kissed her then. His lips were warm and tentative at first. Then, when she did not resist, his mouth became demanding, claiming her. She clung to him, inviting everything, her hands winding through his thick dark hair, and pressing her body against the hard planes of him.

She moaned as the kiss deepened again. Coals flamed deep within her. But abruptly, Dacian pushed her away, holding her at arm's length.

"That does seem familiar." His voice was gravelly. "Like something from a dream."

"Yes."

"But I still don't remember you."

She blinked. "You want me to undo my bodice now?"

"Lady Avely!" He dropped his arms and his eyes swept down her body appreciatively. "Would I remember the sight?"

"You might," she confessed, blushing. "You watched me undress a week ago, though that was as far as it went."

He gaped, disbelieving. "Are you saying that you removed your clothes and I didn't make love to you? What sort of lily-livered fellow am I?"

"We had other concerns at the time," she said primly.

"What could possibly be more important?"

"Ah, well, we were trying to catch a murderer."

"Hm." He eyed her. "Well, if you wish to remove your bodice, I won't stop you. It might be the crucial step to regaining my memory. I think we should attempt it at once."

She blushed again. "No, it is too improper. I am essentially a stranger to you. I cannot possibly undo my bodice, even if you have seen me do so before."

"In fact, I remember you completely," he declared, staring at her bosom, which was still covered. "I utterly adore you. Let us repair to the bed at once."

She cocked a disbelieving eyebrow. "Then what is my favourite drink?"

His eyes flickered up. "Tea. Black. Preferably...oolong."

She sighed, her heart disappointed even though she could tell that he did not yet know her. He was looking at her with lust and warmth, certainly, but the light she usually found in his eyes was absent. "Sorry, your grace. Incorrect."

"Sherry? Port?" His voice became desperate. "Rum?"

She shook her head. "Chocolate."

"Damn it. Of course. I knew that."

A part of her thought it might well work to ravish him into himself—from all accounts, if there was anything the duke knew well, it was lovemaking—but she knew she would regret it later. She wanted to make love to the Dacian she knew, the man who knew all the stupid things that had come between them and was determined to have her at last. Not this stranger who had only just met her and was watching her now with amusement and regret.

"Well," he said, with a sigh. "Do we just wait for my memories to return? I can think of all sorts of experiments we might run to assist me, which do not require the removal of your bodice."

She cleared her throat. "We must simply wait. You recovered enough in a day or two after you first doses of Lethe, enough to write me that letter. We must be patient."

He picked up the letter, running his eyes over it again. Then he looked up accusingly. "It says here, '*Please, I beg of you, do not entertain any foolish plans to somehow breach the walls of this fort.*' And yet that is exactly what you did." He paused. "I suspect you do not show the ducal authority proper respect, Lady Avely."

"It was necessary! You must see that now. Captain Drumpellier made you another false promise—he swore he would give you your mind back, and now see where you are. It was imperative that I remove you from his clutches."

"And yet..." murmured Dacian. "How do I know you aren't just keeping me captive as a servant to your desires?"

"Dacian!"

"I'm locked in, am I not?" He gestured at the sitting room, with its pale cream and lavender walls, and the makeshift mattress set on the floor. "A prettier cell, I grant you, but a prison nonetheless."

She huffed, for the comparison stung, and she felt in her

pockets for his topaz ring. She held it out, hoping he would take it as a sign of her good faith. "Take this: you may not remember, but it is yours, a Travel Ring. If you twist it with the word *veho*, it will transport you out of here, in a blink. Though I am afraid it will only take you back to a tower in Fort Pendennis."

Dacian grimaced as he slipped the ring onto his finger. "Not exactly an enticing prospect."

"And you may have a brief stroll in the corridors, if you like," she added reluctantly. "Ltn Greene told me that the captain is away for a day or two, so we have a small respite. Though the lieutenant himself might pay us a visit, so you must be careful."

Turning, she tried the handle of the door, only to find it immovable. After some banging, however, Trebellow (who must have followed her to the eastern master bedroom to stand guard) opened it and stood aside, blinking blearily. Clearly the butler was under the influence of the Humdrum Spell, for he barely restrained a yawn at the sight of her.

She was relieved, however, that he was distracted from her flushed face and missing mobcap. "Trebellow," she said with some dignity. "The duke is going to take a turn about the castle. I have explained matters to him, and I expect you to treat him with all due respect. And please reverse the Defence spells on the door so he can come and go as he likes."

Trebellow bowed extremely low. "It will be an honour, your grace."

Dacian eyed him. "No more tackling me to the ground, you huge hill of flesh."

"Shakespeare?" remarked Judith. "A pity you can't remember something more to the point." Briskly she led the way through the Humdrum Spell and gave herself a little shake once she was out into the corridor. Boredom was an odd sensation to experience, however briefly, after all that had happened. She turned to see Dacian blinking and frowning. "Yes, that was a Diplomacy spell," she explained. "Set up by my housekeeper to turn away prying eyes."

"Ah, the redoubtable Mrs Ulrich? The battle-axe who brought our fisticuffs to an end? She's certainly a force to be reckoned with. Is there any food to be had, by the way?"

She was glad to see this as a sign he was recovering his spirits. "I'm going to the breakfast room now. The boys are there: the ones who kidnapped you, but please be polite. You know Robert; perhaps the sight of him now might recall something."

Dacian followed close behind. "If the taste of your lips does not trigger any recollection," he murmured in her ear, "I highly doubt that some lad will do so."

In which there is brief respite

A nap cures all ills. Usually.
— from *Lady Avely's Guide to Guile and Peril*

WHEN THEY REACHED the breakfast room, Judith went in first, into the smell of freshly baked apple pie, cream, and coffee. She saw Perry slouched by the window, looking rather sulky and spooning cream into his mouth. Robert was on the floor, his back against the wall, a hand tightly clasped to his wounded leg and a bowl of apple pie on the ground next to him. She was glad that Mrs Ulrich had bestirred herself enough to provide suitable rations, even at this late hour. In the dark outside, she could hear wind whistling past the windows.

"My dear boys!" she said. "You did superbly!"

Perry looked over. "I didn't realise that I'd have to wrestle two mountains at once! You need to keep your butler in check, Mother!"

"I do apologise," she said sympathetically. "Any lasting damage done?"

"No, but Robert's leg pains him."

"It's fine," said Robert, though he looked a little pale. Then he started in surprise. "Your grace!"

He began to clamber to his feet, for Dacian had come into the room with Trebellow. The duke put up a staying hand, and Robert sank back against the wall, staring.

Dacian looked between them. "You pair of rampallians! How dare you assault the ducal person?"

Robert looked pained. "Lady Avely's orders, your grace. I sincerely apologise."

Perry spoke up. "I said you might not like it. But she was convinced we shouldn't leave you there." He examined the duke closely, then his eyes moved curiously to Judith, who suddenly wished she had put her mobcap back on.

Dacian went over to pour himself some coffee. "Which one of you is Robert?"

"Me." Robert's eyes widened. "You don't remember?"

"No." Dacian spoke calmly, but Judith could tell he was uncomfortable to be at such a disadvantage. He stirred some sugar into his coffee. "*How* do I know you, exactly?"

Robert's lips clamped together, and he shot a glance at Judith. She gave a slight shrug of her shoulders. Robert would not want to announce the nature of their history before Perry, but she did not want to lie to Dacian.

"You saw to my schooling," said Robert finally. "I am greatly in your debt."

Perry's head snapped around. "*His grace* saw to your schooling at Taunton? How on earth...? My Uncle Gerald has no connection with the Duke of Sargen!"

There was an awkward silence as Dacian raised his eyebrows. He clearly didn't have the answer.

"It's complicated," said Robert hastily. "It doesn't matter now. Lady Avely, shouldn't we be afraid of pursuit?"

She shook her head. "Apparently Drumpellier is away in Ireland for a couple of days," she explained, pouring herself a cup of coffee and spooning in a liberal amount of cream, "so we have a small reprieve, for he only left this morning. But Perry, you must leave at once. Lieutenant Greene will recognise you if he pays us a visit."

"What about Robert? The lieutenant saw him too." Perry brightened. "Maybe I should take Robert with me back to Devonshire! He could meet his cousin Elinor too, and she won't even be sick all over you now, Bob."

Robert looked startled at this charming offer (and possibly the nickname) and opened his mouth to refuse.

But Judith shook her head. "No, Robert must stay here and rest, not further strain his injury. He has the advantage, don't forget, of being able to melt into the wall if need be."

"Oh?" Dacian also helped himself to a bowl of cream and apple pie. "Is that some sort of vanishing spell?"

"No, Illusion," she explained. "Robert is very Gifted. He conjured up the uniforms the boys were wearing when they rescued you. Perry is the one who transported you all to the castle, and he must transport himself off now."

Perry yawned. "I confess, I'm a bit weary. And I'm looking forward to sleeping in a proper bed at Beresford House, now that we've berthed."

"Off you go, I insist," said Judith.

Perry made his farewells and vanished sleepily. Judith frowned down at Robert with concern and offered to bandage up his leg again.

"It's fine." Robert glanced at the duke uneasily. "Why can't you remember us, your grace? I thought that your memory had returned."

Dacian shrugged. "I don't remember that either, I'm afraid. Completely undone."

"The captain is a traitorous dog," said Judith darkly. "He betrayed his agreement to you. I'll wring his false, lying neck when I see him again."

"It doesn't make sense," objected Robert. "Drumpellier had obtained the duke's cooperation; why undo all his negotiations?"

"Because he wanted blind obedience," Judith snapped, "not a compromise. He wanted to throw Dacian to the wolves. It would be far more difficult to bring him safely out of Austria once the deed was done."

"I don't know what you're talking about," said Dacian, around a mouthful of apple pie. "But you should try this, Lady Avely, it is superb."

She sat down at the breakfast table, ignoring the pang she felt as he continued to use her title. The pie *was* delicious: the warm, sweet apple covered in thick pastry and slathered with the richest cream she had ever tasted. It seemed that the young cook, while terrible at soups, had a talent for apple pie. It was almost enough to make up for the awful suppers so far.

As they ate, she and Robert explained things further to Dacian. He listened with interest but showed no flashes of recognition at their convoluted tale. Eventually, she sighed and gave up.

"You are much better off trying to sleep," she advised. "Rest is likely the best cure. And I'd feel better if you were tucked away safely."

Robert had limped over to sit at the table with her. "Shouldn't we smuggle him out of the castle, while we have the chance?"

She had considered this, but rejected the notion. "Why risk it, when we have the best hidey-hole in all of Cornwall? His grace will be like a lost lamb wandering around without his memory."

"I'm happy to stay here," said Dacian, draining the rest of his coffee. "Especially if we undertake several attempts to jog my memory."

Judith tried not to blush and failed.

Robert looked between them. "There must be some remedy we can try, an herb or tincture. Perhaps Mrs Ulrich will know."

When summoned to the breakfast room, Mrs Ulrich suggested green tea infused with sage and promised to deliver a pot to the secret sitting room. Judith led Dacian back to it and installed him once more, bidding him to go to sleep after his tea.

"One more kiss," he suggested. "It might work this time."

She obliged, stepping into his arms and pressing her lips against his. He took his time, slowly savouring, until their embrace became heated once more.

Judith stepped back, flushed and wanting. "Still nothing?"

His pupils were dilated, his breath ragged. "I remember everything."

She smiled, hearing the lie. "Truly?"

"No." His shoulders sank. "Curse it."

She didn't trust herself to stay in the room any longer. So she left him sitting on the makeshift bed, his hair dishevelled, his shirt undone, and scowling at the suggestion that he should sleep.

YET, in the morning, he still did not know her.

Judith awoke late and sat up in alarm as the events of the night rushed back into consciousness. They must expect the lieutenant today, or even the captain.

She cast aside her blankets, slipped a robe over her night-dress, then hurried down to Dacian's room. This time she found that the door would not budge an inch when she tried the hidden handle, and she had to call for Dacian to let her in.

He opened the door, standing before her in an equal state of immodesty: his chest bare under a silk dressing gown. A cup of coffee sat by the window seat, its aroma filling the room along with that of a plate of eggs, bacon, and toast.

"Well?" she demanded.

He swept her with an admiring gaze. "You are still a beautiful stranger." He sighed at her disappointed look. "But I do remember a bit more of my estate, and my family. Are my parents alive?"

"No," she said. "I'm sorry."

His lips twisted. "I suspected as much; the memories have a childish quality to them." He appraised her. "You look lovely this morning. Do come in."

She clasped the dressing gown before her as he shut the door. "You look rather charming yourself. Can you not remember how to tie a cravat?"

She had thought about reuniting Dacian with Wooten, but she dared not while they were both so out of sorts. Dacian might call Wooten a flittermouse again and cause the little bat to have an apoplexy. Or worse, Wooten might not blink an eye at the appellation, or inform Dacian that the ducal person was a mild improvement on a bovine.

Now Dacian preened, pushing a lock of black hair aside, and did nothing to cover his bare chest. "Shall we resume our attempts to recover my memory?"

Judith huffed a laugh. "Some of your character remains."

"Oh? Am I a lustful degenerate?" He grinned. "I am merely seeking truth, by whatever means possible."

"First some food."

"Indeed, my lady." He led her to the window seat, poured her a cup of coffee, and they shared his plate. They talked amiably together, but it plucked at her heart to see that he still, subtly, spoke to her as a stranger, albeit one whose bosoms he admired. Dear, cursed libertine. His tone remained a little cool, flirtatious to be sure, but in the manner of a nobleman parlaying at court, with a practiced dexterity rather than real passion.

He seemed to sense her disconsolation, for after a while he set his cup of coffee aside and eyed her. "Time for another reprise, I think. Come here."

The authority of the order made her shiver with desire. Yet, when she didn't move, he stood and came to her side, holding out a hand. "May I?" His smile was teasing. "I think I should become reacquainted with your delightful curves."

He was so handsome and had such a gleam in his eye that Judith could not resist. It *might* work, after all. She stepped into his arms again and surrendered to his kisses. They were long, sensuous, and practiced. This, she reasoned, was more of his character returning: the treatment all his widows had received. Her heart gave a pang. She was in the unenviable position where if he dallied with her now, he was effectively betraying her with herself. She consoled herself with the thought that flirting was like breathing to him, and she shouldn't take it amiss. Especially as he couldn't remember her at all.

Soon his strong hands moved to grasp her hips. She decided that was permissible, seeing as Dacian had already taken such liberties. Perhaps the shape of her *derrière* would remind him.

But no. He merely groaned again, pulling her hard against him, then pushing her away again, his dark eyes molten. "I'm certain I haven't been satisfied for years. Was I a monk in Spain?"

She started. "Yes! You were! Have you remembered?"

"God, no." He was aghast. "I was a *monk*? I don't believe it! I was a complete namby-pamby of a man!"

"The vows take great self-discipline," she said, prim once

more. "And it wasn't for the whole nine years, I'm certain of that. You told me you also spent some time incognito as the Count of Querrento."

"He sounds more virile, if somewhat ridiculous." He rubbed his brow. "But how am I to remember myself if I have several selves?"

"I assure you, there was a constant Dacian beneath all of them." She brushed her robe down, reluctantly conceding that further kisses would be unwise. And at that moment, the sound of distant voices and hurried footsteps intruded.

They both looked over as a knock sounded sharply on the hidden door.

"Ma'am," came Mrs Ulrich's disapproving voice. "Lady Avely? I'm afraid that you have a visitor."

"Who?" she asked nervously.

"It is Ltn Greene," came the reply. "He says it is a matter of extreme urgency."

"Oh dear." Judith looked over to Dacian. "The lieutenant has discovered your absence. I must be under suspicion."

"Will you let me in?" demanded Mrs Ulrich. "I cannot be seen out here talking to the wall."

Judith winced, and grabbed at her dressing gown, tying it tightly. She opened the door, holding her head high as Mrs Ulrich marched in.

Her housekeeper majestically ignored her state of undress. "Quickly, ma'am. You need to be ready to receive guests. And your grace must stay as quiet as a newt until they have gone."

"Yes, ma'am," he replied meekly.

Judith gave him a small smile, then hurried out after Mrs Ulrich, leaving Dacian sitting morosely on the window seat.

Hot water and a clean gown were laid out in the Captain's Cabin, along with a fresh mobcap. Hastily she washed herself down and dressed in the black chiffon, while the housekeeper informed her of everyone's whereabouts. The lieutenant was impatiently waiting in the Blue Drawing Room, guarded by Trebellow. Robert was hiding in the ballroom in plain sight, and the rest of the staff had been instructed to forget they had ever met him. Miss Onslow had been escorted to the secret room in the cellars and locked in from both sides, with Kade outside 'cleaning' the underground hall. Baron Quarles was still missing, and Judith hoped he was far away.

"Have you tidied Robert's room, so it looks unused?" Judith carefully fixed her new mobcap on: a pretty black velvet one with lace edges. A widow's cap, which would be a further lure for the duke, except that she couldn't think of that now.

"Of course," said Mrs Ulrich. "I should mention that your companion, Miss Cultor, returned very early this morning, accompanied by another lady vampiri, by the name of Miss Belfleur."

"Oh?" Judith was surprised. "Did they fly all night? They must be exhausted."

"They are both asleep in the cupboard compartment." Mrs Ulrich nodded at the wardrobe. "Together."

Judith did not comment, though she was glad that Marigold had softened a little towards Miss Belfleur, enough to invite her into her hidden chamber. She told herself that the two of them would be far too exhausted to attempt any scenes of seduction, then remembered that vampiri had supernatural healing powers. Oh well. At least *someone* might be properly seduced today, if not her. She sighed.

"Thank you, Mrs Ulrich." Judith stood, brushing down her skirts. "Now, let us confound the lieutenant."

But when they reached the Blue Drawing Room, Ltn Greene was nowhere to be seen.

In which the castle is inundated

In the thrust and parry of heated argument, we can overlook the obvious.

— from *Lady Avely's Guide to Guile and Peril*

INSTEAD, Trebellow was there, looking outraged.

"I tried to stop him, but he vanished!" The butler held out a note. "He left you this, ma'am."

Judith snatched it and unfolded it quickly.

Dear Lady A,

The captain is looking for the duke. I will do my best to hold him off, but he will be at Castle Lanyon shortly.

Play innocent, and keep your prize hidden.

Also, I mentioned Miss Onslow's perfidy, and he refused to believe it. I advise you to wait until he has vented some of his spleen before broaching the subject again.

Yours faithfully,

G.

Judith looked up, staring at Trebellow. "Ltn Greene knows!"

"Knows what?" said Mrs Ulrich grimly.

"He knows we have the duke, but he seems to want to help us." She thrust the note at her housekeeper, guessing by Trebellow's lack of surprise that he had already acquainted himself with the contents. "*Why* is he helping us?"

She frowned, tapping her foot as Mrs Ulrich read the note with frowning confusion. Ltn Greene had always seemed sympathetic to them, right from the start, with his disapproval at how Drumpellier had treated the duke. Was it due to his reverence for nobility? Or his sympathy at Drumpellier's high-handed tactics?

Whatever the reason, she would take his help and ask questions later.

She turned with resolution to her housekeeper. "Quick," she said. "Warn his grace we must expect the captain. And then, Mrs Ulrich, we must launch the rest of our plan."

Mrs Ulrich left. Judith glanced around the Blue Drawing Room, seeing that while she had been indulging in attempts to revive the duke's memory, her retainers had put the room to rights. There was no sign of the recent violence wrought there. She nodded in approval, and then hurried up to the Tea Tower Room, this time finding her way with ease.

She did *not* want to be in the Blue Drawing Room when Drumpellier arrived. Furthermore, the comforting glow of the Tea Tower Room might soothe her nerves. She had a part to play now, and she stopped by her room first to fetch her embroidery—it would have to do, along with her black mobcap and widow's gown, to cast a veneer of matronly respectability.

Mrs Ulrich had also set out a tea tray for her, which was very thoughtful. Judith found that her hands were shaking as she poured the boiling water from the hearth into the teapot, but the strong brew calmed her, pleasantly hot. She drank a full cup and then picked up her embroidery, giving herself a sharp dressing down: there was no need to worry. Dacian was out of harm's way, and she had the tools to negotiate with Drumpellier. She was just lucky that Ltn Greene had given them all sufficient warning. And in the meanwhile, she could work on Elinor's wedding handkerchiefs.

She didn't have long to wait. Within a quarter of an hour, she heard booted heels marching up the tower stairs. Trebellow's voice protested loudly further below.

A moment later, Drumpellier burst in. He glared around the circular, beautiful room, then fixed a fulminating look on Judith.

"*Where is he?*"

Judith calmly laid down her embroidery. "Where is who?"

"You know very well who: the duke!"

She drew a deep breath, widening her eyes, feigning surprise. "The duke? Don't tell me you've lost him!"

"You snatched him! I know it!"

"My dear sir," she said, with great hauteur. "How dare you suggest such a thing? How could I possibly *snatch* his grace? I would never be so vulgar!"

"You were there last night! Ltn Greene told me! With your Travel charm!"

Judith's lips twisted. Obviously, the lieutenant had not felt he could lie about her presence, which was probably wise, as it had been witnessed by several other soldiers. "If you know that," she said icily, "you also know that Ltn Greene escorted me home—without the duke."

"What were you doing at the fort, then?"

Trebellow burst into the room, puffing from his pursuit up the stairs. "My apologies, ma'am. He arrived precipitately!"

"Never mind, Trebellow, I am well aware of the captain's tendency to treat my drawing room as his own," she said coolly. "I was just explaining to him why I was at the Fort Pendennis last night. I wished to speak to his grace, which I did. And I have strong remarks to make to you in return! His grace had lost his memory again! How dare you make false promises to him, then undo his wits once more!"

"Nonsense," snapped Drumpellier. "Do not accuse me of dishonourable conduct when you have been shamefully opprobrious!"

"Explain to me then, why he did not recognise me at all! He was utterly blank when I saw him on guard duty!"

Drumpellier's eyes slitted. "You told me that he did not know you, in the cell when you saw him last."

With a start, she remembered that Drumpellier did not know of Dacian's letter, and the secret signal he had given her. "Nonetheless, I heard you offer him a compromise. Why was it abandoned? What has happened since then?"

Captain Drumpellier ground his teeth. "I don't know what happened, but I wager you do." He began striding around the room, twitching at curtains and glaring at the couches as if Dacian might be tucked underneath one.

Judith grew angrier, or at least put on the assumption of it, grateful for Ltn Greene's warning. "I know nothing! Unless it is that you have foolishly lost him! Did you ply him with Lethe again? It would not surprise me if he went wild, and broke his way out of that dreadful fort, with his mind addled and his Gift untrammelled."

"As far as I can tell," gritted out Drumpellier, "his grace vanished into thin air. He must have had help, and I know exactly where to look for that!"

"You flatter me," said Judith, keeping her hands firmly folded over her embroidery needle. Drumpellier certainly had a very angry bee in his bonnet. "Perhaps I hid his grace under my skirts when Ltn Greene escorted me home?"

"Do not mock me," growled Drumpellier, "I will search this

castle high and low until I find him. *And* whoever helped him—some lackey of yours, I assume. And then you will *all* be hanged for treason!"

Judith stiffened, glad that Perry was now far away, but feeling a little anxious for Robert. And the mention of treason recalled her bargaining chip: Miss Onslow, imprisoned deep below, and the certain knowledge that Drumpellier's plans were wrecked in a far more decisive manner. She was mindful, however, of Ltn Greene's advice that this was a touchy subject and best avoided for the moment. Looking at the captain's red face, she didn't think the negotiation would be well received. He was in too much of a frothing rage. Better to wait, as the lieutenant suggested, until he had vented some of his spleen flinging himself all over the castle, and then they could have a rational conversation.

At that moment, too, Ltn Greene himself appeared in the door. He darted a questioning look at Judith, then turned respectfully to his captain, throwing out a hasty salute. "Sir, the platoon is assembled outside, as you requested."

"Bring them in," snarled Drumpellier. "I want every nook and cranny searched, do you hear me? And guards at every door. This castle is under military watch until we find him."

"Yes, sir!"

Slightly mollified, Drumpellier turned and gave Judith a savage smile. "The lieutenant here is a Healor, ma'am, in case you were unaware."

"Yes, I was aware," said Judith, "but I am incognisant of the relevance, unless you find his grace injured, which would not surprise me at all. He has probably gone utterly mad under your ill treatment."

"Some healors can sense blood and bone, and Ltn Green is one of them," replied Drumpellier with some satisfaction, "and he will personally search this castle from top to bottom."

Judith stared back, as impassively as she could manage. Behind Drumpellier, the lieutenant gave her a wink, so she was hard put to remain expressionless.

"You will find nothing," she said coldly. "And if his grace has managed to effect an escape, I say good luck to him. He is probably already in London."

Drumpellier narrowed his eyes. "*You* stay here until I say you can leave, and I expect your servants to assist me in every way. Trebellow, follow me."

The butler ignored him and looked to Judith. She gave a short nod. Drumpellier spun angrily on his heel, ordering Ltn Greene to come with him too. The three men left.

Judith sat very still, listening to their heavy treads receding. She recalled Ltn Greene's wink, and remembered how he had winked before, on the ramparts last night. Had he known even *then* that she had snatched the duke away? What game was he playing?

Shakily, she picked up her embroidery and made a valiant attempt to continue with it. After a few minutes, her efforts paid off, as she managed to focus on the delicate stitches and calm herself. Far beneath the Tea Tower Room, she could hear soldiers tramping all over the castle, shouting instructions. It was a very big castle. It would take them a while to exhaust themselves searching all one hundred and twenty-one rooms. One hoped they would all become as lost as she had done.

One thing puzzled her more and more: why Ltn Greene had taken the unprecedented step of acting against his superior. In concealing the duke, his actions amounted to nothing less than mutiny. Did Ltn Greene know something that she did not? Did he feel he would be granted immunity by the Custos command further up the chain once Drumpellier's outrageous plot was revealed? Her needles clacked quietly as she pondered the question, wondering how she could turn this alliance to her further advantage. If the lieutenant sensed Dacian's hiding place, would he stay silent? Devoutly, she hoped Dacian would stay quiet. Drumpellier had been very angry. If he found the duke, he might hurl him into Austria at once.

A small smile tugged at her lips. "Opprobrious conduct" indeed! How dare Drumpellier call *her* actions shameful, when he had erased Dacian's memories again, despite his gentlemen's agreement.

Suddenly, she put her embroidery down in her lap, as a thought occurred to her. Drumpellier had denied the charge, calling it nonsense. Her brow creased, trying to recall the tenor of his denial. Oddly, she could not remember it ringing with the hollowness of a lie, though she had readily assumed it at the time, being so angry herself. "Nonsense!" he had declared, and the more she thought about it, the less she was certain it had been mendacious.

Had Drumpellier indeed being telling the truth?

She didn't want to believe it, and it didn't make sense. If Drumpellier had not drugged the duke, then how had Dacian lost his memories again?

Judith bit on her lower lip. It could have been a relapse, a delayed effect. *Or* someone else could have given him the dose.

An uneasy feeling trickled through her veins. Ltn Greene had been in charge of Fort Pendennis in Drumpellier's absence. He would have had access to Lethe. He could have slipped it into Dacian's food or wine. He could have done it at the barracks, either at supper or breakfast while Drumpellier was away. Dacian would not have suspected him.

Judith stared out the window, her embroidered handkerchief lax in her hands, her heart beating rather hard. Ltn Greene had shrugged her question off last night, and at the time she had thought he was protecting his captain, not willing to admit the truth. But what if the truth was that *he* had done the deed himself?

But why would Ltn Greene want to undo Dacian's mind again?

The answer struck her with sudden clarity, and a swooping sensation of dismay. Dacian and the captain had finally come to an agreement. What if the lieutenant had been trying to *undo* that compromise? What if he was eager to hide the duke because he didn't want that weapon in Drumpellier's hands to be wielded against Bonaparte?

Her pulse beat in her throat. She finally realised the awful truth: Ltn Greene was acting for the enemy. It was he, not Quarles, who was Miss Onslow's minder. He was a French spy, working from within Fort Pendennis itself. And now he was prowling around Castle Lanyon, under her own aegis.

Shakily, she thrust her embroidery aside and stood. But even as she took a step towards the door, she heard boots again on the stairs. Wringing her hands together, she hoped desperately it would be Drumpellier, so she could come clean and lay the whole tangle before him.

But it was not Drumpellier who appeared at the door, but his lieutenant.

In which a captain is resolute

A generous action might conceal an injurious intent.
  — from *Lady Avely's Guide to Guile and Peril*

LTN GREENE SHUT the door behind him and turned to smile at Judith. She stood still, trying to paste a welcoming expression upon her face. Words stuck in her throat like dry wool.

"You've done a wonderful job of concealment," he said, admiringly, and came into the room. "I would never have known that sitting room was there, if I could not sense the duke inside. Who cast such a brilliant Illusion?"

She ignored the question. "Is the duke safe?"

"Yes, I haven't told anyone." He bowed his head. "Drumpellier's plot is abhorrent, as I'm sure you agree."

She was reminded of Miss Onslow's careful half-truths. Of course, it must have been Ltn Greene who had warned Miss Onslow that she was dealing with a Truth Discernor. The two of them had been working together all along.

"Thank you." Judith licked her lips. "I am grateful for your help."

Ltn Greene gave her a close look. "It is the least I could do." He tipped his head. "Has his grace recovered his memory yet?"

"Not yet."

"How *did* you whisk him out of there?"

"I had help. Friends." She hesitated. "They've gone now."

Ltn Greene raised his brows. "Both of them?"

"Yes," she said. "They Travelled out of here."

There was a long pause, and too late Judith realised her mistake, for as a Healor he would have found Robert's hiding place. He sighed, tapping a finger against his thigh. "A Truth Discernor, lying to me. Why would you do that, ma'am?"

She said nothing, and he took a step towards her. Watching him, it was as if her vision wavered then straightened. Ltn Greene's friendly, faintly apologetic look vanished, to be replaced with grim determination. The blinking eyes hardened, his lips thinned, and even his cheeks seemed to grow hollower.

"You've figured it out, haven't you?" His voice was no longer friendly. "A clever little Discernor."

"Figured what out?" she said stupidly, in a bid to play innocence. But her eyes darted to the door.

He stepped in front of it. "Ah, suddenly you wish to leave! But not yet, I'm afraid. Though you've been most helpful," he added. "My poor captain is so focused on your meddling that he hasn't noticed mine."

She swallowed. How could she have been fooled by his act of boyish charm? "What do you mean? What meddling?"

"There is no need to look so worried: our interests align, Lady Avely. I tried to help his grace from the start, surely you know that? I gave him some untainted food, in a bid to help him recover his memories. It worked for a while, and he became quite recalcitrant." He sighed. "Then Drumpellier got to him, with some sort of gentleman's agreement, if you can believe it." Disdain smeared the lieutenant's features, as if he did not believe it possible for Drumpellier to behave with nobility.

Judith said nothing. Dacian had written of an unexpected ally. She had thought he meant Yvette, but he must have been referring to Greene, trying to muddy the waters by helping him.

"And then you undid it all," she said finally. "Why?"

"Oh, I hoped that the duke might skewer the assassination plot, if he lost his memory again." Ltn Greene paused. "But then you appeared, with your little rescue attempt! So I turned a blind eye while you whisked him away. It was quite pleasing to sit back and watch the chaos unfold."

She turned her back to him and walked to the window. Anger swirled through her, clouding her vision. Anger at Ltn Greene, as well as with herself. She should have questioned the circumstances more. Instead, she had eagerly accepted his help and assumed the worst of Drumpellier.

"I suppose you ordered Miss Onslow to kill Sgt Finlay," she said calmly.

"Oh no. She did that all by herself, stupid girl. Finlay might have worked for *us* if we gave him enough inducement. Who cares if he was a libertine? She didn't need to murder him for it. Still, she managed it quite well—except then she tried to kill me. I suppose she decided she wanted to end the game and make amends."

Judith turned her head. "Why didn't she tell me yesterday then, when I interrogated her?"

Ltn Greene shrugged. "I suppose she didn't want to admit to another crime. Or she thought I would rescue her. She saw my man yesterday morning, after all, and she had the latest dispatch, so perhaps she thought she had some bargaining power over me. But I've got all that now. I found her in your little tunnel, deep in the earth, which suits her well enough." He smiled at Judith's expression. "Don't worry, I haven't killed her, though she might deserve it." Ltn Greene pursed his lips. "She might still be useful, if she doesn't try shooting at me again."

Judith cursed herself now for not telling Drumpellier about Miss Onslow, and trusting Ltn Greene's instructions. What a fool she had been. She put her chin in the air. "And what are you going to do with *me*?"

"Continue to help you, of course," said Ltn Greene pleasantly. "As I mentioned, we have the same aim, as much as you may abhor it. I don't want such a powerful weapon in Drumpellier's hands, and you want the duke far from here. So we shall work together."

Judith grimaced, an odd mixture of interest and repulsion warring within her. She could *not* accept the help of this weasel; Dacian would never forgive her. And yet, right at this moment, Dacian was curiously impotent, stuck behind a wallpapered door without his wits. Which made him all the more vulnerable to the lieutenant's plots.

Still, her heart balked at helping this traitor.

"I refuse." She turned to gaze out the window. "We can do without your help, thank you very much."

Ltn Greene sighed, coming up to stand close behind her. She repressed the urge to lean away.

"I thought you might say that." His voice was soft. "So I took the liberty of taking that young man into my custody. Robert Avely, I think his name is?"

Judith's head snapped around, in mute question.

"I found him pretending to be a pillar in the ballroom: a

good disguise, but I could sniff him out easily, at the rate his heart was thumping. I waited for the troops to leave, then I confronted him and bound his wrists."

To her horror, she saw him lift a finger to pull a chain out from his breast pocket. It looked very much like the chain that had hung from Drumpellier's: the mechanism that connected to the wristbreaker cuffs.

"Yes," said Ltn Greene, smiling at her appalled look. "The bracelets fit him quite snugly."

Her heart leapt with terror. "He's just a boy! Leave him out of this!"

"He is a rather talented Illusor," Greene corrected her. "Such prodigious talent could be most useful. But I haven't got the time to chat about that. The point is that you must help me, or his wrists will snap with a yank of this chain."

To her utter dismay, she could hear that he was telling the truth. Her skin crawled at the thought of Robert's artist's hands being destroyed so cavalierly. She gritted out, "I don't believe you. Take me to him and show me that he still lives."

Ltn Greene laughed, amused. "My dear lady, you are a Truth Discernor, so you know very well that I am not lying. I'll add, for your elucidation, that Mr Avely is rather frightened at the moment, because I've also tied a cloth round his eyes. Regardless, you will have to trust me on the matter: he is bound and at my mercy."

Judith was silent a long moment, hearing the bell of truth, and trying to keep her rage leashed. "What is it that you want me to do?"

"You must stay quiet about Miss Onslow. And keep your duke hidden, which I'm certain you will be only too glad to do. Once we have the dear captain clear of the place, we can negotiate further."

Judith narrowed her eyes. Negotiate further? What reason would this snivelling snake have to keep them all alive, when they could betray him in the future? But she could hear no lie in his voice, and further, she could see no alternative but to go along with him for now. Not while Robert was captive.

"Very well," she said coldly. "How do you want me to fend off Drumpellier?"

"He is growing too curious about the cellars. I fear that he is about to discover the secret passageway where you stashed Miss Onslow, despite that handy little Illusion over the arch. You must distract him."

She looked away. "It will simply make him more suspicious if I approach him now."

"Exactly." Ltn Greene said approvingly. "Instead, I will tell him I sense an unknown presence moving over our heads, and he will rush to investigate, only to find you surreptitiously lurking in the northern corridor. I believe you already have a decoy set up there?"

Judith scowled. "We cannot run that trick if we do not have Robert's help with his Illusions. Hand him back, and we will do better."

"No," said Ltn Greene. "You'll have to stage your little show without him, I'm afraid. But I have every confidence in you, Lady Avely. Your duke and your boy are at stake."

THE FIRST PART of the plan worked rather well, much to Judith's irritation. But what else had she expected? She had put it all in place herself.

She trod along the norther corridor, heavily. It was a long corridor, the allegedly haunted one, and gloomily she imagined herself as the Crimson Lady, stomping along in a ghostly huff.

Mrs Ulrich had installed the Dread Spell over one of the doors, so it was quite easy to fall into the right mood: one of bleak despair and grief.

It was mixed with her own anger and guilt that she had not realised the truth earlier. She had so stupidly trusted the lieutenant. And now, because of her idiocy, Robert was cuffed and frightened, somewhere in the far reaches of the castle. She couldn't even send Marigold to look for him, as the vampiri was currently fast asleep, probably in the cosy embrace of Miss Belfleur.

Never had Judith cursed the daylight more. The tall windows along the northern corridor let in long slanting rectangles of light, showing the dust motes floating in the air. She swished her skirts to stir them to greater eddies and stomped slowly along the wooden floorboards. She had to enact this plan without any support and with a crucial piece missing: Robert's Illusion. It was doubtful that it would work, but for Robert's sake, she had to try.

Dourly, she thought of Ghastagon and his goat-like keening. If only he could usefully project a suitable wail at an opportune moment to support her performance! But like all cats, he existed to bask in adoration, and not to be useful.

At least, she reflected as she trudged along, this diversion kept the search away from Dacian. That had been its original intention, after all.

Within minutes of her dreary promenade, just as predicted, Captain Drumpellier stormed into the far entrance, bursting through the archway like an avenging angel.

She started guiltily, without even having to pretend.

"What are you doing here?" he shouted, his sensitive brow creased into a thunderous frown.

"Nothing at all," she said, without any conviction whatsoever.

His booted heels clicked loudly as he marched across the wooden floor. "I told you to stay in the tower room."

"I was hungry for luncheon." It was an obvious half-truth, for there was no food to be found in the northern corridor, only dust and shrouded rooms. "I am looking for my housekeeper or my butler," she added with hauteur.

"You won't find them here," he retorted with suspicion.

She gave a small grimace, then let her shoulders droop. "If you *must* know, I am lost."

"Oh, really?" His suspicion grew.

"I can never find my way around this cursed castle," she confessed. "I thought I was heading towards the Blue Drawing Room, but now I'm here. It is most infuriating! I've spent the last three days wandering around in circles."

The truth of this, and the real irritation in her voice, seemed to allay some of Drumpellier's scepticism. "You shouldn't be wandering around at all! I told you to stay put."

"I tried to ring the bell for assistance," she flung back. "My servants seem to have become deaf. Have you seen them?"

"I have restrained them until further notice," he snapped. "Your housekeeper seems to have aged a century since I saw her last: her notion of assistance has been to move as slowly as humanly possible. And your butler has become as clever as a cannonball left too long in the neck. So I've put them in the cellar."

This was bad news. Judith looked down her nose at him. "How dare you lock up my servants! You go too far, Captain!"

"Well, I will only release your servants once I have the duke in custody," he said implacably. "And I would also like to know why the cellar is laid out in carpets, with paintings on the walls. It looks as if you intend to hold a royal reception there. A residence for a duke perhaps?"

Judith drew herself up. "Nonsense. That is the business of Castle Lanyon, and I am not bound to divulge it."

They scowled at each other: the matron and the captain both exerting their authority. It seemed as if it would be a stalemate, but then Drumpellier seemed to notice the Dread Spell for the first time. His blazing anger had protected him initially, but now he twisted his head round, frowning deeply.

"What is *that*?"

His shoulders hunched slightly as he felt the full force of Mrs Ulrich's worst. Judith sympathised. She quite felt like bursting into tears herself.

Instead, she tilted her head in polite enquiry. "To what do you refer, precisely?"

"You sense it too." His eyes darted around the corridor. "That dreadful feeling. As if I'm about to die of misery. Are you doing it to me?"

"Ah no," she replied blandly. "That would be the Lady. She haunts these corridors. You warned me about her, except you misdirected me to the cellars."

His head snapped back to stare at her. "Oh, is that so?"

"You can feel it, can you not? I've heard her footsteps in the night, too, when I was wandering around. The story goes that she was killed hundreds of years ago: her suitor, Lord Lanyon, threw a boulder and unfortunately it landed on her head. You must be sensitive to her presence," she added kindly. "Most feel a simple brush of sorrow, or the faint shiver of grief."

Drumpellier shuddered. The spell was currently more like an avalanche of despair. His face went pale above his red coat. Yet he squared his shoulders and, just as she suspected, he was not deterred. In fact, like her, he was suspicious of such an excessive display.

Resolutely, he turned to face the direction of the Dread Spell. He took firm steps towards it, bracing against the onslaught. Judith watched with some fellow feeling. Mrs Ulrich could really lay it on thick. Judith felt as if she might throw herself on the floor in a paroxysm of despair at any moment now, especially if she let her thoughts turn to Robert's plight. Yet Drumpellier marched on, grim and unflinching, towards the site of the charm.

In which the lady walks

It is particularly confounding when our lies turn out to be truths.
— from *Lady Avely's Guide to Guile and Peril*

MRS ULRICH HAD POSITIONED the Cork of Doom above a doorway, as per Judith's instructions. As Drumpellier drew closer, his posture became ramrod straight, his movements jerkier. Yet his soldier's training prevailed, and he grasped the door handle and shoved it open with a grunt.

The room inside, as Judith well knew, was dim and crowded. The curtains were closed, the furniture covered in sheets: mysterious white shapes loomed, including the recent addition of a hat stand, which lent itself as a tall, ghostly figure. The *piece de resistance*, of course, was the Illusionary oil painting on the far wall, hung with care to be clearly seen from the door.

By the captain's gasp, his sharp eyes had seen the painting flicker into view. He took a shaky step backward and looked over his shoulder at Judith.

"What trickery is this?"

"Trickery?" Judith blinked innocently. "Where?"

"I saw something. A charm, no doubt. Stuck to the wall."

Curse the man, he was far too acute. This was the point where Robert was supposed to Illuse an actual ghostly figure, adorned in misty tendrils, emerging from the painting and staring with accusation.

Judith frowned. "Really? I've only ever felt it, not seen it. What did you see?"

Captain Drumpellier did not answer. He stared grimly into the room.

Judith approached, willing herself to appear unbothered by the Dread Spell, even as it twisted her innards with anguish. "You *saw* the Lady? I would congratulate you on your sensitivity, Captain, but it may be quite unfortunate." At Drumpellier's continued silence, she prattled on. "I gather that the Lady doesn't like Impactors very much, so perhaps that is why she is showing you such attention. She died at the hands of the Gift, after all, a violent, sudden death, so they say that she curses any Impactor who comes within her reach." She paused. "Does it feel as if she is cursing you?"

"Flummery," said Drumpellier, but he took another step back from the Cork of Doom.

"Oh, most certainly it is nonsense," said Judith, peering over his shoulder. "I don't feel much at all, just a whiff of dismay. Nothing to worry about. She wouldn't curse to kill you, I'm sure. Nothing so melodramatic. Just a bit of bad luck. Consigning your endeavours to the devil and promising your actions come to grief, and so forth. I wouldn't worry."

Drumpellier, sweating under the heavy toll of the Dread Spell, grimaced. "I don't believe it for a minute."

"Of course not," agreed Judith, stepping into the room with an air of unconcern and looking around curiously. "Where did you see her? I'm not an Impactor, so I don't mind if I catch a glimpse."

"You're lying." He inched backwards. "You're tricking me."

Judith turned to face him. She opened her mouth, and then, in quite an indecorous fashion, left it open. She could see the Crimson Lady behind him.

It was a female figure, her outline indistinct. She was clad in a wine-red gown, broad with petticoats and trimmed with fur. A black fur stole adorned her pale shoulders, pinned at her throat with a ruby. Her dark hair was shot through with silver, but her face had a pretty softness despite her age. She was behind Drumpellier, but looked directly at Judith. The faintest impression of a wink fluttered at one eye.

Judith's own eyes widened in shock. Could this be Robert's work? Had he been freed and come to help? Yet the costume was ornate, rich with detail. The face was alive with interest, and the whole of her somehow transparent at the same time, the edges shivering into being.

Drumpellier saw Judith's expression, and his shoulders canted upwards.

The lady slowly lifted a slender finger. Very gently, she ran it along the captain's neck.

Drumpellier almost jumped out of his skin. He spun around. Nose to nose with him, the lady glared and wagged her finger at him.

He gulped, motionless. She turned then, dismissive, and promenaded down the corridor. Her feet were enclosed in wooden soles, and Judith realised with a shock that she could hear them tapping faintly.

Drumpellier remained stock-still. Judith rushed to the door to watch the Crimson Lady go. With amazement, she saw the figure vanish into the far wall, as if she had never been.

There was a long, shocked silence.

"I saw her!" Judith whispered. The awe in her voice was unfeigned.

Beside her, Drumpellier gave an involuntary shiver. "What in damnation...?"

Judith turned to look at him. "Did she tell you to leave?"

"She was *your* doing!"

"I swear to you, she was not!" Judith put her hand on her heart. "She appeared of her own accord."

The Dread Spell was still thick in the air where they stood, pouring gloom down upon them. Beads of sweat appeared on Drumpellier's brow. Casually, Judith pushed past him. "Do as you will, Captain. I would heed her warning, if I were you," she said airily. "Now, I suppose this means I must fetch my own tea, if you have locked up Mrs Ulrich. How irksome."

At that moment, Ltn Greene chose to make his entrance. He strode through the same door Drumpellier had come by, looking around cheerfully. For a moment, Judith almost felt relief at the sight of him, then she remembered his perfidy. She came to an abrupt halt. The chain was hidden now, but she knew it was coiled in his pocket.

"Sir!" Ltn Greene saluted. "I checked the cellars again and did not find anyone else. Ah!" He bowed to Judith. "The owner of the footsteps, I presume?"

Drumpellier threw a look of distrust at Judith. "Yes, escort her back to the Tower Room at once, please. And search all the rooms along this corridor with extreme thoroughness. I suspect the duke might be hidden in this one." He jerked a thumb towards the door at his back, while at the same time edging away from it.

"Yes, sir." Ltn Greene looked curious. "Any reason for that, sir?"

"You can't feel the enchantment?"

Ltn Greene cocked his head. "Ah...yes. Some nostalgia, perhaps? A sense of longing?"

Drumpellier's jaw tightened at this mild description. "Something like that." He took another step away. "Search it *very* carefully. And no one comes or goes from this castle until I say so, do you understand me? I won't rest until the duke is found."

"Yes, sir." Ltn Greene saluted sharply.

Judith's throat was tight with tension. This was when she should speak up, announce the lieutenant's treason, and throw the whole sorry tale at Drumpellier's feet. But she could not do it, not with Robert's life tethered to Ltn Greene's pocket.

"Where is Miss Onslow?" snapped Drumpellier. "I must speak with her."

"I haven't seen her." Ltn Greene lifted his hands, and the lie was like a tin cup clattering. "Perhaps she went out for a walk; I know she is fond of them."

"Is that true?" Drumpellier demanded of Judith.

Ltn Greene brought his hand to rest over his lapel with a questioning look: a posture of concern.

Judith nodded. "Yes." She could not give Miss Onslow away now, not when it would come at the cost of Robert's pain.

"Odd," said Drumpellier, frowning. "If you see her, tell her to wait for me in the Blue Drawing Room." He scowled at Judith and Ltn Greene. "I will go back to the fort now—in case the duke is hiding there," he added hastily, "and to see to my responsibilities."

Judith remained carefully neutral. She did not want to provoke Drumpellier's pride now by implying that he was afraid of a ghost.

"Greene," said Drumpellier, "you are in charge until I return. I expect you to keep a very close watch."

"Yes, sir."

"And you—back in the Tower Room." He glared at Judith. "I will return soon." Then he reached into his pocket and muttered one more word. "*Veho.*"

As soon as he vanished, Judith marched away from the Dread Spell, eager to put it behind her, as well as some distance between her and Ltn Greene. His falsely vacuous face was giving her chills, and she was still shaky from seeing the Crimson Lady in the flesh, as it were.

The lieutenant followed her, however, chatting amiably as she strode out of the northern corridor.

"That went well, I must say! What did you do to frighten him so? I've never seen Drumpy so pale."

"It wasn't me," she replied shortly. She took a turn towards the centre of the castle, blindly heading towards Dacian.

"Ah yes, your team of players. Mrs Ulrich's ghastly mood! But how did you manage without your Illusionist?"

She swung around. "Is Robert still safe? Unharmed?"

"Yes, yes." His voice rang true, and her shoulders sank with relief. "Now, we must do as the captain requested and take you back to the Tower Room."

"Why?" she demanded. "Our association ends here. You have Miss Onslow, and I have the duke. Let us be done with it and go our separate ways. You can be gone far from here, within minutes, I am certain."

"Ah, but I have plans in motion," objected Ltn Greene mildly. "I need to guarantee your silence for three more days. Surely you can give me that."

"Three days?" Judith stared, taken aback for a moment. Then she swooped on the opportunity. "I will do so, if you hand Robert over at once."

"I think not." Ltn Greene winced regretfully. He reached up to pull the silver chain from his pocket and let it fall upon his lapel. It gleamed dully, and he caressed it with that awful false air of regret. "I do apologise, but the boy is my hostage for your silence. I know very well that as soon as I release him, you will rush off to Drumpellier with your tale. Or worse, you will wreak your own version of justice, the thought of which quite frankly terrifies me."

Judith could not deny it. She tried anyway, by saying stiffly, "We both have something to lose—we each stand to be accused of treason—so we can both keep our silence."

Ltn Greene ruefully shook his head. "That won't do, I'm afraid." He dropped his hand from the chain and pushed past her, taking the right-hand avenue and leading the way towards the Tea Tower. "Come with me. I'm sure we can reach *some* sort of agreement."

Furiously, Judith followed. She had no choice, not with that cursed silver chain hanging from his pocket. Briefly, she considered tackling him to the ground and wrenching it away but reluctantly rejected the notion. She might accidentally pull the chain the wrong way, and she could not bear to think of the consequences.

"Where is Robert?" she demanded.

"He's tucked away in a linen closet. I can fetch him for you, if you like—if you promise to wait quietly in the Tower Room, like a good matron."

Judith bared her teeth at his back. "I will do so, but only if you promise to bring him to me, unharmed."

"I swear it."

Reluctantly, she heard the truth in his voice again. He *did* intend to bring Robert to the Tower Room, though God knew what he meant to do then.

They began mounting the stairs. The stairwell was close and suffocating.

"And then what?" she asked carefully. "You will make us both jump out of the tower?"

Ltn Greene shuddered. "Nothing so dreadful. Besides, I would be hard put to explain such a scene." He turned to face her, two steps above, and reached into his trouser pocket.

Judith flinched back, half expecting a pistol. Instead, he withdrew a small vial. It was made of glass, a dark purple liquid gleaming within. Her mouth went dry, for she guessed the contents at once. "You wouldn't dare."

"I would, indeed." Ltn Greene shook the bottle gently. "Your turn to drink the Lethe. And Robert's too, of course. But I think you would rather him witless than handless."

Judith said nothing for a moment. She was at a dreadful disadvantage being two steps lower than him, for one thing. And she was full of a twisting fear at the sight of that purple tincture. She knew what it represented: her mind gone, her memories lost, even if only for three days. Dacian would be lost to her again, in a different way that was even more frightening. And she would be powerless without her recollection: she would know nothing and be useless. Anything could happen in those three days. And she didn't trust the lieutenant an inch.

"You can't be serious," she said at last.

"Why not? It is a brilliant solution." He stepped back and gestured for her to pass him, putting his hand over his chest— over the chain. "After you, my lady. Your choice."

Leadenly, she did so. Too late, she realised she ought to have gone to Dacian immediately. He might have been able to restrain Ltn Greene while she extricated the chain. But now she was trapped in this unfolding nightmare.

Ltn Greene continued, his voice soft behind her. "You and Robert are the only ones who know the truth about me, so you are the only ones who need to forget. All your other servants are locked up, and so is your duke. You haven't had a chance to talk to them yet, have you?"

It was true. She had stayed away from Dacian to keep him safe. And now she would be taken very far from him indeed.

She finished the rest of the climb in numb silence, as if she was mounting a scaffold.

In which a terrible bargain is struck

Memories can be full of guile. Yet, without memory, we have no truth.
— from *Lady Avely's Guide to Guile and Peril*

THE LIEUTENANT ESCORTED her to the top of the stairs. When Judith pushed the Tower Room door open, the familiar comfort washed over her, the jewelled colours of the tapestries and rugs bright and beautiful. But there was no comfort to be found this time—except for a slim skerrick of hope. Ltn Greene had promised to bring Robert to her. A chance still remained, she told herself. Together, they might overpower Greene, or confound him somehow, with Illusion or argument. She had to believe that.

She went to stand by the window, staring out over the ocean. The blue expanse of earlier was now grey-green, white-tipped, and choppy. Clouds had crept in to smother the sun, and wind harried the waves.

"So," said Ltn Greene from the door, "I will fetch the manacled Robert, and you will drink the Lethe together. Only then will I remove the wristbreakers. I believe you will have the satisfaction of seeing him free, before you forget him." He let out a little chuckle, as if this was amusing.

She swung round to face him. "What is to stop you murdering us, once we've lost our memories?"

He took the key out of the inside lock and waved it casually. "Oh, I don't want to kill you. Much too messy. Where would I dispose of the bodies? I am a Healor, recall: I don't like murdering people."

Again Judith could tell that he was telling the truth. Still, she frowned, distrustful. "You might not like it, but you could easily arrange it, especially when my mind is emptied."

"If you know nothing, why would I want you dead?" he protested. "If you die, Drumpellier will have run of the castle again. This is much better: you'll still be able to fulfil your function—you just won't remember anything to do with *me*. Miss Onslow will be a great support to you. Drumpellier will be enraged, but he will most likely blame the duke or even suspect that you took the dose yourself as a precaution against accusation."

Judith's lips twisted. She imagined the captain would be all too keen to believe the worst of her. "He will be watching the place like a hawk."

"Let him. He doesn't know about the underground causeway yet, and I don't intend him to discover it. I will be able to come and go as I please. In fact, Drumpellier will send me here often, which suits me well enough. I'm sure we will become wonderful acquaintances, just as we were before. You will rely upon my cheerful presence."

Judith clenched her hands tightly together. "You're a guileful, snivelling dog."

"That may be, but I'll be back soon with your boy." He touched the chain at his lapel once more. "Don't try anything when I return. He will still be shackled, so if you attack me with a teapot, I shall know what to do."

The door shut behind him. She heard the click of the iron lock, and she sank down on the windowsill, her hands coming up to cover her face. She would have to follow his instructions. Trying to overpower him was too risky. She could not bear to not wrench the chain from his lapel and hear Robert scream in pain. She looked around for some sort of other weapon, but the circular, cosy room seemed particularly unhelpful now, with its charming waves of soothing Diplomacy. And she had given Dacian's ring back to him.

She must resign herself to losing her mind.

It might only be for three days, she told herself. But in heart she feared it would be much longer. Why would Ltn Greene ever let her recover, when she knew so much?

Tipping her head back against the glass, she allowed herself to think of Dacian. He still waited innocently below, in his secret room. Perhaps, by now, he even remembered her: brief snatches, or whole years. He would be impatient to see her.

Her mind drifted to when she had first met him, in his arrogant youth: powerful, virile, and all too conscious of his charms. Yet despite his station, he had courted *her*, a mere rector's daughter, charming her with his stories and relentless flirtation. His warm eyes and teasing smile. The kiss he stole, and the slow realisation that he was her own personal lodestone, impossible to resist.

Then she had believed the worst of him, and thus she had lost him.

And now they would both be adrift, their minds untrammelled, their hearts untethered. She didn't know if she could bear the thought of it, except that Robert needed her to do it. She had already betrayed Robert once, and she could not do it again. And so, she would drink her own undoing.

The window felt cool behind her, her back stiff. She stayed still for a long moment, until she heard the approach on the stairs. The footsteps were hurried, impatient, and singular. And somehow familiar. Her eyes blinked open. Surely the lieutenant should have Robert with him? Was this someone else?

Then she heard the unexpected, familiar voice through the door.

"Mother!" Perry rattled at the knob. "Are you in there?"

She sat up, scarcely believing her ears. "Perry! Is that you?"

"I came back for some afternoon tea, hoping to nab some cream," he confessed through the door jamb. "But I find that everyone is locked up! What's going on? Mrs Ulrich spoke to me through the wall and told me to look for you. Where's the key?"

Her heart thudded with sudden hope, and she strode over to the door. "The lieutenant took it. He is a villain, and he has Robert in wristbreakers. Quick, you must fetch the duke."

"What about you?" Perry rattled the knob again. "I can snatch you out of there. I'm pretty certain I can Travel into a room sight unseen, if I imagine you before me."

"Thank you, my dear, but I must not abandon Robert, and he will be here any moment. You must fetch his grace and tell him to use his power to pin down Lieutenant Greene. Then we can disengage the wristbreakers."

Perry let out a low whistle. "Where is his grace?"

Judith hesitated. It would be difficult to explain the location of the secret sitting room, tucked away as it was, and deliberately well hidden. "If you free Mrs Ulrich first, she can show you. Quickly."

"But how? She is locked in the cellars." There was a pause, then an indrawn breath that Judith heard through the door. "I'll use the shatterstone!"

She grimaced. "If you must."

"Where is it?"

"Still on the Blue Drawing Room mantelpiece, behind the clock, unless someone has taken it."

"I'll pop over there at once." Satisfaction warmed his voice. "So: fetch the stone, smash open the cellars, free Mrs U, release the duke, then back to you. Anything else?"

"Yes, be careful! Listen outside the door before you all burst in. And hurry!"

"Righto."

"And Perry—"

"Yes?"

"You're a good son."

"Yes, Mother." His voice dipped into uncertainty. "Will you be all right?"

"I might have to drink some Lethe and forget you for a moment. But I'll be fine."

There was another indrawn breath, then silence from beyond the door. As the quiet extended, she realised Perry had gone, vanishing hastily into thin air. Very faintly, footsteps echoed further below.

This time, there were two pairs, and one was limping.

She backed away from the door, gnawing on her lip. Quickly, she sat by the window as before, arranging her features into an expression of despair, instead of the hope that pulsed under her skin.

Eventually, the key slid into the lock, and the handle turned.

Robert came through the door first. His hands were bound in front in the heavily wrought metal, and his chestnut hair fell across his face. He looked over to her. His blue eyes were frightened, his face pale. Behind him came Ltn Greene, cheerful in his red uniform.

"Release him," said Judith shakily. "At once, do you hear me?"

"Never fear, I will do so." Ltn Greene escorted Robert over to a chair, then rather forcefully pushed him into it. "You know my terms."

Robert twisted so that he fell sideways into the armchair. Judith rushed over to his side and put a reassuring hand on his shoulder. She squeezed it twice, quickly, trying to convey that all was not lost. If only Perry would hurry, and Dacian could grasp the situation quickly.

"What terms?" said Robert, his voice rasping.

"You both drink deeply of this." Ltn Greene pulled out the small, ominous bottle from his jacket. "You both forget, and then you both live. A rather good deal, I would say."

Robert's head reared back in aversion. "No!"

"You'd rather die?" Ltn Greene raised his brows. "With broken wrists?"

Robert did not flinch this time. "You will kill us anyway."

"So untrusting!" Ltn Greene shook his head mournfully. "I swear I won't. It doesn't suit my character. Ask your mother here: she knows I speak the truth."

"She's not my mother," said Robert, then he flushed a painful red. He looked over to Judith. "*Is* he speaking the truth?"

She nodded slowly. "For now." She squeezed his shoulder again, then paced away from him, biding for time. "I suspect we must do as he says. As much as we abhor it."

"A sensible woman." Ltn Greene held out the bottle. "Ladies first."

She eyed it. "At least let me use a proper receptacle." She went over to the tea tray, the one from earlier, which Mrs Ulrich had not yet had a chance to remove. It bore two cream cups, one a quarter full of tea. "We can mix it with tea, can we not? It will make it more palatable."

Ltn Greene shrugged. "If you wish. But do not dawdle."

Robert was watching her, a tiny frown on his brow. With her back to the lieutenant, she allowed herself the ghost of wink. Robert's frown only deepened.

Judith was too busy listening for Perry's shatterstone, tense with the effort. She picked up the teapot and poured a large measure of cold tea. Then she set it down again with a clunk. Just as she did so, she caught the faint sound of a rumble, far below. She coughed, clearing her throat. Perry was blowing open the cellars, the good boy.

"What was that?" said Ltn Greene sharply.

Judith looked over. "The rumble? That is the waves. They crash right against the castle, you know. It quite unnerved me the first time I felt it, too. I suppose the tide must be in."

Ltn Greene narrowed his eyes. "Get on with it." He marched over, opened the bottle, and proceeded to pour a hefty dose of the purple liquid into her cup.

Judith licked her lips. "Sugar is required, I think." Slowly, she spooned in crystals, hoping that her reluctance would be read as a natural aversion to losing her mind.

Deliberately, she stirred the tea and looked up. "Drumpellier will suspect something. You won't get away with it."

"As long as I get away with it for another three days," he replied, unperturbed. "If I can hold my position for that long, it will all be worth it. Then Drumpellier will really gnash his teeth."

"Why?" asked Robert. "What is happening in three days?"

Ltn Greene hesitated, but the opportunity to boast was too much. "Bonaparte's troops are sneaking into England. Into this very castle."

There was a shocked silence.

"Into the cellars?" Judith was aghast. "You're going to Travel them in?"

"Indeed. From a turncoat ship in the channel. We can only

shift a few soldiers at a time, but if we work night and day, we should manage a fair few before anyone notices. This castle can hide a whole regiment or two, I believe, before we make our presence known."

"It won't work," said Robert faintly. "It's a mad idea."

"Fortunately, you won't remember anything about it." Ltn Greene smirked. "Now, come along, drink up. I still have to deal with Miss Onslow, and she is no doubt feeling a little anxious in her dingy tunnel. I don't want her chatting to your servants through the door either, Lady Avely, in case she lets anything slip."

Judith raised the cup. She strained her ears, listening. Had she heard a footstep? Was Dacian creeping up the stairs right now? Would he and Perry burst in? All she could hear, however, was the gulls screaming outside, and the wind keening against the windows. It was a lonely sound now.

"Hurry up, woman." Ltn Greene grew impatient. "If you don't, I'll pull on the wristbreakers now, and then Robert will have no memory *and* no hands."

She took a sip.

The tea was over-brewed and very strong. Underneath the bitterness was a rich, tangy taste. It was sweet, like port. She could sense its potency as she let it roll round her mouth. Then, bracing herself, she swallowed.

She glanced over to Robert. He looked the same as ever, his clefted chin pugnacious, his blue eyes worried. "Not so bad," she said calmly. "Quite delicious, actually."

Robert grimaced. "My turn." He put out his manacled hands, reaching for the cup. "We can take it sip by sip."

Reluctantly, Judith handed him the cup. It was a good idea: eke it out, slow it down. Still, it was difficult to watch Robert take his turn, his eyes widening at the rich taste, his throat bobbing.

Solemnly, they passed the cup to one another, both taking tiny mouthfuls. Her ears were pricked, wondering if Perry and Dacian had reached the door yet. They would need to listen for the lieutenant's voice, to locate his whereabouts in the room. She held up the cup to ostentatiously examine it, hoping to provoke him into comment.

It worked. Ltn Greene spoke impatiently. "Enough of this stalling." His voice was loud and suspicious, and his eyes shot to the door. "Drink up." He raised his hand and hooked a finger through the chain at his lapel, glaring at Judith. "Or else."

She lowered the cup and took a larger mouthful. The liquid burned her tongue, and tears started to her eyes. She could feel herself becoming hazy already, a slight softening around the edges. Vagueness was creeping upon her, like dusk darkening the sky over the bay. Yet she must keep talking, so Dacian knew where she was.

"May I say one thing?" She did not wait for the lieutenant's permission, and held up a hand to foil his anger, turning to Robert. "My dear boy, it pains me to think we will be strangers again. But I hope I will do better next time. And I think Perry could be a good brother to you, if you would only let him."

Robert blinked owlishly. "Thank you." His eyes were wet. "Pass me the damn cup. Let's get this over with."

"I concur," snapped Ltn Greene.

She gave it to him. Resolutely, he lifted it and took a gulp.

He passed it back.

Judith carried it to her lips, waiting, hoping. Where was Dacian? Who, exactly, was Dacian? The thought swum through her mind, and with it, the image of his handsome, smiling face. She didn't want to forget him. She was waiting for him. Waiting for *something*.

"Finish it up," said Ltn Greene harshly.

Under his hard stare, she took another gulp. She held it in

her mouth, then swallowed. She pushed the cup back towards Robert.

"Bottoms up," she said.

It really was quite delicious. Could do with a bit of cream, perhaps.

Robert gave her a dreamy glance, lifting the teacup, but at that moment, the room burst into movement.

Right in front of her, two men appeared. One was tall and dark-haired, his jaw set, his black eyes furious. The other was younger, his arms wrapped around the older man's waist. His blond head peered out from under one arm, his boyish face contorted in alarm.

Under Judith's bemused gaze, the young man released his hold and dropped to the ground. The dark-haired man spun around, and power swept through the room.

Everyone froze, held into place by an implacable force. A red-coated soldier stood transfixed by a bookshelf, a snarl upon his face, his hand lifting to his breast pocket.

The dark-haired man stalked forward.

"You bastard." His voice was vicious as he leaned in. "You're lucky I don't crush your bones to dust." Carefully, at odds with the fury in his voice, he extracted a chain from the soldier's lapel. Judith watched with interest, despite her inability to move. At the end of it, a flat iron key dangled.

"Here you go, Perry," said the man grimly. "Unlock Robert. Be bloody careful about it."

The blond man tried to grimace, but he was unable to move. The dark-haired man sighed, and the stone wall of force dropped away from everyone, except the soldier. *He* was still fixed in place, glaring, his skin turning a blotchy red, his eyes bulging.

The blond man scrambled to his feet. "Right away, your grace." Gingerly, he took the key and went over to a young man sitting in an armchair, manacles on his wrists. Judith, horrified, watched as the cuffs were unlocked. The young man let out a sigh of relief, stretching out his fingers and hands.

Then the blond boy came over, his brow creasing above hazel eyes. "Mother! Did I hear you say that Robert and I are *brothers?*"

"Oh dear," said Judith, frowning. "Did I say that?" She paused. "Do I know you?"

The dark-haired man took a hasty step towards her. "How much did you drink?" he demanded. He really was *quite* handsome.

Judith looked down at the cup in her hand. "I'm not sure," she said, and she slid into a hazy, soft glow of oblivion.

In which Judith enjoys a piece of theatre

Even the most courageous souls, brave in the face of physical danger, cower before the prospect of losing their memories. But really, it isn't so bad.

— from *Lady Avely's Guide to Guile and Peril*

JUDITH AWOKE on a couch in an unfamiliar room.

The room was oddly round, with tall windows and beautiful tapestries hung upon the walls. Beside her, a curving bookshelf brimmed with books, and a fire crackled in the opposite hearth. A very large, fluffy cat sat on her feet, and a strong sense of peace and calm enveloped her. It felt like home, though she didn't recognise it.

Moreover, she was surrounded by strangers.

A stern looking housekeeper stood by the door, her lips pursed. A very handsome, middle-aged man stood a few feet away, looking down at Judith a curious expression of longing and fierceness. He had dark eyes and dark hair, laugh lines at his eyes, and firm lips. Her gaze dwelt upon him for several moments, then she looked away in embarrassment.

"Do you remember me?" he asked, with a strange intensity.

"I am afraid not," she replied, and immediately became concerned that she had been impolite. "I'm sorry, have we been introduced?"

His face fell, but he rearranged it into a semblance of civility and gave a low bow. "I am the Duke of Sargen. You may call me Dacian."

She inclined her head. Something like pain flashed across his face. She was distracted, however, by an argument that was growing louder between two younger men, who were discussing something over by the fire.

"I heard her say it!" said a young blond man furiously. "She said that we could be *brothers*. Did she mean it *literally*? Or figuratively? Come on, Robert, I'm sure you can remember. And I find it damn odd that she should think we could be brothers on such a short acquaintance!"

The other young man, with chestnut hair and blue eyes, seemed to be confused. "I don't know!" he said. "How long is our acquaintance? Are we friends?"

The duke—Dacian—sighed. "Yes, Perry, Robert is your half-brother."

Perry swung around. "*What?* How do *you* know?"

"I was good friends with your father. He sired Robert before you were born, and he trusted me with his welfare."

Judith listened with interest. Somehow, without knowing how, she could sense that the duke was telling the truth. Clearly there was some family scandal unfolding before her. A secret brother! How intriguing.

"Oh, really!" Perry was incensed. "A pretty thing it is for me to discover my own brother now! What was Father thinking! And Mother! She knew, didn't she? How long has she known?"

Judith realised that Perry had turned his accusing gaze towards her. *She* had nothing to do with it! She didn't even know his mother! To avoid his militant look, she glanced away, and her eyes landed on a soldier tucked into the corner behind the bookshelf. To her surprise, he was bound and gagged, tied to a chair. His wrists were cuffed before him, and his face was a picture of fuming rage.

"Oh dear," she exclaimed. "Why is an officer of the Crown bound? Your grace, please untie him immediately!"

Perry let out a huff of despair. Before anyone could explain the matter to her, however, footsteps could be heard marching up the stairs just outside the room. The housekeeper edged away from the door nervously, her silver head turning, and Judith felt some of her own calm slip away.

"Damn," said the duke. "That will be the cursed captain. Robert, this would be a good time to remember your Illusions. Can you make me into that ugly valet fellow of Garvey's, with the long nose and bald pate? Now would be the moment to try."

Robert frowned. "I can cast Illusions?" He lifted his hands experimentally and waggled his fingers towards the duke.

A yew hedge suddenly leapt into being. It missed the duke and took up residence over the bookshelf. Judith blinked, admiring the crisp green leaves and small red berries. It really was most life-like, though it encroached on the muzzled soldier, who looked as if he might explode beneath his gag.

The duke rolled his eyes. "Not the hedgery again. Try something human, for God's sake."

Robert frowned, but before he could comply, the door flung open.

Another red-clad soldier stood there, the epaulettes on his shoulders marking him as a captain. He also wore an expression of extreme displeasure. It twisted into a look of comic surprise as his eyes landed on the duke.

Dacian threw up a hand. Suddenly, the room was a battle-ground, for the captain immediately retaliated. Power rushed from both of them, clashing in the middle. Judith hunched back into her couch, feeling the energy of it upon her skin and the threat of it to her bones. Everyone stared as the two men strained against each other. Force for force, scowl for scowl, they gritted their teeth, trying to overpower one another.

"Wait a minute!" shouted Perry, who had once more ducked to the ground. "Now look here, Captain—I assume that's who you must be, Drumpelly or whatever your name is—you're making a mistake. You've got two traitors in your midst! Why do you think your lieutenant is all tied up? He is feeding infor-mation to the French, that's why! And your Miss Onslow helped him; she is a devilish young lady, and so I can tell you! There's been all sorts of havey-cavey things going on under your nose!"

Taken aback, the captain's gaze flickered towards Perry and his lieutenant, then caught upon the yew hedge. His eyes widened, and that moment of distraction was all that the duke needed. He slammed an incisive Impact past the captain's guard, pushing him against the wall.

"He's right." The duke was panting. "French spies. They are the enemy. Let us stop this."

The captain's jaw was hard, two spots of colour in his cheek-bones. "Lady Avely, what piece of theatre is this?"

Judith blinked, for he appeared to be addressing her. "Pardon me? Is it a play? That explains it! How delightful." She frowned. It had all seemed very real.

"She doesn't know anything about it," growled the duke. "Your lieutenant just gave her a very strong dose of Lethe. If she doesn't recover, I'll burn your whole goddamn fort to the ground."

"No, no," said Judith. "I am quite well recovered, thank you very much. Pray do continue with the performance."

The captain's brow creased. "You don't seem to be yourself, Lady Avely."

"No, she is not," growled the duke. "And I have your rank foolishness to thank for it."

Perry straightened, throwing his hands up in exasperation. "Your grace, this is not the time for threats. And Captain, your traitorous Miss Onslow had a long chat with the housekeeper here and told us about a plot to ferry Bonaparte's troops into England via Travellors. You're about to fend off an invasion, so in my humble opinion you two should stop fighting like dogs and work together."

"Bravo!" said Judith.

"Indeed," said the housekeeper, who had retreated to stand under a far tapestry. "Most advisable."

Judith was suddenly aware of a strong desire to co-operate with her fellow man, and she clasped her hands together.

Even the captain seemed to crumple a little, even as he was still pressed against the wall. "Did you say *ferrying Bonaparte's troops* into England?"

"Into this very castle," said Perry, "using Travellors, stopping on a ship in the Channel. It's how I arrived here, so I know it is possible."

The duke lowered his hand, turning it over in a gesture of surrender. "I will release you, if you will promise to listen."

The captain scowled. "Fine. You have five minutes of my undivided attention."

The force holding him fixed abruptly fell away. The captain stumbled, irritably brushing himself down. He eyed the soldier trussed up in the chair. "Now, please explain why my lieutenant is tied up like a turkey."

Perry launched into a garbled explanation, punctuated by

the duke's pithy remarks. Even before two minutes of it, the captain's demeanour had begun to change, his ire now directed towards his lieutenant, and his gaze avoiding the duke's.

At the end of the tale, Dacian spread his hands out again. "I'm perfectly willing to help you, Drumpellier, if you forfeit all threats against myself and Lady Avely. I am as patriotic as the next man, and I have no desire to see Bonaparte succeed, but I will not stand for any accusations of treason against myself or those I hold dear."

The captain chewed on his lip for a moment, stubbornly silent. Then abruptly he expelled a breath and met his eyes. "I appreciate your forbearance, your grace. You have a deal."

"You will continue to uphold my immunity and drop all allegations against myself and the marchioness," repeated the duke implacably.

Judith looked around for the marchioness. She feared that she was in rather exalted company, but it appeared that her ladyship was not currently in the room. Perhaps she was below-stairs ordering refreshments. Some cream tea would be nice for the intermission.

The captain gritted his teeth together but nodded. "Agreed. I suppose I may need your help to stop this devilish scheme."

"You can start," said Perry crossly, "by chatting to this slippery Miss Onslow, and put her to good use. She can find out the details of the plan. Then whenever these damn Frenchies pop into our cellars, we can take them prisoner."

Judith was confused by this new barrage of information. Her head ached, and she felt very vague, as if she had consumed a whole bottle of wine. Perhaps she had. She couldn't quite remember. Cream tea would be *much* appreciated. Or drinking chocolate.

The housekeeper spoke up. "I can show you where Miss

Onslow is being kept under guard by Cador, Captain. I suppose you will need to know all about the cellars."

"I most certainly will," snapped the captain. "I know you were hiding something from me, with all your tottering about!"

"One is permitted to lie about one's age." The housekeeper smiled, and Judith became aware of a faint wave of amusement rolling through the room. Really, the housekeeper was quite a wit.

Even the Captain gave a reluctant smile, though his eyebrows quirked in confusion.

The servant turned with a regal air. "Come then. Though I warn you that some of the cellar walls are now destroyed by this young man's efforts to unlock the door."

"Ha," said Perry. "You loved it, Mrs U."

"I most certainly did not." She gave him a reproving look.

The vague sense of hilarity vanished as she left the room. The captain followed the housekeeper, after one more admonishing look and extracting a vow of honour from the duke not to disappear again.

Once the captain had gone, his grace let out a sigh of relief. "Thank God for that. I thought he might overrule me and arrest us all on the spot." Then, in two strides, he crossed to Judith, kneeled beside her, and stared into her eyes. "Do you remember me yet?"

"No," she said apologetically. "Are you really a duke? Or are you play-acting?"

"I'm really a duke." He smiled, taking her hand between his. "I am your suitor, and your lover. I've been courting you for years, waiting for you to love me—and I will do so again, if I must."

Judith's heart fluttered. He was so very handsome and intent. His hands were strong and capable, his eyes dark with passion, and she felt a tingle of warmth run through her...

Perry spluttered. "I say! Hands off, your grace!"

"You can leave now," said the duke, without looking at him, and continuing to stare into Judith's eyes with adoration.

"I'm not leaving you alone together! You'll take advantage of my mother, while she is in this vulnerable state! You—you—libertine!"

"I love your mother. I'm not going to take advantage of her. I want to marry her."

Judith blinked. "You love me?"

"Yes, dearly, and completely. So I won't ravish you just yet."

Judith felt a distant sense of regret.

"However," he added, "you could take off that mobcap, as a gesture of your favour."

Judith patted her head with her free hand, finding it adorned with some lacy contraption. She pulled it off, examined it distastefully, then cast it aside without further thought.

"Oh God," said Perry in despair. "She's completely lost to us."

Dacian ignored him and smiled at her. "Judith, my love, shall I pick you up and take you to your room? You probably need to sleep it off."

Judith examined his broad shoulders doubtfully. "If you are sure you can manage it."

The duke slid his strong arms under her and lifted her as if she were a feather bolster. She leaned her head upon his shoulder, and he brushed a kiss against her cheek.

"Your grace!" said Perry in outrage.

"Oh shush," she said. "It's fine. I accept him as my suitor. He's very handsome."

"Mother!"

"Well," said the duke, "that was a very quick courtship. Much quicker than our last one."

She nuzzled into his chest, feeling the lovely heat of him, his strong arms, and the smell of him: whisky, leather, and smoke.

"Mmm, is that whisky?"

He carried her over to the door. "Yes, I found some in my sitting room. It was quite helpful in regaining my memory; something about the scent of it, and the taste." He paused. "I think you will require some drinking chocolate."

"An excellent idea," she murmured.

"See?" said Dacian, over his shoulder to Perry. "She's coming back to us already."

Perry folded his arms in disapproval and watched them leave. As the door shut behind them, Judith heard him say, "This is what happens when I leave Mother alone for a few weeks!"

"Yes, yes," said Robert dreamily. "Just look at that yew hedge! Quite remarkable!"

In which familial bonds are renewed

To be utterly without guile is a lovely place indeed.
— from *Lady Avely's Guide to Guile and Peril*

OVER THE NEXT THREE DAYS, Judith recovered her memory.

In truth, she would always think fondly of that day and a half where she did not know the duke, and she was meeting him for the first time again. After that first declaration, he withdrew a little, allowing her to sleep and eat in a strange room that looked like a ship's cabin. When she rejoined him in the break-fast room, he was all urbane charm and flirtatious coaxing, a mysterious dark stranger who nonetheless seemed to be completely devoted to her.

Rather than tell her tales of her past, however, he insisted they stroll around the castle, walking arm in arm. Exercise and blood flow, he said with a rueful grin, would help speed the eradication of the drug. So they set about exploring the myriad rooms and passageways, walked down to the quaint little dairy and cosy harbour, and inspected the cellars, which seemed to have been partially destroyed by some explosion.

They even promenaded across the causeway when the tide was out, the stones slippery beneath their feet, the sea air blowing into their faces. Her heart beat rather fast as he put an arm around her to shield her from the breeze, and she couldn't help but admire his masculine beauty, aged into authority and warmth.

Despite his attempts to keep the conversation general, sometimes she would catch him looking at her hungrily, or tracing a finger longingly over her arm. She would blush and look away, uncertain what to do with this passion, even as lust stirred within her. But she knew he was right. They must not rush into intimacy until they both knew themselves properly.

Peregrine (her son, apparently) followed them around at first in a very grouchy, suspicious fashion, muttering remarks about rakes and matrons, but he soon conceded that the duke was not going to press any advantage. And when the duke wasn't with Judith, he had his head together with Captain Drumpellier and Perry, as they plotted how to best foil Ltn Greene's dastardly plans. Apparently, a young woman called Miss Onslow was helping them with her French connections, though she was being kept under close guard, so Judith had yet to meet her. And there was one other eccentric guest, the Baron Quarles, who had kept to himself and his telescope since he arrived that morning.

Matters had apparently been further complicated by the arrival by a whole roost of vampiri bats, who had allegedly swept down upon Castle Lanyon in a dark, fluttering cloud in the middle of the night. They, too, claimed a right to the hospitality of the castle, and the butler and housekeeper had seemed to know where to put them, though from all reports, Captain

Drumpellier was seething about it. Judith shook her head at such a muddle, but Perry said that the bats might come in useful in foiling the French.

Judith let them sort it out. She contented herself with ambling dreamily around the lovely old castle, eating food leavened with oodles of cream, and drinking chocolate three times a day. The duke had insisted the housekeeper source some cocoa tablets as a matter of urgent priority, and he prepared the drink himself. Judith enjoyed watching him grind the tablets down and froth the cream, and the expectant look in his eye as she drank it.

Of course, the first memory that returned was of Perry: as a small boy, running along a river after his sister, Elinor, and somehow managing to somersault into the water. It slammed into her with the force of a whirlwind, taking her breath away with the sudden love and affection that swept through her. That sweet little boy was this young man! Bit by bit, her knowledge of Perry trickled back, and she made him walk with her too, holding his arm tightly, reaching around blindly in her mind for further jewels, and laughing at the strangeness of it all.

She and Perry were walking along the ramparts that second morning when they bumped into Robert. He started back, chestnut hair falling over blue eyes, greeting them uncertainly.

Ah, yes, this was the young Illusor who cast the yew hedge... who was also Perry's half-brother. Judith blinked, trying to remember what had been said. When the argument had unfolded in the Tea Tower Room, she had assumed it was nothing to do with her, or all play-acting, but now she realised with interest that this boy must be *related* to her somehow, just as Perry was. They were half-brothers. By a different father? Good Lord. She must have led quite a chequered youth, even *before* she got to the duke.

Robert's eye had fallen upon Judith's arm, which was wrapped possessively around Perry's elbow. Hastily, she put out her other hand in supplication. "My dear boy, you must walk with me too. I am so very sorry that I cannot remember my other son. I have only just recalled Perry, and that is because he executed a particularly impressive fall into the river at age six. However, I'm sure you managed to get up to mischief too and will shortly make yourself known."

Perry coughed violently. "Er, that's all right, Mother, he doesn't remember you either yet."

"Oh?" She smiled. "Then we are in the same dreadful boat."

Robert tentatively accepted Judith's arm. "It is an odd circumstance that we find ourselves in, is it not?" He smiled shyly. "I'm sure we will laugh about it later, Mother."

Perry coughed awkwardly again, but he said nothing, merely darting an anxious look between them.

Judith proceeded to stroll along, quite dwarfed by the two of them, but feeling oddly happy. The sparkling ocean and the distant horizon lifted the spirits, and she must count herself proud to have raised two such admirable young men. She said so.

Perry cleared his throat. "Indeed. Of course you must take credit for it, Mother."

Robert cocked his head to look at Perry. "Can you tell us of years gone by? It might help us to remember you and Elinor."

Perry shook his head vehemently. "Oh no. The duke has told me it is better if you recall such things naturally, your-selves." He paused. "But surely you remember the more recent, chaotic events? Bob, do you recall how you made us both into soldiers, with those sharp red uniforms? And the duke's shocked face when we embraced him in the fort?"

The conversation ambled on, full of laughter and disbelief.

Really, the two boys looked remarkably similar for being of different fathers, though Robert seemed to be the more thoughtful and reserved of the two, compared to Perry's cheerful disposition. Judith hoped they were ordinarily close.

"What about Elinor, my daughter?" she asked eventually. "Did you say she is in Devonshire? Can she Travel over to see me too? It would be lovely to be all together."

"I haven't told her about your condition yet," Perry confessed. "She is busy preparing for her wedding, and I didn't want her to panic."

"I can't remember Elinor either," said Robert, with a trace of melancholy. "When *is* the wedding?"

"In two days," said Perry grimly. "You're cutting it fine, Mother. And you are lucky you have me, otherwise you'd be terribly late. We'll pop in at the last minute."

Judith drew a shocked breath. "Two days? But I don't know myself! And I can only remember Elinor as a ten-year-old child!"

That seemed a trifling concern, however, when that evening at supper, Robert became entirely cold and distant. He sat down at the far end of the table and ate his meal of roast lamb in silence, refusing to look at Judith or Perry.

Judith, between Peregrine and the duke, frowned down the table, puzzled. "What's the matter with Robert?"

Perry sighed, clattering his fork. "Leave him be, Mother. He's still growing accustomed to being part of the family."

She nodded sagely. It *was* passingly strange, to be part of a family one did not recognise, and then to go from darkness to the light of recognition. However, when the covers were removed on the orange pudding and jellies, she deemed that Robert had quite enough time to stew on his discomfort and raised her voice to address him. "It is quite the odd feeling, isn't it? A sudden felicity!"

Robert's head snapped up. "It is not a felicity. You are *not* my family, as much as you like to playact it."

Judith blinked. "Excuse me?"

"You misled me! I am not your son! My mother is Anna Steer, and my father is a blacksmith." Two spots of colour burned angrily in his cheek. "It was a low trick pretend we are a real family, even for a day."

Judith turned in consternation to Dacian, who explained the matter to her in a low tone. Mortified, she stared down at the table, feeling as if black holes had appeared in the ground around her. Her dear Nicholas had sired Robert with someone *else*? Robert was not her son? Various emotions crashed through her: anger, humiliation, grief. And yet, when she looked over to Robert again, her heart wrenched at the suffering in his face.

"It wasn't a trick!" she protested. "I didn't know! I thought you *were* my son! You are Perry's brother, after all."

"Ha!" said Robert. "You might not remember it, but you pestered me to come here. In plain disregard to my feelings on the matter! Well, I'm leaving tomorrow. And I certainly won't be going to any Avely family wedding, you can be sure of that." He stood, throwing his napkin upon the table, glaring at them.

She took a hasty sip of wine to hide her feelings. The liquid was bitter at the back of her throat, and she bowed her head in acquiescence. Robert turned to leave, his jaw locked in a grim line.

"Wait a moment." Perry put down a large spoonful of pudding, looking between them. "I'm sorry for misleading you, Bob, but aren't you being a bit...hasty? I wouldn't advise you to toss an offer of friendship aside so readily. Mother saved your life, you know."

"She did not." Robert put clenched fists on top of his chair. "You and the duke did that, bursting into the room like a platoon of bulls."

"Yes, but Mother stayed back for you, when that lieutenant had you in cuffs." Perry continued inexorably, despite Robert's disbelieving expression. "I found her in the Tea Tower Room before you were hauled in there. I begged her to come with me, to whisk her out of danger, and she refused. She told me she had to wait for *you*, to prevent the lieutenant from snapping your wrists."

Robert looked down at his hands curled on the chair. "Is that true?" he asked, in a low voice.

"Yes," averred Perry. "And Mother stayed with you and drank the Lethe, for your sake, risking her mind. She would rather have saved you than come with me, her blood kin. So don't tell me that you're not family, you ungrateful dog."

Robert swallowed. There was a long silence, then he cleared his throat. "I thank you for that, Judith."

"You are most welcome, but I confess I have no memory of any of it," she admitted awkwardly. She tried for a tentative smile. Robert didn't go so far as to return it, but his step was a little less angry as he left the room.

And the next morning, he was still there for breakfast. As he was pouring coffee, the duke took the opportunity to remark, "Robert, I don't know if you recall it yet, but until recently, you've been in my employ as a footman. I take leave to inform you that you are now summarily dismissed. Hence you might as well stay in this draughty castle a little longer."

Robert nodded slowly, buttering a piece of bread. "Very good, your grace."

"And," his grace added, "you shall have to give up that stiff mode of address and start calling me Father, for I intend to marry Judith. We shall all have to grow accustomed to being part of a rather singular family."

Robert raised his brows and looked between them, but his

hostility seemed to have abated a little. "A singular family indeed," he said stiffly. "I congratulate you, your grace."

"Oh hoh," said Perry, in his usual spot by the window. "We'll see about that! I might accept Robert as my brother, but I don't accept you as my father, you dissolute malt-worm!"

"Peregrine!" said Judith, shocked.

"Shakespeare!" said Dacian, with approval. "You clay-brained jack-a-napes, you will find you have no choice in the matter."

"You can't propose to Mother until she is in her right senses," Perry retorted, "you rough-hewn puttock!"

A smile tugged at Robert's lips. Judith blushed and took a sip of coffee. "His grace may propose to me as many times as he likes. And he is not rough-hewn!"

Dacian smiled at her. "What am I, then?" he said, brazenly fishing.

"Very handsome. And brave. And charming." She fluttered her eyelashes at him.

Perry gagged. "Oh God, Robert, let us drink our coffee elsewhere." He stood abruptly, and marched over to Robert, gesturing. Robert grinned and poured himself a cup and followed Perry out the door.

"Trebellow," said Dacian. "You may also leave us now."

The butler had been standing at the breakfast board, listening avidly. Now he gave a worshipful bow and quietly removed himself.

Judith was left alone in the breakfast room with the duke. "Why does my butler regard you as some sort of god?" she demanded.

Dacian shrugged. "He respects my wrassling abilities. We had a rematch."

"A rematch?"

"Not in the Blue Drawing Room this time, you'll be pleased to know."

Judith sighed and took another mouthful of coffee. "I don't think I want to know."

"No, it's quite irrelevant." Dacian leaned towards her. "How much do you remember, my dear?"

She licked her lips. "I remember you flirting with me in the Sargen woods. And kissing me by a river. It was quite...memorable." It was utterly riveting. How could she have turned away from him to Nicholas? It was like reading a book to which she did not know the ending.

"Ah yes. I didn't know you were betrothed to Nicholas then, in my defence."

She looked down, embarrassed. "I did, however. I do apologise."

"Never mind. There have been awful errors on both sides." He looked as if he wanted to take her hand again but curtailed the impulse. "It is all in the past now."

For her, however, the story unfolded as if it was all new: that day she recalled their fatal encounter in the Sargen library, and her subsequent marriage to Nicholas, and wept anew at the pain of it. Then, gradually, the events of Garvey House, both nine years ago and more recently, returned to her. By the end of the third day—which Dacian spent mostly with Drumpellier in the Blue Drawing Room, in a series of urgent meetings with various officers—she could remember everything, including that regrettable incident where she had almost bared her breasts in an attempt to jolt Dacian's recollection of her. She rather thought she would pretend *that* was an irrecoverable memory, lost to the mists of Lethe.

Feeling rather overwhelmed as the events of the last few days returned to her, Judith retired early to her room and asked Trebellow to send up some hot water for a bath. Now that she could recall her first impression of the Captain's Cabin, she could see that the dark green quilt had been replaced with a pale green one, edged in primrose. The green and gold rugs were also recent additions, put in by Mrs Ulrich, along with the vases of flowers, and the wall hanging of embroidered yellow roses. The room was more welcoming now, with the wood panelling freshly dusted and the heavy curtains replaced by creamy silk, framing the soothing view of the ocean.

The hot bath was even more calming, with Kadee providing extra buckets of steaming water. The girl was eager to please, grateful that Judith had kept her secret and allowed her to stay on as a footman, though Judith had hopes she might convince her to become a lady's maid. Or a lady's footman, at least. Or some new category of servant altogether, she mused. Castle Lanyon would be a singular sort of establishment, if all went to plan: exempt from the Edicts, now home to a roost of bats, and eventually to be a school for young, budding Musors.

She had not yet had an interview with the French vampiri queen; while she had been indisposed it had been left to Perry to play the role of the diplomat and settle Her Majesty into her new abode. And now the queen had declared she must sleep for three days in order to recover from the turbulent crossing from Sark. Judith hoped to be granted an audience after that. There was much to organise after Elinor's wedding, though according to Elinor's letter, she was planning on a long honeymoon.

Perhaps while she was away, Judith could begin writing some introductory pamphlets or guides to Truth Discernment for the new school. Absorbed in various contemplations, she stayed in the bath until the water cooled. Then she stepped out and surveyed her gowns. The dark fabrics of a widowed matron no longer felt right. Even the pale lilac seemed too drab. Mrs Ulrich had put an old-fashioned, rose-coloured muslin gown on the armchair, which Judith slipped over her shift. It was rather scandalously low-cut with ties down the front. Thoughtfully, she pulled them tight and flung a soft, grey shawl over her shoulders to retain her modesty. There were no matching rose mobcaps, so she left her head bare, her hair loose.

Then she sat at the table near the window, and considered the huge ship's bell in the corner. The pulley ran to the bed, and after a moment she yanked it with both hands, giving it an almighty pull.

In which a hat is symbolic

Patience is a virtue, until it is not.
— from *Lady Avely's Guide to Guile and Peril*

THE SOUND RANG OUT SO LOUDLY that she had to cover her ears, reverberating through the room and into the rest of the castle. Soon pounding footsteps announced the presence of Trebellow, who looked in anxiously.

"Ma'am, you rang?"

"Yes, thank you, Trebellow." Judith drew a breath, tucking her grey shawl closer. "I find myself somewhat displeased about a certain matter."

"Yes, ma'am." Trebellow looked anxious. "Which matter would that be?"

"The irksome Captain Drumpellier," she replied darkly. "My memories have returned, and I now recall that he incarcerated the duke, bound him, and attempted to sacrifice his life in some foolhardy plan. And yet I understand that the captain continues to treat this castle as if he is a welcome guest?"

"Indeed, ma'am." Trebellow added, "He has been working together with his grace. They appear to have reached some understanding."

Judith grimaced. "I suppose Dacian thinks that the French plot must supersede his grievances." She knew that Dacian also felt some guilt about his own past, and he might have some sympathy with Drumpellier's motives, if not his means. "Yet I am reluctant to let the matter slide. The Custos cannot be allowed to treat people in such a fashion, even as they pursue their mandate of justice."

Trebellow nodded. "I quite agree, ma'am. It was shocking how they treated his grace. Quite shocking."

"I want you to send Baron Quarles to talk with me."

Trebellow stared. "Baron Quarles, ma'am?"

"I have reason to believe that he is also ranked within the Custos. I want to discuss the matter with him."

"Certainly, ma'am." Trebellow withdrew, eyes wide.

Twenty minutes later, a soft tap on the door heralded the entry of the baron. His tall form sidled in, and he made a low bow.

"Lady Avely," he murmured. "I am glad to hear that you have recovered. Do you wish to borrow my telescope again?"

Judith ignore this parry and eyed him. "Tell me, are you higher or lower than Drumpellier in your Custos rank?"

The baron looked momentarily taken aback. Then he smiled wryly. "Lower, I am afraid."

"Please sit." She gestured to the windowsill settee, and the baron sat, crossing his thin ankles. Judith leaned forward. "So you do not have any power to immediately discipline the captain?"

"No, but I assure you that I am making a thorough report." The baron paused delicately. "As you appear to have guessed, I am what you might call an internal affairs officer. I've been tasked by the highest rank in the Custos to keep an eye on the lower orders."

"Did they suspect that Drumpellier was taking liberties?" Judith demanded.

The baron shook his head. "No. We knew that he was running an intelligence operation out of Castle Lanyon, and I was sent to check on it. I did not inform him of our investigation, especially after Sgt Finlay died. And thanks to you, I have now discovered how much leeway the captain has been taking in the execution of his duties."

"Thank the Lord there is *some* oversight," said Judith bitterly. "I suppose you are Gifted in Memory, to assist your reports?"

"Indeed." The baron tipped his head. "May I enquire how you guessed my secret?"

"You are a friend of the king's," replied Judith. "You knew of the Musing: I could tell that you lied when I first met you in the drawing room, though I was a bit Bemused at the time. I knew you must have your own Gift, and Memors are often drawn to astronomy, with its complex charts and changes. Yet Drumpellier did not seem to realise your Gift or your interest in the castle. And I knew you were questioning all my servants, and Miss Onslow."

The baron bowed again. "Not much slips past a Truth Discernor. I will be grateful to hear your full account of the recent events."

Judith nodded and rang the hand bell for tea. "We might be here for a while."

Two hours later, she dismissed him to her satisfaction. At least some steps were being taken to hold Drumpellier to account, even if Dacian wanted to simply slap him on the back and move on. There were some things that were unforgivable, and that included leaving a man in wristbreakers and no memory.

She shuddered. Glancing to the window, she saw that the sun had set, streaking the sky with gold. Right on time, a commotion came from her cupboard. Yesterday evening, the same rattle had given her a fright, but now she turned with gladness to see Marigold emerge, recognisable as her own dear companion. Her curly head peeped out next to the smooth dark one of Miss Yvette Belfleur.

"Judith!" Marigold peered down at her. "Do you remember me yet?"

"I do." Judith smiled. "I remember *everything* now, and I'm quite put to the blush by our adventures. I must thank you again for flying all the way out to Perry. We couldn't have managed any of it without you. And you too, Miss Belfleur, for taking care of the duke and dear Wooten."

She crossed to the cupboard and put up both her hands, one for each vampiri, and carried them over to the massive bed. They were both wearing capes, and Marigold informed her that they planned to investigate the broken-down tower as a suitable residence for Yvette.

"You don't want to join the roost in the cellar?" enquired Judith. "They might welcome one more to their ranks."

"I'd prefer to have my own quarters," replied Yvette politely. "Marigold is sufficient company for me."

Marigold blushed a little, and Judith asked what she had been doing for sustenance the last two nights.

"I shared a cow with Yvette." She waved an airy hand. "The Lanyon breed are quite tasty, though quite beset now, with the roost also requiring nourishment."

"Yes," said Judith, "and I'd be honoured if you would continue as my companion, dear Marigold, if you will have me."

She paused diffidently. "I know this was always intended to be a temporary arrangement, and you may leave now, if you wish it."

Marigold's eyes widened. "Pfft! You need my sobering influence. If it wasn't for me, you might have blown up Fort Pendennis!"

Yvette picked up Marigold's hand and kissed it affectionately. "We are in trouble if *you* are the sobering influence, my dear."

"Well, you must admit I did better than Wooten," said Marigold. "Strutting about without his clothes on! That's twice now!"

"How is Wooten?" Judith asked, gratefully removing her grey shawl and offering her wrist to Marigold, who leapt onto her lap. "He was quite the hero too."

"Fully recovered, unfortunately," said Marigold, baring her fangs. "He keeps telling me to put on my clothes, even though he has no wing to fly with anymore. And he is continually making pointed remarks about the duke's cravat. Dacian calls him a flittermouse in retaliation, though he seems to be quite fond of the little fop. But Judith, you must tell me your account of what happened while we were asleep. All we know is Perry's version, and he seemed to think *he* was the hero of the piece."

"He was, indeed," said Judith, and she recounted the tale, forced to pause on the encounter with the Crimson Lady, for Marigold withdrew her head from the vein to remark that she had also met the ghost of Castle Lanyon, the night before in the northern corridor.

"Strolling around as if she owns the place," said Marigold, "but she was friendly enough, and winked at me."

"She was quite helpful," agreed Judith, "almost as if she knew exactly what we required."

Marigold almost choked at Judith's wry description of the

'theatrical' that unfolded in the Tea Tower Room, and Yvette tutted at Robert's excessive deployment of a yew hedge.

Once Marigold was fed, Judith carried the vampiri over to the windowsill and watched them squabble fondly about how Marigold's cape should be arranged. Then she unlatched the window, letting in the fresh ocean breeze, and they flew off into the night.

Sighing, Judith shut the window again, and stoked the fire into a blaze. Then once more she gave the silver bell a hefty tug. The sound boomed out, and Trebellow soon appeared, puffing, at her door.

"Trebellow, please ask the duke to join me." She paused. "And then we are not to be disturbed, even if the castle is set on fire by the French."

"Indeed, ma'am." A small twinkle showed in his eye as he retreated.

She stood and paced slowly along the windows as she waited, looking out over the glimmering sea. What should she say to him now, after all that had passed? Her heart beat with anticipation and it suddenly felt as if champagne ran in her veins. How dearly she loved him, and it seemed—if her memories were to be trusted—that he loved her in return. Yet unaccountably, she felt nervous, like a girl meeting a suitor for the first time. She was past forty, for goodness's sake! Age had not dulled the exhilaration of love; if anything, it felt richer and sweeter for it.

She straightened her rose-coloured skirts, leaving the grey shawl where she had flung it, and sat down on the bed, leaning against the pillows. She was wise enough, now, to know how to seduce a man. And Dacian knew exactly what to do with a widow. Yet this was more than a dalliance. It was her whole heart and being that she was to lay before him.

Finally, she heard his firm tread on the stairs. The door

opened, and Dacian stepped inside. He was wearing a fitted blue waistcoat over a white linen shirt, though without a cravat. His black hair was damp and curling, as if he had also recently had a bath.

He saw Judith on the bed, and his face lit up in a devastating smile. Carefully, he shut the door behind him. A small silence lay between them, while she greedily took him in, all her memories once more making his face so dear. And he was so handsome, damn him. If he hadn't been so handsome from the beginning, she might have trusted his affection more.

He was examining her low-cut muslin gown with appreciation. Then he spoke. "No mobcap, marchioness?"

"Not today, your grace." Her voice was surprisingly calm.

"Must I assume, then, that you still do not recall yourself?"

"Quite the contrary: I remember everything." She paused. "I even recall an incident when I tried to kiss you, and you snored like a donkey."

"Ah." He took a few steps closer to the bed, raising his brows. "Believe me, I was not bored at the time. Indeed, I was in a state of torturous conflict, torn between your heavenly lips and the role of a slumbering mule." He grinned. "Not even Bonaparte could have put me at such a disadvantage."

She ran a hand over the quilt, thoughtfully. "Yet as far as I recall, *I* was the one who undressed." She had been removing a disguise at the time, while the two of them hid in the Garvey House master bedroom.

His lips twitched. "Indeed. I have very fond memories of it. Thankfully, they have all returned to me now."

"Yet I have no such memory of you." She considered his tall form and tipped her head consideringly, her heart beating rather fast. "I believe it is your turn now."

There was a moment's silence, then he mirrored her movement. "Are you certain, Judith? Has the Lethe addled your brain?"

"I've never been more certain." Her voice softened. "We've waited long enough. You will oblige me now by not wasting another moment."

Dacian, loath to disappoint, immediately began unbuttoning his blue waistcoat with great haste. "Certainly, my lady."

Seeing her riveted gaze, his long fingers slowed. He slipped the last two buttons out with tantalising deliberation, and eased the waistcoat off his broad shoulders. Judith did not lick her lips, but he smiled and swept the linen shirt over his head in one fluid motion, revealing the sculpted breadth of his chest.

Judith blinked, admiring his dark curls and the lean taper of his waist. He kicked off his shoes, and the huge room now seemed exactly the right size, with him in it.

"Judith." His voice deepened. "Those were the darkest hours of my existence, my dear, when I could not remember you."

"Mine too." She climbed off the bed and stepped up to him, placing her hands on his bare shoulders. "It was awful seeing the blankness in your face." Her voice quavered. "I thought I had lost you forever."

He cupped her cheek tenderly. "I would have simply fallen in love with you all over again. I think I had already begun, in that miserable cell when I didn't even know your name."

She pressed her body into his then, steadying herself in the warmth of him, resting her head on his chest. Her whole being thrummed with happiness and deep contentment. They stood there a long moment, satisfied to simply hold one another. Then she turned her face up to his, and he kissed her gently, as if for the first time.

The world fell away. The fire between them, long banked, leapt eagerly to life. Their kisses became deeper, his hands pulling her closer and ardently canvassing her curves through the soft muslin. Eventually, impatient, Judith reached for the tie on his breeches and slipped it loose. Dacian stepped away, letting his trousers fall.

"My goodness," she said. Her memory from Garvey House had not deceived her. He was indeed rather...well endowed.

He grinned. "An Impactor trait."

"I approve." She blushed like a maiden, but that only seemed to please him. Without giving her time to admire him further, he gathered her up in his arms and carried her to the bed.

"Well, marchioness," he murmured. "I have a thousand lustful fantasies which have waited far too long to be realised. You have tortured me for twenty years. Now it's my turn. And you are wearing too many clothes."

This time, Judith did lick her lips. His eyes followed the movement hungrily, but his hands were unhurried as he slid her silk ribbons undone to part her gown, trailing a fiery path down her body.

"I haven't tortured you," she objected, as her hips arched in response. "I've barely seen you!"

"You didn't have to be present to consume my thoughts," he retorted, placing devoted kisses along her collarbone. "And when you *were* there, you delighted in making me take on ridiculous disguises, while you sailed around looking beautifully unattainable." Slowly, he slipped her rose gown off, leaving her in the whisper-thin shift. "Now I shall take my revenge."

He grasped her hips and tilted her towards him with possessive authority, bracing her against him.

"Nonsense," she managed, as heat flamed deep within her. "A yew tree isn't ridiculous. It is a fine upstanding specimen of... botany."

He rocked her pelvis, making her bones melt, his own gaze molten.

"You'll pay for that remark," he said conversationally. Then he settled her back into the bed, slipping her shift off, and made good on his promise to torture her. Her eyelids fluttered closed with pleasure and she surrendered to his expert touch.

Delicious sensations swept through her. Dacian murmured encouragement and endearments against her throat, saying outrageous and perfectly reasonable things: that she was his to do with as he liked now, and he wanted to see her completely undone and ready for him. Soon she was writhing in pleasure, threading her hands through his thick, dark hair as if to anchor herself. When he took her breasts in his mouth, she gasped, helpless as he tantalised her with his long, warm fingers.

She arched in desperate invitation, and he groaned in response, his knee coming up to part her legs wider. The long, hard length of him pressed against her thigh, and she put a tentative hand down to tease him in return. He groaned again, his muscled arm flexing against her cheek.

Then they were sliding under the sea-green quilt in a tangle of limbs. Hands sure, gaze hot, Dacian guided them together. They fit exactly right, and the sense of fullness and completion made Judith's heart pound. The pleasure was an exquisite pressure, demanding release, but Dacian moved slowly, his eyes intent.

Outside, the sound of the waves crashing made the room seem even more like a ship's cabin, a private bubble where they could be wholly together. Under his deliberate rhythm, they surged together like the tides on the ocean, relentless and inevitable. Slowly, then quickly, waves of sensation spun through Judith, until release shattered through both of them.

Afterwards, she was utterly limp and shaken. Dacian collapsed beside her and pulled her into him with a possessive arm and a deeply satisfied sigh. She rested her head on his shoulder, in a safe harbour at last.

He ran a tender hand over her hip. "That's only the beginning of your punishments, you realise."

She murmured something inarticulate, still speechless.

His breath warmed her ear. "You do know that I have always adored you, Judith. Ever since I met you."

She revelled in the fact that they should feel exactly the same. For so long she had pretended to herself that she did not love him, to keep her heart safe from hurt.

"I adore you too, my love," she admitted. Then she added, "Even if you *are* terribly vain."

He scoffed. "If I am vain, it's your fault."

She lifted her head. "Because I gaze at you so worshipfully?" She suited action to words.

He laughed, gaze warm. "No, because I have inexplicably won you, despite my terrible character."

Judith gave him a chastising kiss, and arrayed herself across his broad chest complacently. "You were too noble for your own good."

He returned her kiss deeply, then sighed. "Yes, you are very right, as usual, my love. I managed to refrain from killing Captain Drumpellier, so I am a model of saintly restraint."

"Yet you were far too restrained with me," she remarked thoughtfully. "Next time, I expect you to claim me with ducal arrogance."

He let out a groan and ran a reverent hand down her body. "It is true I've spent far too much time curbing my base impulses around you. All I wanted was to drag you away and claim you as mine, even when you were another's."

Judith sighed happily and surrendered to his caress. "I *am* yours, my dear. As long as you understand that you are mine too."

"Completely," he murmured, and leaned in to kiss her again.

THE NEXT DAY, Perry was to transport them all to Elinor's wedding in London (in stages, to save his Bemusement). They gathered in the Tea Tower Room, looking out onto a rainswept ocean. Judith wore a sky-blue gown trimmed with cream, which Perry had fetched from a dressmaker in London the afternoon before. She was rather pleased with it, especially when Dacian murmured in her ear that she looked exquisite.

"What a delightful hat," he added. "Where did you find one of such good taste?"

Her hand self-consciously lifted to pat the blue satin. Dacian had previously bought the pretty confection for her in Stokesford, in an effort to distract her. At the time she had thought it was far too frivolous for a matron of her station, with its cream lace and ribbons. Now it suited her mood perfectly.

Perry gave them both a very suspicious look. He and Robert wore matching swallowtail coats, and Robert fidgeted with his cravat uncomfortably. Sadly, Marigold, Yvette, and Wooten would miss the wedding breakfast, being fast asleep, but Judith had promised to bring back posies of flowers for them.

"Well!" She looked around approvingly, ignoring Perry's glower. "We are all very smart. No one would guess that you were blowing up a cellar a few days ago, Perry."

"Or that the duke was tussling around with the butler," he retorted.

Trebellow, standing by the door, drew himself up further, so that he loomed over all of them. "Wrassling is not tussling."

The duke grinned, also finely dressed in his tight buckskin breeches and a tailored coat that set off his shoulders admirably. Judith thought he looked like the epitome of noble masculinity, even when he said, "We can demonstrate the difference, if you wish."

"Not here," reproved Mrs Ulrich, from where she was stoking the fire. "I've only just finished mending the curtains in the Blue Drawing Room."

Ghastagon stalked in at the door. He leapt onto the windowsill, with a miaow like a goat scaling a mountain, perhaps to express his disapproval that the Tea Tower Room was so full of people. Or perhaps he was expressing his admiration for their smart clothes. It was hard to tell.

The soothing, cheerful Diplomacy charm on the Tea Tower Room was in full force at the moment, possibly strengthened by the housekeeper's benevolent gaze and the blazing fire that warmed the room, in defiance of the sweeping autumnal rain. Yet Robert still had a frown on his face.

"I really don't like this," he said uneasily. "It is not fair on Elinor, to spring an additional brother on her at her own wedding. Even if I go with the story of being Uncle Gerald's byblow, she might guess the truth. She sounds like a very discerning young woman."

Perry snorted. "Literally, I'm afraid. It's best not to say anything at all, in case she's trying out her budding Truth Discernment on you. But trust me, Bobsy, she will be so taken up with marrying her precious Lord Beresford that she won't notice anything amiss. And if worse comes to worst, simply disguise yourself as a yew hedge."

Robert jostled his shoulder. "At least I know how to carry off a military disguise and still breathe at the same time."

They began squabbling about who made the best infantry-man. This soon devolved into Perry's scornful insults about the army in general, and Robert's sceptical remarks about the navy. Judith looked on fondly, grateful to see that they were bickering like brothers.

Dacian's arm slid round her waist. "Will they have drinking chocolate at the wedding breakfast?" he murmured. "I want to ensure that my beloved is happy."

Judith rested her head on his shoulder. "I am happy, my dear."

"How happy?"

"Extraordinarily, supremely, blissfully."

"Even without chocolate?"

She considered. "Perhaps I could still do with some chocolate."

"I'll pour it myself."

"Nonsense." She took a step away, straightening her blue satin hat. "It isn't appropriate for a duke to serve a marchioness."

"But that's all I did last night." His eyes gleamed.

Judith blushed and ran a teasing finger over his lips. "Not *all* night."

Unable to resist his handsome smirk, she leaned up and kissed him. Perry and Robert let out identical shocked gasps behind her, but she ignored them, and the risk to her gown and hat, and leaned into him with a sigh, like a cat with the cream. "This night and every night, my love. We have plenty of lost time to make up for."

"Indeed," said Dacian, and crushed her to him in a most satisfying manner.

— The End —

Author's Note

'Flittermouse' is indeed an old English name for bats!

Cornish wrassling did, in fact, always begin with an oath, stating 'Sweet play is fair play'. Traditionally, contestants formally renounce the use of any magic before the match.

There were several assassination attempts upon Napoleon, including a cart that exploded near his carriage on the way to the opera in Paris, and an attempt to infiltrate his *Guides Consulaires* in copied uniforms, among others. Some of these attempts have been linked to British secret agents, or were financially supported by the British government, who had spies established in Jersey.

Castle Lanyon is based on St Michael's Mount, a castle on a tidal island off the coast of Cornwall, though I took the liberty of adding various rooms and features that are not part of the original!

What I call Arloedhes Karek is in fact Chapel Rock, near the causeway to St Michael's Mount. The real-world Cornish myth tells that Cormelian, a giantess, dropped the green rocks out of her huge apron when her husband Cormoran scolded her for not carrying granite to build their fort. I wanted a tale with more romantic overtones! The Cornish translation of Arloedhes Karek is Lady's Rock.

And one last note: although the Cornish technically live in England, to this day many regard themselves as a different breed to the 'English', having their own language, history, and heritage, including rebellions against the English in the distant past. In 2014, the UK government recognised the Cornish as a national minority, similar to the Welsh and Irish.

I hope you enjoyed this final instalment of the Matronly Misadventures!

If you want to see more of these characters, they will reappear in the next book in the Lady Diviner series, *The Emerald Teapot*, where (one hopes) Elinor will finally be married! Pre-order the ebook now at the special pre-order price of $4.99, or join my newsletter to stay tuned for updates, as well as claim your free prequel novella *A Pendant for Trouble*.

Thanks so much for reading! I had a real lark with this one, and I hope you did too.

Rosalie

The Lady Jewel Diviner

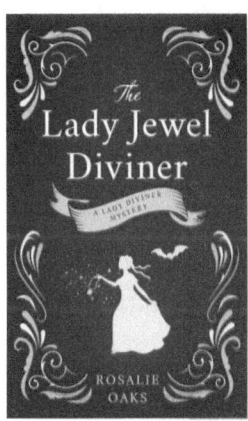

Follow the adventures of Judith's daughter, Elinor, which starts with *The Lady Jewel Diviner*.

Diamonds, Death, and Devonshire tea... in a magical Regency England

Miss Elinor Avely's proper upbringing cannot prepare her for the tiny, spinster vampire who crashes into her sitting room and demands to be fed with a sheep.

Elinor already has enough troubles without having to catch ruminants.

First, her gift for divining jewels has landed her in scandal and exiled her from London society.

Second, a nobleman of dubious repute has asked her to find a cache of smuggled jewels, hidden somewhere along the Devon coastline.

Last – and worst – Elinor has been invited to cream tea at the local manor. And while the autocratic and magnificent Earl of Beresford might be there (and perhaps the jewels themselves too), Beresford is the last person Elinor wants to meet over cream tea.

When a dead body is discovered along the cliffs, of course, such delicate considerations become secondary. Fortunately, Elinor now has a small vampiric chaperone – even if said spinster has a habit of appearing stark naked – and together they are ready to risk the hard questions.

Where are the jewels hidden? Who killed the smuggler? And just when *is* the cream tea being served?

Or if you are already up-to-date with Elinor's adventures, you can pre-order her next one in *The Emerald Teapot*, for the special ebook pre-order price of $4.99.

Thank you to Patrons

Deepest thanks to my Patrons for their generous support.

Annelise Bauer
Tania Clucas
Ria D.
Katie Forrest
Anna Fridlund
Ginny Farris
Cori Gonzalez
Linda Hawkins
Nathalia Hjordt
Megan Hodge
Susan Mason
Cortney McInerney
Marcela Mets-Chamberlain
Tamara Ng
Kristin Rafe
Danita Rambo
Eva Schiffer
Kimberly Shore
Karen Slater
Lauren Sullivan
Sarah Swarbrick
Fiona Tewson
Taylor Trenchard
Mary Lee Vacca
Anneke Rebecca Van Belle

A. B. Warwik
Ginny Williams

Many thanks also to my beta readers who helped shape the final manuscript, as well as catching many a typo and inconsistency; my continuity reader, Allen Schroeter, for his keen eye; and my proof-readers, Xenia Tashlitsky and Anne Kavcic, who caught the remaining errors. You all helped to ensure this book conducts itself with decent literary propriety!

With love,
Rosalie

Rosalie's Private Tea Parlour

If you'd like to be part of the lovely community who support my authorly endeavours, please call into my Private Tea Parlour, where you may read my books before anyone else, as well as peruse deleted scenes, short stories, join in the Castle Lanyon Book Club, and much more.

You can even read a scene from Dacian's POV, as well as the letter he wrote to Judith while he was in exile in Spain!

My wonderful Patrons also gain a secret key to the Lamplighters' Guild Discord community, filled with delightful bookish folk and conversations.

I'd be thrilled to have your support. Pop along to patreon.com/rosalieoaks to have a peep.

Happy tea drinking,

Rosalie

About the Author

Rosalie Oaks writes novels set in a magical Regency England full of good manners, mysteries, and soothing beverages. As a child, she loved conducting home-made theatre productions with her three younger brothers. Now she directs her characters instead, but like her brothers, they don't always do what she says.

While writing, Rosalie consumes vast quantities of tea and chocolate, and steadfastly ignores the housework.

Further intimate details, such as her favourite books and recipes, can be found in her Private Tea Parlour on Patreon.

Books by Rosalie Oaks

Lady Diviner

A Pendant for Trouble (prequel novella)

The Lady Jewel Diviner

The Moria Pearls

The Sapphire Library

The Golden Flute

The Emerald Teapot (forthcoming)

The Selkie Scandal (an internovella)

Matronly Misadventures

Lady Avely's Guide to Truth and Magic

Lady Avely's Guide to Lies and Charms

Lady Avely's Guide to Guile and Peril

rosalieoaks.com